CW00419150

STILL

Howard Evans

Double Dorje

Cover illustration by Graeme Chambers
Cover design by Marie Tilbert

Double Dorje
34 Marley House
London, W11 4DJ
UK

ISBN: 978-1916201200

For my children

Oscar Blue and Elizabeth Rose

With special thanks to

Sarah Walton

One

1

A warm breeze carried the scent of sewage and salt and the occasional wisp of jasmine blossom to the place where I gazed out over the sea from the restaurant terrace. Children played noisily on the street below. I sipped cold beer as I waited for my meal.

My wife was in bed with an upset stomach, yet another expression of her interminable discontent. Still, after all these years, I could not tell if it was with life in general or only with me. I had done what I always did and retreated into solitude and separation. I had grown to relish these times alone - to think, to watch the world, to enjoy the undemanding familiarity of my own company. It was good to be free from my wife's endless chatter about all the other places she wanted to visit and her complete lack of interest in where we were.

My reverie was broken as two people entered the restaurant, neither locals nor the occasional tourists who were lucky enough to find this place. The man caught my attention first, his face familiar in the moment before he sat with his back towards me. Long, thick, black hair fell loosely plaited against his dark blue, linen jacket.

The woman faced me - slim and graceful with a tangled mane of wind-swept blond hair. Gold jewellery shone like the sun against her skin. She looked about twenty-five but her eyes seemed old as they coldly surveyed the terrace. The couple had an intimacy, an aura of complicity, a magnetism that constantly drew my eyes to them.

They ordered red wine and mineral water. The man drank only water. I willed him to turn towards me, to confirm what my gut already knew.

I recalled the uneven little road from David's house where I had been living, past Prakash's store to Rafa and Jasmine's house and their garden on top of the world. That was twenty years ago but the sights and smells of Mussoorie still remained fresh. Rafa and Jasmine's garden sat high above the village with views out across the tropical heat of the valleys, out towards the snow-capped mountain peaks beyond which lay Tibet, still a secret land back then. Whenever I thought back to those days I always pictured Rafa and Jasmine playing in the garden with Ganesha, the son they named after the universally loved Hindu god.

I felt again the longing I had always felt when I was with them, a longing for a love like theirs, for their closeness, for their satisfaction with the simple life they chose. We shared so many meals together, meals cooked with time and patience, special dahls prepared with seven types of lentils picked clean of grit by Rafa as the sun set over the mountains. I always hoped their simplicity would rub off on me and wipe away my own innate unease. It never did. I smelled again the rich scents of flowers that cast their fragrance only at dusk.

A woman arrived in the restaurant and was led to their table. She had an air of darkness about her, more animal than human, a presence that seemed to push the air before her.

My couscous arrived but I no longer wanted it; my stomach was suddenly closed by a surge of panic that made me want to run from that place, made me want to run back to the secure indifference of my wife.

I couldn't leave, I had to know. I walked across to the table and found myself gazing into familiar eyes, into Rafael's eyes but in a face so changed. His soft, round, beautiful features had hardened into a look of resigned sadness. Tears filled my eyes and the world around me began to disappear. On the point of weeping I was pulled back as Rafa said my name and stood to embrace me.

He invited me to join them, called for another glass and introduced his friends. Christina sat opposite him. The dark woman was Kali. As I took the seat facing her that presence, at first so frightening, became deeply reassuring. The air filled with the smell of her Turkish tobacco. It was too delicious to resist and I broke a four-year abstinence to accept the cigarette she offered from a filigreed silver case. As she held the lighter, I saw the ring she wore on her little finger - antique gold, hand beaten, with Tibetan letters carved around its circumference.

Rafa asked about my life since we were together in Mussoorie. I hurried through that futile tale, told him about the import business I set up with David's help in India and its inevitable collapse through my own lack of commitment. I told him of the string of other failures of my life. I told him of my marriage into a wealthy family that seemed to save me from myself, of the endless round of travel, hotels, dinners and parties. I told him of my wife, the woman who, despite so much activity, seemed tired of life and tired of me and was now lying in bed in our hotel room. My story bored me with its aimlessness. I wanted to know about Rafa and Jasmine and Ganesha. I wanted to know about the two women with whom we shared the table. I wanted to hear about the fulfilling lives I assumed everybody but me was living. As I talked, quickly relating the empty facts of the past twenty years, Rafa removed his jacket, slipped it onto the back of his chair, folded back the cuffs of his shirt and revealed two watches - both Rolex, one silver, one gold.

They showed different times, neither correct for Tunisia. Rafa asked me to tell him more about my wife. I could think of nothing to say except, "Perhaps you could meet her tomorrow." But Kali replied, "We leave tomorrow."

Finally, I found the moment to ask Rafa about himself. "And you, are you still with Jasmine?" Although the answer was 'yes', his reply was vague and uncertain. "And Ganesha, he must be more than twenty now?"

Rafa's sadness deepened. He nodded and looked away. As I waited to hear more he became nervous, kept looking towards Kali, finally dismissed my question to order more wine.

"What is it Rafa? I want to know about you. You were always so important to me. I thought of you often over these years."

Rafa heaved with a huge sigh and took a cigarette from Kali's case. "Please Kali, let me tell him. It's too lonely and painful like this. He's an old friend, he knows so much of my story already."

Kali took me with her eyes. I felt entered to my soul, seen for the first time in my life. A deep sense of ease filled my body. She nodded toward Rafa. "Tell him, he'll understand."

Rafa let out a deep sighing, "Thank you," to Kali.

I could not make Kali out. Although the sense of danger had gone I felt her power and, although that power was now balanced by compassion it still felt as if she had us all in her control. Rafa poured a glass of wine and turned his chair a little more towards me.

2

"I am so glad to see you. I knew someone was coming - this morning in my meditations I kept receiving a visitor. I felt uneasy all day and now you're here I'm not sure where to begin." Rafa lit another cigarette from the glowing end of the last. "How well did you know David?" he asked.

"Well enough for him to let me live in his house in Mussoorie. I worked with him for a while and then he helped me set up my own business. After I bankrupted the business we lost touch. I wrote from time to time but never received a reply."

"Do you know what David really did?" Rafa asked.

I told him what little I knew. Publicly, David dealt in antiques and handicrafts. I knew that some of his business was illegal and involved exporting antiquities that were not permitted to leave the country. I once helped him prepare the paperwork for part of a consignment he was shipping. Some crates would pass through five or six countries before reaching Germany. There were different papers for each leg of the journey. It helped that David had good connections in India including close friendship with one of the ruling families. That was pretty much the limit of my knowledge.

Rafa nodded and asked if I had ever met David's Tibetan girlfriend. I did meet a Tibetan woman with him in Mussoorie but I couldn't remember her name.

"Then I have a lot to tell you. David's girlfriend was Tamdin. She was raised in a refugee camp in Bodh Gaya. They met in Kathmandu. You are right about the illegal nature of David's business and about the level of his connections. In fact, that Indian family were minor players in David's world - he just made use of them. David smuggled antiques out of India as well as silver and ivory. As you know, he was very successful at it, so successful that he had no fear of the authorities. In many ways he lived the perfect life - he had his house in Mussoorie, the one you know, and others in Rishikesh, New Delhi and near Goa. His reputation was such that his business almost ran itself. He had no need to find buyers - they came to him, and only then through a complex network of introductions.

"Some time after you left Mussoorie David started to spend much more time there. Although he was rich he was never ostentatious. Sure, he had a driver but he lived simply and often travelled quite humbly, by foot or by bus. You probably know he was always torn between his business and the ascetic life. He spent a lot of time with us - eating, sharing stories, practicing yoga in the garden. He was like family. After he met Tamdin, all that changed. She was strange; it is difficult to say quite how. She had an uneasiness about her, or rather, she made everybody around her uneasy. Perhaps that's not surprising, considering her story. Jasmine said she felt haunted. That's still the best description. When Tamdin was around David was quieter, more withdrawn. He was devoted to her but the relationship was imbalanced. He always seemed unsatisfied by her but he never stopped trying to make her happy. To be honest, I didn't expect it to last very long - he never was very good at staying with women anyway. When winter came David and Tamdin left for the plains. It was more than six months before we saw them again. During that time things became difficult for Jasmine and me. If you remember, we made money by shipping handicrafts to Columbia.

"A friend of ours, Jorge, used to sell the goods and cable us the money. Jorge was arrested; nobody could tell us why. He died two months later in jail. We had just sent a new consignment that cost us most of our money. We were told it never arrived. Friends in Columbia tried to find out what had happened, to Jorge, to the money, to the shipment. They could find no answer. Some friends blamed us for Jorge's death. There was no reason for that but it frightened us, made it difficult for us to find answers.

"By the time David returned we had very little money left, enough for a month or two in India and not enough to get us back to Columbia. I told David what happened. He was strangely detached, more interested in what was happening politically in Columbia than our situation. Finally, I had to ask if I could do some work for him but he was vague and wouldn't give an answer. I was really hurt by that; we had always been so generous with him. We saw him again a week later. He was very formal, no longer the ascetic, very much the businessman. He asked me to meet him later in his office. I didn't even know he had an office but he explained where to find it and left. Jasmine became nervous. She made me promise to tell her everything and agree to nothing without talking with her. That wasn't like Jasmine - we always shared everything, I never had secrets from her, but I promised anyway. By the time I left home for the meeting I too was feeling nervous. I left plenty of time for a slow walk down into town, hoping it might calm me. It didn't calm me. In fact, that day remains one of the most memorable of my life. It felt as if a cloud of darkness had settled over Mussoorie. There was an uncanny quietness. I didn't hear any birds. I didn't hear the usual sounds of the children from the school. As I walked through the main street it was as if I was invisible. Nobody called to me or asked after Ganesha as was usual. I cannot tell you how many times I wanted to turn around and go home but I was already caught in a web of inevitability.

"I found myself at the door to David's office without knowing quite how I got there. The door opened as I arrived and a young Tibetan boy invited me in. He led me to a room where David was sitting cross-legged on the floor. He gestured for me to join him. We sat in silence until the boy brought tea. The room was very simple - wood-panelled and windowless, lit by candles. Against one wall was a small Buddhist shrine. There were rugs on the floor and nothing more. David told me that he had some work for me, something to be delivered to Columbia, something too precious to go any other way but by personal courier. I told him about my fear of going there after what happened to Jorge. He assured me that everything would be taken care of, that I had nothing to fear. He told me that I would be in and out of Columbia in two days, that I would be met upon arrival and escorted at all times until I left. He told me what he would pay. It was a lot, too much in fact, enough for another year in India. I thanked him for the offer and told him that I would talk it over with Jasmine and let him know tomorrow. David exploded with a fury I had never seen before. He told me there was no time to think it over, that he wanted my decision now or I could leave immediately. I agreed to his offer. Only later did I realise that I only agreed out of fear. My fear of him, of that anger which bordered on the murderous, was bigger than my fear of the trip or of how Jasmine would react. As soon as I agreed, David calmed down again and continued as if he had never been angry at all. My fear of him deepened. He rang a bell on the tea-tray and the house-boy came into the room with an envelope which he handed to David.

"David told me that in two days his driver would collect me and take me down to his house in Delhi where I would spend the night. The following day I would be given a small package. I would be taken to the airport and accompanied to my plane. I would not pass through immigration. In Bogotá I would be met from the plane and, again, I would not pass through immigration.

"I would be taken to a hotel where I would wait. The same day a visitor would come to exchange the package for one I would bring back to David in India. I would return to India the following day in the same manner. I would be met at the airport and brought directly home. David gave me the envelope and asked me to open it. Inside was a plane ticket in my name, an itinerary and full payment in new twenty-dollar bills. He offered his driver to take me home but I really needed to walk.

"I almost collapsed when I stepped out onto the street. I could not believe what I had done. The envelope in my hand felt heavy and toxic. I wanted to throw it away but I stuffed it in the pocket inside my jacket. At the tea stall halfway back to the house I stopped and sat at a table across the road. From there I could gaze across the plains and watch the buses and trucks wind their perilous way up to Mussoorie. I ordered chai and two cigarettes. Back then I never smoked cigarettes, never drank anything stronger than water but that was when I started. As I sipped the sweet, spiced tea and smoked the harsh, unfiltered cigarette I tried to reassure myself. I knew I had been bullied and manipulated but I still could not reconcile what had just happened with my feelings for David. He had been our closest friend in India for so long. I told myself that my apprehension was completely unfounded, that it was nothing to do with David, that it was just my fear of being apart from Jasmine and Ganesha. By the second cup of chai and the second cigarette I had rewritten the whole encounter and suppressed my sense of foreboding.

"It would be okay, just a quick trip and I would be back and then we could all live peacefully for another year. I paid the boy and continued my journey home. Jasmine was waiting for me on the garden wall. I sat behind her and wrapped myself around her body but she pushed me off and turned to face me. She demanded that I tell her everything.

"I tried to lighten her up, started to tell her about the walk back up from the village but she stopped me, gazed at me with tears in her eyes and begged me to tell her everything. I related the facts, the details of the meeting but nothing of David's behaviour and nothing of my fear. She started to cry. 'Rafa, I'm scared. Something awful is happening, please don't go.' I told her everything would be fine, that David was trying to help us and cared about us, that he was being very generous and was asking little of me. I began to believe everything I was saying and my certainty silenced Jasmine. But I knew in my heart she was right. It was a strange experience. When I look back, I think I was under some sort of spell - I was lying to Jasmine and I was lying to myself. I knew that David had betrayed us and I was now betraying the people I loved. I had never lied to Jasmine before. I could even see myself lying but I could not break out of it, tell her the truth and abandon the whole deal. I was trapped and I did not understand how.

"That night I lay awake in a strange sort of half-sleep. I felt awake and very aware but I could not move. I sensed that Jasmine was awake but I could not talk with her. It was as if we were frozen in time. The night drifted on until the birds began to sing and the morning light crept into our bedroom. I got up and made breakfast. Ganesha was already awake and playing in the garden with the dog. I brought breakfast back to the bedroom and sat on the bed with Jasmine. Ganesha came and joined us. I told Jasmine and Ganesha they were the most important people in the world, that we would never be apart again, that we must be strong for each other. I told them that, although I would be away for a few days, we would stay in contact, that we would keep each other in our thoughts, that we must keep our minds positive. I promised this would be the only journey I would make for David. When I returned, we would use the money to build a new future for ourselves, to take the uncertainty out of our lives.

"We spent the day walking - through the village, beyond David's house, down into the valley past the vegetable gardens. The first rhododendrons were flowering and colour was returning to Mussoorie. The thin, spring light began to dispel the shadows along our path. We stepped out into the clearing where the Tibetans went to pray. Strings of prayer flags hung between the trees, tattered flags from years ago and new ones added quite recently. We went to that place many times and, although we had never seen anyone else there the place always felt inhabited, as if someone had just left. Our entire journey had been in silence, even Ganesha and the dog were quiet, unusually quiet. It felt as if we were on a sacred journey, a pilgrimage. The clearing was peaceful. I took Jasmine and Ganesha's hands. We stood linked in a circle. The dog sat down. I asked the gods to take care of us, to make sure I returned, to take care of Jasmine and Ganesha in my absence, to free us from this unease.

"On the way home we met the vegetable man - that long spider of a man with the huge basket on his head. We stopped him and bought some fruit. We squatted with him on the ground for a while, talking of the spring and the year ahead, while he smoked a bidi. At home we cooked a meal together. Ganesha was tired and went to bed early. Jasmine and I sat up until late. Things were easier between us. We talked of the future. I had long been thinking of teaching more English classes and we talked of using the money to set up a proper classroom. I wanted a way for us to live in Mussoorie without depending on David. We also talked about having another child. Jasmine always said she wanted a big family, at least five children. We talked until sunrise when Ganesha got up and came to lie down with us, gazing out through the window to the mountains. We decided that when I returned, we would go on a trek into the mountains. Nando, our chockidar, had been offering to take us ever since we moved into the house. Soon it was time to pack and leave.

"David's driver arrived and Jasmine and Ganesha drove down with us into the village. The cloud had left us and our parting was peaceful and easy. Jasmine and Ganesha left to walk back through the village while I continued on the treacherous descent to the plains below. David's driver barely spoke English and for the long journey to Delhi he was mostly silent but for his occasional wild outbursts as he maneuvered to overtake a truck or a bus.

"We arrived with the sunset at David's new house in Delhi. His housekeeper welcomed me and showed me to my room. It was a wonderful house, a beautiful piece of colonial English extravagance surrounded by a high-walled garden, furnished with a perfect balance of English and Indian antiques. There were formal rooms for dining and lounging European style and other rooms furnished exclusively in old Indian style with low platforms and rugs and heaps of bolsters and cushions. My room was very English, with dark mahogany furniture and thick velvet curtains. In one corner was a shrine to the god Ganesha with newly lit sandalwood incense. It made me smile. I lay on the bed and let my body find its stillness again after the ceaseless vibration of the journey. I must have fallen asleep and leapt up at the sound of a dinner gong calling from downstairs. I quickly washed my face in the bowl of water on the washstand and hurried down. I expected company but the dining table was set only for me. I ate well - South Indian vegetarian food served on English china with silver cutlery. I retired to the Indian lounge where David's cook served me tea. I had only been in there for a few minutes when Tamdin arrived - she must have been in the house all the time.

"I had only ever met her before with David and she had always seemed aloof, even elusive. Now she was much friendlier and sat down beside me. She told me that she was very happy that I was working for David, that he worked too hard and needed someone to help him.

"She told me that I was one of the few people he could trust. I explained that this was just a one-off trip, that I didn't like to be away from my family and when I returned, I would try to find another way to live. Tamdin said she understood. She told me she would also like to have a family but it was not possible. She didn't say why but there was sadness in her words. She told me this trip was very important. Once it was over everything would be different, she and David would spend more time in Mussoorie and she hoped that we would all see more of each other. She said she would see me in the morning, wished me good night and left.

"I went to my room soon after and slept soundly until the housekeeper woke me in the morning with a tray set for breakfast in bed. I prepared myself for the journey and went downstairs to the dining room. Tamdin was waiting for me there and asked me to join her in the lounge. She closed the door behind her, reached into the folds of her kira, brought out a small package. 'This is what you will be carrying,' she said. 'I want you to see it. You must understand how to carry it with respect.' We squatted down on the floor and she unwound the fabric to reveal a small, carved wooden object. Tamdin told me it was a phurba - a ceremonial knife. She explained that most phurbas are made of metal but this one was very old, 'from a time before metal'. I reached out to take it but she pulled back. 'Not yet,' she said. She held out the phurba for me to look. Although it was obviously carved it was so old and worn that the design was no longer clear. All I could say for certain was that the handle seemed to resemble a human figure and the blade was formed with three sides. Tamdin rolled the phurba up in the fabric and retied it. She told me very firmly that I was not to open it, that I was not touch the phurba, but that I should carry it at all times next to my body. She then told me that I had to complete a ritual before taking the phurba. I would have to repeat the ritual before handing it over in Bogota.

"Tamdin asked me to repeat the words she said. It was a mantra, rhythmic and repetitive. I repeated the words. Tamdin asked me to lift my shirt. She took a roll of medical tape and taped the package to the left side of my chest. 'Near your heart,' she said. 'Do not remove it until your contact meets you and instructs you.' She wished me a good journey and led me out of the room to the hall where the driver was waiting.

"The journey unfolded exactly as David said it would. I do not know how these things are done but I was taken to the airport and to my plane without ever checking in or passing immigration or customs. I was welcomed onto the plane and seated in first class in advance of the other passengers. When we arrived in Bogota I was asked to wait on the plane until the other passengers disembarked. A driver escorted me from the plane to a car that was waiting on the tarmac and drove me from the airport to my hotel. He took me directly to my suite without the need to check in. It was only then that I realised the power of the people David was dealing with. I had never suspected that he moved in such a world, a world where even immigration controls didn't matter. I could not understand the value given to the object I was carrying. How could that little wooden knife be worth the cost of this journey?

"A short while after my arrival a tall, thin man let himself into my room. I think he was Tibetan but he dressed in Western style with black business suit, white shirt and a necktie, subtly patterned in shades of green. He greeted me with a handshake and spoke in perfect English. He asked me to remove the package I had brought. He asked me to repeat the ritual words he said. Once the ceremony was complete, he accepted the phurba from me and handed over a thick envelope which I was to deliver to David. He wished me a good journey and asked that I remain in my room at all times. Shortly after he left room service arrived with dinner and bowls of fruits and chocolates.

"The journey back to India was as simple. At Delhi airport David's driver met me and drove me directly back to Mussoorie. It was such a relief to find myself back in lands that now felt more like home than my own. As we slowly drove up the twisting road to Mussoorie I started to relax and only then realised just how tense I had been. It was wonderful to see Jasmine and Ganesha again. I wanted to complete my work for David as soon as possible so we agreed to walk down to his house to deliver the envelope. The gate to the courtyard was open. We went straight in and called out, but nobody answered. We crossed the courtyard to the kitchen. Inside we found David's maid crouched in the corner under the sink. She was catatonic, her body rigid and her eyes staring into space. We talked to her but she didn't respond. Jasmine and Ganesha stayed with her while I went to search the rooms for David. I found him in what was left of his study. The room looked as if it had been hit by a tornado, everything reduced to splinters, walls stripped of shelves and books, stripped bare to the stone, nothing left of the furniture. In the middle of the dust and fine debris I found David. He was dead, his body completely unmarked, eyes open and an expression frozen into a strange, child-like smile.

"Jasmine and Ganesha went to the Prakash store to phone for help while I waited with the maid. She didn't respond to my being there and died later that day in hospital without saying another word. The doctor said she died of shock. An autopsy on David revealed no known cause of death. The pathologist said he just stopped living. An investigation concluded that there had been a gas bottle explosion which killed David and traumatised the maid. Everybody involved knew it wasn't true. David's neighbour had been at home at the time and heard nothing. But it was the best solution to a deeply disturbing case, a best attempt to allay the fear felt by everyone who bore witness to the scene in David's study."

3

I couldn't believe what I had just heard. A thousand images raced through my mind. A thousand questions infiltrated the images. I found myself trying to calculate dates, when I last saw David in India, when I saw him in London, when I received letters, when I didn't receive replies. I found myself indignant, then sad, then furious that I had heard nothing before. Finally, I resorted to disbelief. Such is the strangeness of the mind when confronted with death; it's as if it tries every possibility to disprove the fact.

A hand on my hand brought me back to the table, back to my companions and away from the imagination I was desperately trying to escape into. It was Kali's hand, her touch so reassuring I wanted to be in her arms, to be held by her, to be protected from the world by her. I looked up into her eyes through the tears that had flooded my eyes.

"It's alright," she said and at once everything felt all right.

Rafa wasn't sure if he should continue and I had to insist. I needed to know the rest. He continued.

"When we got home, I remembered the envelope I had carried from Columbia. It contained four hundred thousand dollars in bearer bonds and cash, and a small, green, subtly patterned business card. There was nothing written on it. We didn't know what to do. We had always considered ourselves to be close friends of David and yet now realised how little we knew about him.

"We knew nothing of his family or his other friends. Was it up to us to arrange his funeral or, perhaps, return his body to England? Was it up to us to attend to his affairs in India? Too soon we knew it didn't really matter. What really mattered was us. We were terrified by what we had seen and I already sensed it was connected with my trip to Columbia.

"I woke up during the night, to a strange light in the room, a light I had never seen before, neither dawn nor dusk, neither sun nor moon. I heard my name. It came as a whisper, repeated and repeated. I followed the call out into the garden. The same light filled the garden. Even now as I think back I cannot be sure that it was actually a light. Although the house and the garden were the same, nothing was familiar. I followed the whisper until I came face to face with an old man sitting cross-legged on the wall. He looked like a monk, dressed in simple brown robes with a hood covering his head. He summoned me to him with a wave of his hand. 'Rafa, come - sit beside me.'

"I sat beside the old man, my fear eased by being in his presence as he spoke. 'Rafa, you are a good man, perhaps a little stupid but with a good heart. For that you are still alive. For that you don't go the same way as David. David was not just stupid. David was also bad. David took something very important to me. Phurba! My phurba! My phurba is now with enemies! This is very bad for the world! You must repair it.'

"Although I had read a lot about reincarnation I thought it described a psychological possibility, not a physical truth. But the old man told me that he lived in Tibet long before it was called Tibet, long before it embraced Buddhism and that now he was in his final incarnation.

"He said he belonged to a group of 'permanents' - people who no longer needed to reincarnate through the body of a baby, people who could recreate their being at will, wherever and whenever they chose. However, despite appearing human, he could exert only a little physical influence in this world because his energy was so fine. For this reason, he and his group acted as guides, or lamas, to tulkus - reincarnates who were not yet permanent and still had to go through the process of physical death and rebirth.

"The old man told me that the earth was not as we imagined it to be. It was not a planet in the true sense but really the embryo of a planet, a planet in potential, like a baby yet to be born. As such, the earth was not a stable place but a place caught in conflict between the forces of life and death. If the earth reached a certain level of development it would ignite with a new energy in exactly the same way as a baby's nervous system ignites as it takes its first breath. If that happened, the earth would become a stable presence in the universe. He said this was similar to the process of growth and rebirth that humans had to go through to become free from decay and death.

"Although many of the lamas present on the planet today are concerned with guiding this process on the human scale, the old man and his group were concerned with work on the planetary scale. In reality, he said, there was little difference between the life of humans on the earth and the life of the earth itself. As long as the earth remained a planet in potential so would its inhabitants remain human only in potential. As long as the earth remained caught in the conflict between life and death so too would humanity be caught in that conflict. If the earth could be brought to a higher level of development, the planet and its inhabitants would become free from conflict. They would all be permanently connected to the forces of growth and freed from their suffering.

"However, as much as there were beings like him who were concerned with encouraging growth and permanence, there were others pursuing the opposite aim. He said this was a lawful consequence of the conflict.

"I was lost and the old man knew it. He told me to close my eyes. He described a staircase that lay before me and told me to walk up it. It was a simple staircase, made of white stone and without a balustrade. There was nothing either side, just emptiness. I continued walking upwards until the old man described a temple above me, a small round temple also built of white stone, no more than a circle of columns supporting a cupola. I found myself at the entrance and stepped inside. He told me to look down. I looked down and saw that below my feet was nothing but empty space.

"Way below me I could see the earth, just as it appeared in photographs from the moon. The old man told me to look round. Now there was no temple and no stairs; I was suspended in emptiness. I could see the earth and beyond it the sun and other planets. He explained that I was looking at a tiny portion of the universe. 'No more than a twig to an oak tree. Earth is a bud, ready to burst with life.'

"The old man said he would take me a little higher, to give me another perspective. Again, he asked me to look down and now I could see many suns, each surrounded by its own planets and moons. He said he would clear my vision to allow me to see things as they really are. I could see white strands lacing across space between suns and planets and moons. 'These,' he said, 'are like canals, like in a rice field - some irrigating, some draining. He asked me to turn around. Now I was looking into an incredible vortex, the white strands spiralling outwards and spiralling inwards. 'This,' he said, 'is the centre of the universe, a place of unlimited giving and receiving.'

"When the old man asked me to open my eyes again, I was sitting on the wall of the garden in Mussoorie which was still filled with a strange light. He put his arm around me. 'What do you understand, Rafa?' I told him that I could see that everything depended on everything else, that the earth was a very long way from the centre, that the threads reaching to the earth were more fragile and feebler than those closer to the centre. He nodded. 'This is so, the earth is beginning to die, like a tree bud in the frost.' He told me this was normal and had happened many times before, but this time was more critical and there was no guarantee that the earth would be reborn. If this happened, the human souls would be lost forever. I asked him why? It didn't make sense that the earth and all its people should just be wiped out. He said it was the result of a long and ancient conflict.

"As much as there were people like him who worked for the growth and development of the earth there were others aligned with the forces of death and decay. Many were just ignorant - scientists, politicians, industrialists - people who saw the earth only in terms of their hunger for wealth and power. Behind these people though, were others like the old lama who had seen many lives and many ages and whose intentions were much more dangerous. If the universe had unfolded naturally there would have been no difficulty; the earth would have gone through its process of death and rebirth until it became a self-sustaining planet capable of nurturing human life. Unfortunately, a community of souls accidentally incarnated on the earth before it was ready. They found themselves caught in the conflict between development and decay expressed by the planet. While many of them strived to evolve and play their part in the universal process of giving and receiving, some fell under the influence of the devolutionary force and developed unusual qualities like greed, envy and competitiveness.

“Some people, including the old lama, succeeded in raising themselves beyond the level of the earth and found freedom from the cycle of death and rebirth as well as the freedom to travel to other planets in the solar system. They were not free to leave the solar system but they were able to communicate with what lay beyond. They were given responsibility for the evolution of the humans who remained on the earth and for the survival of as many of them as possible whenever the earth went through one of its processes of death and rebirth. They became teachers and some are still remembered by name. More often, they suffered at the hands of humans opposed to their teachings.

“Some of them tired of the struggle and became disillusioned with the results. They decided it would be better if the population of the earth were wiped out. They encouraged all forms of selfish and destructive behaviours. They introduced technologies that didn’t belong to the earth and taught people to use them to manipulate the foundations of life. They hoped they would release a power so enormous or a disease so virulent that humanity would never survive. But, for reasons nobody could explain, it wasn’t so simple. For years the earth and its people have been balanced on a knife-edge, never quite falling into the expected cataclysm. It was as if there were a mechanism in the universe that none of them understood, a mechanism that magnified the work of the evolvers and diminished the effects of the devolvers. The earth hovers in a state of balance, but a balance so fine that it could be pushed either way, into death or into rebirth. The evolvers and the devolvers have been looking for an extra force with which to finally push the planet one way or the other.

“The lama’s phurba had a dual purpose. It could be used as a receiver, to draw universal energies down to the planet and to help him in his work. The lama said this was similar in effect to the domes and spires built at many places of prayer but, because it was so ancient and had been used by the lama for so many incarnations, its power was immense. The lama believed it was unlikely that any more powerful tool still existed on the planet. In the hands of the devolvers, the phurba could be used as a transmitter. They could gather energy from people and drive it into the earth to speed up the death of the planet and its people. This is the reason why the phurba was taken to Columbia; it was one of many places where natural geological faults gave access to the very core of the earth. The lama was sure the phurba would not stay there. He thought it more likely that the devolvers would take it from place to place, shaking the earth through many faults rather than just one.

"The lama always had with him an assistant, a tulku who remained when he died and was there to meet him when he reappeared. It was the assistant's duty to protect the phurba during his absence and return it to him when he returned. David's girlfriend, Tamdin, was that tulku. She achieved permanence under the guidance of the old lama and became free from the need to reincarnate. She accepted the lama's invitation to assist him in his work but he didn't realise until too late that she had been damaged, either from the pain of being born in exile or from the difficulties of life in the refugee camp. When the old lama died Tamdin disappeared with the phurba. She had heard that David supplied the devolvers with ancient and sacred objects. She used him. I think David knew it but he was too weak to resist her. David then used me. I think I also knew it but I too was too weak to resist. When I took the phurba to Columbia I was met by another assistant, someone in very much the same position as Tamdin.

"The lama said that as I was partially responsible for the loss of the phurba it was up to me to recover it. Although he could assist me, he could do no more because the problem was now a human problem. To ensure my commitment he took Jasmine and Ganesha away from me as surety.

"I am only permitted to see them once a year for one day. When we meet it is always the day before I travel to Columbia, repeated over and over. During that day nothing has changed. We are all the same age as we were when we were last together. We have no anticipation of David's death or of the lama appearing in our garden and I have no memory of this life that I live outside of that day. In this life I remember everything. In that life, the future remains a mystery. The lama promised that if I return the phurba our life together will begin again from that day. The future that I am now living will no longer exist. Does this make sense?"

4

When I lifted my head from the table I saw the sun rising over the sea. I couldn't believe it - I had spent the entire night in the restaurant. I looked around. All the tables were clear. The restaurant was closed. I felt a sense of panic; I had left my wife alone all night. I hurried from the restaurant, down the hillside path to our hotel. I unlocked the door as quietly as I could, hoping to find my wife still sleeping. She was sitting on the bed, facing me. I felt nothing but guilt and then the force of her fury filling the room. I couldn't say where I'd been for a string of other stories racing through my head. I felt like a child trying to think of anything to say apart from the truth - as if the truth itself were nothing but lies. Perhaps she had been waiting for this moment, been waiting for this one last straw, this one final sin.

"You bastard."

I knew she was right and yet I couldn't think why. I wanted to laugh. I always wanted to laugh when she swore in English. When I think back, I suspect I had always been pushing her to end it because I wasn't strong enough to do it myself. When the end came, when I heard her tell me she was leaving for Rome, that she didn't want to see me again, that I would hear from her lawyers, I felt an enormous sense of relief. A car-horn sounded outside. I stepped aside from the door in silence as she left with her cases and climbed inside the taxi. I knew in that moment I was losing everything - my home, my wife, her family, the money, the travel, the parties, the friends. Everything I possessed deserted me in the back of the old Mercedes, which pulled away from the hotel.

I waved feebly at the back of Marisa's head as the taxi turned the corner on the coast road and was gone. I closed the door and dropped my body onto the bed. I wanted to sleep but I was not tired. I looked around the room. The wardrobe doors were open, emptied of my wife's clothes. She had left my passport and ten one-hundred-dollar bills on the bedside table. That was it, my worldly wealth. There would be no more stipend from my wife's family; I could be sure my wife would fix that the moment she set foot in Rome. There would be no more extravagant voyages and shopping trips, no more bailing out my credit cards.

I had always been well aware of the insecurities of being a kept husband and now I would have to face them with a vengeance. Even if my conscience permitted me to sue her for divorce I knew I could never penetrate the defences her family would construct. Strangely, in the face of my imminent fall from grace, I felt at ease. I sat on the end of the bed and savoured the silence and peace and the sense of freedom, knowing that from this moment on I would no longer have to account for my every move.

I thought back to the evening's events. I had so many questions left unasked. I was confused now, unsure of what was real and what was dream. I couldn't understand why they had left me there or even when they had left me, with my head asleep on the table. What I knew for sure was the longing I had to be with them again and, compared to that, the loss of my wife was nothing. I had no idea what I would do now. I had no home to go to; the years of travel had cost me my friends and the acquaintances I had acquired meant nothing to me. I didn't even want to be in Tunisia now. I was only here because of my wife's need to top up her sun tan. I decided to go to the cafe just along the beach from the hotel to consider my future over breakfast. I stepped back out into the bright morning sun. Its touch exhilarated me. I was alive and I loved it.

I arrived at the cafe at the same moment as Rafa and Kali. Across the road Christina was parking a Land Rover, loaded up like an old camel. We sat together and, over coffee, I told them what had happened. They didn't waste their sympathy. Perhaps they could see my relief and, for once in my life, I actually didn't feel the need for sympathy. I never knew at this point whether or not I was being manipulated but to my enormous surprise when I asked them to take me with them they all agreed without hesitation. And so, I found myself in the back of a Land Rover heading south through Tunis and onto the desert road beyond.

5

As the sun went down, the cold gripped my body in its clutch as it rose like death from beneath the sand. We all moved in around the fire we had built between the tent and the Land Rover and I pulled my blanket closer. We had finished a meal of lamb and bread, which Kali cooked on skewers over the fire. There was a stillness - a stillness so profound it seemed to suck the noise from my mind and reveal an inner silence. Within that silence I realised that my anxiety had gone. I felt so at ease as I sat between Kali and Christina facing Rafa across the flames. I looked at his beautiful face. The sadness seemed to have slipped away and I saw again the round, happy face of my friend. He was looking down. I realised he was looking at the watches.

I finally asked him what it was with those two watches. "Whose time are they set to anyway?"

He looked at me with that soft smile that never left him in all the time I knew him in Mussoorie. "My time and Jasmine's time. When they meet, so do we."

He turned to Kali. "It's almost time. Which way?"

Kali raised her head and turned her face from the fire. She seemed to sniff the air and then simply, silently pointed. Rafa stood up and wished us all good night before following her direction. I now knew it was not a trick of the firelight – Rafa's face had shed its sadness and now he looked exactly as he was when I first met him. I watched him walk away.

He didn't go far, perhaps twenty meters and then he just stood facing out into the desert. The three of us remained, quietly watching the fire, watching the flames released from the wood, watching the red glow race back and forth across the ashes and embers. As the fire died Kali suggested that the warmest place for us now would be in bed.

I already knew she was right. I already knew that inside the black Bedouin tent we had set this afternoon was only one bed, built on layers of felt and stacked with blankets of wool and fur. I needed to take a pee and walked from the fire, beyond the tent towards a brilliant new moon which was just breaking the horizon. It's difficult to know where to pee in the desert; there's a strange feeling someone might be watching. When I finished, I walked back to the tent. Inside Kali and Christina were already in bed. By the soft, dark light of the oil lamp I checked for signs of clothes - I wasn't sure of what was correct. I hated sleeping with clothes on but I didn't want to offend anyone.

I noticed some clothes at the end of the bed, stripped down to my underwear and climbed into the space left for me beside Kali. Her back was towards me. I wanted to wrap myself around her warmth. When I used to enjoy sleeping with my wife I loved to wrap myself round her back. For a moment I missed her, wished she were here beside me in this beautiful tent in the middle of the desert. But with her I would never have been in this beautiful tent in the middle of the desert; I would be in the best hotel in the nearest city or by the beach. I lay on my back, a little apart from Kali, longing to roll in towards her body, remembering the moment in the restaurant when she put her hand on my hand. I must have fallen asleep immediately, into a deep dreamless sleep. When I woke it was hot. I supposed it was morning but I had no idea of how long I had been asleep.

Kali was wrapped around my back, one hand lying loosely against my stomach. I gently turned over to face her. She was still asleep. As I looked at her I knew that I loved her, that I wanted her. I realised I had no idea how to love a woman like her. I watched her sleeping - followed her deep, smooth breath, studied her beautiful face, resisted pulling her body to my body, let my hand rest on the curve of her hip.

Kali opened her eyes and I gazed into their green depths. They smiled at me. Her whole face smiled at me. She brought her face close to my face, gently rested her lips against my lips and then turned to whisper in my ear, "I know you love me."

She pulled herself up out of the bed and stood above me in her beautiful nakedness. As she leaned across the bed to gather her clothes I noticed a tattoo following the line of one shoulder blade - a line of Tibetan letters like birds on a cornfield. I asked her what it said.

"It's my name." I asked what it was and she answered, "You tell me."

She stepped outside the tent. Christina was still asleep. I stayed in bed a short while longer. It was too hot. I put on my trousers and stepped out into the sunlight. Kali was lighting the fire. Beyond her, Rafa was still standing in his place. I wanted to stare at him, to try to understand what was happening. I knew I should not and turned my gaze back to Kali. She asked me to bring the food and water from the Land Rover. In the moments it took, Kali had the fire ablaze. She hooked the kettle on the bar above the flames and prepared butter-tea and toast. When it was ready, she left me to eat alone while she took breakfast into the tent for her and Christina.

I sat alone, feeling like a puppy, wanting to run after her, wanting to leap and wag my tail for a moment more of her attention. I knew I had a lot to learn from her. I sat by the fire, trying to enjoy my breakfast, trying to enjoy the beauty of where I was, trying to enjoy my own company and find the value of my place in all this. I felt like a fraud. I could suddenly see how much I depended on others to know who I was. I didn't know what I wanted. I just waited to be wanted - waited to be defined by the want of another. Now I knew that I wanted Kali and I was scared. I didn't know how to ask, how to choose someone. I feared refusal so much I would never ask. I looked over to Rafa. I had always envied his life with Jasmine. Now, even in the midst of this tragic story, I was still envious of him. He was giving everything for the ones he loved. He knew what he wanted and in that knowing, his life was defined. His life had meaning - mine had none.

Kali and Christina joined me by the fire. Kali handed me my shirt. "You'll need this." She was right. I hadn't even noticed the heat of the sun. I couldn't keep my eyes off her. She was dressed in a long, black, hooded dishdasha. She acknowledged my gaze. "What is it?"

I wanted to know about her and about Christina. I wanted to know about their life with Rafa. I wanted information to feed my curiosity. Really, I just wanted to know about Kali. She could see through me. She could see the childish need behind my asking. She was kind with me, careful with my sensitivity. "Well," she said, "we have nothing else to do. Let's entertain you for a while. Christina, why don't you start."

I had barely heard a word from Christina since our first meeting. She had maintained a constant seal on herself, neither contributing to the conversations nor inviting any attention.

As she looked up from the fire, I was reminded of how lovely she looked. I was reminded of the first moments when I saw her enter the restaurant with Rafa. Since then it was as if she had become invisible. Now she reappeared and as I looked at her face I saw that what I had thought was wisdom was sadness - a perfect, impenetrable sadness.

"There is very little to say. I am David's daughter. When my father was killed I was staying in our house in Rishikesh. The maid looked after me when David was away. Rafa and Kali came for me. I've lived with them ever since. I am trapped, as trapped as Rafa. David was my father. I carry the responsibility for what he did. His sin is my burden. If we find the phurba I will be released. Until then I cannot live my own life."

Christina looked down again, returned to the cocoon of her sadness, resealed that lovely face that never smiled. I wanted to hold her. There was no possibility. There was no point. She didn't need a hug. I didn't even know that David had a daughter. My heart ached for her, wanted to weep for her. There were no tears, just a feeling of hopelessness. I wanted to tell her that I could help, that I could find the phurba, that I could give her back her soul. I knew I couldn't. I told her I was happy to meet her, told her I was sorry, told her how I felt her pain, how I wanted to be able to help.

My words sounded stupid, sounded so small and pathetic in the face of a situation that was mostly beyond my comprehension. I stopped talking and felt the meaningless of my life begin to swallow me up. Kali's hand took mine, called me back, rescued me from my own despair. "It's not your fault. Why do you take everything personally?"

"I can't help it," I said. "David was my friend. I care about his daughter. Rafa is my friend. I love him and Jasmine and Ganesha. I can't bear what is happening. It is personal."

Kali turned towards me. I was filled with fear. Suddenly I saw again the woman who frightened me when I first saw her in the restaurant. In that glance I knew just how pathetic were the words I had just spoken. She didn't need to say anything but she did.

"You understand nothing. You see everything according to your own little needs. You don't know how to care for somebody else. You talk of love and you know nothing about love. All you know is how to feel sorry for yourself. You use what you imagine about other people to help you feel sorry for yourself. If it is sympathy you want you have my sympathy. If you had listened to Rafa in the restaurant you would have understood something. Instead you think you are witnessing some tragic little drama. In truth, you are living some tragic little drama when you could be living your life. Do you understand?"

I understood. Caught in the grip of Kali's eyes I felt a veil lift. In the silence in which she held me my history unravelled. It was a history defined by insecurity, a history of relentless taking. The strange thing about the experience was my sense of detachment. I was like an observer, curious but uninvolved. I was being shown the truth of my life. Despite the ugliness of it, there was no sense of criticism, neither from myself nor from Kali. When she released me, I was looking at her at her most compassionate. I bowed my head and tears rolled down my cheeks.

6

We spent the day resting - mostly avoiding the sun, which, curiously, seemed not to shine on Rafa. Christina kept herself to herself while I helped Kali clean and prepare the Land Rover. Kali explained that we must prepare to leave before we slept, that we would strike camp with the sunrise. We shared little more than chatter, my mind too full of questions I dared not ask.

As the sun disappeared and plunged us once again into the cold desert night Rafa returned, joining us beside the fire. He looked exhausted and silently took the cup of butter-tea that Kali held out to him. He quickly drank it and without a word left and went into the tent. Kali prepared flasks of tea for the morning and together we packed what was left into the Land Rover. The two women retired to the tent. I wanted to stay outside for a while. I returned to the fire, which now was nothing more than a pile of glowing embers. I squatted down and stared into them. Tomorrow we would leave this place. I had no idea what I would do next. I felt at home with Christina and Kali and Rafa and the thought of parting company with them frightened me - I wasn't ready to be alone. They felt like family. I felt like I belonged with them even if I didn't know my place. They seemed to live between two worlds and I could participate in only one of those worlds.

I walked across to the place where Rafa had been standing. I could smell the scent of Mussoorie's evening blossoms. I stood for a moment. As I turned back towards the tent, I caught the flutter of fabric in the corner of my eye. It was a quick movement as if someone were running away.

I spun round but there was nobody there. I had the feeling of being watched. I called out but there was no answer. I called again. "I want to see you, I want to talk with you." I waited. I could hear nothing but my agitated heart. I returned to the tent. Rafa was asleep between Kali and Christina. He still looked young and very vulnerable. A place was left for me next to Kali. I undressed and climbed into the bed beside her. As I did, Kali rolled over towards me and rested her head on my shoulder. I put my arm around her and she continued to sleep. I don't remember sleeping that night; I had too many thoughts - repetitive, circular thoughts. I lay awake, listening to the thoughts and the sounds of the others sleeping. I felt my perception shift outward from the comfort of the bed and the sounds of sleep to the desert. Now I could only hear the huge silent breathing of the desert. Now I could hear only a silence from within me. Within that silence I felt a question emerge, a huge question that I had been hiding from all my life. "Why am I here?"

From the silence of the desert I heard my name, whispered like a breath, over and over. I eased my body gently from beneath Kali's weight and sat up, preparing to step outside. I felt Kali's grip on my wrist, pulling me back towards her. "Don't go. You don't belong here. Don't give up your freedom. What you want to know might poison you forever."

I turned back towards her and gave myself to her arms. I felt the seduction of her lips, which she offered, to my mouth. I wanted her so much but already knew that I would never have her like this, that I would lose her the moment we left the desert. I whispered in her ear, "I am already poisoned by my freedom, poisoned by my ability to run. I want you and I want to sacrifice my freedom." She let me go without another word and I stepped out of the tent into a strange light already familiar from Rafa's story.

I followed the whisper of my name back to the place where Rafa had stood and I waited cold and naked in the desert night. I heard a laugh and turned to meet the old man Rafa had described.

"So, my friend, you are serious. You leave the arms of a woman you desire and you leave your clothes. What do you want?"

I told the lama of the question I now felt burning inside me. I told him how my life had become pointless and lacked meaning. I told him how, in the company of Rafa and Christine and Kali, I felt a longing I had never felt before - that I envied their sense of community and purpose. I told him how I had lost everything, how I had no place to go and no one to go to.

"Then you have nothing to offer me," he said. "Go back to bed and enjoy what you have while you have it."

The old man turned away from me and started walking into the darkness. He was right. I had nothing. Rafa had no choice, he was trapped. Rafa couldn't give up because he would have to give up the only things that mattered to him. Christina was also trapped; she had nothing to lose but everything to gain in finding the phurba. I wasn't sure about Kali. I already had a sense that she was indifferent to human wants but it was clear that she had something to gain from her involvement in the search. I felt desolate as I watched the form of the old man fading. I wanted to curse him. I hated him for telling me the truth. I hated myself for the truth that he told me. Kali appeared behind me and draped a fur blanket over my shoulders. "Come." I followed her to the tent like a child. She offered me her arms, her body. I accepted but lay rigid in her embrace until it was time to leave.

We struck the camp and loaded the Land Rover. I was cloaked in the silence of my misery and remained so for hours as Kali drove us on our journey out of the desert. Rafa and Christina sat up front with Kali. I wallowed alone in the back, resenting them, envying them, loathing them.

It was getting hot. The sun was at its mid-point and the air-conditioning struggled to keep us cool. Suddenly the Land Rover lost power and stopped. Kali made a few attempts to restart the engine but it was futile - no response at all. I offered to go out and check the cables but I couldn't open the door. An ominous silence settled over us. Within a few moments the vehicle was like an oven as the mid-day sun continued to bear down on us. I heard Kali say, "It's too late," just as the brilliant daylight faded into an eerie purple darkness and the temperature in the cab plummeted to that of the desert night. I reached over behind the seat to pull out some blankets and saw the cloud just as it hit us. The Land Rover began to rock ferociously in the fury of the sandstorm. The interior filled up with a fine dust, which forced its way through every crack and crevice in the vehicle. The others clambered over the seat and we all huddled together on the floor under a layer of blankets. There was nothing to say and we cowered there together until an immense gust tipped the Land Rover and threw it onto its side.

There was an awful sound of cracking metal and glass and we were thrown into a desolate pile against one of the sides. The sandstorm was inside the cab and we could do nothing but cling together as the sand filled the cab and buried us. It was impossible to know how we were, whether injured from the fall or cut by broken glass. I heard Kali's voice, her head close to mine. She was speaking in Tibetan, repeating a mantra over and over. I focused on the sound and the dreadful roar of the wind faded in my awareness. Hearing her voice reassured me and released me from my fear that we would all die in the storm.

It took some minutes before I realised that the storm was no longer in the vehicle. When I did, I lifted my head and saw that the storm was still raging outside. It was as if we were in a bubble of safety and quiet. I watched as that quiet space expanded beyond the vehicle and then filled with the same light I had seen before in the desert night. I lifted myself from the pile of debris and pulled at the blankets and scraped at the sand until I freed Kali. We worked frantically to uncover Rafa and Christina, clearing the sand from their faces. They were both lifeless. As I was feeling Christina's neck for a pulse that was not there I heard the voice of the old lama. "Leave them, they are free now. Come."

I climbed from the shattered wreck and helped Kali up until we were both standing on the side of the Land Rover. The lama was standing there, the storm still raging behind him. I looked around and realised that we were standing in the eye of the storm. He waved us over and we climbed down and followed him as he cut a swathe through the chaos. I turned back to see the storm swallow the Land Rover, turning it into a dune.

The lama led us through a tunnel of clear air and we walked for hours until the tunnel opened out into an oasis, a little patch of peacefulness carved out of the melee. In front of us was a small pool surrounded by rocks and trees. Pitched beside it a Bedouin tent like the one in which we had slept the previous nights. On the other side of the tent a fire burned in a pit.

"Bathe and rest," the lama said. "Come to the fire when you are ready."

The lama turned his back and walked away while Kali and I stripped and plunged into the hot, sweet water. As we washed the sand from each other I asked Kali, "Do you know what's happening? Is this how the world ends?"

"I'm not sure," she said. "Let's wait for the lama to tell us. I'm sure he can tell us more than I can guess."

"And Rafa and Christina, are they dead? And Jasmine and Ganesha?"

"I don't know. Please be patient and enjoy the moment," Kali said and, as she sealed my lips with her lips, I accepted to follow her advice and enjoy that beautiful moment. We left the pool and found white dishdashas where our clothes had been. We dressed and walked over to where the lama was sitting beside the fire. He handed us tea as we sat down next to him. It was the strangest experience to be in that place. It was so peaceful and so safe with the lama and yet in every direction the fury continued to blow. There was now something familiar about being with him and the strange light that accompanied him seemed normal. I sat in the warmth of the fire and my questions returned and the awfulness of what had happened became clear. As it began to sink in and I began to sink into despair the lama called to me.

"That's enough of that; we do not have time for your little miseries. Rafa and Christina are gone. That is that. We have lost many good people and many more are at risk. You are only here because Kali chose to keep you alive, but that is between you two. You wanted some meaning to your life, now you find it. Kali works for me. It is up to her what she wants with you."

The lama explained that the search for the phurba was over, that it was already too late. The phurba had been plunged into the earth. Rafa and Christina had failed in their mission and, because their fate was tied to finding the phurba, there was nothing that he nor Kali could do to save them. The storm we were in was one of many raging around the planet. In a day or two they would subside but only temporarily. The earth was now poised on the brink of death.

He said he had to go to gather what was left of his people and would send for us when he could. “In the meantime,” he said, “perhaps Kali will tell you why she chose to keep you alive.”

With that the lama turned and walked toward the wall of fury. As he faded so too did the light he brought with him. Kali and I were left in the firelight.

7

Before the question had fully formed in my mind Kali began to answer it for me. "Before I can tell you something about you I must tell you something about me. Twenty years ago, when I was still at school, I was picked up in the street by a talent scout for a modelling agency. I did a camera test and was offered a contract. I had never considered work as a model and never thought of myself as a beauty, but I saw a way out of a life that offered me nothing but pain. I immediately accepted without consulting my family. A week later I was working my first assignment in Milan and, after a hectic year of work and travel, I moved to New York.

"My new life unfolded so quickly that I never had time to think. I travelled the world from show to show, hotel to hotel, party to party. When the novelty faded I realised the shallowness of my life and the world in which I was moving. An old familiar sense of despair settled in. For a while I carried on, turning on the smiles when I was in public but more and more retreating to my hotel room and an increasingly awful sense of futility. One of the girls I worked with persuaded me to try cocaine. It had always been around and I had always refused the offers before, not because I had any particular attitude to using drugs but simply because I knew nothing about them. At this point in my life I was prepared to try anything and, to my joy, cocaine seemed to help. I still suffered from despair but now I had a way to shift it fast when I needed to work or socialise. To start with I just used it when I had to be out and I accepted the despair when I was alone, but it wasn't long before I was using cocaine all day long. I felt more in control of my life and it took a long time for me to see just how much it damaged my judgment.

"I started sleeping with anyone who would have me, just to help me through the night and then I would do my first line as soon as I woke up, to help me deal with the shame of the night before. Over time I could see that I was caught in a circle. It took a while longer to realise it was a downward spiral. Finally, I noticed that I was getting less and less work. It was at this point that I met a guy. I tried to treat him just like any of the others who passed through my bed but he wouldn't accept it. He wouldn't accept the lifeless body I offered him in the dark. He wouldn't just leave in the morning like the others. He insisted on spending the daylight hours with me, on taking me to galleries and exhibitions, on walks in the park. I don't know why he tolerated me. I offered him nothing but he saved my life. He took me on a trip to India, to seek a healthy life by the beach.

"In the first days away from the city I realised my dependency on cocaine. I couldn't see the beauty. I didn't even want to leave my room beside the beach. I felt frail and empty. I treated him with all the contempt I felt for myself. But little by little I emerged from the awful tensions and anxieties and paranoia of the withdrawal. After a couple of weeks, I found my appetite again and began to put on weight and find some energy. I started walking and swimming and meeting people. Unfortunately, I didn't lose my sense of despair. Although I was feeling healthier, I still felt that something was missing from my life. I now knew that whatever it was could not be filled by the lifestyle I had been living, not by cocaine, not even by life on the beach. However, the simplicity of that life away from the distractions and complexities of the city did help me define the despair a little better. In part it felt like a hunger but I could never be sure for what. In part it was the feeling of being in the wrong place wherever I was. Somehow, and I don't remember how, I decided to leave India and travel to Nepal. I left behind the guy who had been so kind to me without any thought or thanks.

"I arrived in Kathmandu and checked into a travellers' hotel. Within a few days I picked up a stomach bug and after a week with dysentery I was too weak to leave my room. A woman who was in the room next to mine noticed my absence from the world and climbed across the balcony to look for me. She found me slumped across the bathroom floor. I think I was ready to die at that point and the dysentery had become the easy way to do it. I was barely conscious and had no will to help her as she tried to help me. She arranged to have me taken to a hospital which was attached to one of the monasteries.

"The monks nursed me back to life, although I remember little of those days. The first strong recollection I have is when one of the monks woke me one morning. He was very old, his body twisted like a vine and his skin parched and creased with age. He came and sat on my mattress on the floor. He didn't seem to speak any English but his hands communicated well and he soon had me lying with my head in his lap. He started singing to me in his own language. The song was incredibly familiar and I relaxed totally under its charm until I was suddenly aware of the child that I was still. The song changed into a rhythmic chant like a mantra and I was amazed to find that I knew the words and chanted with him. Then he clasped my head, put his mouth to my forehead and started sucking. I felt an awful darkness being drawn from every cell of my body. When he blew his breath out across the room toward the window, I saw a movement in the air, like black storm clouds. He repeated this process many times and with each breath I felt my body and mind get lighter until I was so relaxed that I drifted off to sleep.

"When I woke again I felt wonderful. I was alone in a room filled with the light of the morning sun. I was ready to go. I wanted to go back to the beach in Goa, back to the man I had left behind and now wanted so much to be with. When I left the room, I found myself in a small stone courtyard.

"I saw a large door across the other side and headed for it. Before I reached it, the old monk appeared and blocked my way. He refused to let me past. I thought he wanted money for his work and I gabbled something about going back to my hotel to fetch some. He refused to budge and I started to get anxious. I tried to push past him but he beat me back, knocking me to the ground. As I was lying there, he shouted at me. 'Death gone. Wish to die not gone. You stay here.'

"I was still too weak to fight and the old man's frail appearance belied his strength. I gave in and went back to my room. This scene was repeated many times over the following weeks. Many times, I tried to sneak out but it didn't matter how silent I was nor at what time I tried, every time I reached the door the monk would appear and beat me into submission.

"Finally, I lost my will to escape and my fantasy of whatever it was I thought I was going to escape to. I resigned myself to staying in the monastery and came to realise that I was happy to be there.

"It was around this time that another monk started to visit me. He introduced himself as the head of the monastery and as my teacher. He told me something that, despite its craziness, made sense and immediately calmed my anxious spirit. He told me that many years prior to the Chinese invasion of Tibet, the Tibetan religious leaders were already convinced of the inevitability of that event. They arranged for many of their lamas to die and to reincarnate outside of Tibet, in countries where they would be safe. They also arranged to set up a network of monks and lamas around the world whose job it would be to identify the new born tulkus and prepare the conditions for their protection and education.

"Unfortunately, the network took longer to prepare than was anticipated and many of the new tulkus were lost. Many, like me, found themselves as outsiders in the normal world, unable to fit in but not sure what it was they were lacking. I was one of the lucky ones who, through a series of accidents, found people who could recover me to some degree and prepare me for the life I was born to live. Many others died as drug addicts or suffered mental afflictions or fell into the hands of bad teachers who manipulated what little memory or skill they had.

"I was introduced to a small group of people who, like me, were reincarnated into the West. I spent seven years training with this group under the guidance of my teacher. We were subjected to a punishing regime. There was so much to learn, so many memories to revive, so much to be undone from our former lives and time was limited. From time to time, like the others, I would reach breaking point and try to escape. We were always caught before we reached the door and beaten senseless by the old monk.

"Most of my time was spent in the monastery but, occasionally, we made secret trips through the mountains to Tibet to meet other teachers or to visit sacred places that were necessary for our development. It was not the ideal education but it was the best available."

Kali at last acknowledged the state I was in and stopped. "Does this make any sense?"

It took quite some time before I could tell Kali just how much sense it made. That time was occupied with a flurry of mental and emotional activity. For a while I was sure she was just playing with me, as if she already knew as much about me as there was to know and was now throwing it back to me piece by piece, just for fun, just to pass the time in the desert. For a while I couldn't imagine why she had kept me alive, kept me here with her in the midst of this chaos when even the old lama couldn't understand her motive. For a while I was aware of my withdrawal, aware of the way I would withdraw into my complex thoughts and away from any possibility of spontaneity or conflict. This habit had been with me most of my life - much to the annoyance of so many of my friends. And here I was again in its grip at this, the most profound moment of my life.

Finally, slowly, I re-emerged towards my surface, to face the world outside, to face the smiling eyes that had watched the whole process and waited for me to return. In the middle of that strange place, lit by the flames of the fire I watched as Kali's face softened and changed its form and for a moment took a prior form and became the face I had been drawn to so long ago at a party in London.

As Kali's face returned, she whispered, "So now, tell me my name."

Softly, I said the name I had called her by from that first night. I never knew where it came from but it was all I could ever call her by. All these years I had forgotten it, never said it again after she left me on the beach in Goa. I never even knew what it was that drew me to her in the first place; she wasn't really my type. I could see that she was a mess and I really did not need another mess in my life. I was only in London briefly, only at that party by chance. I had closed my business and was intending to go back to India but this time not for business. This time I wanted to return for all the reasons I had gone in the first place - I wanted to find my spiritual home and I imagined it was there. Since that first trip I had done everything to avoid the search but now it felt that a circle was complete and the opportunity had come around again. At the last moment, just as I was ready to leave, I had received a call from an old friend.

He was staging his first fashion show in London and wanted me to be there. On an impulse I said yes and delayed my flight to Bombay. I decided to spend a few extra days in a hotel in London and then pick up my already packed bags and start my journey east. Beyond that I had no plans. I had rented out my flat and had nothing to call me home from my travels.

She had been modelling for my friend and was introduced to me at the party. As we kissed a cheek-to-cheek greeting, I heard myself whisper that name to her and I never remembered the name she was introduced to me by. We spent the entire night together on a sofa on the edge of the party and I went back with her to her hotel. She offered me her body and I refused. I told her then that I couldn't because she wasn't really in it. We did spend the night together and I remember holding her and watching over her as she slept a dream filled sleep. In the morning I didn't want to leave. I couldn't understand why, she had nothing that I wanted and I already had my plans. But I couldn't leave.

I'm not even sure why she let me stay beyond that first night. It seemed obvious I also had nothing to offer her. I refused her body and I refused her drugs. For both these refusals she paid a price in discomfort. Perhaps for the first time she felt her addiction to both but she accepted the discomfort to stay with me. I think we were together a week in London before I told her my plans to go to India and she said she wanted to come with me. Again, without knowing why, I agreed and we arranged to leave a few days later.

She left behind her drugs and the first weeks in Goa were pretty scary and not what I had planned. I stayed beside her through her sickness and shakes and mood-swings. It seemed to be the opportunity she had been waiting for and she went through the pain of withdrawal with an amazing determination. As she became stronger, I found the peace and quiet I had been longing for.

Now we spent our days together on the beach or sleeping in the shade of our beach hut. We attended yoga classes with a local teacher who lived near the beach and followed his instructions on diet. Soon we both looked a little healthier. We were not lovers and I never imagined that changing. Regardless of the changes she had gone through it never felt quite right to explore that level of intimacy.

Despite this, despite everything, it still came as a massive blow when she left. I was out at the time, out with some friends along the beach and came back to find her gone, came back to a note that said little more than that. I spent days searching for her, asking everyone on the beach if they had seen her but she had disappeared like a breath. It was only then that I knew how much I loved her and how I had used my altruism to disguise what I truly felt. It didn't take long before I knew I wouldn't find her; India is the perfect place to disappear and I resigned myself to the loss.

Soon after I met the woman who was to become my wife. By chance she was staying on the same beach and she moved into my life with such speed that we were getting married before I even noticed how she had taken me over.

"But you know, I never forgot you."

Kali laughed. "And you never found your spiritual home?"

"No, I never did. I married a rich woman who was looking for a man like me - a lost soul who could accompany her on her aimless search for experience. After losing you I was happy to take that role, to live a life without responsibility and without direction."

Marisa had just enough enthusiasm for the both of us and enough money to make it look as if we had some direction. Years later she told me how she had been stalking me on the beach and couldn't believe her luck when my partner left without her having to chase her away.

8

I don't know how many days Kali and I spent by the oasis but, at some point, the wind died down and the silence was more disturbing than the wind. I was fearful that there was nothing left in the world but the two of us. Our oasis felt like a glorious prison, the last place on earth with nowhere else to go. We spent the time sleeping and telling stories about our lives apart.

It became clear that we had crossed paths many times since Kali had left and she always knew when I was close. Kali's intuition brought her to the restaurant in Sidi Bou Said. Rafa and Christina wanted to go straight to the desert but Kali knew she had some business of her own to take care of. Her timing was impeccable, as was her sense of discretion. I would never have guessed that she was the same woman I knew on the beach. Her years of training and preparation had made her so different and it was only occasionally, when she chose, that I saw a glimpse of the waif she had been. And so, we became lovers.

After Kali had completed her training she had been assigned to the old lama as his assistant. Although she didn't yet have the same level of power as Tamdin she was to take over her responsibilities. The old lama continued to teach her as and when he could but the demands on her were enormous. Although she had strong psychic powers, they still took a lot of effort and left her exhausted. The old lama had himself told her that she would benefit from the company of a husband. He offered to find her one but she was satisfied that she could find him again herself. It was a mixed feeling that came with the return of the old lama. I was happy in the desert with Kali and happy to continue living forever those days of talking and sleeping and making love.

I was also happy to finally receive some news of what was happening in the world and what was expected of us. The old lama laughed when he looked at me. "Ah, welcome back," he said.

I wanted to know what he meant and he took an old silver case from inside his robe, polished it against the fabric and held it to my face. Apart from the beard that had grown, apart from the suntan, apart from the bleaching of my hair, my face had transformed and I too couldn't help laughing. The years of worry and anxiety that had creased my face had disappeared.

The old lama told us that we would soon move from the desert. Someone would come for us and take us to the road where a vehicle was waiting. We would drive to the coast and a boat would pick us up and take us to Italy. From there we would drive to a house near Florence where we would meet other survivors from his group. He told us that at the time the storm came to us there had been a series of small earthquakes around the world. Tokyo and Los Angeles had been shaken, as had many towns in Central and South America, China and Central Asia. There had simultaneously been a global magnetic storm and many transport and communication systems had been disrupted.

As far as governments around the world were concerned this was just a series of natural disasters caused by sunspot activity. But the lama told us that this was the beginning of the complete destruction of the earth as we knew it. The energy that would be released by the destruction of the earth and all its life forms would be used in a way that none of them could imagine. Despite being privy to all this bad news I too could in no way imagine why anyone should either want to or even be capable of destroying the planet. If all of this were true, I certainly couldn't see what I had to offer in a disaster of such epic proportions.

I wanted the lama to leave, to take his bad news with him and leave me in the desert with my lover. But I knew that I had finally found my path.

After the lama left I quizzed Kali on what she knew. It was very little. Since she had been working with the old lama, her main responsibility was to help Rafa and Christina in their search for the phurba. Her psychic powers had kept them in touch with its location and they had travelled the world together in pursuit. They knew that the phurba had been brought to Tunisia but they hadn't realised that the devolvers had assembled enough people to put it to use. If they had, they would never have set off to the desert for Rafa's encounter with his family. Kali confessed that even after all these years she still had a sentimental tendency, a tendency that may have cost the lives of Rafa and Jasmine and Ganesha and Christina. I tried to reassure Kali but gave up quickly as her glance cut through the futility of my words.

"So, what do you want from me?" I asked. "What can I do to help you?"

With a smile and a voice that made me feel like the hero of the story, Kali answered. "Already, without knowing it, you have done so much. I will ask more when I need it and you are ready to give it. In the meantime, come and sit with me and let's watch this new moon rise over the desert."

9

The following morning our guide shook us from our sleep. He brought a change of clothes for the journey and as soon as we were dressed he silently beckoned us to follow him and abandon our little oasis. We followed, struggling to keep up with this man who seemed to float above the sand as we laboured across its shifting surface. In a surprisingly short time, we found the remains of a road and an old jeep parked beside it. Inside we found food and water and a roughly drawn map of our route. Our driver showed us how to start the jeep using a cranking handle and pointed out our initial direction before wandering back into the desert.

We travelled in near silence except for occasional discussions about the route. I suppose we shared the same sense of anticipation and foreboding about what lay ahead. By the time we arrived at the coast we were both exhausted from the noise and vibration of the jeep. I felt as if my insides had been turned to liquid and it was a relief to be helped aboard the fishing boat that was waiting for us at the beach. Its gentle motion over the surface of the Mediterranean soon rocked us to sleep in the place where we lay together amongst the nets and tarpaulins.

I didn't wake again until sunrise and I woke to a complete panic. It suddenly dawned on me that apart from our desert guide and the skipper of the boat we hadn't seen another soul, not another sign of life. I woke Kali, desperate for reassurance that we were not the only people left alive. She couldn't say it, couldn't tell me it wasn't true. My panic increased.

I took Kali by the shoulders and shook her, tried to shake the words I wanted to hear from her half-sleeping body. I stopped as suddenly as I started when I saw her restful face turn to fear and I realised what a complete idiot I was, how I was always demanding reassurance from her and never able to give it in return. I turned away, let my body flop over the side of the boat towards the water, let the spray soak my face and let the coldness of the water bring some sense to my deranged mind. I turned back to Kali, took her in my arms and begged her forgiveness for my failure, for my weakness.

As my tears mingled with the seawater a voice interrupted my thoughts - the voice of the old lama. "Trust me. If you can trust me you can help her in her work. If you cannot, better you leave her to do what she must do alone."

The words and the sense of the old lama that came with the words reassured me and I replied out loud that I was okay now, that I knew I could continue. Kali was now fully awake, staring at me, asking who I was talking to. I told her that I was talking with the lama. Her concern gave way to a broad smile. "Then we will be alright. You're in touch now and that contact can only get stronger from now on. I'm sorry, I had to know you were with me. Of course there are other people apart from us but we have to be careful. Whatever it is the lama wants us to do will be resisted. The more discrete our journey can be the more possibility we have of reaching our destination and beginning our work together. Now you have established your contact I can start to teach you. I feel happy today."

And with her words I too felt happy as I suddenly awoke to the beauty of our journey as the fishing boat cut across the sea and porpoises played in between the wake and the rays of the morning sun. Our skipper brought us glasses of hot sweet tea and life felt good.

10

My lessons with Kali started as the boat continued its slow journey to Italy. Kali borrowed a pack of playing cards from the skipper. "The idea is simple," she said. "I will pick out a card and you can tell me which card it is."

I thought she was joking when she told me. I couldn't imagine doing anything of the sort. Although I was willing to accept psychic powers in other people I had no pretensions of such powers in myself. Kali gently insisted that I try and in return for her kind encouragement I agreed. To start with I didn't manage to get a single card right.

"Stop guessing and stop trying. Simply open your mind to the possibility of the image of a card appearing."

I followed her instructions and was amazed to find one time after another the correct card appeared. By the twentieth correct card in a row I was jumping up and down in a childish ecstasy of achievement, much to the annoyance of the skipper. I quickly regained my composure under his gaze and sat back down on the tarpaulins to face Kali again. In the style of the best teachers she congratulated me on my success before telling me how that was the easy part. "I had been pushing the image into your mind. Now you have to learn to reach out and take the image from my mind without any assistance."

It took a long time before I could follow Kali's instructions but, little by little, I learned to concentrate my mind and send it out in a strand that could search Kali's thoughts and find the image of the card that she kept hidden within.

In the process I found more and more freedom to rummage through her other thoughts as well. Although what I was learning was extraordinary, my excitement wasn't so great as before because the whole exercise was exhausting. Very soon I could hardly keep my eyes open and Kali ended the lesson and told me to sleep.

We continued the rest of our sea journey in this way. Each time we practised Kali moved us further apart until I could see every card with us seated at opposite ends of the boat. Each session ended with sweet tea or another nap. One of the stranger things that happened was that I started to see three or four cards in advance. At this point Kali became very excited and finished my first training session with an enormous hug.

It was early morning when our skipper finally beached the boat somewhere on the coast of Italy. We bade him farewell and he took straight back to the water as our driver appeared out of the half-light and called us across to where a car was waiting behind the dunes. In the back of the car we found blankets, food and flasks of strong black coffee. Our driver, a young Tibetan man who spoke no English, told Kali that we should take no more than a few minutes break before we started our journey. We used those minutes well by removing our shoes and socks and dashing into the warm sea before leaping into the soft leather interior of the old car to start our journey north. Kali quizzed our driver but he knew very little. All we could find was that he had made this journey a few times before as he collected others like ourselves from the beach. As we reached the main road it came as a huge relief to see other vehicles and town lights and people walking. I don't quite know what I was expecting but life outside did at least look normal. Kali and I ate some of the food, which the driver refused, and then she suggested we rest. "We might yet need all our energy on this journey."

By now I was used to her enigmatic statements and needed to know no more as I snuggled into the back seat and closed my eyes. When I woke again, we were speeding along. Our driver had all the driving skills of a local as he pushed his way past car after car, flashing his lights and clinging to the car in front until he could get by. I felt at ease with him and could relax and enjoy the scenery. Soon we were on familiar roads, roads heading north into the hills above Rome, roads I had travelled many times before with my wife as we were driven up to her father's palazzo with its electric fences and guards and dogs. For a moment I felt a pang of nervous guilt, half expecting to see her on the road, remembering the first meeting with her father who put the fear of God into me when we went to tell him we were married. I never knew what it was she told him but when they emerged from his study, he treated me with the congeniality afforded a simpleton and withdrew his threat to have me taken into the garden and shot. We were often at the house but I was never privy to the many meetings that took place there. I was always kept apart from the other guests who converged on the main house, but I used to watch in awe from the safety of the garden cottage that was always reserved for us. My wife told me they were 'trustee' meetings. I always assumed that to be code for mafia and I was happy to keep a low profile.

As we reached Umbria I felt more at ease until I heard a siren and turned to see a police car closing in on us. Kali said something to the driver and he pulled over to the side of the road. She turned to me. "Do nothing. Keep very still and withdraw your attention from the world."

I sat there in silence as the two Carabinieri checked the car. I heard them try to open the boot and the doors. I watched as they recorded the registration number, as they peered into the car and noted details of the tax. Then I heard them walk away, start their car and speed off into the distance.

"What happened?"

Kali smiled. "They didn't see us."

Before I could say any more we were back on the road. As we continued our journey Kali explained the ways of invisibility. As the driver and I withdrew our attention from the world Kali inserted into the minds of the two policemen the scene she wanted them to see, an empty car, parked by the side of the road.

I didn't get it. "How could they see an empty car when they had just been chasing us a moment before?"

Kali's answer was so ludicrously simple it made me laugh. "Because in the light of their new experience it was easier for them to forget their previous experience. Do you think two Umbrian Carabinieri could cope with people disappearing before their eyes?"

Kali went on to explain the different ways to become invisible and the importance of understanding 'the psychology of the simpleton'. I wanted to know how she could know who she was dealing with. "Simple," she said. "I take a look."

Kali explained that 'taking a look' was not much different from what I was doing with the cards. I just had to clear my own mind and then reach out to the mind of the other person, but this time without any specific aim. She said it was more like general tourism than specific sightseeing. My first guinea pig was the driver. I followed Kali's instructions and reached out into his mind. He must have felt something because he looked up, caught my eyes through the rear-view mirror, flashed me a smile.

There really wasn't much going on in there. In fact, I was quite envious of the sense of peacefulness I wandered into. I reported my findings to Kali and she agreed. "Why do you think he's a driver? Next time try and be a little more discrete, he felt you coming."

I wanted to try it with Kali but she told me to wait. Instead she had the driver stop in Assisi and took me to a cafe near the basilica. As we sat there with our coffee I took a tour of the other customers. In some cases, as with our driver, there really was almost nothing going on. The patron's wife was a bit of a shock, with her plan to poison her husband and take up life with her young lover. I would never have guessed from her affectionate performance.

I felt sorry for the girl sitting at the next table from us, carrying a baby fathered by an unknown farm-worker she had slept with for just one night, unable to tell her family, unable to seek help in such a small community. I think she was right to run away and I couldn't resist leaving a small affirmation in her thoughts.

What I didn't understand was how I could know what was going on when I didn't know the language. Kali explained. "Because all thought is the same language. Language as you think of it is only the surface and we're always looking deeper than that, at thoughts before they become words."

We were preparing to leave when a newcomer caught my attention. He reminded me of the men who used to associate with my father-in-law, with his black suit and sunglasses and his hair preened and greased to hold the curls in check. As he disappeared behind his newspaper I sneaked into his mind. Before I had a chance to see anything I felt a darkness surging around me. My vision began to close down and I felt my body rapidly draining of life.

I couldn't disconnect, couldn't take back my mind as I felt a stronger force than me wrestling with it, dragging it out of me. Suddenly Kali was on her feet and all hell broke loose. I felt my mind snap back into place and turned to see a flurry of activity around the man in the suit who was now lying on the pavement.

In the chaos, Kali helped me from my chair and half dragged me to our car that had screeched to a halt nearby. The last thing I remember before I blacked out was the squeal of tyres as our car set off even before the door had closed.

When I came around it was dark. I was sprawled across the back seat of the car with my head on Kali's lap. My brain was split in half with migraine and I didn't even have enough energy to raise myself. Kali reassured me that everything was under control and under the soft touch of her hands I drifted back into sleep. I woke again when we finally reached our destination and I was helped from the car to our room in the old farmhouse. After some hours in the comfort of a bed I felt strong enough to sit up. Kali was sitting beside me in a chair. She looked exhausted and was clearly relieved to see that I was finally all there. In the soft candle light of the warm stone room she explained what had happened.

"You tangled minds with someone much stronger and much better prepared than you are ready for. If I hadn't stopped him he would have sucked the life right out of you in a few seconds. Thankfully he was no match for me and soon gave in to the heart attack that I thrust upon him. I only realised who he was after you blundered in."

I felt like a fool but Kali reassured me. "Your action probably saved us. A few more minutes and we would have been surrounded by other 'minds' and we would never have survived their consolidated attack."

This was for me the first shocking realisation that we really were at war, that we had real enemies and that those enemies were already way ahead of me in their psychic powers. I wanted to start straight back in with my training now that I saw how important it was. But Kali was too tired from her night of taking care of me while my body recovered. While she slept I took my turn in watching over her, caressing her tired body with my mind.

11

Morning broke and our driver arrived at the door. Behind him stood a burly Italian grandmother with a tray laden with coffee, bread and pastries. As she set the tray down I couldn't resist practicing my new skills and found what was obvious from the first. Here was a good country woman, a mother of many and a godmother to many more, a woman who liked nothing better than to open her home, her kitchen and her heart to the people who were sent to her. As she stood up she wagged her finger at me. "Naughty boy, keep your mind to yourself."

With an affectionate wink she turned and bustled out of the room. I ate my breakfast and continued watching over Kali until, sometime in the afternoon, she sat up. She looked radiant after her sleep. After cold coffee and croissants, after a much-needed hot shower, after changing into new clothes, we left our room and stepped out into the clear Florentine light and the long cypress shadows and the buzz of insects. We were called across to lunch served on a big table outside the farmhouse.

Kali and the Italian lady knew each other and after much embracing and cheek pinching and whispered comments and laughs that clearly alluded to me, I was formally introduced to our host, Maria. We sat down to eat and I discovered that Kali had been here many times before. I would never have guessed, but Maria's husband, Ennio, was a tulku. He never even knew it until quite late in his life. He had spent his life as a sculptor. Nobody knew where his passion came from, as there was no artistic lineage in his rural family.

But it was all he ever wanted to do. He taught himself and his work became much sought after. When Maria showed me his studio I could understand why. Just being in the company of his work, facing those stone figures, evoked an incredible sense of calm. Although he had died two years before, his presence still inhabited the space and both Maria and Kali gave their tears to the memory of that very special man. Kali later explained that Ennio's youngest daughter had persuaded him to go with her to Rome to receive teachings from a Bhutanese Rinpoche who was touring Europe. At the end of the day the Rinpoche called Ennio aside, embraced him, touched him forehead to forehead and showed him who he was. Ennio was not surprised by the revelation. He was content with the life he had created but in anticipation of the times that lay ahead he opened his house to anyone in need of refuge. After his death, Maria continued to offer that service but from then on Ennio's studio was closed to all but the special guests she entertained. After lunch we returned to the studio to continue my training.

12

In the days that followed Kali introduced me to many new talents. We continued the work we had started on the boat but now we could extend the distance between us, and this time we worked with many things besides the cards - with objects around the farm, with nature, with ideas and concepts and finally with entire conversations so that Kali and I could communicate directly without words. This was the part I loved the most. There was an incredible sense of intimacy when I talked with Kali in this way, as if we momentarily became one, despite the many fields or buildings between us.

In the studio we started working with visualisation. To begin with Kali taught me how to look more thoroughly at one of Ennio's sculptures, how to really take in the form until I could reproduce it in my mind with my eyes closed. She taught me how to make the visualisation three-dimensional so that I could turn and rotate the image in my mind. She then taught me how to open to more dimensions until I could place the object anywhere in space and time that I chose. During one of these sessions Kali let out a shriek of delight and I opened my eyes to see her dancing like a child around the studio. When she finally calmed down and released me from her embrace I realised that the sculpture I had been working with was gone. There was nothing but a dust-free patch on the floor where it had stood.

"Quick, quick, tell me - where did you put it?"

"Outside, by the kitchen door."

"I'm glad you didn't go too far – let's go."

Kali dragged me out of the studio and round the side to the house where we found Maria staring at the sculpture in its new location. I offered to try and move it back but she said, "No, I like it here." I wasn't sure if she was telling the truth or simply didn't trust me to get it back in place. I never did find out just how much Maria knew about what was going on but she was surprisingly easy going about some of the strange things that were happening around her home. As we walked back to the studio Kali put her arm around my shoulder. "Do you know what you just did? I knew I was right - I knew you had it in you."

After that giant leap in my training things just got better and better. Now I learned to do the same things with sculptures I had not yet seen, those under dustsheets and those in packing cases. Later Kali took me outside and taught me how to see behind trees and buildings, how to look down on the farm from above and, finally, how to extend my field of vision until I could see all the lanes and roads and fields for miles around the farm-house. When I described a coffee shop on the edge of the market in Florence she said, "Let's go there - you need a break and the driver's back."

I had been so occupied that I didn't even notice his absence but when we got to the house he was waiting for us there. Kali told me that he had just brought some more people up from the coast but that they were resting after the journey. We set off to Florence and found the café. It was exactly as I had seen it even down to the girl working the tables. Despite the change of venue, Kali didn't let up on my training. I think she was on a roll and determined to push me as fast as she could.

Perhaps she already knew what was in store for us. Over fresh orange juice and sandwiches Kali explained that we had to start work with energies. "When you collapsed in the back of car, I used my own energy to keep you alive while your body repaired itself from the attack. To a lesser extent and without really knowing it, you did the same for me when I had to rest after the journey. It is all to do with attention. You could feed me with your attention while I slept simply because you love me. Now you must learn to do it with more consciousness and without regard for your feelings for the person."

Without looking she described a man who was sitting behind her. She asked me to take him in, in the same way I had already done with the sculptures, until I could close my eyes and visualise him in all dimensions. "Ok, now I'm going to give you a little gift."

She took my hand and I felt a strange tingling sensation deep inside my head. She then told me to visualise his energy. Without knowing quite what she meant I closed my eyes and now I could see the man but this time he appeared as a web of glowing threads which formed a three-dimensional human figure. I described what I saw and Kali told me I was looking at 'threads of life'.

"This is the energetic field which holds his physical structure in place. Now try and look directly at the man but only see this energy body."

To my amazement I could do as she asked. Here I was sitting drinking coffee in this ordinary street cafe and looking at someone else's energy system. As I looked around, I found that I could do it with everyone and even with the annoying little dog that begged crumbs from the table next to ours. Kali called me back from my reverie. "Listen, we haven't much time. Take a look at the man again and tell me if you see any weaknesses in his system."

I related what I saw. "Around the area of his heart the threads seem to be weaker and some of them look broken. There is something similar happening around one side of his pelvis."

"Ok, go for the heart and pull at the energy. Use the same method you used to take images from my mind."

I started to do what Kali asked and to my horror I watched as the man's life force seeped out from the area of his heart and started reaching out towards me. I switched my attention from the energy body to the man himself and watched as the colour drained from his face. Just before he closed his eyes and slumped in the chair he looked at me with a pained and accusatory look.

"Oh my god Kali, I've killed him. Do something."

Kali grabbed my hand and dragged me towards the car as people started gathering around the man.

"He saw me, he knew it was me."

As I jumped in the back of the car Kali stopped for a moment and faced the man and then calmly climbed in beside me. "It's okay," she said. "He'll come around soon. He was due for a heart attack anyway but now he'll avoid it for a few more years."

As we drove back to the farm Kali congratulated me on my work. I had just learned to do what she had done with the man who attacked me in Assisi. "We will practise this work much more so you can heal as well as damage energy structures."

I was relieved to hear that but I really didn't want to hear any more. I was tired from the effort and still shocked by what I had done. I couldn't get rid of the image of the man's face when he realised what was happening. Now the work felt dangerous and dirty and my head was filled with doubts about what I was doing. Kali must have been aware of what I was going through and left me in silence for the rest of the journey back.

13

The old lama was waiting for us at the farmhouse. He greeted us with a warmth I had never seen in him before. He told Kali and the driver to meet us later at the dinner table and then, with his arm around my shoulder, he led me out to the fields, to the shade of a walnut tree. As we sat and talked he settled many of my fears and very quickly reinspired my confidence and enthusiasm for my training. During the time we had been at the farmhouse he had been out visiting groups around the world. He still believed there was a chance to save the planet. Although many of his people had been killed recently, much of the work they had been doing was still intact and useful. It seemed that the war, which I had only recently become aware of, had always been going on. Mostly it was an invisible war, a war of energies, a war which very few people ever even noticed. It had nothing to do with the crude military wars that broke out incessantly around the planet. They had another purpose that meant nothing in the face of the current crisis.

The earth had an energy structure very similar to the one I had seen in the man in the cafe and which Rafa had described to me in Sidi Bou Said. This energy system was constantly changing and adapting to conditions in the universe. As long as it remained fundamentally intact the physical integrity of the planet was guaranteed. Occasionally, and quite naturally, this energy field was damaged or had to make major adaptations. These shifts in the energy field caused earthquakes and volcanic eruptions and, to a lesser degree, storms, as the physical structure of the earth adapted to the change. The phurba that had been stolen from the lama had been used to damage the energy structure of the earth. Holes had been torn in the web in Columbia and Tunisia.

Fortunately, the phurba had been mishandled in Tunisia and had been destroyed in the process. But for this, the devolvers would probably have succeeded in completing their plan to open up wounds elsewhere on the planet and there would have been nothing we could do to repair the damage. Now we had a chance.

The lama explained that we would be using a very ancient technology, one that people had been using for thousands of years to assist the planet in its repair and growth. We still had many remnants of this technology scattered around the world although, as the true purpose behind these projects was secret, most people never realised their significance. He gave me a string of examples, projects which still amazed people for their audacity but which remained a mystery in their purpose. He included the great pyramid and related constructions in ancient Egypt, the Mayan Temples, the ley line and standing stone projects in England and France, even the old observatory I had once seen in Jaipur. He said there were many more, as yet undiscovered. All of these projects had been undertaken to maintain the energetic balance of the earth and its relationship with the rest of the universe. Even in more recent times, the governments of America and England had been seduced into setting ancient Egyptian obelisks in their capital cities. Although on the face of it this project looked like nothing more than an act of extreme vanity on the part of its participants, it was actually the completion of an energy system that had been started long before in Rome and continued later in Istanbul.

It was this that saved the world from certain destruction during one of its previous deaths. The project almost failed at the last moment when the devolvers nearly managed to consign one of the obelisks to the bottom of the sea, but an enormous effort on the part of the evolvers recovered the situation just in time.

A similar project had been started in our own time. The design for it had been drawn up many hundreds of years ago along with many other constructions, any of which could have been undertaken in response to the prevalent conditions. Part of the project was physical and this had long been completed. It consisted of a network of structures erected around the world. One of these was in my own city, in London. I remember it being built.

At the time I was surprised at the raising of a stupa on the banks of the Thames, with its golden Buddhas gazing out to the four directions. I was living in London at the time and often used to go down to the site. Once when I was there I joined the monks who were doing the work and drank tea with them in the little canvas shantytown where they lived in Battersea Park. None of them could speak English and I never did find out who was organising or paying for the beautiful stone and wood construction. I did hear later that other such stupas were being built in many cities but I knew no more.

During this time many Buddhist centres were being opened around the world, places where very advanced lamas and tulkus could offer their teachings and transmissions. This was the energetic part of the work. When it became apparent that this process was moving too slowly a new system of transmissions was introduced under various guises.

The system proved so simple and effective that it became self-regulating with transmissions being passed from person to person with very little further work from the initiating lamas. These two processes resulted in two new energetic webs around the planet. One carried unconsciously through the newly attuned minds and one carried through a network of special buildings. The next part would be to energise the entire system and this was now the task that the old lama had to undertake with the help of his group.

After the lama had told me all this, he left me in silence for a while, clearly understanding my need to digest such an unusual meal. Once the pieces had fallen into place he called for my attention again. He told me that he had hidden a ring in the field. It was a ring very similar to the one that Kali wore but this one belonged to me and he wanted me to find it. To begin the process, he asked me to close my eyes and he put an image of the ring in my mind. Then he got up, told me to get on with it and join him at the table when I had found it.

I was left alone and perplexed in the middle of the field. Too much had happened. I hadn't really had a moment to reflect on it all. When I thought through the whole chain of events from my first meeting with Rafa in the restaurant I could no longer believe that all this was happening to me. I thought back to my wife and the simple idiot's life I had lived with her. Suddenly it seemed so attractive. I wasn't looking to be a hero. I didn't want to save the planet or even concern myself with such huge issues. I felt a terrible sense of loneliness overcome me. These people - the lama, Kali, Maria, all seemed to be so at ease with their roles. I was a novice and these were still just stories to me. I felt a powerful urge to walk from that field, away from the house and out to the road. I imagined hitchhiking down to my father-in-law's house, seeing my wife, begging her forgiveness, beginning again that pointless life that now seemed so attractive and easy.

My dreams were broken by Kali's voice, calling from inside my head, urging me to find the ring so that they could all get on and eat. I sent my mind out across to the farmhouse and saw them all sitting, chatting around the table - Maria and Kali, the lama and a man and woman I hadn't yet met who must have been the people the driver brought back from the coast. I called my mind back and reformed the image of the ring. I could see it perfectly in all its detail.

I could turn it and rotate it in my mind but I couldn't see where it was. One by one I added other dimensions so that I could see it in other moments in time until I saw the ring on the lama's finger. I watched him walk out from beneath the tree, scrape a hole in the ground and drop the ring in. I changed my view so that I was looking down on the field and again followed the lama on his mission. I repeated this a few times until I was totally clear about the direction in which he walked and could count his paces and could see the little yellow flower next to the hole.

I stood up, walked straight to the spot and recovered my ring from its place in the soil. There was a loud cheer from the farmhouse and I felt elated, happy once more to be here, happy to be part of this mysterious process. As I put the ring on my finger a thin column of light wound down from the sky. As its warmth coursed momentarily through my body I remembered my name. I ran to the house, arriving at the table just as Maria set the last plate of pasta down at my place.

14

Over lunch I met the new people. Robert was another Englishman. He looked pale and studious and spoke with great reluctance. Much of the time he ate in silence and it was never clear if he was listening. But from time to time his contribution simply gushed out in a string of words that took many minutes of real effort to make sense of. It didn't take long before I realised his brilliance. When his words finally fell into place they did so like gemstones on a necklace. The depth of his knowledge and understanding constantly amazed me. Once I was familiar with his words I warmed to him, became aware of making more room in the conversation, hoping he would fill it.

Robert had been in Tunisia at the same time as us. He had been there with our other new arrival, a woman called Remi. They had been sent there when the lama knew that the phurba was going to be used again. They had been within an hour of reaching us when the phurba was plunged into the ground. It seems that we had come very close to retrieving the phurba without ever realising it. The devolvers were also in the desert waiting for the arrival of the rest of their group. They became aware of us and plunged the phurba into the ground before their circle was complete. This is how they destroyed the phurba and three of the group involved.

Robert and Remi had sat out the storm much the same as us but the old lama had kept us apart for fear that our combined presences would alert the devolvers to our location. While we were making our journey to the farmhouse they had remained behind to create a temporary repair to the new earth wound.

This, it emerged, was Remi's speciality. She came from an old Berber family who for centuries drifted between Morocco, Algeria and Tunisia. She carried the ancient wisdom of her family, an intimate knowledge of planetary energetics and healing talents that extended from the human to the universal. She was a delight to listen to. She spoke as if in song and each of her stories carried such a weight of history that even the most minor event evoked the epic.

I would have had that lunch last forever, such was the quality of Maria's cooking and the stories punctuating each course. My little experiments with telepathy and casual murder seemed meagre compared with the scale of events being recounted by Robert and Remi. It was only after the coffee arrived that I realised that Kali had remained unusually quiet throughout the meal. I turned to her, to check that she was all right.

"I'm fine," she said, "but we don't have much time. They're onto us and there is so much to do."

It was agreed that we would work through the night. Nobody else would be joining us, as it was already too dangerous. The old lama would visit the others where they were. The lunch was finished and I was immediately sent to the studio with Robert. He explained that we didn't have enough time for me to continue my training with Kali; it was too slow. He would finish the work directly through a series of transmissions and attunements. He apologised in advance if it hurt and promised that Remi would quickly alleviate any discomfort. Once the changes were made Kali could introduce me to my new skills as and when they were required. He told me that, among other things, he would reconfigure me so that I could switch time-scales. This would permit me to work much faster in this time-realm.

He would also reorganise my attention so that I could undertake many simultaneous tasks. If these explanations hadn't come from Robert they would have seemed farcical but there was something so benignly professorial about his description of the mind and its possible enhancement that I accepted them as if he were about to upgrade my computer and not reorganise my entire nervous system which, for so long, I had accepted as the only true representation of me.

Robert asked me to sit in the old leather armchair with its deep and permanent imprint of Ennio. As I sat there I felt the quiet reassurance of the old sculptor's energy and immediately sank into an easy state and closed my eyes. I heard Robert's voice explaining that he would work quickly and without stopping. If it became too much for me, I was to call out, 'Stop, I mean it!' Otherwise he would continue regardless of what I said or did.

I nodded my acceptance of the conditions and a moment later felt a surge of light energy enter through the top of my head and down through every nerve fibre of my being. I detached from my physical body and hovered nearby from where I could see the light body sitting in the chair. A fantastic blue colour defined the nervous system, while the energy body shone pure white. The few minor holes and tears in the energy body quickly closed up until the entire system appeared complete and intact. Robert's body also had the same appearance but for the strands of light that reached out from the bright area around his solar plexus and connected to the same area in my body. I began to feel afraid as I watched him draw my energy away until all that was left was a faint white glow around the brilliant blue of the nervous system. Somehow, I knew that I was watching the first stages in the death of my physical body. I wanted to shout out but I had nothing to shout with. The panic subsided when I realised that Robert was also draining his own energy body.

Everything that once constituted our physical presence was poured into one of the marble figures in the studio. When the process was complete the two brilliant, blue nervous systems inverted. They looked like the twigs and branches of winter trees growing out from the seedpod of the brain.

What was immediately apparent was that Robert's nervous system was much denser and more complex than my own but in a matter of a few seconds through an amazing process of rapid growth they both looked the same. The two systems flipped over again and, suspended in the space of the studio, looked like complex root systems. As I continued watching, vast swathes of brilliant colours cut through the studio. Each new colour brought a new rhythm to the movement in the nervous systems until they were pulsing and undulating where they hung in space.

Suddenly there was no light, just darkness, just two pulsing systems floating in the darkness. Then there was no more studio, just the sense of space before the studio was ever built, before the farmhouse was built, before the land was farmed, before anybody even thought to live here. In those last seconds before a soul lived on the earth two fiery strands of energy shot down from the heavens and everything plunged back into place. Just before my spirit was hauled back into my body I had time to notice that the strand of light that touched the crown of my head remained. I was now permanently connected to my past and to my fate. In the darkness where I sat, eyes closed in the armchair I heard Robert's voice. "Lucky you, you saw the whole show. Wait a few minutes until Remi checks you over."

I heard Robert leave and then felt Remi's soft touch on my head.

15

Back at the farmhouse there was a frenzy of activity. Everyone, even Maria, was preparing to leave. The lama was already gone. Maria, Robert and Remi would leave with our driver. Another car would come for Kali and me. Robert took time out to check that I was feeling all right. I told him, 'Yes,' but in truth I was feeling quite resentful. I felt like a pawn in someone else's game. I was constantly being told what to do. Clearly everybody else knew what the big plan was except me. I felt as if I simply wasn't good enough as I was, I was always being pushed to learn some new skill and now I had just had my entire system ripped to bits and rebuilt according to someone else's whim.

It wasn't until the car pulled away that I finally exploded. Kali was just about to hand me yet another task when I turned on her. "I feel totally manipulated by you. Since our days together in the desert, you've barely given me more than a moment's affection. Maybe that's okay for lamas or other super-beings but it isn't good enough for me. I thought I'd finally found the woman of my life, finally found real love. I have needs and I'm tired of being a martyr to the survival of the planet. I'm not even sure I care if it survives or not; it doesn't seem that special a place. If I really understood what it meant I'd probably side with the devolvers and blow the whole damned place to hell."

Kali tried to pacify me but I was having none of it. She tried to reach out but I pushed her away. Now I knew she simply had a job to do and would do anything to get it done – including being sweet with me. As I turned away, I knew she was still talking but I refused to listen.

I ran out into the fields and felt her trying to follow me with her thoughts. I closed all the doors and windows to my mind and refused to let her in. When she started running after me, I threw up a wall so she could run no further. When I reached the walnut tree, I slumped against its bark - my body sobbing, tears blinding my eyes. I was starving for Kali's touch, dying to feel her close to me. I wanted to die there, untouched, unloved, unwanted, with the only person who could make it alright rejected by my stronger mind, incapable of finding her way through. I stayed there as dusk settled, unsure of what to do, wanting a way out of the mess but unable to drop my defence.

Car-lights pierced the darkness. Our driver was coming and whatever it was we were supposed to do remained undone. The car stopped before the house and a familiar voice called my name. It was Marisa and behind her, her father and two of his men. She called again, called me to her. "I've been looking for you for weeks. I want to apologise for how I've been. I want you back. My father used all his resources searching for you. He realised you were the best thing that ever happened to me. I want you back. He wants you to join his company, to have a proper job, a position in the family. He's sorry that he didn't really appreciate you before but now everything will be different. I want your child. I want to stop all this stupid travelling and make a proper life with you. You can have it any way you want. You deserve it, putting up with my childishness for so long. Since you left, I've had time to think, time to grow, time to talk with my family, time to realise how important you are to me."

It went on like a poem, a beautiful poem, a poem I had always longed to hear. I pushed myself away from the tree and started walking towards the car, towards the life I had always wanted - with the wife, the home, the family, the money and status and travel, the parties, the friends.

As I walked I dropped the energy field I had thrown around me. I felt the ease of normality returning. I felt lightness as the burden of all the crazy past weeks lifted. As I glanced up towards the farmhouse I could see Kali still standing there. She looked smaller, more insignificant. I turned back towards my wife. She looked more beautiful than ever, free of the make-up I so detested, dressed simply, the way I liked her - Marisa in all the natural beauty I had fallen for on the beach.

I turned to take one last look at Kali. She was on her knees. Without breaking pace, I changed view and saw that Marisa and her father were ripping the life energy from her. I threw an energy field around us both, started running up towards the house. Behind me, I heard my wife screaming. "You arsehole! I wasted ten years of my life keeping you away from that bitch! She'll be no good to you now."

By the time I reached Kali she was sprawled on the ground and as pale as death. In the faintest whisper she asked me to hold her but save my energy until they had gone. A few moments later the car was reversing at speed down the track. I heard Kali's whisper again. "Was that your wife? You need to be careful; she's still got some powerful threads knotted into you."

I carried Kali back to our room. I was filled with remorse and frightened by the seduction I had fallen for. After all Robert's work I was still nothing but a arsehole. I was still occupied by the same stupid little needs and fantasies that had always run my life. I was more frightened still to find that my wife was involved in all this. I knew that her father was a scary man but I always thought it was something banal like organised crime. I never suspected my wife of being more than a spoilt child. It was unbelievable that she could be a killer and one who could kill at a distance - like Kali.

I snapped out of the misery when I realised that Kali was unconscious. I didn't know if I had the skill to save her but I put my hands on her head in the way that Remi had done with me and called on all the energy I had access to. I closed my eyes and concentrated on the strand of energy still attached to the crown of my head. After a few moments the colour returned to her face and she opened her eyes. I felt the tears well up in my eyes as I looked into them and realised that I had almost killed the most important person in my life.

I started to beg her forgiveness but she sealed my lips with her fingers and told me that it was a necessary part of the changes I had gone through. Robert could only reorganise the matrices of my thoughts and memories and powers. I had to fight the inner battle to make the change complete and it was better that I had the opportunity to do that sooner than later.

"Now you are as good as it gets."

I wanted to continue my work on Kali but she told me to save my energy.

"There is something more important to be done and only you can do it. Come back to help me when you have finished, I can hold on. You must work fast and be on your guard. Your wife will return with reinforcements. She and her father didn't have enough power to take you on but they will be back. Before he died, Ennio completed one last project under the supervision of his teacher, the Bhutanese Rinpoche. He made nine marble vases to a design that was specified many centuries before. The Rinpoche sealed amulets brought from his kingdom into each of the vases and between them they buried the vases somewhere near the farmhouse. Nobody else knew where they were hidden.

"You already showed that you are still a treasure seeker when you found your ring in the field and before that when you uncovered some of Ennio's sculptures during your first days here. Now you must find the vases. We will take them to England. Robert knows where they have to be placed."

I protested. "I don't want to leave you alone. I don't want to be left alone with this responsibility. I don't know how to do this."

But Kali insisted and insisted with such a force that I really had no choice but to get out and start. I left our room and went out to the studio. I sat in Ennio's chair and tried to open myself up to his presence. It was a struggle - my mind constantly drawn away. I knew that the damage done to Kali by my wife and her father was serious and I was afraid that I would lose her. I was still deeply disturbed by the appearance of my wife and the implications of what she had said. I was torn in half; the seduction of her words had been so powerful that even the events that followed failed to destroy their effect completely. It took a super effort to call all my energies back from where they were tangled in my thoughts and feelings.

I called on the memory of Ennio, that wonderful man I had never met. The first image that came was of one of the vases. It had the characteristic simplicity of Ennio's work and the vision of its form calmed my mind. I gazed at it until I could picture it in all dimensions. With the memory lurking in my mind I left the studio and walked out into the darkness of the evening. I found the first vase with little effort. I could see it glowing with a pale white light beneath the stones that formed the path to the house. I raised the flagstone with a crowbar from the studio and exposed a wooden box, set quite close to the surface. I broke away the top where it rested and opened the box to reveal the vase.

It was perfect in every way - not just in shape but clean and pristine as if only just finished and placed there by the hands of the master. I raised it up and my hands marvelled at the smoothness of the surface and perceived warmth, unfamiliar in marble. At first sight, the vase looked to be of one solid piece but as I looked a little closer I could see the separation of a lid from a base defined by a very thin line of bright red that I presumed to be wax. With my first find I ran back to our room to show it to Kali. She was asleep - still pale but deeply resting. Inspired by my find I couldn't resist laying my hands upon her head and channelling a stream of energy into her body. As I watched I could see the threads of her energy, tattered and torn from the attack, seek each other out and reconnect. Her energy field was still weak but was, nevertheless, intact when I finished.

I remembered Kali's words and decided not to continue for too long but to save my energy for the night's work. I was now confident that she would survive and left her asleep in the company of the vase that rested in all its beauty by her head, in all its beauty.

I left our room to continue my search and had only taken a few steps before I saw another vase glowing behind the base of one wall of the garage. With the crowbar I broke away the stones and mortar and pulled it out still in its box. I opened it back in our room. At first sight the new vase looked very much like the previous one but when I put them side by side they were clearly quite different. Although they were identical in size and shape and although they were both made of the same warm marble with a thin line of red wax delineating lid from base, once in the other's company they began to glow with different shades of red - one tending more towards the vibrant red of a wild poppy and the other towards orange.

My night continued in this way. Each time I discovered a vase it seemed to inspire the next vase in the series to glow. Each time I brought a new vase into the room, in the presence of the others, it also started to glow with its own unique colour - inevitably the next in the sequence of colours forming a rainbow. When the seventh vase joined the circle that surrounded Kali she woke up with a smile, unable to contain the joy inspired by the play of colours and form which filled the room, unable to resist the joy which had grown in me, vase by vase throughout the night. I rolled onto the bed beside her, rolled into a big strong hug that made me so happy, so relieved to feel her again in all her strength. I knew I didn't have long to lie with her but I really wanted to share that moment and to share my amazement at the way in which the vases shone their light. It was only then, when Kali drew my attention to it, that I realised that each vase also had its own unique sound. Not only was the room awash with the purest of colours but also vibrating with a harmony of sounds more beautiful than anything I had ever heard.

With a quick kiss I rolled off the bed to the floor and out again into the night with my heart singing. It wasn't long before the singing stopped, as I searched for the eighth vase. It didn't appear as the others had. I searched the buildings and the paths and the courtyards looking for the glow. My search became more frantic and repetitive with desperation. I caught myself just as I entered the studio for the fourth time and stopped. I sank down in Ennio's armchair. I realised that the last two vases could not appear as the others had. If I had already found seven vases for each of the colours of the rainbow, it seemed that the final two vases were bound to be different and would have to be found in a different way. I ran through in my mind where I had found each of the other seven until I could form a picture of them, each in a place that divided a circle that cut through the farm. As I separated the circle out from the buildings of the farm, I could see that the division of its circumference was perfect.

There was no place for the other two vases in the circle. It was then that I realised that the place where I sat was in the centre of that circle. It was so obvious that Ennio's chair should be the centre. I looked up and for the first time noticed that the ceiling of the studio formed a pyramid. From the outside, a decorative dovecote capped the roof. I dragged a ladder from the studio and climbed up onto the roof. The top of the dovecote lifted away quite easily to reveal the vase wrapped in saffron silk. I carried it down and placed it in the studio, determined to find the final vase, which I now knew had to be hidden in the ground beneath Ennio's chair.

I lifted the stones of the floor, knowing that the last vase would have to be as deep beneath the earth as the eighth vase was above it. I feared spending the rest of the night digging but was relived to find beneath the stones a small stairway leading into a cellar. I lit a candle and cautiously made my way down.

The stairs led into another studio. In one corner was a shrine with water and rice bowls gleaming in the candle light as if they had just been polished and filled that day. Against one wall was a workbench and an array of stone-working tools lined up as if ready to begin. This must have been the place where Ennio made the vases - the atmosphere of the place certainly had the feel of a sacred space. Beneath the stairs I found what I knew to be the final vase sealed in a case made of polished wood. I knew I had no time to squander and carried the vase back up the stairs.

I carried the eighth vase still wrapped in silk back to our room where I found Kali sitting in meditation on the bed. She looked calm and radiant in the fabulous light of the vases and opened her eyes as I entered the room. "Is it done?" she asked.

"It is. The last vase is waiting in the studio."

"Unwrap the eighth before you fetch the ninth."

I untied the knots and unwound the fabric from the vase. As the silk fell away and the vase revealed itself, a new light entered the room. All the colours faded into white and the entire room seemed to glow and pulsate, not so much with light but as if with presence. It was as if I were able to see life and movement in everything. When I stepped outside again to fetch the last vase I noticed that this phenomenon extended beyond the room and way beyond the farm. As far as I could see the world seemed to be vibrating to a different song. I returned with the last vase still in its case and checked with Kali that what I saw was really there.

"Yes, but as yet the energy doesn't extend for more than a few kilometres. Once the vases are installed in their proper places the entire world will feel their influence and be saturated with a new energy that will hold it together into its new incarnation."

Kali asked me to open the case and I prised away the lid. I gazed into blackness, a blackness that seemed to draw all light into it. The light in the room faded. Everything returned to its normal state. I drew the vase from its container. The black material it was made from was icy cold and unlike anything I had seen before. It was neither shiny nor matt and although the shape was like the others it was as if it had no shape, no form. It was more an absence of form, a shape carved away from matter, like something missing from the universe. I placed the vase in the circle with the others and became aware of the sense of peace in the room - stillness imbued with immense potential

16

It felt like my work was done but Kali reminded me that it had only just begun; we had yet to get the vases back to England. She suggested that I sleep for a while and within a moment of the suggestion I was overcome by the exhaustion of the night and was fast asleep. She woke me some time later. The room was cleared and fresh clothes were laid out for me at the end of the bed. I quickly showered and dressed and drank the strong coffee that Kali had left beside the bed.

When I stepped out it was still dark. Kali was packing things into the back of a muddy old Range Rover. We had a new driver, an older man, a friend of Ennio from the village. His wife was there too, a robust country-woman who was busy closing up the house. Kali hustled me into the back seat of the vehicle. As we left the farm, via a dirt track that led the opposite way from the main road, I caught the flicker of headlamps coming up the drive. The woman up front must have seen them too and gave her husband a slap on the shoulder. He responded by jamming the accelerator to the floor and we slithered and skidded our way into the darkness.

"Why doesn't he put on the headlights?" I wondered.

"Because he doesn't need them and we need the darkness," came Kali's reply in my thoughts. We both spontaneously reached for the seat belts and snapped them into place. "This is Peppi's land, he's walked it since he was a child, he knows it intimately and it loves him."

As we careered onward, I cast my mind back to the farmhouse. Marisa's father was shouting orders to groups of men gathered by their cars. Marisa was directing another group, men with sledgehammers and axes who were smashing their way into the studio. I reported my vision to Kali but she reassured me. "Don't worry, Maria has another home and we've already taken the soul from that one. There's nothing but rubble left for them to find."

After some minutes we pulled onto a small tarmac road. Peppi increased the speed but continued still in darkness. Just as suddenly he stopped - switched off the engine. All was silent.

"What's happening?"

There was no reply. I turned to Kali. She was silent, her eyes fixed on the distance. I leaned forward, shook Peppi by the shoulder. No response. I yelled out in fear, "What the hell is happening?"

Kali's voice, distant and weak, found its way into my mind. "Do something. Please do something."

I was alone. I turned away from my terror, quieted my mind, looked out into the world beyond the car. Ahead of us, hidden behind the crest of a small hill, three men stood hand in hand beside their car. Their minds were linked as one. A stream of thought wrapped our car, held my friends in its grip, emptied their minds of all possibilities.

"But why not me?" I turned back to my friends. Life was ebbing away. Even the possibility to breathe, to beat blood, was fading.

I reached out, tried to invade the minds of the men. Their protection was too strong. I reached up, tried to block the stream of their thought but it pushed its way through me, effortlessly, as if all I had was tissue paper. I was tiring. I needed help. I called out to the old lama, but nothing, only silence. I was alone. Death was creeping closer to my friends. I was passive. Possibilities were disappearing fast. I felt comfort in that state, abandoned, content, willing to let it all go. I felt a prickling in my scalp, the place where the strand of light connected with me back in the studio with Robert.

I pushed against that place, felt a softening in the membranes, a small space opening between the bones and, suddenly a sense of connection - a cool breeze flowing down through the channels in my body. Possibilities crept in. I reached out again to the men at the car. The tissue paper had thickened. I began to deflect their mind. Breathing deepened in my friends. Death stepped back a little but continued to wait nearby. I watched as the men released their hands. Their fingers reached out, seeking energy points in each other's bodies. Their force increased, pushing harder against me. I felt my deflection weakening, watched hopelessly as their fingers worked their magic in their web of mind and force. I was tiring. My deflection began to buckle under their weight.

In the distance I heard the lama's voice. "Pull harder on the cord."

I reached up towards the heavens, pulling harder on the strand of energy reaching down towards my crown. The old lama's voice grew louder. "Pull more. Don't stop until you feel the ocean flow."

I intensified my effort, felt the strand thicken into a cord, watched the men counter me with the play of their hands and fingers. Anger built in my belly.

Words began to gather and roar inside. "I will not give in. I will not succumb to these men and their dirty ways."

The words remained within me, not yet ready explode into the world. I pulled still harder and felt the cord thicken into a torrent, felt the wind turn to a gale, blasting its way through my body. "I will beat these men. Nothing they can do will stop me."

I watched the men as they worked feverishly to thwart me. I felt the joy of power, wanted more, pulled harder, felt the gale increase and focus into a tidal wave of pure force. "I will destroy you."

I heard the pure clarity of my words, felt my body anchored deep within the ocean, watched as the men's energies collapsed, disintegrated and dispersed, watched with pleasure as their bodies crashed to the ground.

In front of me Peppi and his wife were furiously crossing themselves, muttering their prayers. Beside me Kali whispered, "Oh my gods!"

The storm receded. Normality returned. Peppi and his wife didn't want to go on. "Take the car," they said. "We want to walk. We need to sit on the land."

We embraced and the old couple set off across the fields, a basket of provisions held between them. Kali took the wheel and we continued in silence to the prow of the hill. I stared forward in trepidation. As we crested the hill my fear was confirmed. To the side of the road sat the car and beside it three lifeless bodies. "Are they dead?" I asked.

"Yes."

Kali carried on, gathering speed as we passed the bodies. I was swamped and silent, desperately trying to consolidate the sensation of profound joy in the presence of so much power and the real consequences of my actions. Kali reached out to take my hand. "In the grander scheme of things their deaths are neither here nor there."

"Have you ever killed?" I asked.

"No… But if it wasn't them it would have been us."

"Why didn't you do anything?"

"I couldn't… What you did was awesome."

She was right, it was awesome, but it still didn't make it okay. Suddenly I felt more apart from Kali than ever before. I was fearful, afraid that what I had done had set me far apart, not just from Kali, but also from the whole of humanity. I tried hard to recall Rafa's story, tried hard to believe it, to believe the 'grander scheme' as Kali called it. I needed to sleep. Not because I was tired - in fact I was far from tired, I was more awake and alive than ever before. I needed to sleep to escape, hoping that all would become clear as I slept. I climbed into the back of the car and curled as best I could across the seat.

17

When Kali shook me awake it was late afternoon. She offered me a baguette with ham and cheese and a glass of steaming hot black coffee. I needed her arms around me more. She climbed into the back, held me close until I realised I was holding her, until I realised she needed me as much as I needed her. Tears drenched our faces. The incident on the road remained as silence held between us, a huge unfathomable question that would forever set us both apart. In the silence of that embrace we sealed our complicity.

When I finally turned to feed my belly, Kali explained the route I had to drive. She had to sleep. Suddenly I saw her exhaustion, was struck by her stamina and courage and was only too happy to take the wheel and drive her to the sea.

We made our rendezvous with time to spare, time enough for me to take on provisions as Kali slept, and still time for me to brace the Atlantic air before our boat arrived. We had to wade out to where the boat could anchor. One trip was enough for Kali and in no time she was back asleep in the cabin. I repeated the freezing trip until the car was unloaded while the captain kept his watch. We abandoned the car to the lick of the sea and chugged out into the darkness. I was soon asleep with Kali and our precious cargo as our clothes dried on a line above the heat of the engine.

When the captain woke us it was still dark. The enormous hull of a tanker towered above us. A net, lowered from one of its cranes, hauled us and our cargo aboard. Our captain waved and drew his little boat away.

We settled in our cabin as the tanker lumbered on towards the English Channel and onwards to the River Thames. In that grey, metal cabin I felt the urge to open the cases, to fill that dreary space with light, to hear that vibrant harmony again. Kali counselled me against it. "We're not yet safe. We dare not call attention to ourselves. You have to accept that nobody will see or hear the vases together again. We are the last. Let's confine that privilege to our memory."

One more night-time transfer brought us by launch to the shore of the Thames near Battersea. Marianne was waiting with a car. She took us across the river to a small shop near Piccadilly where she dropped Kali and me. Marianne left immediately with the vases. Kali secured the street door and led me upstairs to the apartment. "Welcome home," she said. "If you want it this is your new home. You have to share it with Marianne and me. You also get me, of course, and the business downstairs."

I needed no time to think. "I want you and if this is how I can have you I want it all."

Over tea, Kali told me about my new home. "This shop was originally set up by David, as was the smuggling network that brought us into London. Rafa and Christina also used this place as a base and as their source of income. Marianne took care of everything in their absence. The shop is never open; customers only ever come by appointment and even then, rarely. None of them had ever met David so it makes no difference who answers the door and completes the trade."

It was clearly quite a brilliant setup and when I thought of the man, my friend, who organised it I felt a pang of sadness at the terrible waste.

Kali showed me our room, a large room with a curtained bed and a sitting area arranged around an open fireplace. We had our own bathroom. There was another bedroom for Marianne, another large room filled with bunks for guests, a living room, meditation room, kitchen, office and another bathroom. There was also a large dressing room filled with clothes of every style and size.

"This is communal," Kali said. "Help yourself to whatever you need."

While I was searching through the drawers, I found one stuffed with cash and a collection of Rolex watches, both old and new. I turned to Kali. "What's this about?"

She laughed as she explained. "When Rafa started his search for the phurba he assumed that David's business would attract the connections he needed in pursuit of his quest. It soon became clear that it would not. Rafa remembered that his contact in Bogota was wearing an expensive Rolex, as did David, despite his humble taste in most other things. Rafa correctly guessed that it was a more attractive possession to these people than any oriental antique. From then on Rafa operated a second business trading in watches. Help yourself," said Kali as she headed back to the kitchen. I couldn't resist.

18

For now, we were confined to the flat. We had to wait for Marianne to get back. If she delivered the vases safely the plan had a very good chance of success. It was a week before she came home, a lazy week recovering. Marianne had laid up a good supply of food and Kali and I did little more than eat and sleep. Nothing was said of the events in Italy.

Marianne returned with bundles of herbs that she left in the kitchen. She had delivered all the vases, attended ceremonies that saw them installed in their secret resting places, and driven back. There was something reassuringly simple about her. She described her journey as if she had just gone out to the market. She drank a tea and went to bed. While she slept Kali told me more about her.

"Marianne comes from a large country family from the south-west of France. When she was sixteen she attended a talk given by a rinpoche. She took refuge and that was that. She accepted to live entirely according to the guidance of her teacher. She was sent to take over David's affairs when he died and since then she has lived here and maintained this place as a refuge, happy to play her small part in a network about which she knows very little."

In the days following her return Marianne taught me about the business while Kali introduced me to the extraordinary stock we kept in the shop. One afternoon I heard the lama's voice. "It is done. Sit quietly tonight with your friends. You will know when to celebrate. We thank you."

The three of us gathered quietly together in the meditation room, sat in our little triangle, and waited. From my perspective I was aware of a sudden softening of the whole of my being. Physical tension simply melted away from my muscles and nerves and my mind fell still. There was a palpable sense of magic in the room. That was it. Marianne left and returned with Champagne and glasses. We drank quietly without a toast. What was there to toast? Had we saved the world? Were the devolvers defeated? We couldn't know. All I knew was that I had done my part and now, sitting in that room, it hardly seemed heroic; I had just followed instructions.

Life became normal. I was content living with Kali and Marianne. I continued to study the business and the stock and started to learn Tibetan. Occasionally, a visitor would come and buy a piece, always a specific piece, identified and reserved by phone. Occasionally a shipment would arrive but I never did find out how that part of the business worked. As I became more able, I answered the phone and met buyers, interesting or curious people who came only for what they wanted and not for idle chat. I had no more training from Kali, no more words from the lama, not even silent conversations with my lover. It was as if all that were behind me, no longer needed. I asked Kali one day, "Is this it?"

"Perhaps it is. Is it enough for you?"

It was enough. It dawned on me that I was mostly content. I say mostly, because I knew that somewhere, not far behind me lurked a thousand unanswered questions. But the undivided attention of Kali more than compensated for that. The days turned to weeks and the weeks turned to months and our little community in the heart of London smiled and gracefully passed the days.

Marianne went to a meditation group twice a week. Kali and I remained around the neighbourhood, walking in the park or occasionally loitering in cafes or shops, even if all we ever needed to buy was food.

19

I never had an inkling that Kali would leave. Nothing was said, not even hinted at. Nothing prepared me for the note I found beside me when I woke alone one morning. "I have to leave. It is my shame that I cannot even tell you face to face. Marianne will take good care of you. I love you always."

A rock landed on my heart. I searched the apartment. Marianne was still asleep. In that communal home I could never know if she took her clothes, or packed a case. Nothing but the note said that Kali was no longer there. I shook Marianne awake, begged her to tell me it wasn't true. But it was true. Kali didn't play tricks or games; she had gone.

Marianne told me what Kali could not. "She is dying. She was mortally wounded in the fight in Italy, her life is seeping away. She has gone into retreat for what remains of her days."

Marianne couldn't say where - she didn't know.

I argued furiously against this version of the truth. "I healed her myself after the battle with my wife and her father. Her system was intact. I checked her again in the car with Peppi and his wife. They were all well, I had mended the harm."

"I'm sorry," said Marianne. "That's what she said. I'm sure neither of us have any reason to doubt her word."

She was right of course but still, inside, I fought the truth. I returned to my room to think and rethink those days, looking for clues, looking for anything that might prove it wrong. The more I thought the more I could see it was true. Now I remembered how Kali could do nothing in the fight in the car. Now I remembered that she never reported words from the lama again. Now I remembered her weakness, her tiredness, how much she slept after Italy. Now I remembered how I never heard her words in my mind again. Now I was angry. Now I was furious at myself for not seeing it before, for accepting my ordinariness, for not reaching out to her mind, for not looking at her energy body again.

"Don't go there. Kali told me how you like to go there. There was nothing you could do. There was nothing anyone could do. She gave as much time as she could to be with you. Let her go. Let her prepare for her dying."

It was the first time I had heard Marianne's voice in my mind. I found her sitting in the meditation room. "You can do it too?"

"Of course," she replied.

Her observation of me, the mention of Kali, her words in my mind brought me to weep. Marianne stood up and collected me in her arms as I lost it. Marianne's embrace was too inviting, too comforting, too reassuring. I pulled away, gathered my things and ran downstairs to the street. I kept running until I reached the park, kept running until I was exhausted, kept walking, searching, refusing to accept that I wouldn't see her again, convinced that if only I looked hard enough, she would have to appear. When that failed, I went to our café, sure I would find her at our table, but only inviting more suffering when the waiter asked if she would be joining me.

I said 'no,' and left. I found another café, not one of ours - a fake, a chain, a place for people who didn't know better. I ordered coffee and scanned the room. I scanned the energies of the room. I scanned the minds of the room. I found one I didn't like - a nasty man, mean with his children and mean to his wife. I found his weak spot, his liver seething with anger. I would rip its energy to pieces. I wanted to kill. I wanted to know that power again.

It was too easy. I leaned against the crown of my head, pressed apart the membranes and bones, called on the thread of energy and pulled. I would take them all, not just one. I would show the world real power. I felt the stream, the river, the ocean, the tide within the ocean, the immensity of the power coursing through my system.

But I couldn't do it; I couldn't kill like this. I wasn't angry with these people, with this man, not even with myself. It was something else; the futility of it all. After all that time with Kali - the experiences, the training, the work with Robert, I couldn't even see that my lover was sick, let alone do anything to save her. I left the money, traipsed home through the back streets and took to my bed.

Marianne looked in from time to time over the days but I always sent her on her way. "No, I don't want anything.

"No food."

"I'm not thirsty. Just leave me alone."

One night, late into the night I found the quietness and concentration to reach out for Kali. I found her energy, a weak but alive vibration, far away, or well protected. I couldn't look inside. I couldn't even see where she was.

I called down more energy. I would find a way to leave her a thought, to look gently through her mind and find out where she was. Marianne burst into my room - furious. "Why don't you leave her alone! She has already done more than enough for you, for all of us. Now she needs to do her own work. Just wake up and move on."

Anger from a gentle soul is a powerful thing. Marianne's words hammered home, cut through my selfish story and brought me crashing to the ground.

"She said you'd find it hard to cope alone. She asked me to take care of you. If you want me I'm yours. Tell me when you've made up your mind."

I reached up and Marianne led me to her room, secured me with her embrace, lowered me gently into my first real sleep for weeks. We weren't lovers, sleeping with Marianne was like sleeping with a sister but she helped me through the nights and then more and more through the days. She helped restore my need to live again. I still longed for Kali but came to accept the way it was, to accept her need for me to let her go.

Marianne tried to explain the process of conscious dying. It sounded a little like what I did with the cord at the crown of my head, only the other way around, releasing upwards rather than pulling down. It was a bit more complex of course, but these Buddhist ideas didn't really resonate deeply with me.

20

The days with Marianne crept by. From time to time we'd take delivery of a new consignment. From time to time we'd entertain a client. And that was all. Sometimes I shared her bed; often I slept alone. My longing for Kali wouldn't disappear. My desire for Marianne wouldn't materialise. Many times, as I lay alone I wanted to reach out for Kali but I always felt the sense of Marianne listening in, ready to pounce. I realised I was scared of her. I realised that, although alive, my days were nothing but a slow dying, days passed, waiting for nothing in particular.

Marianne did her best with me. She tried, in her gentle way to bring some life to me, with a taste, with a flower, with her touch, with her laugh. Finally, she gave me a telephone number. "Go and see him. I think you need his help."

I made an appointment and met Christopher at the door to his dingy basement flat. He seemed to know more about me than I did. Some things I was willing to believe. Much of it I could do without believing. He had me undress and lie on a couch in the corner of his living room. He covered me with oils and spices from jars on the shelves. He laid slices of ginger root on my heart and solar plexus and burned cones of oily seeds and herbs until the hot oils burned and scarred my skin. All the time he talked, a strange hesitant ramble of ideas and suggestions, unspecific and infiltrating. I didn't think to reach out, didn't think to check him out. I felt powerless, like a child, well held but still fearful. I left with oil seeping into my clothes and another appointment for the following week.

His last words as I left stayed with me for that week. "No time for dying - still too much to do."

At home I threw away my clothes, reeking as they were with oil and smoke. In the dressing room I changed my style, suddenly preferring white to the dowdy browns and greys I had worn since Kali left. I didn't want to talk with Marianne about my experience. She could see a positive change but I felt unease. The week passed quickly and when the day arrived I realised I had been looking forward to my next appointment.

It was a bright and smiling Christopher who met me this time. He had me wait in his hallway, choosing a chair from the row that lined one wall. In the next room I could hear him talking. I expected to see another patient leave but Christopher called me in, called me across to where his patient lay on the couch. He handed me a jar, instructed me on how to apply the thick ferment to her body. I was hesitant, this wasn't why I came, but he insisted. Again, like the child, I gave in and followed his instructions. When I'd finished, both Christopher and his patient commended my technique and touch. I felt conned, felt like a joke was about to be sprung. But no joke sprung. When his patient paid, Christopher gave half the money to me.

"That's fair isn't it?" he said.

I didn't know what was fair. I hadn't come to work and I didn't need the money.

"See, you have good hands, you have the touch. I'll teach you, I'll show you how to make the preparations."

I didn't know what to say. I just wanted to say 'no,' but it wouldn't come out. As I stood, silently waiting to see what would come my way the doorbell rang. Christopher showed Andy into the room. After a brief introduction and to the surprise of us both, Christopher announced, "Andy will teach you 'rlung ta'".

Still I had nothing to say. Neither, it seemed, did Andy. Christopher filled the space, explained that I was to learn a martial art, something like tai chi, but older - from Tibet. "It translates as 'wind horse'," he said.

He told Andy just to teach me the circling, the meditation, not the martial part. "He doesn't need to fight; he just needs grounding. He already knows how to kill."

By the time I left I had two more appointments scheduled that week with Christopher and two with Andy. Once more I was on the street, breathless, annoyed, angry and confused. I stopped at a café nearby, tried to calm myself, tried to reach out, to reach back and explore the apartment, explore Christopher. I wanted to know what he knew about me. I couldn't reach out. There was a fog in my mind. I couldn't gather my thinking, it was weak and dispersed. I wanted Kali there, wanted to draw on her strength and clarity. I settled for Marianne but it didn't help. She had nothing but positive things to say, thought it wonderful for me to learn with him. Reluctantly I kept my appointments.

I started walking circles with Andy. He explained that it was more like the Chinese system of pa kua than tai chi but even more powerful. He had been studying martial arts since he was a child and was something of an expert, a champion in several styles.

"I've only been training with Christopher for a few months but I've learned more in those months than in all the previous years. He knows something. I don't know where it comes from. I think he's channelling."

Andy was nice enough but had no interest in the sense of unease that had begun to blight my days. Like Marianne, he was not one to share that with.

Back at Christopher's flat we sat at the table in his tiny kitchen as he instructed me on how to prepare the oils. They were not complex, just marinades of garlic or ginger or chili, but he was meticulous in the ritual of preparation - where to cut first, which direction, how thick. Once again, I had the feeling that it would all be exposed as a big joke, almost that he was testing me for my gullibility.

I carried the jars of oil back home, installed them in the kitchen, feigned my interest in the whole process with Marianne. From time to time I practised the steps that Andy had shown me but they seemed futile and meaningless to me.

Still Marianne reached out to me. Still I couldn't respond. Still I couldn't reach out at all. When I mentioned this to Marianne, she thought it strange, insisted that her own powers had got stronger since working with Christopher. "I think he's preparing you for something bigger."

Next time I sat in Christopher's kitchen I had a moment where I thought she might be right. He had me close my eyes and asked me to look at my own energy body. It was easy enough for me to do after the experience with Robert back in Ennio's studio. Christopher then asked me to concentrate on the energy vortices spinning at various points along my central axis and limbs. He showed me how to adjust them, how to open them and close them and how to feed the energies from the central axis through my arms to the palms of my hands. He then asked me to reach up through the crown of my head to connect with the energy thread. "It's a 'sky-cord,'" he said.

As I did what I hadn't done for a long time I felt an old familiar surge of energy through my system. In a moment it turned into a torrent, unstoppable, without any pulling from me. Far away I heard Christopher's voice. "Now you are permanently connected to your own sky-cord. Let's hope you can use it for healing instead of killing."

His words jolted me back, back to the kitchen where Christopher sat smiling across the table. Again, that mention of killing. How did he know? I resented his knowing, resented anyone knowing. I felt disturbed by its mention, as if, unmentioned, it never really happened. When he left to go to the bathroom I used the new force seething through me to reach out to him. All I could find was darkness.

He wanted me to stay for dinner, wanted me to meet his wife. I invented a prior appointment, promised I'd be there tomorrow and fled up the stairs to the light.

21

I didn't see Marianne that night; she had her meditation class. I locked myself in my room. In the morning I left early. I needed to walk. I thought walking would clear my mind, would lead me to a decision I knew I had to make. An hour of walking found me outside his flat. Christopher was waiting at the top of the stair. He called me down. He led me into the kitchen where hot coffee and croissants waited for me on the table. He was bright and funny and disarming. Nothing I wanted to say could be said.

When the doorbell rang he left me there with my breakfast. After a short while he called me into his sitting room. Marianne was lying naked on his table. It was the first time I had seen her naked. She was beautiful, eyes closed and tranquil. He handed me an open jar, filled with a dark and aromatic preparation, something I'd never used before. He instructed me on how to smooth it onto her body, into every crease, over every mound, with long continuous strokes following every line and contour of her muscles. I followed the instructions but all the time I wanted to run. I felt myself pushed closer to something I didn't want, into an intimacy that I wanted to refuse, which should remain private. When I finished, he gave me a small foil package. "Take this and go. Marianne knows what to do. You must help her and keep her safe. This is important for her development."

With that I left. Marianne joined me later at home. Nothing was said as she packed the car. Little was said as we left the city, driving west into the sunset. "I can't tell you where we're going," she said. "I'm not even sure, but I know I'll know when we get there."

After a couple of hours, we pulled off the motorway and continued into the darkness of lanes and then a small track leading down towards a river. Between us we carried the packs, Marianne leading the way deeper into the woodland beside the river. She finally found her place, a clearing by the water, silent and secret, reserved from the sounds and light of habitation. She asked me to light a fire while she gathered more wood and explored her territory.

When the fire was blazing she told me more. Christopher had sent her on this mission, a ceremony to prepare herself for her work in the world. "I need you to protect the space, to keep the fire burning and to make sure I am not disturbed."

It was a simple enough request and I was happy to tend the fire and enjoy the awesome sense of peace after months of living in the city. Marianne shed her clothes and left them in a pile beside the fire. She walked down to the river and immersed herself. She gathered handfuls of mud from its banks, covered herself slowly, meticulously, in what looked like an ordained pattern. My gaze drifted between her and the fire and the edges of the clearing as I sipped mint tea from the flask. A deer entered the clearing, a small female deer, curious and courageous. It stood for a moment on the border with the trees, and then slowly walked to the edge of the water as Marianne lowered herself into the river. The deer lay down and watched as Marianne's body disappeared beneath the surface. A spell crackled through the clearing, a palpable change in the air, as if the air were crystallising. Magic was happening in this place, but not for me, I was only there to tend the fire and protect the space. And yet I felt the honour of that duty, ignorant and blessed. The deer kept its place even as Marianne pulled herself back from the grip of the water and brought her body to the fire. She dried herself in its heat, wrapped herself in the bedding, sat in silence sipping the tea I offered.

After a while she asked for the package that Christopher gave me. I handed it over and Marianne threw it into the embers on the edge of the fire. She asked me to time four minutes on my watch. When the time was up she hooked the package out with a stick. She unfolded the foil to reveal two small cubes darkened by the heat, one for her and one for me. I swallowed mine as instructed and accepted the invitation to lie down beside her to pass the rest of the night.

In the warmth of the covers, in the dying of the fire, I felt our breathing synchronise. As I moved closer, I smelt a new Marianne, not the usual lightly scented one. This one darker, a blend of smoke and soil, salt and leaf-mould, cat breath and musk. I moved closer, nuzzled the leather of my nose into the thick pelt at the back of her neck. I felt a ripple run through the muscles of her flanks. I sank my teeth into her ruff, tasted the sweetness of iron, felt my pads and claws draw her closer, felt her body arch to pull me deeper. Our bodies merged, now human, now cat, now flying, now falling, now one, now none, now air, now power. In the dense rhythms of that night, our spirits, liberated from mind, liberated from flesh, surged and swelled like the tide, permeating all, permeated by all.

We woke in the damp of the morning dew. The fire smouldered still. The deer was gone. We drank coffee, stewed and bitter from its night in the flask. Marianne seemed bigger, brighter, more complete. She thanked me for the night. I accepted, but not sure for what. For keeping the fire and the space, or did we fly together in a dream? I checked my hands - no pads, no claws. I wanted to inspect her neck for blood but she was already dressed when I woke. I didn't know how to ask, chose melancholy instead; my old friend, protecting me as ever.

22

Back in London, Christopher was more affable than ever, his jokes and jibes constantly over-riding my doubts. He chided me for my resistance to Marianne, pushed me constantly to see what she could offer. Each time I prepared to leave he would thrust another of his patients upon me. He knew I could still leave him but had too much pride to abandon a patient. The work was easy enough; these people were not sick, just curious or insecure. I tidied up the little tears or stains in their energy, tried to send them on their way, only to have Christopher meet them at the door and book them in again. I watched him weave his way into their lives, reading their weaknesses, vanities and dreams, stitching his thoughts into their minds, nurturing their dependence on him, as he nurtured my own dependence on him.

More and more of my days were eaten in this way. Each time a new trick to get me back, another promise to make me stay, more money thrust into my hands to make it seem like a fair exchange. I began to hear him calling in my dreams. I vowed not to return, planned a journey away, to put a sea between him and me. The more Marianne encouraged me to stay with him the more I suspected her too.

I was woken by his call. "I have a difficult patient coming today. I need your help. Please don't say no."

I set off immediately. We both knew that vanity was one of my greatest weaknesses. A man lay on the couch in the sitting room. Christopher asked me to scan him and tell him what I saw.

His system was intact, no holes, no tears, no leaks, no infiltrations. I had seen him there many times before. There was nothing wrong with this man, or nothing I could see. Christopher stepped behind me. I felt his hand brush lightly across the base of my spine and a cool breeze entered. "Now look again."

Now I could see another energy system, a brighter web some distance from the body.

"Look to the right of his chest, about a metre away." He said.

I could see a core of threads, beating, communicating through waves of energy both in towards the man and outwards into space.

"That is his heart; the one inside is just a pump. This one manifests at conception and the physical body unfolds around its call. Do you see the dark patch?"

I did indeed. It looked like a thumbprint pressed into the fabric of the energy.

"He's been attacked. Unless that is repaired nothing can make him well again."

I heard the significance of his words, thought of Kali and the thumbprint that must have been left on her heart. I watched as he took one of the gold needles he liked to use, opened the energy wheels from the base of his spine to his crown, front and back, called on the force of his sky-cord and began the process of repairing the dent. It was too fast for me to catch what he was doing but he caught me, with the one thing he knew I needed to learn.

My training with Christopher and with Andy continued. It became a subtle dance, learning as much as I could while hiding what I'd learned. I continued to walk the circles with Andy, searching for the precise configurations and angles of my joints, trying to find the secret mudras that could connect and enhance my energy system.

With Andy I walked slowly, the walk of the willing but inept student, forever goading him into showing me more than he intended. Back home, when Marianne was out, I practised alone, sometimes moving, sometimes still, but always visualising the movements inside. I brought the training from my days at Ennio's house to bear on what I was learning, playing with views and dimensions and speeds, until, at last, I cracked a code.

I spent more days with Christopher now; I didn't want to miss a thing. He began to train me in the use of needles. "Needles are the same as swords," he said. "Useful tools but not necessary to a master."

Often, we would work with a group of people gathered in his hallway. He taught me how to embed the gold needles in special patterns in their scalp. Then we'd leave them sitting silently in the hall while we worked with another patient in the living room. I had always thought that this was simply another way to see more people, to make more money while Christopher reserved his attention for the more useful clients he'd attend to personally. As I started to watch him at a faster speed I realised that it was not so simple. For sure every new client got his undivided attention, albeit augmented with my own, but some of these were quickly destined for the treatment in the hall while some were clearly of more significance to a plan I could not yet see.

One Sunday morning Christopher's phone call woke me from my sleep. He instructed me to meet him at an address not far from where he lived. I was shocked when Robert opened the door but his greeting betrayed no acknowledgement of our previous time together. Not knowing why, I accepted to meet him as a stranger. Robert led me into his garden where Christopher was stirring a thick concoction boiling in a barrel over an open fire. I was introduced to Chris, another student, but one I hadn't met before.

On instruction, Chris explained the ingredients of the brew, various spices, tree barks and roots, minerals and oils, and a deer - everything of a deer but its flesh. The flesh was slowly cooking in the oven for our lunch. As was so often the case when I was with Christopher, my head was alive with questions and confusions. I had no idea what knowledge about me Robert and Christopher shared. Nothing was betrayed and I assumed my usual demeanour of the willing but not too curious student.

Chris was instructed to add more ingredients from paper bags as Christopher continued stirring. I felt a pang of jealously as I watched him, wondering if he knew more than me, received more teaching than me. I saw the foolishness, recognised the results of Christopher's way of meddling with the emotions of others. I remembered why I was here, the only reason I was here and I hid the thought away. Finally, Christopher finished his stirring and set the stick aside. The mixture continued boiling, thick and yellow and viscous. Christopher muttered one of his prayers and then explained to Chris and me that we had to plunge both arms in up to the elbows and retrieve a bone. Thankfully Chris went first and quickly withdrew with a bone from the cervical spine of the deer. It didn't look too painful so I rolled up my sleeves and followed suit.

Very quickly I felt a bone between my fingers, a small rib, and was ready to withdraw as the heat began to bite into my skin. A voice in my head stopped me, Robert's voice. "Not that one… Keep looking."

I let the bone slide from between my fingers, caught sight of Christopher who noticed my hesitation, not sure if he knew the reason. I reached deeper into the mud, the heat now searing deeper into my flesh, sweat breaking on my body in response to the heat and pain. Christopher was mumbling his strange prayers again. I felt urged by him to withdraw but heard Robert's voice again. "Keep going… Nearly there."

In the darkness of the mud I felt another hand meet mine, press a bone into my palm, close my fingers around its shape. "This one is yours."

I withdrew my arms. Christopher passed me a spatula to scrape the paste from my skin. I expected to scrape the skin away too but all was well, the pain receded, no burn remained. I opened my palm and examined the bone, from the spine, broad and solid, a lumbar vertebra, the foramen wide enough to slide my little finger in.

Christopher turned away, asked Robert for a baking tray. He ladled the brew into the tray and asked for more. Ten trays of various shapes and sizes sat cooling in the garden while we ate our lunch of venison. After lunch Christopher sent me away. I saw the paste again, carved into cubes and dispensed to Christopher's many patients.

I left with the bone clutched in my palm, more confused than ever. That night I slept with the bone in my hand, my little finger pressed inside the foramen. I had the first of the dreams.

Although I was in the dream I was also watching from a distance. I was with Christopher, on a long, stone ledge high up in the mountains. Above us stood a high, stone wall, below us the rock plummeted into the valley.

Beyond the valley were more mountains - tall, rocky, snow-capped and austere. It would be too easy to say it was Tibet but I couldn't really know. We were both wearing thick brown woollen robes and carrying heavy sticks. To begin with we were simply walking and talking. I could not hear what was being said. As the dream progressed it became clear that we were arguing, our actions becoming more and more heated and erratic. At one point I turned my back to Christopher, gazing out from the ledge towards the mountains.

Christopher took up his stick and swung it with both hands towards my head. It was a deathblow. Had it connected I would have plunged lifeless into the deep ravine below. Perhaps I heard the sound, perhaps I felt the wind, perhaps then I already had the powers I was only just discovering now. I ducked, just as Christopher's staff flailed over my head. He lost his balance and crashed painfully to the stone floor. I turned and stared down at him crumpled on the ground. We were at war.

When I woke I knew we were still at war. What I didn't know was how much of this Christopher remembered. In the dream it looked as if I had the advantage. In my relationship with him now I suspect he had that edge. After the dream I sensed an increasing paranoia in Christopher. Often, he would ask if I'd been followed. Often, he would rush up the stairs from his basement and search the streets for hidden enemies. Sometimes he would tell me stories, furtive and incomplete stories whispered in his kitchen. He talked of the Vril, a small, invisible and ancient people who inhabited tunnels deep beneath the earth that spanned the planet from Tibet to Norway.

He told me of the underground wars that raged continuously, unknown to most of humanity. He told me how from time to time the Vril would send one of their numbers to instigate wars on the surface.

He warned me to look out for men who wore green, a colour favoured by the servants of the Vril, that they were out to stop him in his work. I had little interest in his stories. I already had enough of my own thoughts of conspiracy but I was curious to know what Christopher thought was his work.

"To shock people," he said. "To wake them up."

"But why?" I asked.

"Because there is little time left."

23

As Christopher's paranoia increased so too did my clarity. Now I knew I was involved in a game with him. I had much to learn about this game and, especially, about my opponent. I gave in to Marianne's offer. I couldn't be sure if she was with me or with him but it seemed the best way to discover that was to let down my defences with her. Christopher was right, at least in that, she was good for me. She brought a new calmness and simplicity to my life. I was happy to come home to her. I didn't feel the least pang of guilt when she moved into the bed I'd shared with Kali. She opened herself like a book, answered my every question and let me be with my own dark secrets.

She said she had met Christopher by chance, in the park where she practised Tai Chi on Wednesdays. It was summer. "He watched me practise from beneath the beech tree. He called me over and corrected my moves. I agreed to let him teach me. That's all he taught me, only Tai Chi. He said he approved of my choice of meditation teacher, said he'd met him twice before."

Marianne said she'd been practicing with him every week since then. It was not so long, just a few months, just a few months before Kali returned to London with me. She was sure he was a sword master. "Already he's taught me more than I've learned in seven years of practice. When I told him I wanted to be a sword fighter he said I already had been in a previous life. He promised to start me back on that path quite soon."

It was refreshing to talk with Marianne, rare to meet someone so simple, open and pure.

I soon knew she had nothing to tell me about Christopher but everything to show me about humility. I worked around her routine, always arranging to stay at home when she went to practise Tai Chi or to meditate. I knew at these times she was fully occupied, had no attention left to keep an ear to me.

These were the times I reserved for correspondence and for practising with the wind horse. Now as I stood, silently visualising the moves Chris had taught me I could feel the wind on my face. With one part of my attention I could hold the series, faster and faster, impregnable. With another part of my attention I could send out a stream of life force to Kali. I still could not see where she was, still could not receive from her but I knew the energy touched her, could feel the slight quickening and strengthening of her system in response. I used another part of my attention to call out to the lama. Three times each week I practised like this, each time faster, each time stronger, each time clearer, but I didn't receive a reply from the lama.

Now as I worked with Christopher I never missed a thing. Whatever he was doing, whatever he asked me to do, I was secretly practising the wind horse, studying his every move, learning to know my enemy and understand the weaknesses in his system. My methods worked and he became more and more available to me. The defences that had stopped me from infiltrating his mind softened as he worked in another room. Occasionally, he would flinch or stumble on his words when I was clumsy in my approach but even so, he didn't seem to realise it was me.

Only once did he come close to understanding what was going on. I felt him catch my thread where I had hooked it in his mind. I felt a tug, like a fish on a line, as he began to take measure of the strength and source of the infiltration.

In a moment I slipped away as I overwhelmed with anger the patient Christopher was treating, flooded Christopher's mind with confusion that he later ascribed to his patient and set up a ripple of discontent in the small group gathered in the hallway.

As Christopher struggled to regain control of his space, I focused my attention once again on the little task at hand, thinly slicing ginger root to marinade in peanut oil. I think it was this incident that brought me to see Robert more often. He was often at Christopher's flat but only ever as a patient, at least when I was there and only ever sitting in the hall with gold needles embedded in his scalp. Like so many of the patients, he was usually submissive to Christopher's orders and demands. Whatever power he had when I first met him seemed lost or forgotten. But now Robert's discontent was the loudest and Christopher had to work hard to stop him leaving.

I so much wanted to question Robert. It would have been easy; I knew where he lived, but something held me back. I still wasn't sure if he was under the spell of Christopher, in collusion with him or, perhaps like me, hiding what he knew. From then on Robert was always there when I arrived; Christopher was teaching him too. Now, instead of sitting with needles in his head he was learning how to use them, learning the various patterns: the five-point star, the seven-point star, the eleven-point vortex. Christopher never let me put the needles in but seemed to want me to know the patterns. Unsurprisingly to me, Robert learned fast and soon came the day when Christopher left him in charge of a hall-full of patients and led me into the kitchen.

He sat beside me at the table and asked me to close my eyes. He described a staircase that lay before me and told me to walk up it.

It was a simple staircase, made of white stone, without a balustrade. There was nothing either side, just emptiness. I kept on walking upwards.

Christopher then described a temple above me, a small round temple also built of white stone, nothing more than a circle of columns supporting a cupola. I found myself at the entrance. I stepped inside. He told me to look down. I looked down and saw that my feet were standing on nothing, only space.

Christopher told me he was going to take me a little higher, to give me another perspective. But I didn't want to go a little higher; I didn't want to follow his direction. An eagle was hovering beside me, an enormous eagle surfing the updraft, calling me to step upon its feathered back. I detached a little of myself to remain with Christopher in the kitchen while the rest of me stepped onto the back of the eagle. Its soft feathers wrapped around my bare feet where I squatted and we became one as it glided out towards familiar mountains, mountains I used to see from Rafa and Jasmine's garden in Mussoorie. We travelled fast, the heat of that enormous bird's body warming me as we soared across the icy peaks.

We swooped down between the peaks into a dark valley devoid of signs of human life: no lights, no roads, just bare rock and, far below, wild nature. As we moved in closer I could see a tiny wooden hut clinging to the rock-face. No path led to it, no ladder, no rope. No metal held it in place, just wood, fitted into crevices, swollen by the water that seeped through the rock. The hut had a window but no door. Above it I could see a wild beehive and the nectar that leaked from it dribbled down the rock face into the hut.

As the eagle reeled past, I caught a glimpse inside, a glimpse of Kali deep in meditation, a meditation essential to preserve her own life.

The wild bees would turn on her and sting her to death were in not for that constant meditation that kept her invisible. No wonder she had nothing spare with which to reach out to me.

As we reeled by once more the bees began to agitate and we had to pull away for fear of upsetting the delicate balance of that ingenious prison, but not before Kali opened her eyes and momentarily engaged with me, a moment that caused her prison to creak against the rock and the bees to swarm.

In the last fly-by I took in the incredible subtlety of the engineering. There was nothing in the rock face that permitted a person to climb up or down. The hut must have been lowered into place by rope with Kali already inside. If she moved from where she sat she would imbalance the structure and tear it from the rock face. If she allowed her attention to wander from inside for more than a moment the bees would feel her and attack. All that sustained her was the water and honey that seeped down the rock to where she sat.

I wanted to fly once again on the crest above the hut but the eagle soared on an updraft and powered back to the place where we met. I could hear Christopher's voice and other voices shouting from somewhere else. I was pulled so quickly back into the kitchen that I almost puked. Christopher was gone, the door open, chaos beyond it in the hall, Robert shouting, patients crying.

One of the patients lay spread-eagled on the floor, the life draining from his face. Robert stood petrified, begging Christopher to help, a look of terror in his eyes. Christopher plucked gold needles from patients' heads and ushered them quickly one by one out of the flat until all that remained were the dying patient, Robert and him. From the kitchen I watched, unnoticed through a crack in the door as Christopher set to work.

"What is it?" cried Robert, tears streaming down his face. "What did I do?"

Christopher reassured him. "It's not your fault, he was already wounded. He was lucky to find his way here."

I changed my view and almost gave myself away as I saw the thumbprint on the man's heart. I silenced my breath and my attention and sank deep into invisibility as Christopher worked to repair the damage. I studied every tiny gesture he made as Christopher sucked the man's essence from the crown of his head, holding it safe within his own body, as he wove the torn threads of life that formed the web of the patient's energy heart.

I watched as Christopher opened and closed the vortices along his own spine modulating his colour and sound to match the colour and sound of the layer with which he was working.

I watched as Christopher tuned himself to white and poured white light into the completed weave. I watched as that whiteness filled the energy threads and jump-started a healing process that had been stalled by the damage. I watched as Christopher breathed the man's essence back into his physical form and the colour returned to his cheeks.

As he woke, not quite sure of where he was, Christopher cradled the man in his arms and Robert sank down into a chair in relief. I seized the moment to leave the kitchen and head quickly past Christopher and Robert to exit the flat.

I needed nothing more and was afraid that Christopher would realise what I had learned. I didn't want to take the chance and left without another word.

24

I decided to walk home rather than take my usual bus, aware of a fear that now sat heavy in my stomach. I headed into the park and stopped to drink a tea, to settle myself down again, to search for the reason for that fear. It took very little time for me to understand. Now I had no reason to stay, neither with Christopher, nor with Marianne, but I was not yet sure of where I had to go.

I finished my tea and headed out across the Tai Chi lawn. Halfway across I saw Christopher and Robert heading straight towards me. I scanned the field to see which way to run and saw three other people heading in my direction. I slowed down my breath, opened the vortices throughout my energy body and pulled on the sky-cord just to remind myself of what that power felt like. As I pulled a little stronger on the sky-cord and readied for action I heard Robert's voice inside my mind. "Relax, it's okay, they're not coming for you."

As all the players in this mystery converged in the centre of the lawn I saw the sweat and panic on Christopher's face. On the periphery of my vision I caught the moment when the three strangers synchronised the mudras of their hands and the world stood still. The panic fell from Christopher's face as he relaxed into that stillness. I looked around and saw that it extended way beyond our circle. Out, as far as I could see across the park, all life stood still - people, pets and wildlife suspended in a heartbeat. As the three strangers worked their magic Robert worked his, reconfiguring Christopher's energy body, closing windows and vortices, disconnecting his sky-cord, and finally, with a press of his right middle finger against Christopher's breastbone, the work was complete. Where the finger had been a red sore erupted. "Years of bad use," Robert said.

The three newcomers stopped their work and life in the park continued as if the stillness had never been there. Everyone went about their business as before - everyone except for Christopher who now walked alone. He seemed confused and didn't recognise Robert or me as he continued his walk across the Tai Chi field.

"Has he forgotten everything?" I asked.

"Only temporarily," Robert said. "An effect of the stillness. His memory will come back but not his power."

"But surely he'll recover his powers, somebody will heal him?"

"Not a chance, I took his powers and now they're mine."

"Are you serious?" I asked. "You can take away someone's power?"

"We all can, you just have to seize the right moment, but it helps to have stillness workers on your side."

"Can you show me how?" I asked.

"Not now, you have to begin your work, you have to find Kali and we don't have much time." Robert replied.

"But where? How?"

"That's your work - you're the treasure seeker."

"And you, what are you?" I asked.

Robert smiled. "A light worker."

As we continued across the park Robert explained how he had drained and hidden away his skills and powers and come to Christopher as a patient, although a patient with some advantages - money and connections, two things that Christopher could not resist. Only today had he taken the risk of reinstalling his powers.

"We're running short of time," he said and went on to explain. "The devolvers have awakened an army of demigods like Christopher, individuals who possess some powers but are easily manipulated through their greed for money and influence. They are building a human network to overwhelm the effect of the vases installed by the old lama. The golden needles are part of that process. Traces of gold remain embedded in the scalps of those patients. They will be pulled into a network when the time is right. Those innocent people form one tier, unaware but living only one step removed from the devolvers.

"Just one small gesture is all that is needed to ignite and connect that golden web. Others, like you and me were intended to form another tier, which involved a more intense work reconfiguring the threads of life to create an open channel with which to pull down the root sky-cords. Thankfully, you had intuited the need to hide your skills and Christopher had not yet discerned your power as a treasure seeker. He had plans for us and had not yet realised that we already belonged to another plan. The sudden urgency arose because your wife is in town and was due to call on Christopher."

I paled at the mention of her. "She really is that important?" I asked.

"Yes, very important," Robert replied. "From one of the deep old families. I hear you have already scrapped with her?"

"Yes, but she ran," I said.

"You were lucky, she wasn't expecting you, she wasn't prepared. You ain't seen nothing yet."

What I had already seen was shocking enough. The thought that she might yet have more power filled me with fear.

"Don't worry, she needs her family. Hopefully by the time you see her next you will have your family ready."

"My family? I have a family?" I asked.

"You don't think you came alone?" Robert replied.

"But who are they, where are they? I only know of you and Kali, and Kali is dying alone in a prison on the dark side of the Himalayas."

Robert explained: "I know we belong to the same family because we were both recognised and called by Kali, but it is your work to find the others. As a light worker, my duty is to be called and not to call. It is your duty as a treasure seeker to call the rest of the family together."

He went on to explain the final tier of the devolver's network - a hoard of unwitting sitters was being prepared by false teachers and their twisted teachings, meditations and energy techniques.

"These are people whose search for meaning and connection might once have led them to the truth but who were now tricked into sitting in groups, withdrawing themselves from real life and real struggle and the truth of their own feelings into the comfort of dissociation, fantasy and dream.

"Where once they could have discerned the taste of truth, now they are prepared to believe anything that comes from the mouth of a man with a beard, a book or a saffron shirt. Like the vase network, this human network has been in preparation for decades, but only now is the full design being implemented through the creation of the golden tier and the sky-cord tier."

Just today Robert had received news of Marisa's visit and reinstalled his powers. It was Robert who sent the eagle to where I was sitting in the kitchen and it was he who ripped at the heart of the patient who then collapsed in the hallway. He had set up the conditions necessary for me to find Kali and to learn the skills I needed to save her. Without me, Kali was lost forever and without Kali, so too was the old lama.

"Nobody knows where the old lama is - probably caught between worlds, but a big battle has begun and we need as many families with us as we can get."

25

I went home and took the dreaming bone from where I had hidden it amongst the wardrobes. I packed and hid a travel bag with clothes, passports and money. I prepared supper for Marianne and waited for her to come home from her meditation. I fed her and seduced her and softened her body in my arms and when she fell into a deep sleep I slipped the dreaming bone onto my little finger and let myself go.

I sat on the step of a cabin and watched as day and night passed me by. I watched the sun rise each day and carve a new arc across the sky. I watched the moon wax, grow full, wane and disappear into shadow. I watched the constellations spin on their axis. I watched bees pass by in search of blossom, returning with legs laden with pollen. I watched leaves unfold from sticky buds, expand and swell, dry out and fall to earth. I watched birds courting, mating, feeding their young and teaching them to catch the winds that would take them far away to other lands. I watched as the whiskers grew from my face and my body became weak and thin and frail. I watched as the clothes disappeared from my body, eaten by insects. I watched as my nails grew in curls until they pierced my own flesh.

As the world froze beneath a thick layer of snow I entered the cabin. The space inside was warm and dry. There was food and water and wood. I lit the stove and heated water. I washed my skinny body and cut my hair and nails. I cooked food and ate. I drank whiskey and danced. I sang songs whose origins I had forgotten and finally I lay down and slept.

I woke to the sound of bird-song and, when I opened the cabin door, I saw the vivid green of spring. I drank strong coffee and smoked Turkish tobacco. When I looked in the mirror I saw that I was beautiful. My long, black hair oiled and shining, my body full and strong. My eyes were clear and bright and when I gazed at their reflection I started to weep. I turned away and noticed a single book on the shelf above the bed. I took it down and looked at the spine. I didn't know what it said. I opened the book and gazed at the pages and realised that I didn't know how to read. I was filled with an immense longing to understand.

I tried to stare at a page but my eyes began to drift to the side and focus on another world. I saw immense red fires blazing beside a familiar lake. In the smoke I could smell dark and exotic fragrances. As I stepped closer to the fire, I could see it consuming gorgeous books bound with leather and hasped with fine silver. I could see caskets of wonderful woods break open, spilling manuscripts into the flames. As I fell to my knees in the wet sand I saw carriages drawn by magnificent horses. They were driven by our people, a people of beauty, graceful and serene with long straight hair and eyes glowing in the firelight.

As each carriage arrived, the people unloaded their cargoes of writings into the flames, freed the horses and stepped calmly into the inferno. I watched, frozen and horrified, as this awesome and horrendous scene continued throughout the night into the following day. At last the final carriage arrived with the passengers I had been waiting for. I gave Kali the last book, which she clutched to her chest as she took my hand and we stepped into the pyre. The devolvers reached the beach to find our peoples' knowledge blowing as fine white ash across the lake.

I sobbed as I remembered what we had done, although I knew that in this awful act, we had prevented the accumulated knowledge of our people from falling into the hands of the devolvers.

For thousands of years they had been searching and stealing and inventing and experimenting in their vain attempt to bring together what we had taken from the world. I knew now that, according to a plan we had made then, I was back. I knew now that if I was here the others must be here too. I turned from this scene and out into the sunshine. I closed the cabin and left. I knew I would not return here until my work was done.

As I returned from the dream, images from my past began to emerge. I recalled the people whose significance I had felt but who in ignorance I had let pass by. I rolled quietly from the bed and gathered my things from the dressing room. I looked in one last time on Marianne, a woman who now touched my heart even as I prepared to abandon her. I sneaked out through the kitchen and unlocked the front door. Before I opened it, a powerful hand pulled me back. I was facing Marianne at her softest and most beautiful, hair tousled from the pillow, skin a little creased by sleep. "Where are you going?" she asked.

"I don't know," I lied. "I need some air".

"With a bag?"

"I have to go. I have to find my family. I will come back for you soon."

She knew my lies and started to cry. "Please don't leave me now; I am your family."

"I must go Marianne. I don't know what I can tell you. I don't know what you know. I don't know who you're with."

"I'm with you," she cried. "I'm your woman, just as Kali asked me to be."

"But I don't know if I can trust you; you were with Christopher."

"You idiot!" she said. "How could you doubt me? How could you doubt Kali's choice? How could you doubt the woman who carries your baby in her belly?"

I sank to the floor with Marianne, all urgency gone, tears soaking my face, confusion paralysing all but my hands that found my way to her belly, to the roundness I had touched so many times without ever thinking there might be a child in there.

"From the night of the deer," she said. "A sacred child - your son. He's a tulku of course."

As her words, and her belly, and the little boy inside conspired to keep me there I barely noticed the slight tremble in the air around us. But thankfully, some part of me remained alert and recognised that change in the atmosphere. In an instant that part discerned the truth - Marianne was indeed carrying our child but she couldn't come with me.

I pressed two sky points above her clavicles sending her instantly to sleep. I pressed for a moment a point just below her navel and sent a wave of love to the little boy inside. I dragged them both to safety, away from the door that would soon be turned to splinters, to the shelter of the kitchen.

I ran to the dressing room and, following instructions Kali gave me on my first day in the apartment, I pulled a shelf on one of the wardrobes by the door and the wardrobe fell to seal the door exactly as she said it would. I pulled on the lever set in the wall behind and a trapdoor dropped open to reveal the ladder to my freedom.

I slid down the ladder and the trapdoor sprang shut again as the garage doors opened. The morning light streamed in to reveal my ride, an old Mercedes, fully fuelled and ready to go. On the passenger seat was a leather holdall. I was sure Kali had left it for me but I had no time to look inside. The trembling of the floor above intensified and I heard the door splinter as I started the engine. I pulled out onto the road and followed the directions that Kali had made me memorise long ago, heading east out of the city.

I finally breathed again when the ferry pulled out into the night. I opened the holdall and the smell of Kali filled my cabin. Inside I found changes of clothes that made me smile, white no more for me, just green shirts and everything else black, including thick down-filled jacket and trousers. There was also a toiletries bag with everything a man could need, two passports, exact replicas of the one I left in the apartment and a set of keys with an address in Paris.

26

As soon as the boat docked, I set off for Amsterdam, heading straight for the little bar whose name I no longer remembered. Before I had even started drinking my coffee Judith walked in to begin her shift. She drank a short, strong coffee, grabbed a bag that she said she always kept hidden behind the bar and we left for Paris.

I met Judith twelve years before in Cannes. I was hanging out with some friends who had business in the film market. Judith had won a trip to the festival in a writing competition. She recognised me then but I was still lost. I had bought a beer in the Petit Carlton and she followed me out onto the street. She took me down to the beach. We walked and talked until sunrise. She was young and very beautiful but her hands were dry and wrinkled like the hands of an old lady.

As the sun came up, I tried to make love with her but it was futile. That wasn't our story but I still knew of no other way to be intimate and she didn't have the power to call me out from my sleep. I left in confusion when my driver came to take me to the airport. I left her crying in my hotel bed.

Judith and I drove all day, stopping only to pick up supplies and swap the driving. Now we had an intimacy that needed few words. In Paris we followed the directions written by Kali on the label attached to the keys. We let ourselves into another perfect home, a first-floor apartment that opened out onto a beautiful square. The place was fresh and clean and felt as if someone had left just moments before our arrival.

We slept the night in an embrace that softened our bodies and I knew another piece of my life was in place. In the morning Judith showed me her hands. They were beautiful like the rest of her, no longer cracked and sore with eczema. I had nothing to show but I knew something in me had also healed.

We hid away for a few days eating picnics prepared from food we brought with us. I taught Judith the wind horse and we practised for hours every day, sometimes in movement, sometimes in stillness. She couldn't remember doing the dance before but she learned fast as if waking a memory in her body. Practicing with her beside me, I learned new skills and taught her things I didn't know I knew.

Soon we could work as a team, completely in synchrony as if one body. Soon we could practise in stillness and throw our collective consciousness outside the room, beyond the plaza, to the very edges of the city where man and nature struggled to rule. The days passed quickly and the information that poured into our systems during practice was phenomenal. Neither of us quite understood the process involved but we both had the same feeling, that this practice together of wind horse magnified our individual capacity and opened us to a level of consciousness where everything is known, and that 'everything' became a part of us, or us a part of it.

On the third day Judith stopped and said, "It's time."

She called Alice's number and caught her just as she returned home after three months working in Tokyo. We had both met Alice that same year in Cannes. Judith had interviewed her for a Dutch magazine and I met her when she came to discuss a project with my friends. We had not met again since then but I often saw articles about her in magazines.

She arrived at our apartment the following morning with a small travel bag. She had just abandoned her husband and home. She had become a woman and lost the childish pout I most remembered her for.

"After Judith called, I was suddenly freed from an unease that has haunted me all my life. Nothing I had to do was important anymore. I cancelled all my appointments and went to bed where I dreamt of fire. When I woke I knew I had to leave. I told my husband and he knew it was true."

Alice was interrupted by a call on her phone. She quickly scribbled down some notes. When she finished the call, she removed the battery and threw the phone to the floor. "We've got to go right now, danger is here."

We grabbed our bags and ran. As I closed the door behind us I could feel a now familiar low trembling in the fabric of the building and a wind began to roar from under the door. As we pulled away in the car that strange wind poured into the square, throwing café chairs and tables tumbling into the road.

Once we were on the road out of Paris Alice explained. "The call was from Mireille. I haven't seen her for years but I always loved her. Now I know why, she's one of us. We have to meet her in Barcelona, I have the address."

We stopped as we left Paris to fill the car with petrol and to buy water and cigarettes. After that we drove through the night until we reached our destination the following morning. We shared the driving and when Alice drove Judith and I continued our practice. I taught her all I had learned from Kali. Soon we could communicate in silence and leave thoughts, suggestions and skills in each other's mind. Together we slid undetected into Alice's mind.

She didn't feel us coming and didn't sense us there, just continued driving unperturbed. There wasn't much to find there, just quietness, stillness. I didn't understand why she was with us, why Judith had called her. I asked her directly, "Do you know why you're here? Are you a stillness worker?"

The term meant nothing to her and she couldn't find an answer. "I don't know yet, but I know we'll know when we get to Barcelona. I know that I never forgot my meeting with you both all those years ago and I know I have a strong connection with Mireille. It feels as if, for all these years I have just been passing time, waiting for a call, waiting for this moment and yet now it has come I still don't know what it means. Maybe I'm just a driver."

Alice lapsed back into silence and returned her attention to the road ahead having spoken for us all and raised a question that we all hoped would be answered in Barcelona. Judith and I continued with our practice and soon she was teaching me new skills. She showed me how to extend my attention and my ability to act at a distance. To begin with I was scared and resistant, reminded of the killing on the road near Maria's home. Judith brought her soft hands to my hands and unfolded a wave of healing and reassurance into me.

Through her silent touch she helped me understand that, within the realm of this fight, an individual death was neither here nor there, no more than an exhalation freed from the need to inhale. Again, I was reminded how Kali had tried to do the same but could not, the attack to her heart had taken her power.

Soon we realised that Judith knew my whole story since the moment Kali had found me in that restaurant by the sea in Sidi Bou Said, everything I had seen and done, everything I had learned. Soon we realised that since I had come to find her in that Amsterdam café her powers had increased enormously.

Her healing touch, which until then she had reserved for a few customers and friends, now had a force and clarity that seemed to drive demons and ghosts from every corner of my being.

Under Judith's guidance I extended my attention back to Paris, back to the apartment and Alice's phone lying on the floor. From there I stretched out to the London apartment where all was well, a new door fitted, the changing room open again and Marianne sitting alone in the meditation room, singing to our unborn son. Now I could visit that space without Marianne feeling the least hint of my presence.

Much as I longed to, I refrained from reaching out to Kali, now aware of just how fine a thread of attention held her life in balance. I was afraid my contact would unsettle her balance and cause her prison to crash to the ground or distract her and cause the hive of bees to perceive her presence and attack.

When I took over the driving, Judith brought her hands to Alice's hands where they sat in the back of the car and I felt the wave of bliss as Judith cleared Alice of her demons. I watched in the mirror as that adrenalised face she wore fell away and she drifted into sleep in Judith's arms. Judith and I exchanged a smile just as she too fell asleep and I drove the last stretch to Barcelona, not stopping until we reached the address Alice had been given.

27

The concierge let us into the building and we took the stairs to the first-floor apartment where we waited, listening to the music being played on the piano inside. It was completely entrancing and we silently agreed to hear it out. When the music stopped the door swung open to reveal a large, dark man with an enormous smile on his face.

"Come, come," he said, beckoning us into a darkened room lit only by the morning light squeezing between shutters. Juan introduced himself and introduced us to Mireille who was sitting at the piano. She stood to embrace Alice while Juan brought coffee and pastries and set them on the table. He tried to gather us all together but Mireille hushed him, took his hand and led him to where Alice was waiting by the piano.

Judith and I watched as they linked hands. Mireille began to sing and soon Juan and Alice joined in. As the three of them found their song together an extraordinary light filled the room. It was a light I had seen before, like the light of the old lama and the light of the eighth vase that seemed to reveal the life and pulsation of the air and of everything in the room.

I turned questioningly towards Judith and she whispered, "Three become one."

Later, as we shared breakfast in the calm atmosphere of his home Juan explained. "Although I wrote music I had never heard any of it played until I met Mireille. I was born with stiff fingers and a head full of songs. I met Mireille last year and she was the first person who could hear what I heard in my head.

"She has been coming to visit every month since then. She told me about her dreams, about the fires and about Alice and I knew we had to meet. Two days ago, I dreamed of Alice for the first time and I woke up knowing she was in danger, knowing that an important moment had arrived. I called Mireille and she already knew what to do.

"When I was a child in Chile I discovered that I could heal sick animals. I would put my hands on them and let the music play and they would become well. I found I could do the same for people. In no time at all I was overwhelmed. So many people wanted something from me. Soon it was not just sick people coming to me but people wanting my blessing, my advice, my help, wanting me to see the future and give them charms for wealth and power and love. I became exhausted with their constant demands and ill through the clouds of resentment they left when I refused.

"I moved from Chile to Barcelona and lived here without telling a soul what I could do, until I met Mireille in a gallery. With one touch I cured her asthma and she cured my sadness. Now that Alice is with us, I know that our triangle is complete. I can feel my brain softening and my mind expanding and information lost long ago is pouring back in. Already I know we have a lot to do and many skills to revive but it is too dangerous to do that here. I know a small farm tucked away from the world on an island where I know we will be safe. Mireille, Alice and I will meet you there but for now we have some things to prepare. Others will join us. Now rest."

Mireille showed Judith and me to the bedroom and we slept until late afternoon. When we woke we showered and prepared for the next leg of our journey. Juan gave us tickets for the boat and explained how to find the farm and wake it from its hibernation.

On the way to the port we loaded the car with provisions from the list Mireille had prepared for us. We ate on the dockside and waited for our boat. We behaved as any other travellers waiting for the ferry, knowing that now was not the moment to talk of precious things nor practise anything other than ordinariness.

As the boat eased out of the dock and forced its way into the darkness of the sea, we exhaled a unified sigh of relief, and then laughed at the realisation that we had both sensed the danger, both sensed the need for silence and both sensed the safety of being at sea. We retired to our cabin where we shared a bottle of wine before falling into a comfortable sleep. In the morning we went up onto the deck to watch the sun rise over the sea.

We drove straight from the harbour to the farm and unloaded the car. We cleaned the kitchen, brought water from the well and fruit from the garden. We swept spiders webs from the bedrooms and made a list of things we still needed from town. We shopped and, in the afternoon, we drove down to a beach. It was almost empty and the late sun threw a rosy light across the sea. We swam and floated and dived. We played together on the sand and collected shells and pebbles. As the sun set, we headed back to the farm.

28

When we reached the dirt track leading to the farm I could see lights in the distance. We left the car on the roadside and quietly walked around the edge of the orchard until we were near the house, until I could see Juan and Mireille in the kitchen. We broke cover and joined them. Juan was making tea and suggested we wait in the lounge. I could not believe what I saw as we stepped through the door. Sitting around the dining table were Robert, Remi and a newcomer who was introduced as Herve.

"How on earth did you get here?" I asked Robert but, before he could answer, Juan, Alice and Mireille joined us in the lounge. A moment later three more people joined us. I recognised them as the stillness workers from the Tai Chi field.

Juan set down a tray with silver pots of mint tea and fine Moroccan glasses. He grinned. "I am so moved and honoured to be here with you all. Welcome to this house. It is now our home."

As Mireille poured the tea, he turned to me and said, "Perhaps you would like to tell us all why we are here?"

To which I replied, "If I could I would, but I still need a little help to piece this all together."

I turned to Robert. "Can you help me?"

Robert sipped his tea and slipped into one of those silences that I now knew had an extraordinary way of awakening the attention. As usual, he didn't disappoint.

"Well, for me, this story began ten years ago. I had long known I didn't fit into normal life. For years I hid behind a camera and found a good way to make money while travelling. But I never could capture what I really saw. What the books and magazines published was what they wanted, pictures of places, people, landscapes and things. But what I saw was beyond the light and colour. I could see vibrations, relationships, interdependencies, but I could find no way to share that.

"I was alone in the world until I met Remi in the High Atlas Mountains. I hadn't intended to go there. I had a job in Marrakesh, but I was drawn into the mountains by a strange light that nobody else seemed to see. Remi knew what I was looking at. Not only could she see it but she taught me a language to describe it and to understand it. Remi told me she was the last in a line of nomads, originally from Persia, who travelled the planet as the seers and interpreters of celestial signs. Remi can tell you more about that but I can tell you that our meeting brought us both not only the companionship that we each had longed for throughout our lives, but a meaning and purpose that we could never have imagined.

"The light that drew us high into the mountains drew us also to our destiny. It was there that we met Kali and it was Kali who awakened us to that purpose. And the first part of that purpose was to help the old lama reincarnate far from where the devolvers were expecting him."

I looked around the room and realised that I was the only one with a question.

"So, am I right to assume we all know Kali and the lama?"

"Not at all," said Robert and continued.

"It seems that Kali was expecting us and we were quickly prepared for our duties. Remi's lineage skills as a healer of planet and people were needed to prepare the land to receive the lama, to make sure he came through intact. Remi had never done such a thing and there was no knowledge carried within the songs and stories of her people. But that didn't matter. When Kali brought us together that knowledge revealed itself to us, and Remi was obliged to create a new song which I hope one day she will sing to our children.

"Once the lama was safely through, he and Kali taught us to use our skills as light workers. The old style of tulku training that Kali went through was too slow for the current emergency. Kali and the lama needed to travel to gather our family together and they relied on Remi and me to prepare each of them for their work."

"So you did the same to everyone here as you did to me at Maria's?" I asked.

"Not yet. Anyway, everyone is different and has different skills and energy structures."

Robert went on to describe his life studying and practicing with Remi, the trips to Maria's house to work with newly found tulkus as well as their own search for their 'third' which was now complete. He introduced Herve, who they found soon after they left me at Maria's house. Robert turned to me.

"Actually, it was thanks to you that we found Herve. We found him when I was working with you in Ennio's studio. You'd met each other many years before. Although you were not ready to do anything with that knowledge back then, you knew he belonged to our family.

"You kept his memory bundled up as a jewel in your energy web, tucked away in the fibres and fluids of your body. We found him exactly where you saw him last - waiting, as he had waited his entire life to be found."

I turned toward Herve, met his eyes, and recognised him in an instant now that Robert had removed yet another veil from my eyes. Too many people around that table obliged us to save our embrace for later but the tears and smiles were enough for now. Robert continued. "That was what confirmed Kali's belief that you were a treasure seeker."

"So you know everything I know?" I asked.

"Not at all. Obviously that treasure was meant for us and you gave it to us. Your system is filled with such treasures and only you and the other treasure seekers can choose to share them."

"The other treasure seekers?" I asked.

"You and Kali and Judith - a three."

"But one is always missing!"

"Only so far!" Robert said. "But wait until your three is complete. You ain't seen nothing yet."

Robert turned toward Remi and asked her, "Is there anything more you want to add?"

She turned to me and replied, "Not much for now, apart from my thanks to you for helping us complete our three. And, I feel I need to say, trust yourself. Trust that inner wisdom that, despite the chaos of your past life, recognised and protected treasures. You might feel like you need us to guide you now but soon enough it will be you who guides us."

A silence settled over us all, a silence in which I felt not only the enormity of our task but also the strength of the family that now gathered in that room. In that silence I felt myself grow. I knew that Remi was right. I turned to her and said, "And you ain't seen nothing yet!"

Laughter cracked the solemnity.

Juan stood up. "I think we need more than mint tea to drink to that."

He reached up to the top shelf of the library and brought down a bottle. "Island medicine," he said as he topped up our glasses with an amber liqueur flavoured with wild herbs gathered from the land around the farm. He raised his glass.

"To the gifts of the summer past and the promise of the summer to come."

As we drained our glasses and returned the empties to the table Herve leaned forward and addressed me.

"Just to add to what Remi said. I remember you so well from those years when we were neighbours. I could see the struggle you were living. It was something we shared but you turned outward for answers and I turned inward.

"We spent only a little time together but you brought peace to my troubled soul. Back then I didn't know why, and I didn't know how to tell you. Now I can thank you for the strength you brought me then. And now I can thank you again for holding me within yourself as a treasure for all these years. You are my brother and I love you."

I reached across the table to take the hands Herve offered. As I held them, he added.

"Just one more thing - about our three. Although we are all light workers we work in different realms. Remi's realm is the earth, Robert's realm is the human. Mine is the air. When Robert sent you an eagle, I was that eagle. I will always be ready for your call, brother."

With a smile Robert answered my question. "That is how we came to be here with you; we had an eagle to follow you."

29

That first night together continued until daybreak as we each revealed our place in our family. Remi, Robert and Herve were light workers, Alice, Mireille and Juan sound workers. In their case Juan's medium was music, Alice's was words and Mireille's was movement. Once again, it seemed, I was a catalyst in the completion of their three. All these years I carried Judith and Alice as treasures. My night with the dreaming bone released the memory of Judith and led me back to the café she described so many years before where, despite her success as a writer, she patiently continued her morning job and waited for me to come for her. During Judith's first night with me in Paris I gave her the treasure-memory of Alice, and when Alice joined Judith and me in the apartment Mireille felt something in the air and just had to contact her.

The last to talk that night were the stillness workers. They were two sisters and a brother, orphaned and abandoned at an early age, who survived through their gifts of silence and stillness. They shared the same mother, a remarkable woman who gave passage to three tulkus. Each had a different father. Mariam's father, himself a master of stillness, had not been seen since her mother had to flee to save their child. Hawa's father, a drum master from Mali disappeared on a trip to his village. Rafiq's father, a Sufi, died with their mother in a car-crash, leaving the children to fend for themselves. Mariam was just fourteen years old but amply equipped for the task. She led her siblings into the mountains before they could be taken into care. She woke them all to their talents and they flourished in the secret world they created, invisible to the world from which they stole everything they needed.

The first outsider to penetrate their world was Kali who came looking for them. She brought Robert and Remi and asked them to prepare their sacred space for the arrival of the lama.

Although the stillness workers were able to understand most languages, they had little need to talk. They communicated with each other instantly and could also read others instantly without the need to enter minds. When they did speak it was usually brief, precise and enthralling, and the stillness and silence they generated with their words left one refreshed and energised - unless that is, they had other intentions.

Throughout the following day we remained close to the house, either resting, preparing meals or responding to the calls of Robert, Remi and Herve who worked tirelessly to reconfigure our energy bodies. More than anything, they needed to strengthen our energy threads so that we could cope with the new skills and powers that were open to us now that our family was nearly complete.

A new confidence began to build in me in the days that followed. I felt a sense of meaning in my life, now that I was surrounded by my family again. Now there was only one aim and that was to liberate Kali. We had no need to think beyond that. The simplicity of one aim was empowering.

When I worked with Robert he told me that families like ours formed a global network. One lama travelled between many families as the means of communication and as the coordinator of action. At quieter times families never quite came together but in times like these it was as if a force awakened in the universe that helped us find one another.

"But what happens to members of families like ours who are not called together? Do they just pass their life a little lost like so many of our family once were?" I asked.

Robert didn't know the answer but assumed it was a mixture of yes and no. "Yes, they probably remain a little lost but on the other hand nothing is lost forever, as long as there are treasure seekers."

Which led me inevitably to my role as a treasure seeker, which I was only just beginning to understand. I now knew that Kali and I had recognised something in each other when we first met. I knew that she had carried that memory of me wrapped up as a jewel within herself as I had done for others. I knew that treasure seekers like us had the capacity to project our attention out into the world or deep into other people's minds. I knew that we could cast our attention back through time or forward to places we had never been before. But what else?

"I cannot tell you what else," Robert said. "I can tell you only what I have seen and what I have heard. I can tell you that, like all family members, you have riches beyond your imagination, many of which you will carry all your life as unused potential but many of which you will discover because you need them and demand that skill."

"But you can look at my energy body and see jewels, right?" I asked.

"Only some of the jewels are clear, and those are the ones that have already come to light. Treasure seekers have a dense energy body in which it is possible to carry many hidden treasures - treasures carried from other times, treasures collected in this life and treasures which others have hidden."

"So, does that mean I lived before, that my dreams are real memories of previous lives?"

"Probably," Robert replied. "It is likely that your energy body is an accumulation of many previous lives. You have to learn to understand the energy body you have entered and learn to use it well."

Robert asked me to look at his energy body to see if I could find anything significant there. I did as he suggested, first looking at the layer closest to the physical body and then progressively further outwards. Everything looked perfect. I softened my gaze, stopped searching for something wrong as I had done so many times when working with Christopher and suddenly I could see jewels sparkling within the fibres and threads. They were like precious stones, but raw, unpolished, unfaceted. Some had strong colours like rubies, emeralds and sapphires but they were clearly not jewels of that kind, their light and colour were stronger and they pulsated when I looked directly at them. Others looked like more like pearls. I described what I saw to Robert and he clapped his hands in delight. He explained their meaning to me.

"You have to understand that I can only tell you what Kali entrusted me to tell you. I can't see jewels myself - the jewels that you see are only visible to treasure seekers. As well as this ability to find things in the material world, treasure seekers are also able to help people find their own jewels. But in this respect, you are more like catalysts than protagonists. In your company, jewels become visible to the person carrying them but only those that fit the treasure seekers purpose."

"You mean we use people?"

Robert laughed. "Yes, treasure seekers are really just a bunch of users!"

He continued. "As you now know, without a family, treasure seekers are lost souls, but with a family you have a purpose, but what you do is not for you. It is the same for all of us, our gifts are more like a curse unless we find our family. Each family has its missions and each three within a family has a specific purpose. Very few families have treasure seekers. When a family does have them, it is the treasure seekers who define the purpose of the family. People like you and Judith and Kali carry knowledge and history through time and, as you have seen, you can recognise qualities in others and awaken them to their destiny. Seeing jewels is just one of the ways you do that."

Robert went on to explain about the pearls. "The pearls are altogether different. They are not treasures. They are skills and powers - some inherent and some stolen from others, like those I took from Christopher that day in the Tai Chi park. What is interesting is that, while treasures are scattered throughout the energy body, the pearls are all gathered in one area, an area specific to the individual and they can be seen by others, not just treasure seekers."

My ears pricked up. "How did you do that? How did you take Christopher's powers?" I asked.

"As I said at the time, it was easy because of the stillness workers. There was nothing Christopher could do to stop me. Without the stillness workers it is almost impossible to take someone's power - but it can be done."

"Do you know about the men I killed in Italy?"

For a moment Robert lost his poise. His silence was his answer. "Kali told me."

I was silent, a little confused, not sure when Kali told him but also relieved that someone else knew.

“She told me soon after you arrived in London. It was important that I know.”

“But if only I’d known then what I know now, perhaps I could have stolen their power, perhaps they would still be alive.”

Robert put his arm around me, reassured me with his contact, assured me like Kali before, that what I did was okay. “You need to let that one go. What you did was incredible. But for you, our family would be finished. When you found that power you saved us all. This is not a soft war, people will die.”

“But if I could kill at a distance I don’t understand why I couldn’t steal their power at a distance?”

“I can’t answer that but I think you need to be close enough to touch. You could never have got close enough. Stealing is a subtle art; it can never be done well in the midst of violence. I’m going to teach you how to steal. But you also have to respect your ability to kill.”

True to his word Robert taught me how to steal pearls, even when he himself could not see them. I realised just how much Kali had prepared the way for me, despite the fact that she knew she was dying and knew she had to leave. My love for her deepened every day, as did my resolve to save her.

30

During those days on the island we learned to steal much more than the occasional jewel. In fact, stealing almost became the theme of our entire stay. It soon became clear that the only resources we had were our skills and powers. Once we entered the island we were cut off from the rest of the world, freed from our phones, bank cards and history. What cash we had was soon finished but we had the stillness workers to show us the way and they showed us how to draw down a veil of invisibility and take what we needed from the world.

During those first days together, Juan said he would take the position as head of the family but made it clear that it was only until I felt ready to take over. "After all, I am the old man and I always wanted to be a father. This may be the only opportunity I have to know what that feels like."

Juan also made it clear that once we could control the island we would be ready to leave. "We will learn that everything on the island is communal property - we will take what we need."

I was already familiar with this idea after my time in the London apartment but extending it to the rest of the world was both challenging and exciting. On the island we had to learn to take what we needed without arousing alarm or suspicion. This meant that everything we took had to be compensated for in some way.

We started simply enough and on the small scale of our nearest village. To begin with we depended on Hawa, Rafiq and Mariam to smooth the way.

They would walk ahead and unfold the stillness. The rest of us would follow in their wake and help ourselves to whatever we needed, just food to begin with.

Little by little the stillness workers extended their web until we could no longer see where they were. Then we had to learn to feel the waxing and waning of the stillness and catch the moment to act unseen. Once we became familiar with this, we took more than we needed, sometimes taking money from the purse of one to put in the pocket of another, sometimes taking just for the pleasure of knowing what we could do.

We had to learn to work together, one unfolding the stillness, another doing the taking and another rearranging the thoughts of our hosts and benefactors to conceal our action and return the favour with a gift. I enjoyed myself so much and quickly came to see that the stillness workers were in no way as austere as their silence and lack of smiles had led me to believe. On the contrary, they revealed themselves as playful and mischievous, always awake to the subtle nuances of our environment, they would sometimes leave us teetering on the edge of disaster but they would never abandon us nor the poor victims of our games.

When I thought of how hard it must have been for them, orphaned at such an early age, I came to appreciate what an extraordinary sense of justice and fair play they had, and little by little I developed a sense of the one amazing mother and three amazing fathers in whose traditions they followed. As much as we took what we needed, the stillness workers arranged things in such a way that our victims always gained more than they lost, even if all they gained was to be touched by deep stillness, we came to see that it was often life changing.

Knowing this allowed the rest of us to become more and more audacious and, as we extended our audacity, so a wave of love and peacefulness unfolded across the island. Wounds were healed, relationships rescued, forgotten gratitude expressed.

As a family we tuned into the communications of the stillness workers and they to us. Their communication was quick, timeless in fact, and we came to rely on them to set the pace in all our activities. We all learned to prepare, to act and to move on in microseconds, so that Hawa, Rafiq or Mariam often only needed to hold the stillness for a moment.

Over the course of a week we played this game together, extending the stillness until we could hold the entire island in its embrace. At this point I no longer knew where Hawa, Rafiq and Mariam were. Robert told me that they had each taken up residence in one of three main observation points of the island. From these places they could, together hold a vision of everything happening in our world. Under their protective gaze the light workers were now free to explore the potential of their three.

And so began the next stage of our preparations. One morning, before sunrise, Juan led us around the edges of the dew-laden fields near the house until we came to a small grassy meadow. In all directions the meadow was surrounded by orchards of almonds, of figs and of citrus trees. It was a private place, invisible from the roads, overlooked by neither house nor hill. I had always wondered how Robert knew so much and was always the first with the news. Now I was privileged to learn. Robert had us all stand in an outward facing circle in the middle of the meadow. I felt him briefly enter my energy system and perform a small tweak. "Now you can see what I see," he said as he called down an aurora that flickered and swayed in greens and reds around us.

Under his direction the aurora organised as translucent curtains. As we watched, Robert left the circle and started running, fast, almost as fast as the light, disappearing and reappearing between the curtains, sometimes disappearing behind us and reappearing in front.

I heard his words inside me. "Relax, I'm going to sweep you up," and suddenly I was looking through Robert's eyes. Now I no longer saw curtains of light and colour but instead an interweaving of times and places. One moment we were passing through the garden of Juan's house, the next we were down at the harbour. Then we were back in the field, then passing Hawa where she sat on a rock gazing back from the sea to the island. Each time we passed back through the field it was clear we had disappeared for no more than a moment, merely slipped behind a curtain and reappeared from behind another. And yet wherever we appeared time seemed to pass normally.

Robert's voice said, from I don't know where, "Prepare yourself."

We were now in the main street of our village, moving in real time. We sat at a table on the street outside the café and Robert ordered us coffee. In the time it took to arrive we listened in to the thoughts and conversations of each and every person around us. Robert took his time drinking his coffee and called for the check. The man on the table next to us leaned across, picked up the bill and smiled. "Please allow me, it would be an honour."

Again, we passed by the harbour before returning to the circle in the field. Again, it seemed, we had disappeared for no more than a moment. Robert repeated the process with each of us in that circle until the transitions between being in the field and watching through Robert's eyes became seamless. And then it was Herve's turn.

Herve used that same expression, whispering within me, "Relax, I'm going to sweep you up." And with a gust of wind and a brush of feather I was looking through the eyes of an eagle, this time from within. We soared high until I could take in the whole of the island.

It is incredible to see through the eyes of an eagle, to have the capacity to switch so quickly from the general to the specific, from a view of the island to the whiskers twitching on a mouse. Although we had no need to eat a mouse, I could see that they and the other small creatures that caught our eyes had more to offer than a tasty snack. They told us of other movements down below, movements on the land and below the earth, and I came to see that they didn't scamper around individually but formed a field of awareness and action. Included in that field was us. But they knew that our purpose was not to hunt them and they communed with us, mapping out magnetic fields and flows of wind and water, teaching us how to read the land and how to move according to its inhalations and exhalations.

Now I could see a large rock jutting from the sea and Hawa, still sitting there. She looked up and smiled. She left her human form behind and joined Herve and me in that eagle form. To share the inner sensation of an eagle so closely with two such wonderful people was incredible, the sense of complicity, of intimacy, of love and potential, and for a while we just chose to experience that. We flew fast across the sea, rising high on a thermal as we reached the land and then volplaning at amazing speed the full length of the island and beyond to another small island sitting alone in the clear blue sea. In the middle of that island was a party - a hundred or more people gathered around the pools, gazebos and dance stages laid out in the gardens of the house.

There were fires burning, roasting lamb, Moroccan tents, Arab horses, dancers, guests dressed in Arab clothes. Boats lay moored offshore from the small harbour, engines switched off so the only sounds were of nature, singers and acoustic musicians. In the middle of the lawn Rafiq was turning, arms outstretched, one hand raised to the sky, one hand hanging loosely towards the earth.

"He's just passing time," Hawa said. "Invisible to this world but at play in another. Ask him to show you sometime, it's truly beautiful what he can do."

Again, I was washed over by the warm wave of Hawa's love. As we reeled around the island Rafiq acknowledged us with just the tiniest of gestures - the smallest flick in his right wrist, visible only to the eyes of an eagle.

"But why there?" I asked. "Why in the midst of a party?"

"He's listening," Hawa said. "There are people there we might need."

"People with power? People like us?"

"No," said Hawa, "not power - just money and things we might need for our journey."

I let many more questions remain, as we swept back towards the land, my heart expanding with love for my family, filled with an intense happiness to be in the company of these beautiful people.

Our journey took us once again low over the harbour and then out towards the lighthouse where Mariam gazed out to sea.

We passed close by her with a ruffle of feathers and a deep-throated call and she waved as we returned once more through a curtain of light. Herve dropped me off and continued his journey with Hawa alone.

No sooner had I settled than I was swept up by Remi in the form of a cat. We leapt through a curtain and appeared again in the party, strolling slowly between the guests - sniffing out details through fine little nostrils, listening through large hairy ears until we knew them all - their names and relationships, their longings and needs, their weaknesses and secrets. We stopped and washed where Rafiq was turning and I understood what he was doing. Beautiful as that party was, beautiful as that island was, Rafiq and his turning added a new dimension previously unknown to them all. Each person there, whether singer or dancer, cook or rider, host or guest, protector or protected, felt themselves at their best, their most alive and open, more relaxed and at ease than they ever had been, their treasures and powers on show for the eyes of a treasure seeker like me.

We continued to practise like this for days until we could merge all of our qualities at will, slipping between stillness and action, appearing and disappearing, changing from human to feathered to fur. We could share forms, share thoughts, think as one, think as family, exchange information in an instant. Now Juan no longer needed to act as our father. We were in harmony, a symphony of shape shifting and sharing. And then we knew that we could control the island and, with that realisation all the fragments of information we had gathered over the previous weeks fell into place and the plan revealed itself.

We gathered again at Juan's house. The stillness workers no longer needed to monitor the island while we practised and played.

We discovered then that it wasn't really Juan's house, he just borrowed it. Juan, it seemed, borrowed everything, including the apartment where we met. And in return for what he borrowed, he healed. Our island house belonged to a family broken by the death of their father. The house remained empty and unappreciated while the family fought over their father's will. Now, during these days Juan had healed that family, bringing them back together to share the house that their father had loved so much. Soon they would return and be surprised to find that it was not crumbling as they feared but was clean and fresh, the garden tended, as if only just abandoned by the spirit of their father.

Now we needed to borrow a boat, a large boat, big enough to take us all to Turkey. Now we needed somebody to stock that boat with the fuel and food and water we would need for the voyage. Now we needed money to grease the way once we made it to Turkey. And we already knew which boat. And we already knew whose boat it was. He had talked about his boat at the party on the island. He had told us of the journey his crew would take and the preparations underway at the quayside.

It was a large sailing boat, big enough for us all but we had yet to persuade him to send the boat with us and to send his crew by plane. Now it was time for the sound workers to practise their skill. Judith and I set off with them by car and, at the far end of the island, we found the jetty and the launch that would take us out to the party island. As we stepped aboard, I heard Alice say to the boatman, "Stefan is expecting us," and in that moment not only did the boatman know it was true but so too did Stefan, and he announced to his chef that five more guests would join him for lunch. On the short ride out to Stefan's island we passed many yachts moored offshore, yachts belonging to the guests who had joined him for his end of season party.

Overshadowing them all was Stefan's boat - the most beautiful, with its single mast reaching skyward from a sleek, uncluttered deck.

"Do you like our Swan?" Alice asked.

"She's beautiful." I smiled and watched as Alice, Juan and Mireille linked hands and between them carried Mireille's intentions deep into the machine room on Stefan's boat and deep into the minds of its captain and engineer. A problem arose on the main computer and they all knew it had been there all season. A problem arose with the boom and they all knew that after Stefan had spent just a little more money on refinements, they stood a good chance of winning all next year's races.

Now they knew that Stefan would stand down his crew and invite them to party. Now they knew he would send his boat away with a substitute crew sent specially by the boat-builders in Turkey. Before we moored at Stefan's island, we pulled alongside his boat to say hello to the crew and, as we shook their hands, I plucked from their webs the skills and powers we would need to sail the boat. I redistributed them between us so that we knew everything about this boat and the crew understood that it was better that we sail the boat, that the problem with the computer was beyond them and better that they didn't risk the journey.

Alice talked to Stefan and he issued instructions from the jetty where he waited to greet us. Over lunch Alice explained the enhancements we would make to the boat and the arrangements that Stefan must make for his crew to meet us.

Stefan was a happy man, happy to spend some more money to improve his boat for next season's racing, happy to let his crew take time off with their families, happy to tell us how he had already arranged to provision the boat for our journey, provisioned as if he himself would be aboard.

Stefan's generosity suddenly seemed to know no bounds and now even his closest friends were surprised. Stefan was known to be a generous man but his generosity was always calculated to benefit himself. But now something was different; his generosity was free from calculation and he understood that the more he gave the happier he felt. For Stefan and his guests this was something new. Stefan had never felt happiness before and, as the lunch continued, tears rolled from his eyes as he felt his own heart and told his guests of his plans to move the lion's share of his wealth into a foundation devoted to the promotion of happiness.

"We will begin at the ground," he said, "and give the money to thousands of small projects and organisations that already know something about happiness."

Under the table Juan and Alice and Mireille completed a circle with their feet.

Three days later we closed and shuttered the house and watered the garden one last time. The owners were on their way for their first ever holiday as a family since their father had died. The stillness workers had already left and were waiting at the lighthouse to be picked up. I dropped Juan, Alice and Mireille at the jetty where the tender waited to take them out to our Swan.

31

Judith and I joined the stillness workers by the lighthouse. We were now standing where, through the eyes of an eagle, I had seen Mariam gazing out to sea. She was sitting in the same place as before with her siblings beside her. They waved us across to sit with them and gaze out to sea.

"What's going on? What are you looking for?" I asked.

"Not looking - listening," came Mariam's reply.

We joined their listening, to the sea lapping around the rocks and concrete blocks beneath the lighthouse, to the light wind and the birds and insects playing on the wind, to the sounds from the quay, of engines and action, of ropes and sails. And we listened deeper into the shifts and movements of the land and the stronger currents beneath the sea and then to a new voice, a rich and musical voice.

"Listen only to the wind. Let go of all the other sounds. Don't try. Don't reach out. Just open your ears and relax. Let the sound come to you."

I did as he said, listening only to the wind, and I could hear the subtleties of sounds within the wind, the echoes and eddies as the wind picked up disturbances from everything in its path. As I closed my eyes and opened my ears I could hear the shape of the island and the quality of the sea. I could hear the chatter of life: human, animal, bird and plant.

And I realised that there was a sound within the wind for each creature and each type of creature. The easiest to hear were the cat and the bird as I already had some experience of being both these creatures. But even when I was cat or bird I hadn't heard their sound. Now I could hear the sound that carried the essence of both. And I could hear the sound that carried insect of both land and air. And I realised that they were all in touch with each other - that there was a layer of cat sound, a layer of bird sound, a layer of insect sound, a layer for every life form, carrying knowledge and information to them all. None lived in isolation.

"But why not human?" I thought, and suddenly I could hear the layer of human sound.

"But why is that not normal for us, like every other creature?"

The new voice answered my thoughts. "Because humans spend too much time listening to themselves. Their minds are so full of their own thoughts there is no room for anything else."

"Who are you?"

"I am a wind watcher."

"But you don't watch - you listen."

"It is true that we listen more than we watch but it was not me who named our people. Perhaps our ways have changed since we were named."

I opened my eyes and looked at the wind watcher standing before us. He was taller than the rest of us - tall and skinny with chalk-white hair dreadlocked by the wind and sea. His small eyes were too close together and brilliantly blue.

As more questions began to form he raised a bony finger to his lips. "Hush. Listen."

Once again, I closed my eyes and listened. Once again, I could hear the sounds of the sea and the island, and the sounds of the creatures within the wind. Again, I could hear the wind watcher. "Relax deeper. Open your ears. Let go of the need for details."

The sound built into a cacophony.

"A little more. Just let go."

I followed the wind watcher's instructions and all the sounds fell away into the background and a new sound emerged to the fore. But this one was not like something heard but, rather, something felt - deep within, a slow rocking of pebbles and reeds on the tide of the inner ear. As I allowed myself to feel it, I could feel a quietness within - a clarity and quietness deep within the tide.

"This is the wind that will carry you east to the next wind watcher. The long wind is rising. Prepare to set sail tonight. Catch this wind and you will need no other."

I opened my eyes and the wind watcher was gone. "Who is he?" I asked.

Mariam answered. "He is one of many. With luck we will travel between wind watchers. They will guide us on the fastest and safest routes."

"So they are with us?" I asked.

"No, they are independent."

"Does that mean they will help anyone?"

"Not at all. First, they can only help those who know of them and know how to wait for them to come. Second they will only help those whose story they like."

"He knows our story?"

"Each one," Mariam said. "As we listened so he read. I guess he likes what he read. But we'll know for sure tonight when we raise our sail."

"You mean he might have been lying?"

"Yes, wind watchers like to lie; they are fickle like the wind. But I think we'll be okay."

We returned to the boat and made the final checks ready for our journey. Stefan had stocked the boat well. The stillness workers took charge and as the sun set, they raised the mainsail even if there was as yet no wind to fill it. They used the thrusters to hold the prow to the east and the stern in direct line to the lighthouse. As the sun disappeared behind us and the island sucked the wind from the sea, they kept the boat steady and let the sail hang loose.

We all sat in silence - waiting, listening. Stillness settled around us. Not the stillness of the stillness workers but the stillness of balance, of poise, of the moment between exhalation and inhalation.

Then from her place at the wheel, Mariam gave a sign and Rafiq and Hawa trimmed the sail. Although the evening breeze continued to blow toward the island, we were pushed by the long wind away and out to sea, out into the darkness. The long wind was steady as she picked up speed and pushed us fast away from land. Soon the island was no more than a flicker of distant lights and soon the moon and the stars outshone them.

I turned to Mariam and asked, "How did you know the right moment to catch this wind?"

She replied. "Stillness workers and wind watchers have a long history of working together. While we were waiting, we were in contact with the wind watcher. He told us the moment. All is good, he likes us. It is an auspicious start to our journey."

If ever there were any reason to doubt that the stillness workers should be in charge of the trip it was now dispelled and we all listened intently while they explained our duties. Each of the threes would stick together. We would rotate four hours on watch, four hours cooking and cleaning and four hours rest. The stillness workers would always remain on deck regardless of which three was on watch.

Hawa warned us, "From now on we need to be attentive when we come close to land. For us the island was a secret place but we're heading back into the world now. The devolvers will have spies seeking us out.

"At sea we're safe but close to land they will sense our presence. If any of us feels anything strange we must sound the alarm immediately. There will be no room for hesitation."

While the stillness workers took the first watch, Judith and I went to the galley and prepared enough food for us all for supper and breakfast. We took the watch four hours later and Mariam explained the little we had to do.

"While the long wind pushes us forward the control systems will handle the fine adjustment of the sails and steering to keep our direction true. You need only remain alert for the unlikely event of errors or alarms. Apart from that, enjoy the ride."

Judith and I sat back in the cockpit and gazed along the clear line of the scrubbed teak deck. Hawa sat with her back to the mast - facing towards us, eyes closed in meditation, fingers held in mudras. Mariam took a place leaning against the mast and facing forward, hair blowing loose in the strong breeze. Rafiq stood at the prow, arms outstretched, his right hand raised to the sky and his left hand hanging loosely at the wrist.

Judith and I huddled closer together and pulled our blankets around us against the wind. We were both touched by a strong impression of Kali and shared a longing to have her there beside us. For a moment it felt as if it were possible for us all to be here, freed from the weight of responsibilities and destiny in this life, here just for the pleasure of the voyage on Stefan's boat.

Our watch passed quickly and peacefully with nothing to do but revel in the sense of family. Judith and I cuddled up close in the cockpit while the stillness workers engaged in their own special magic, untouched by the cold.

Down below, the others were asleep in the simple, beautiful cabins that Stefan himself had designed for his boat.

Robert, Remi and Herve came to relieve us as the first colours of dawn were just beginning to light the horizon sky. Judith and I handed over our warm seats and blankets with now familiar hugs and walked along to the foredeck. It was time for us to find the wind horse again. On the island there was always too much else to do but here and now there was nothing else to do.

We found our circle on the deck and began to walk. Already something was different; new arm movements, gestures and mudras had entered our repertoire - perhaps assimilated as we all studied and practised together on the island. As our circle became a point and our walking settled into an inner movement, Rafiq slowly turned to face us, arms still outstretched, clearly not in the least bit tired from the night standing watch. A new movement evolved as he led us into his world - a world slowed down, where the air was thicker, warmer and more buoyant.

Now the boat plowed smoothly through the surface of a syrupy sea and a warm and viscid spray from the prow caressed us gently. In Rafiq's world time was much slower, nature softer and more supportive, breathing slow and deeply nourishing. It became clear that his standing all night with his arms outstretched was nothing like the equivalent in our world.

Then Rafiq began to turn and Judith and I followed his lead, our arms rising spontaneously to emulate the gesture of his arms and our heads tilting ever so slightly to the right, left ear raised to the heavens and right hand pointing to the sea.

As we turned, the heavens, which only a moment before had been simply a familiar mass of stars and constellations, appeared as a dynamic web of action and relationship. A sense of the enormity of our voyage through space and time became clear. Now it was no longer the sea air that swept on by, nor the steady breath of the long wind pushing us ever eastward, but the immense and unfathomable exhalation of the universe.

I heard Rafiq's voice. "Brahman."

And that one simple word expanded into the enormity of all that existed, a wave of sound that would continue until eternity, until the breath of the universe rested between exhalation and inhalation.

As we turned, Rafiq led our attention beyond the sea, to the coastline, across plains and mountains to a place I had seen before, to a fragile little room ingeniously balanced on a cliff side. Now Kali was turning with us. The sense of power and joy flowing between our three was immense and now I remembered what it was to be one. We continued like this until Rafiq called us all back to our place on the deck and we returned to stillness, cupping our hands to our hearts, heads bowed to the enormity.

Rafiq returned to his place at the prow and Judith and I walked back hand in hand to the cockpit. We passed Mariam whose beaming smile acknowledged the change as two touched upon three. A day had passed and our family had covered for us, all aware of the mission on which Rafiq had taken us. Warm seats, warm blankets and warm food were waiting for us in the cockpit where we started our watch. Now the stillness workers would listen to the physical direction given by the wind watchers while we would listen for the route into the mountains, to the call of Kali.

Now we knew the design by which Kali had to leave and understood that finding her was no more than the first step in a series of events poised to cascade. Now we were more aware than ever of the forces that would be rallied to resist us.

32

The first hint of that resistance revealed itself five days later as we passed between Sardinia and Sicily. Mariam felt it first and sounded the alarm. In the minute it took for us to gather on deck the force was strong enough to affect us all, a pull through the fluids of our inner ears that first manifested as nausea but soon was strong enough to completely destroy all sense of balance.

The boat was still holding true to her course but I could already feel the tendrils of malice reaching out from the islands to interfere with the controls. I braced myself for the fight, pulling lightly on the tendrils to assess their number, strength and location, but Robert intervened from where he lay.

"Not now. That's what they want."

I softened my grip a little and listened to him through the haze of disorientation.

"If we fight now we will win but we will waste time. We need only to weather this storm and protect the Swan until we are out of their range."

I pulled myself up against the dining table to look forward. Already the stillness workers had regained some poise. Rafiq and Hawa had dragged themselves back to sit upright and held themselves to the mast with a rope they were tying between them. Mariam had dragged herself to the cockpit, her hands on the controls, caressing the programs and systems that kept us true.

"All you have to do," said Robert, "is hold the tendrils at bay. Don't push, don't pull, don't think. Give no sense of our direction or position. Let them waste their time and energy searching while we sail on. We will make land before they know they have failed; they know nothing of the long wind."

"How can you be so sure?"

"They don't have stillness workers. They are a rare type and they never belong to devolver families."

"Thank goodness," I thought as I accepted to do as Robert said, holding the tendrils at bay, resisting the impulse to fight, but realising just how much I wanted to fight, how much I yearned to play with that power again.

Now Judith's hand was in my hand and our family circle was complete. We continued to weather the storm, knowing the boat was safe, knowing we would recover from the sickness, knowing a quieter place within each of us - safe from the disorientation and fear of the attack.

As the tendrils weakened and finally disappeared, I felt a simple happiness, to know again the power of our family, to know what it was to fight without violence, to know what it was to win without show and to know how blessed we were to have stillness workers in our family. When I was able to walk again I just had to hug each one of them in turn.

33

Mariam steered the Swan into her mooring. The crew was already on the quayside waiting to catch the ropes and greet us. Along with our handshakes we gave them back their powers and skills and Mariam explained some of the improvements she had made to allow us to make such good time.

"Once the new boom is installed, she will be unbeatable," she said.

As requested, a minibus was waiting for us too. When we climbed aboard, we found another guest, a Turkish man who had installed himself as our driver.

"Were we expecting a driver?" I asked of anyone who cared to reply. The silence said no but the driver said yes. "Don't worry, I'm with you. Let's go, we have an appointment to make."

"An appointment with whom?" I asked, as our driver drove us from the shipyard. "With the wind," he said, accelerating onto the open road.

"You're a wind watcher?" Mariam asked.

"Yes. I know I don't look like one but bear with me for a moment."

As we reached cruising speed he pulled his hair from where it was tucked into his collar and shook his head. There was a flash of chalk-white dreadlocks and pale skin and whiskers and the smell of sea-air carried on the wind.

"It doesn't do to attract too much attention here," he said as the white receded into black and the wind watcher looked once again like a Turkish driver. "Why don't you all just sit back and rest - we have a long journey ahead and you might as well save your energies for more important things."

I turned back to the stillness workers, seeking reassurance, which they gave as a nod from Mariam and a smile from them all.

"Relax brother," said the wind watcher. "The wind is with you. We know the path you are on. We will help you all the way."

I felt a little tearful at the reassurance in his words and manner - as if my family had just extended. "Do you have a name?" I asked.

"You can call me Meltemi today. Tomorrow we will see. Now rest. I know you have a hundred questions but I should tell you, we wind watchers don't much enjoy to talk. Mariam can answer your questions; it was her father who taught her our ways."

I accepted to lapse into silence and soon into sleep, my head resting against Judith's as Meltemi drove us into the darkness. I didn't wake until Meltemi stopped at the entrance to a house and an iron gate slid back to let us pass. He pulled in and parked at the entrance, an arch carved out of the rock face. We unloaded the minibus and Meltemi led us into an ancient house cut into the rock.

"Welcome to Cappadocia," he said. "The land of the wind - a land given to us by the gods to hide our human secrets. We will stay for a day. Please treat this house as your home but do not stray beyond its walls."

With that, Meltemi left with the minibus and the gate slid closed behind him. We explored the house finding a warren of interconnecting rooms. We followed the light and found an arched door opening onto a terrace that looked out across the extraordinary Cappadocian landscape, pierced by dwellings carved into the rock. The table on the terrace was already set for us with fruits, water, coffee, nuts and pastries. We sat together to enjoy the peace and the crystal-clear morning light which highlighted the beauty and detail of everything it touched. Inevitably our conversation turned to the wind watchers and to Mariam who was happy to answer our questions.

"There are many things my father told me that only now begin to make sense. He told me scores of stories in the little time we had together - bedtime stories and daytime stories, stories during meals and stories during walks. He never told me the same story twice and yet he told the stories in such a way that when I remember one I remember it down to the finest detail. I know this place. I know there are caves and tunnels deep beneath this house and I know that Meltemi will soon return and lead us into them. The story of this place is the story of the origin of the wind. It's true what Meltemi says, that the gods created this land. In this case it was the gods of fire and thunder who threw a heavenly rock opening a wound in the earth out of which poured smoke and ash and cinders for hundreds of years until an island rose from the sea. Although, as Meltemi says, the tunnels are used to hide our human secrets, they were built for another purpose.

"Once upon a time, long before the human race had a need to hide its secrets there was a more pressing need. In those days there was no wind, for the earth's atmosphere was thicker and deflected the solar storms and the pull of the moon. The sea was still, disturbed only by the movement of the creatures living within it and in those days, there was much more sea and much less land.

"The humans living here were outgrowing their island and feared the day when they could no longer sustain the trees and bushes and shrubs which gave them food and fire and shelter. Already the birds had learned to avoid the hunter's arrows and too often flew beyond their range. The fish too had become wise to the hunters and often swam beyond the range of their rafts and paddles. The people knew they needed a way to move faster and further on land and on sea.

"The wind watchers learned their craft from the Vril who were tunnelling the earth long before the first humans landed. Meltemi's ancestors were the first to realise the cleverness of the Vril. Others had heard them tunnelling and some had discovered the tiny entrances to their underworld but all assumed they were nothing more than fur covered diggers and not sophisticated creatures more clever than humans. The first Meltemi smelled the smoke from a Vril tunnel and realised they burned fires down in their caves. That first Meltemi also felt the breeze as the fire sucked in air through the hole."

"After much searching, he found a hidden chimney through which the smoke exited as a fine and forceful jet. Meltemi's people had always known of these smoke jets but had never gone close enough to investigate, believing them to be a demon's breath. Close up, Meltemi could smell the juniper wood and sage that the Vril loved to use to feed their fires.

"That first Meltemi took to tunnelling and fire-making - studying and experimenting until he perfected the art of creating a wind. His people thought he was just a crazy man spending his life underground until the day he took them and showed them the wind he had made. One end of his tunnel opened out from a cliff face to the sea.

Deep within the tunnels, Meltemi's son tended a fire of juniper wood and sage, waiting for his father's signal. Resting on the sea was Meltemi's raft on which he had erected a sail of wood and leather.

"Meltemi also learned the art of signalling from the Vril, and when the people had gathered by the water's edge he raised his digging staff and, like the Vril, struck the rock just once with its metal tip. Meltemi's son rolled a great rock wheel in its groove opening one tunnel and closing another. Wind and smoke belched from the tunnel to the amazement of the people and they all shouted with joy as the first wind carried the little raft out to sea. Having never had a wind before the people didn't have a word for it so they called it 'Meltemi,' in honour of its creator. The people immediately saw the potential and decided that the brightest and strangest of their people should join Meltemi in his research and building. They called them the wind-makers and they were relieved of all other duties such as gathering food and hunting and fishing. Everything they needed was brought to them so they could just concentrate on their work. The strange qualities for which they were chosen included obsessiveness, and they all quickly became fascinated by their work in the underworld, and less and less inclined to return to the surface.

"Over time they lost their colour and their skin turned white. Some say it was due to vapours in the underworld. Their hair turned chalk-white and dreadlocked. Their eyes turned blue - better suited to seeing in the underworld but no longer suited to the light. They stopped talking, preferring to communicate through the rock, like the Vril. They taught the people of the over-world the signals for the words that mattered most - words like wood, herbs, food, water.

"Soon the wind-makers were better able to communicate with the Vril than with the people of the over-world. The Vril admired that and shared ever more of their knowledge with the wind-makers. The wind-makers created more and more tunnels and more and more winds until they could send a wind in each of the sixteen directions. They named those winds in recognition of each of the sixteen wind-makers.

"It was at this time that serious problems arose in the over-world. In order to make the winds, the wind-makers needed fire. The over-world people warned them that they were now consuming wood faster than it could grow. To add to the problem the wind-makers could not be sure how far each wind could travel. At first, they thought that the wind would go so far as to find its way back again. They sent out smoke of different aromatic herbs on the winds and waited, hoping to catch a whiff of aroma coming back. But nothing ever came back.

"Meltemi sank into despair. He knew they could make a wind strong enough to push the rafts away from the island but he didn't know if the wind would take them far enough to reach another land.

"The Vril felt moved by his despair and asked after the problem. It is strange that the Vril went on to develop a reputation for meanness and malice for they really were quite compassionate little creatures. No sooner did they understand the problem than they came up with the answer. The Vril tunnels, unlike those of the wind-makers, were not limited to the soft volcanic rock of the island. Their tunnels stretched way beyond, to every corner of the earth and deep into the hot layers below. Over the course of a night they described the world to Meltemi and he carved a map into the walls of one of his caves.

"They described a world of little islands scattered around two great continents - one to the north and one to the south. They said that either one of these continents had resources enough to sustain the people forever. They told Meltemi which wind would take them where. They recommended that the people should divide, with a group heading to each continent.

"They told Meltemi that his people would have to destroy their home in order to reach a new home. They would need to cut down all the wood to build two boats. They would need to kill every last creature and use the skins to make their sails and water containers. 'But how can I be sure that the wind will go far enough to carry the people to their new home? And where will I get wood for our fires if the people use it all for the rafts?' Meltemi asked of the Vril. But the Vril reassured him and told him that they would take care of the wind. So Meltemi returned to the surface and gathered the people together and told them his plan.

"As soon as the tree and bush fruits were harvested and dried the people were to cut all the wood and build two enormous boats - one to the north of the island and one to the south. They were to move from one end of the island to the other and systematically kill every single creature. The meat was to be dried for the journey and the skins prepared to make the sails and water containers.

"The people did as Meltemi instructed but the excitement and hope of the journey ahead could not overcome the sickness they felt for so much death and destruction. When the boats were built and stocked the people divided into two groups according to eye colour - for they could think of no other way of deciding. Those with blue eyes and green eyes would head north and those with hazel eyes and brown eyes would head south.

"The people boarded the boats and raised the sails and sat on the stillness of the sea gazing at the land they had plundered and destroyed, and they wept. Meltemi returned to his tunnels and listened to the Vril. Following their instructions, he sent all the wind-makers except for his son up to the surface. They were to board a boat according to the direction of their wind. When Meltemi and his son were alone the Vril told them they would have no further need for fire to make the winds. The Vril would open a tunnel into theirs and release a wind from deep within the earth. They should set the stone wheels so that only the tunnels to the north and the tunnels to the south were open. Then they should leave, one to the north and one to the south, board their boats and listen for the wind.

"The two Meltemis boarded their boats and announced to the people that they were no longer wind-makers but wind-listeners. And they listened. And as they listened, they heard a new wind emerging from their tunnels, a new wind from deep within the earth that filled their sails and drove them fast away from their now barren land.

"Despite the excitement and hope of the journey, they carried with them the sickness and shame they felt for so much destruction and death. And that was the beginning of the wind and the beginning of the two peoples. All the winds we now have derive from those two first winds. All, that is, apart from the winds that the Vril release from time to time from deep within the earth. Nobody now knows why the Vril do this but the wind watchers still know how to listen for those winds. All the people now on the earth derive from those first two peoples - those from the north with the blue eyes and green eyes and those from the south with the brown eyes and hazel coloured eyes."

As Mariam's story drew to its conclusion we realised that our Meltemi had returned and was leaning with his back to the wall, listening intently to Mariam's tale.

"I have heard enough," he said, "to know you are the ones we have been waiting for. Please follow me, we have a long journey ahead. If you need to eat or drink now is the moment - we can bring nothing with us where we will go."

34

We followed Meltemi back into the house and through to the kitchen where the cook was cleaning up after the meal she had prepared for us. We wanted for nothing but to know what mystery lay ahead for us in Meltemi's world. He led us to a corner in the kitchen. It was, in fact, the only corner in the house - all the other walls and rooms were rounded. But here the walls were carved to meet as a perfect right-angled corner.

"This is the entrance to the caves," Meltemi said. We all exchanged bemused glances. "You must squeeze through," he continued and with that he pressed himself into the corner and disappeared.

We could still hear his voice. "Just follow me and press on through."

We did as he said and, one by one, slid through the finest crack between the two stone walls that met at the corner. It was the strangest sensation, one moment pressing against hard rock, the next unable to differentiate between rock and body, and the next on the other side greeted by the smiles of those already through. Once our family was gathered Meltemi led us down a long passage carved into the solidified lava. I realised there was no light and yet I could see, albeit in an unusual way. I asked Meltemi to explain and he told us that from now on we would depend on the natural glow of our bodies to light the way.

"When you squeezed through the first portal you squeezed the red light from the cells of your body to the surface. It is that light that now lights our way."

And so, in the warm red glow of our own bodies we followed Meltemi into a catacomb of tunnels deep into the earth. The route was strange and complex and, try as I did, I could find no logic in the choice Meltemi made at each division and junction.

Mariam understood my concern and felt my struggle to find a pattern in the route. "There is no pattern," she said. "My father also told me the story of these catacombs. The route is never the same and nobody ever comes back following the same route by which they went. The route unfolds moment by moment and in direct response to the travellers embarking on the journey."

"But what if we get lost or separated, how we will find out way back to the house?" I asked.

"We will not go back to the house," Meltemi said. "We are heading for the mountains to find your woman."

I turned around towards the others and saw that we all shared that same state of bemused trust. For a while we continued in silence and the rock gave way to rich dark earth and the walls of the tunnels were pressed into place by human hands. Following Meltemi's advice we abandoned our shoes and I felt warm earth beneath my feet. As we walked, the earth became damper until we reached a cul-de-sac where the water seeped from the soil and flowed as rivulets between our toes. As before, Meltemi instructed us to press on through and we followed one by one through a muddy portal into a world that now glowed orange and where water poured from the mud and flowed as a stream.

As we followed Meltemi, the waters rose until they were they were lapping around my groins. As the water rose so too did the temperature and I began to enjoy the sensation of moving through that blood-warm river. At Meltemi's suggestion we removed and abandoned more and more clothes as the river continued to rise until, at last, we were swimming naked through its warm, orange waters.

When only our heads were above the water Meltemi called us together. "The next portal will be more frightening than any before. You will have to accept not to breathe through your lungs. The only way you can do that is to allow them to fill with the water. You have another breath that will sustain you but it cannot sustain you until you give up the air."

Following his guidance, we allowed ourselves to sink, exhaling the air as we sank until no breath was left and the weight of the water pressed us against the floor of the tunnel. I heard Meltemi's words over and over in my mind.

"Resist the need to panic. Resist the need to gasp. Open your mouth and your throat and let the water find its own way in."

Finally, I rested comfortably under the river, my lungs no longer working, relaxed for the first time since birth in the warm, soft waters that now filled them. I was at peace, sustained by another breath. I roused myself and joined the pod as our family swam behind Meltemi along the stream that now glowed sulphur yellow.

The tunnel turned abruptly downward and we continued to swim in Meltemi's wake deeper and deeper. The glow of the water changed from sulphur yellow to emerald green. I heard Meltemi's voice inside my mind. "The green you see now is the light squeezed from your heart as we plunge further into the earth.

"The weight of the water will compress your lungs until they are no bigger than your fist and your heart until it is no bigger than the space contained by your fist. You will no longer feel your heartbeat. It will be nothing more than a murmur as the pressure squeezes the oxygen from your blood."

Now we were no longer swimming but falling, no longer active. The weight of the water pushing us, squeezing us, compressing us, until our flesh was dense like meat - barely alive, no longer permeated by tubes and vessels. Barely conscious - just falling, exhaling until the last vestige of air was emptied out. We landed, freed from the need to ever inhale again. The light, electric, vibrant, indigo blue and peaceful.

"This is the final portal. Please take a moment to prepare yourself. Perhaps by now you think you are familiar with strange experiences but nothing any of you have experienced has prepared you for this next transition. Please take a long, slow moment to remember yourselves and each member of your family. When each of you feel strong and stable and safe in the sense of yourself and those you love, let go."

Nothing was left but Meltemi's words. "This is the last voice you will hear until you reach your destination. This next portal leads you into a tunnel built for us humans by the Vril. Please hold that last little spark of life deep within the muscle of your hearts and let go of all else."

We did as instructed and, as always, Meltemi was true to his word. On the other side was a world unlike anything I had seen before - a world of light and colour and movement, a world of eternally unfolding patterns, a world I had glimpsed in churches and mosques and temples, in the stone work and calligraphy, in the stained glass and mandalas, in the paintings and sculptures of masters.

As Meltemi warned, I was utterly overwhelmed - by the vibrancy, the patterns, the machinations and movements of designs and systems too complex to take in and understand.

But for the contact with my family, my capacity to think and to organise my sense of self would have been swept aside by what was unravelling around me. And yet the most shocking thing of all was the realisation that I was no longer looking out through the eyes of a body. I no longer had a body. None of us had a body. There was contact but not through flesh, for we were no longer flesh. And as the reality of this began to fray what little remained of me, I remembered Meltemi's entreaty and, in the midst of this disintegration, found the memories of my family and their images held somewhere within my thoughts. And I held on to this as my thoughts and memories and dreams and hopes became no longer mine, became no more than fragments of colour and movement that was now the entire world.

Then came the wind, a subatomic wind, a neutrino wind channelled by the Vril. A wind that carried all knowledge, of every moment passed, of every moment yet to be, of every thought and every idea from every creature that ever thought and every creature yet to think. We were carried by that wind with no sense of speed or distance but imbued with a sense of universal genius, connectedness, order, correctness and calm.

When the wind died down we found ourselves sitting in a cave that opened onto a ledge high up on a rocky and austere mountainside. We were embodied again but silent, silenced by the nature of the experience, piecing back together our sense of individual selves, separating those selves from the sense of all to which we also belonged.

When I was once again fully conscious, I saw the wind watcher - now certainly not a Turkish driver but a true wind watcher with white dreadlocks and tufted chin, pale skin and piercing blue eyes.

"Where are we Meltemi?" I asked.

"I am not Meltemi. Meltemi did not come with you. His place is Cappadocia. I am Shamal. The White Mountain is my place."

Shamal turned to Mariam. "Welcome to you and your friends. I knew your father and you are exactly as he described."

"You too, Shamal of the White Mountain." Mariam replied. "My father taught me your story and told me of the City of Wisdom to which you hold the key."

"The city is no more." Shamal replied. "Something terrible happened here. The life was sucked from the mountain. Some of the scholars escaped. Some of the books and treasure were saved. Many were lost."

Shamal sank for a long moment into silence, then took a breath and continued. "I am sorry to be the one to tell you, Mariam, but this is where your father died."

The colour drained from Mariam's face and Rafiq and Hawa moved in to support her.

"He was a great man. He came to learn. He stayed to help. The fact that anything remains from the City of Wisdom is thanks to him.

"You have every reason to be proud, and now that I see you and your family, I understand why he was so proud of you."

We all found ourselves spontaneously gathering around Mariam, holding and supporting her, sharing an immense grief that welled up, distributing it between our bodies so each sobbed silently as we understood the danger and the need to keep quiet.

Shamal gave us the space we needed but the moment our attention extended to include him again he spoke. "There is no point in you visiting the grave of this mountain - nothing remains - everything was turned to nothing by a heat we never knew before. The human tunnels are gone and only the Vril tunnels remain."

Shamal led us down to the roadside and asked us to hide. We waited more than half a day until the sound of a truck broke the silence. For an age we could hear the sound of gears grinding and the heavy labour of a well-worn engine until, at last, it appeared - tasselled and mirrored and painted with every good luck symbol and protective deity imaginable. But it was no match for Shamal who leapt into the path of the truck, white dreadlocks flailing, skinny almost bone-like arms gesticulating wildly, leaping on spindly legs, naked and terrifying even to those of us who knew him.

The driver leapt from the still moving truck and Shamal jumped into his place. As the driver ran and slid and tumbled down the mountainside, Shamal brought the truck to a halt.

"Sorry to alarm you," he said as we all caught up with him. "He didn't have any protection from my kind of demon. You might like to turn away while I fetch my clothes."

Shamal came back dressed, now looking like an Afghan driver. Between us we rearranged the boxes and crates in the back to create the space for the rest of us to hide. Shamal taught us the sound he would make in case of danger. If we didn't hear it we were to remain hidden at all times. We seated ourselves in our makeshift cave as Shamal crashed the gears and we started our journey through the mountains.

35

Everything we needed for our journey was onboard. Shamal chose well - the smuggler's truck was fitted with extra tanks for fuel and water. Under the crates of fruits and sacks of grains lay cases of weapons. We had no need of them. When the truck finally stopped after long, slow days crossing the mountains Shamal called us out and into the forest by the side of the road.

"From now on we must travel by foot. There is danger. There are spies and traitors. Death and destruction still come from above. We must move like cats with our eyes on the sky as well as the land. I will lead you but you must use all of your skills to hide your presence."

Our journey through the valley of Mariam's ancestors was cat-like as Shamal suggested it should be. We moved stealthily, wary of everyone and everything. We sharpened our sense of connection and quickly developed into a clowder. The sound workers became our ears and the light workers our eyes. Our bodies retained a faint glow from the journey into the catacomb, making us all the more visible to the light workers' eyes.

We moved mostly at night but sometimes, under Shamal's urgent direction, we changed location during the day - at prayer time, when the attention of the valley was turned to the southwest and our presence was momentarily cloaked by the sound of a common prayer.

"I feel something," he would say. "Eyes watching us, many eyes, like vultures."

The sound workers knew the moment when heads bowed to the ground and a wave of devotion swept from human to heaven, from heaven to earth, from earth to human. In this moment, when the people bowed down, we ran. In the moment that the people raised their heads we stopped and the stillness workers shrouded our presence. When heads bowed down again we ran again until, at the end of the prayer, we could hide in a new place and wait for the night.

One day, as we sheltered in an ample and comfortably furnished cave hidden deep inside the forest, Mariam told us the story of her land.

"Once upon a time, many years ago, one continuous path circled the earth - not a straight path but a crooked path that wound round lakes and rocks, fields and mountains. This path was not built for speed but was trodden into being by the feet of those who were drawn to every sacred place that ever was and in anticipation of every sacred place that ever would be. The path was not designed by humans but reflected a simple truth - that throughout the earth there are special places where earthly love and heavenly love mingle more freely.

"Some people call this path the Silk Road and others the Diamond Way. Some call it the Way of the Light and others the Golden Line. All these names are correct, for this path has all these qualities - it is indeed as fine as silk, as clear as diamond, as precious as gold and as revealing as light. Sadly, the qualities the names describe are often misinterpreted and have caused ignorant people to fight for control of the path - convinced that control will lead to material gain. This valley forms a section of the path and my people have always been here to protect it.

"In good times they are a peaceful people dedicated to the well-being of their family, tribe and land, and to the study of the teachings entrusted to them.

"In difficult times, like now, they become ferocious warriors dedicated to protecting the path, its treasures and the people of the path. The process is cyclical and my people have developed an equanimity to both roles. Studying or killing are equally valid - it is simply a matter of acting according to the needs of the time.

"All the prophets, teachers, mystics and sages of every era were born along this path, and all the great teachings encourage their followers to walk a section of this path - because treasures are hidden along it, available only to those with open heart, open eyes, open ears and a mouth closed against stupidity.

"My father told me of a family of twelve who would travel this valley and gather together the treasures. Now I know we are that family but this is not the moment. One of us is still missing and we must travel this valley twice - once to complete our family and once to gather the treasures. But something strange is happening here, something my father didn't tell me of. Whenever we stop under Shamal's instruction others in this valley prepare to move. When we move under the cover of stillness they move too. I do not know who they are - we cannot hold the stillness and follow their movements."

"They are the scholars," Shamal volunteered. "They can never rest now that the City of Wisdom is lost. But they know you are here and you know they are there, and you are learning how to move together. Do not waste your skills on looking for them and do not worry about the treasures - nothing will stay still in this valley until you return."

Mariam continued. "In the story my father told me he talked of the catacomb years and he talked of the years when the treasures spilled out.

"He said in these spilling-years men with swords would appear and we stillness workers would discover other skills. Do you have a sword Shamal?"

"Better than a sword," said Shamal. "A wind watcher has a digging stick. There are still only sixteen digging sticks and these same sticks were made by the first wind-makers. We do not know which wood they used - perhaps it only ever grew on their little island home but it is harder than ebony and has never decayed over all these years. The Vril taught us how to prepare the wood but that was all. Those original sticks were passed, by our ancestors, into the Vril tunnels where they were finished. The Vril tipped them with a metal we believe fell from the sky. The handle is made from some kind of resin the Vril harvest from deep within the earth - it is so dense it can crack a rock with one whack."

"Where is your stick?" I asked.

"A wind watcher's stick never leaves his side," Shamal replied. "But you cannot see it. When the time is right it will appear and it will be the rallying point for you and your family."

36

For many days we continued our journey through the valley of Mariam's people, dancing with the scholars, moving from secret refuge to secret refuge, sharing the ears and eyes of the clowder. As we learned to move with the scholars, we came to appreciate just how large a community they were, and although we never once caught sight of them, we constantly benefitted from their support. Each refuge we stayed in was warm, with a fire burning and freshly prepared food waiting for our arrival.

Our final refuge in the valley was in a tunnel cut through the rock by a river that had long since changed its course. Mariam found the entrance, hidden by trees and bushes growing along the riverside.

"My father told me of this tunnel," she said. "It marks the end of my peoples' section of the path but it is not a part of the path. It is always kept ready for the spilling-days. We can use it to leave the valley unobserved."

"I don't know this place," Shamal said. "It doesn't feel right. I'm coming with you in case of trouble."

We followed Mariam into the tunnel, still benefitting from the glow of our bodies to light the way, occasionally feeling our way through walls polished smooth by millennia of fast flowing water.

Suddenly there was darkness. Our bodies no longer glowed. The light from the entrance to the tunnel was gone.

I heard Shamal's voice. "Something is wrong. Be still."

We stopped, moved close, found the clowder but could not find our senses, could not find what was happening.

"The tunnel is closed," said Shamal. "We are sealed in."

"But why can we not feel through, it's only rock?" Juan asked.

"It is not only rock," Shamal replied. "It is rich with gold and copper - too rich to be natural. Someone built this tunnel as a trap, arranged the gold and copper to deflect your powers, to build a tomb for you all."

"I'm sorry Shamal," said Mariam. "I should not have let you come. You were not in the story of the tunnel that my father told. And now I've left it too late to learn that they were not simply stories but instructions."

"Fear not Mariam, there are many versions of the same story and, in the version your father told me, you and your family were tricked into entering a capsule built deep in the rock, a capsule laced with gold and copper where your powers would not work. It's true what you say, the stories are instructions, and my instruction was to come with you when my feeling told me to and now, in this moment of doom, to lift my digging stick and strike the ground."

The 'clack' of the metal tip of the digging stick threw up sparks that illuminated our prison and ignited the strands of copper and gold woven through its walls so that we now could see clearly by a soft golden light. Now, for the first time, we could see Shamal's digging stick and its metal point glowing white-hot.

"Interesting!" said Shamal. "I've never seen that before." And he raised the digging stick again and brought it hard down against the floor. 'Clack, clack'.

"In the stories of my people we say that we are never more than a leg-length away from the Vril."

And he raised the digging stick that was now glowing white-hot its entire length.

"I thought as much," he said. "I always suspected there was a metal core inside the wood." And again, he brought the metal down hard against the floor. 'Clack, clack, clack.'

And a crack opened in the rock and a breeze began to blow, and Shamal said. "As we wind watchers like to say - where there's a wind there's a way."

Shamal raised the digging stick and we all watched in awe as the wood burned away revealing a sword blade glowing white-hot.

He turned toward Mariam. "Our stories converge. I think you know what to do."

Mariam, Rafiq and Hawa raised their right hands towards the sword blade while their left palms stretched toward the crack in the floor. Hawa started to ululate and her voice and the wind found a rhythmic unison that pulsed up along their bodies towards the tip of the sword. A little patch of bright light appeared. Hawa continued to sing, the ululation sinking down from her throat to her belly. The sound deepened. The pulsation of her voice and the wind deepened.

The hole widened and through it we could see an austere mountainside and then a dzong - its dark towering walls seemed to grow directly out of the rock.

“What is this?” I whispered.

“A Vril-hole,” Shamal answered.

“I didn't know we could do that,” said Mariam.

“I didn’t know I had a sword,” Shamal replied.

The Vril-hole continued to widen until our tomb was little more than a memory and we stood, finally facing the goal of our journey.

“I must bid you farewell,” said Shamal. “I must return to my duties. Call me when you need me and it will be my pleasure to travel with you again.”

And with that he was gone. And the Vril-hole was gone. And the stillness workers, empowered by their new skill, strode toward the gate.

“Wait for our call,” said Hawa, and the stillness workers were gone.

37

When Judith and I entered the inner quadrangle of the monastery we found the space empty but for one young monk motionless, suspended in the act of lighting the butter lamps. Hawa, Rafiq and Mariam had done their work with their usual elegance, waiting for the boy to light the final lamp and extinguish the taper before they unfolded stillness across the courtyard.

The soft light of the butter lamps flickered in the boy's green eyes as they gazed into another place. The only other movement was from a cat - a white and marmalade cat wearing a necklace of roughly polished turquoise. For a moment a wave of anxiety flowed through me. The cat was untouched by the stillness. This cat belonged to no man. If she belonged her consciousness would be tied to her owner. But the cat was not owned. The cat was a free spirit and presented a threat to our plan.

It is easy to kill a cat but, thankfully, I afforded her a moment's grace and discovered she was with us - a spy who had retained this furry form just for this moment. That is of course the beauty of the cat - their ability to gaze between worlds and times and wait for the perfect moment.

Cat came to me, twirled her long tail around my ankle and led me to one of the buildings. She whispered to me. "All the others are in here, there is a puja. A wealthy man has died and the family can afford to pay them all to chant, to help his soul become free."

Inside, the entire community sat frozen, suspended in time. Although the rice grains had fallen to the floor, many young hands remained in the air - still throwing rice. Others held sticks, poised to strike their bells and chimes and others held their lips to silent trumpets and horns.

All, just like the butter lamp boy, gazed into another place. All, that is, except for the abbot. His eyes followed us even if his body remained held in stillness. I could feel the intention in his gaze. It was ugly, dark and mean - no longer hidden from the world by the veil of well-rehearsed kindness he had learned to portray with his body and smile. His darkness was held in check by his incapacity to reach into his robes and wrap his fingers around the bronze double dorje that had passed through the hands of a long line of abbots practised in darkness and deception.

I took it for myself and I plucked a few gems from within the subtle threads of his energy body. I could feel a little of his darkness touch me and felt a cruel joy as I looked into his eyes and saw evil with no power. I resisted the temptation to gloat once I saw that he had nothing more to tell me.

I turned away, back to Judith and the cat.

"He cannot help us. He has spent his entire life here and played the role of the abbot for years but he is still nothing more than the discipline master. The only tools he ever used were the smile and the whip. The double dorje was wasted on a man with no protection against stillness. There is another. Somewhere here there is another but I cannot feel his breath."

Hawa, Rafiq and Mariam had joined us. Mariam told us that the rest of our family was already searching the monastery.

She warned us that time was not on our side. "Winged messengers have already flown from the roofs. Herve plucked many of them from the sky but some escaped - an eagle's claws are no match for dragonflies and bees and he needed to concentrate on more important things. He said to tell you Kali is well. She knows you're here."

Tears welled in my eyes and I started to reach out to her. "Not yet," Mariam said as she seized my wrist and hauled my attention back to the moment.

"We need you here. There is still too much unknown and Juan, Mireille and Alice are already preparing her."

"I need a second or two," I said and sank cross-legged to the stone floor. I passed the double dorje to Judith. "Hold this, you might need it."

Cat sat beside me and tuned her purr to my breath. With Judith and the stillness workers watching over us, I closed my eyes and turned my attention to my fingertips. They touched the floor and felt the familiarity of the stone. I looked back to when Christopher and I sat side by side in this room, both young monks with little to do but repeat the prayers and wait for the moment to throw some rice. Then, as now, it was the discipline master who dressed like the abbot and led the prayers. Now, as then, the true abbot lived as the slenderest thread of life within a body slowly killed and preserved through a daily draught of tree lacquer. I stood and faced the discipline master and felt a wave of appreciation for the role he played - the most difficult role in this monastery, balancing pure love with an equally pure evil, outwardly wearing the role of the abbot but inwardly obliged to subsume all goodness, all aspiration and all hope. Even as he sat, held in stillness, I caught the faintest flicker of a smile in his eyes and I felt his love.

I turned around towards the altar and passed through the curtain into a long corridor with its row of teak caskets lining one wall. We opened each to reveal a lineage of lignified abbots. Once the last thread of life had departed their bodies they were undressed, painted and polished so that each had the same sheen as the wooden box in which he had sat for the last seven years of his life. Each body was then dressed in the rainbow colours that celebrated their achievement.

When we reached the end of the line, we found the last box open and the current abbot sitting there. Just the faintest flicker in the air betrayed the fact that he had not yet departed and I quickly clasped my hand over his fontanelle to prevent him from doing so. I could feel the gap where his practice had opened the bones and the membrane trembling from just the slightest murmur of life within.

Through the careful consumption of tree lacquer and the practice of esoteric techniques revealed to very few he had gradually withdrawn his life from his body, layer by layer replacing his own fluids with the lacquer, effectively mummifying himself from the outside in. All that remained of the abbot was concentrated in the thread of fluid that reached from his heart to the centre of his brain and was already pushing against the membranes - the last barrier to his total freedom.

Although my light contact was enough to hold him in place the fury contained was immense - the fury of many lifetimes of dedication that had brought him to this place - to the edge of freedom from birth - to a return to the source. That fury began to scramble my thoughts, brought panic to my breathing and sweat to my skin.

I replaced my hand with an old bronze ceremonial bowl that Judith brought from the altar and breathed a sigh of relief as I was able to put a little more space between the abbot and me.

This was the great irony of the practice - that such a strong will could still be contained by such a small resistance. It was why the monastery was hidden from the world and protected against disturbance. We were lucky to arrive in time - the abbot was close to completion and the force of his leaving would have sent a huge wave of energy through this, his last refuge. At such moments there were earthquakes and rock falls and the monks lived with this risk - knowing that if they survived, their own status would be raised enormously as they bathed in the pure rainbow light of the passing abbot.

Cat touched me again with her tail and her whisper reminded me of the tunnel that lay beneath the abbot. Carefully, we slid his casket to one side and opened an entrance into the stony darkness. Cat led the way down a spiral stairway cut through solid rock until we emerged onto a familiar terrace. Above us loomed the outer wall of the monastery and below us, a sheer cliff that seemed to plunge forever. Suspended on that cliff was Kali, sitting in her cell. I knew this terrace from a dream. I knew this terrace as the place I stood arguing with Christopher. And yet still, I could not understand. The rest of our family joined us on the terrace.

Cat touched me again and told me of the Vril tunnels deep in the rock below us, inaccessible from the monastery and too small for any but the Vril. She had never seen them herself but knew of them from other creatures that lived in the monastery. The tunnels were used for the construction of the cell in which Kali now sat. Cat knew of one other tunnel and showed me the place where it opened onto the terrace.

"They use it to blow smoke into the beehive - to sedate the bees in times of transition. The herbs they use are on a shelf in the main kitchen."

She knew no more. A cat needed so much brain for action it didn't have much to spare for memory or mind. It was time for the dreaming bone. I took it from my pocket and my family gathered around me - in part to hold me as I dreamed - in part to share that dream. I slipped the bone onto my finger and let my body soften into the warm embrace of the body of my family. The dream came quickly, vividly - so much confusion cleared simply by being back in this place.

I saw again the scene with Christopher on the terrace and heard the argument clearly. We were brothers - one of us tasked to die and one of us tasked to kill. He was to die. I was to kill. For our entire lives in this monastery we had prepared for this moment and now I refused. Above us, the fifth abbot was about to die. I could hear the puja building to that zenith. What would complete the process was our action. Our abbot was ready to leave forever. The energy accumulated by his sacrifice would bless the entire sangha. All that was needed was for Christopher and me to fulfil our roles. I was to kill and he was to die. He was to die willingly and I was to kill freely. Our entire lives we had prepared and I failed.

He was to stand on the edge of the terrace and I was to push. And I refused. His action was needed to complete the action of the abbot. His action would liberate the abbot forever and raise the status of the entire sangha. His action would guarantee his own rebirth as the seventh abbot of this monastery. My action would lead me to the role of the discipline master - outwardly playing the role of the abbot, inwardly embodying the forces of evil and love, wielding the smile and the whip.

And I failed. I hadn't yet learned how to kill.

And now I saw that cat was wrong - a wealthy man had not died. A poor man with nothing, not even a body, was about to die. The puja suspended in time above us was for the abbot. Now he sat with a singing bowl trapping his soul in his body as I dreamed.

And I saw how I failed. And I saw how I fled. And I saw how the fifth abbot had been left incomplete. And now I knew where to find the old lama, trapped once again in his lignified body. And I saw how I ran. And I saw the lifetimes I was obliged to return over and over to learn how to kill. And I saw how finally, in this life, I had learned how to kill.

And I saw how the system was changed - how my failure then had led to what was unfolding now - how the price I had to pay was the life of Kali, the woman who sat poised between life and death in the cell suspended on the cliff wall far below.

And I saw that what saved me from Christopher's death-blow was not luck nor intuition but the sound of a small gold coin thrown from the parapet above by Kali, the secret consort to the abbot.

And now I knew how she had loved me then and nurtured me through many lives since then and found me once again in this life and loved me and taught me how to kill, knowing it was her I would finally have to kill. And now I turned to the details and I saw the Vril within their tunnels, fires ready to burn the slender poles on which balanced Kali's cell.

And I understood what I saw when Herve first took me to look at the cell - that crafty construction that ensured that the structure would fail and the walls would fall away moments before Kali's seat itself would topple.

And I saw how she sat and prepared for that moment when she would fall head-first through space, gazing out across the mountains, willingly giving up her soul as the abbot gave up his. And I saw that she had to do it - it was the price she would pay for her love of me. And I knew that it had to happen.

When I opened my eyes, we all knew the role we had to play. The light workers remained on the terrace while the rest of us returned to the abbots' corridor. I stopped at the last and put my hand to his heart and assured him that all would be well. Hawa remained with him ready to remove the bowl from his head. Rafiq and Mariam followed cat to the kitchen to fetch the herbs.

I stopped at the fifth abbot and brought my brow to his brow. I felt the faintest stirrings of the old lama within. I removed the gold coin that covered his fontanelle and put it in my pocket. When I stepped back from behind the altar, Juan, Mireille and Alice had already found places amongst the monks. They were ready to lean on the sound to help make up for lost time. I found myself face to face with the discipline master and bowed to him in honour of the difficulty of his role.

Although he hadn't yet had to kill to take this place he was ready for the task. It was he who would tell the Vril to light the fires that would send Kali to her death - a hands-off killing, much easier than in my day. I returned the double dorje to its place in his robes. He would need it to send the signal to the Vril. I didn't return the jewels I stole from him. It didn't work like that.

Rafiq and Mariam returned with the herbs - a tightly packed bundle held together with a red silk thread. They had already set it smouldering on the fire in the kitchen and for a moment I let its smoke carry my prayers to the altar before I returned to the terrace. The stillness workers would remain with the sangha. They had a difficult task - to remove stillness without accident and control each individual's flow of time until we reached unison.

On the terrace I dropped the bundle of smouldering herbs down the hole and could feel the slight breeze that would draw its smoke to the bees and sedate them before the stillness was removed. I joined Judith on the ledge and gazed down at the roof of Kali's cell directly below us. I could see Herve soaring below. Robert and Remi were gazing into the light. We could not afford to lose track of each other.

"Ready?"

I turned to Judith in an embrace. I could feel the stillness receding. The music resumed, momentarily chaotic but soon called into order by the sound workers' voices that were so pure, so beautiful, so in harmony that it felt as if they could bring order into everything. Now I held Judith's hand and we waited. The stillness was gone but another stillness took its place - a rightful stillness, poised, anticipating. The music worked its inevitable way to its zenith - order and time restored by the sound workers. The abbot pressed more forcefully against the last soft spot in his fontanelle, now freed from the pressure of the singing bowl. I took from my pocket one of the jewels I had taken from the discipline master and integrated its knowledge into my web. I felt his hand rise and strike the stone with the double dorje. I felt the fine resonance that touched the Vril and told them the time to light the fires had arrived.

I saw the jets of white smoke either side of Kali's cell as The Winds from the North poured through the Vril tunnels driving furnaces that consumed the poles. The music stopped. All that remained was the unified 'om' of the stillness workers - now no longer with the monks but here beside us on the ledge. The smoke turned to black and the walls fell away from Kali's cell. Herve swooped towards her. The abbot's soul broke through the final membrane. The stones of the monastery began to shake with the force. Judith and I dropped headfirst from the ledge, releasing our hands just as Kali dropped sideways from her seat - hands outstretched to meet our hands. We were three again, our vision as clear as diamond. The stillness workers slowed us for the moments I needed to heal her heart, and then we were one.

We followed Herve's direction and saw where he was leading us - first just a softening in the light, then a pattern in the air that didn't belong, then a Vril-hole that opened out beneath us. We glided our way in, followed by the others, all now hand in hand in their threes.

The cold rushing air of the high Himalayas become soft and warm and viscid. Gravity exerted no force in the Vril-hole and our fall slowed to a soft and gentle caress. Hands reached out and three became twelve - a circle suspended in space and time. Warm air between our toes gave way to soft grass and earth and twelve became thirteen as we stood in a circle around the old lama in the High Atlas mountain retreat that Hawa, Rafiq and Mariam had prepared for us so long before.

Two

1

We stood and waited – timeless, for a moment that none of us could define, for a moment in which the disturbance created by the Vril hole was healed, for the moment when the cleft we had made through the natural order was fully resolved. We waited, quiet and still until the last rock that had to fall had fallen from the walls of the monastery. We waited until the rainbow that wrapped the earth fell as a fine unseasonal sleet and the abbot's soul left the earth forever. We waited until the old lama had fully settled into his new form and we could drop our hands and feel the love of a family complete once more.

On the old lama's instruction, we separated into our threes and went to our quarters to rest - we to the home I had prepared so long before in the hope of finding my three, not knowing if in this lifetime I would ever succeed. The rooms I had prepared were still beautiful, set deep into the walls of the mountainside, furnished with rugs and fabrics and furniture gathered little by little over the years by Mariam and her siblings.

We slept a night, a day, and another night and woke to the call of the dawn chorus as the golden rays of the morning sun sparkled on the fine, freshwater stream that flowed from the mountain, through a pool in the cave and out into the valley. As a three we sank into the pool and let the icy waters carry away the last vestiges of sleep, the last vestiges of the struggles of the fall and, for me, the last vestiges of those days and weeks and months perched on a cliff side, sharpening my sense of the present, unsure if that present would lead to death and rebirth or to the sense of completion I had dreamed of since I was a child.

Memories returned in waves - memories of this life, of the days of love with Dorje in London and the days before in Florence and Tunisia as I woke him to his skills and powers. Memories rolled in of that single day Dorje and Judith shared in Cannes and the days in Paris as they discovered what powers they had between them. Memories returned of the last moments in the monastery as Judith and Dorje fell through space and the first taste of the power of three, as they caught me as I fell. Memories returned faster and faster, of many lives before - lives spent together and lives lived apart, lives in which we missed each other and lived alone and lives lived as couples but somehow incomplete. Finally, the memory returned of the last life we lived and died as three.

We were standing on a beach, facing the fire, Dorje and me hand in hand as I clutched the last book to my heart, Judith behind us singing the spell that would integrate the knowledge of that book into the web of memory that existed only when we became a three.

2

We left our home in the cave and followed the stream that now flowed as a golden light from the pool, through the circle of our family and down the mountainside as liquid gold that brought illumination from river to rock, from rock to earth, from earth to plant, from plant to sky - as swirls and vortices, as pulses and beats, unseen by so many and yet seen by those who were called to raise their eyes to the sky that night.

A glow spread out on the land below and, where it touched the sea, it set the sea afire and where sea touched sky a matrix ignited, a matrix which to varying degrees would touch all of humanity.

The lama explained that all over the planet eyes were clearing, veils falling, unspoken truths could no longer be contained. For some there would be trouble that made no sense and for others there would be trouble that made sense of a lifetime of nonsense.

"Many families will come together tonight," he said. "Some will work with us and some will resist. I must go; there is much for me to understand under the cover of this chaos. Follow the golden thread and we will meet again."

We walked and we ran and we flew like dragonflies, ravens and hawks and I felt a love that I had missed for so long - the love of Dorje and Judith and me as a three, and now as a family sharing ourselves deeper and deeper with each shape shift and creature body.

Out of the sky matrix a page reformed, visible only to the eyes of our three, a page from the last book I held before the fire, a map of the route we had to follow from our mountain lair into the valley, to a sacred path that had long lain dormant, waiting for the caress of our family's fingers.

Mariam had given each of us a leather rucksack prepared long before she knew any of us apart from her brothers, before she had even the slightest hint of the life that would come and make sense of the life they had lived. Their little family completed so many projects guided only by her dreams and visions - the rooms prepared in the mountainside, objects located and stolen from the villages and towns below. What trust she must have had, driven for years by that unclear mission! What trust her brothers must have had to follow every instruction from the mouth of Mariam, their mad magpie of a sister.

Within our bag each of us found a change of clothes, simple toiletries and precious objects and tools from former lives. Opening the bags became a party, a ceremony, a ritual - sometimes solemn, sometimes accompanied by waves of laughter. One moment it was a fashion show as each of us modelled our new clothes, another moment a magic show as we remembered how to use the tools and objects Mariam had returned to us.

One question recurred. How did she do all this without any hint of the reason?

Mariam could never answer that question - she really did not know and she had no stories from her father to guide her.

"Perhaps from my mother," she said. "She was the one with the dreams and visions. I don't remember her teaching me but I must have learned it anyway."

Now, as our family followed the golden thread into the valley, a new sense of joy was shared by Mariam and her brothers. Their once familiar expressions softened as their long and arduous past finally made sense.

Along the route Mariam would often have us rest while she disappeared into the wild, returning with fruits and nuts and fresh water gathered from places she knew even if she had never walked this path before. From time to time one us felt called to lay our hands against a rock or to insert them into a crevice or plunge them beneath the waters of a mountain stream. With each touch, new information returned to our family's library of knowledge and new strands of golden light unfolded the path before us.

We continued like this for days, sleeping like a pack under the stars, walking like a pride along this long-forgotten path. There was no need to hide, there was no sense of eyes watching, but this path revealed abundant treasures for the eyes of treasure seekers like us. On the eighth day of our journey the path ended abruptly with a wall of rock - a towering cliff-face impossible to climb. Herve investigated, flying the length and breadth in numerous winged forms.

"It is smooth like the finest marble," he said. "Apart from one solitary aperture, there is no other place in which to fit a finger, a nail, a claw or a talon. Not a single seed has taken hold. Not a single ant investigates the surface. There is no sign of wasp, no sign of bee, not even the beginning of a nest. Even lichen has failed to find a place to make its mark. We could go around but it would take days of hard work to cut through the wildness, days spent far from the path. It is clearly enchanted, waiting for something from us."

"And thanks to Mariam we have that something with us," I said as I stood and embraced her.

"I'm sure we will all ask this same question of her many times - how did you know?" I removed from my bag a fossil, a belemnite - an ancient squid, perfectly polished, one end ragged and the other end a soft and rounded point.

"I remember finding it, but not in this life. I was just a child, searching the beach for driftwood to keep my family warm and to make the fire on which my mother cooked our family meal - that was my duty. There had been a storm that night and I went to the beach early. There was often a bounty after a storm and I wanted to be there first. At the least, I could be sure I would find more wood but sometimes, I would find fish or crabs thrown ashore by the waves, sometimes enough to fill my basket, enough to salt or smoke and feed us for weeks. That day I didn't find fish. That day I found wood, too much wood for me to manage, enough for the whole village for weeks but it would take many men to cut and carry it. The storm had blown off the land and torn trees from the cliff side. Some of the cliff had collapsed. It was there I found the stone, in the cliff fall. It drew me to it. It didn't belong there. I had never seen anything like it before. My family had never seen anything like it. They told me to keep it, to hide it, not to mention it to anyone. My mother said she thought it might have power - perhaps it belonged to a witch. 'Don't tell a soul,' she said, 'in case folks think it's you that's the witch.'

"This stone remained with me the whole of that life, protected and hidden, waiting for a purpose that never arrived. Before I died, when my death was inevitable, as each day became noticeably harder and even breathing became a chore, it became clear I would never know its purpose but that I had to hide it for another time. I made a journey to our sacred place - the place where our ancestors rest. I knew this would be the last time I would make this walk alone, on my own legs. Next time I would be carried on the legs of others.

"I walked the perimeter of the barrow until I found what I needed - a rabbit hole, long since abandoned by the digger, partly overgrown by brambles. I took the stone and kissed it goodbye before throwing it deep into the hole. The journey home took the last of my breath and I died that night as I slept. Now I know again what I knew before - that this stone is not a wand as my mother thought, but a key to fit a lock, a special lock unlike any crafted by man. This lock was crafted by the Vril and Herve already knows what to do."

I raised the stone to meet the clutch of his eagle's claws as Herve swept above me and surged high up the cliff side until the stone drew him to complete an ancient pair. Silently the wall was gone as easily as a veil falling from eyes and the unseen became seen. Before us the path shined gold and bright, sparkling with treasures for seekers like us and knowledge for all who would follow.

3

Remi stepped forward, excited, stood and faced us from a place that was once a wall. "This is so incredible, my family talked of this path, of a secret way through the mountains known only to our people. They said it was a path that not only crossed the mountains between two lands but also crossed between times. I always thought it was a myth. They said it was this path that kept our people safe. We were always a persecuted people, persecuted for our beliefs, for the way we looked, for our language. Sometimes we were safer on one side of the mountains, sometimes on the other - it all depended on the time. But there is something I must do before we can move forward. At the moment the path we see is as illusory as the wall we saw before."

Remi reached into her bag and brought out a small gold case.

"Again, we must thank Mariam for the magic of her ways. It's a needle case," she said. "It once belonged to my grandmother. I remember holding it as a child. I remember the sensation as I rubbed my thumb over the design engraved into the surface. She told me one day it would be mine but when she died it was never found. I cannot imagine the process by which it was hidden until the moment that Mariam could return it to my hands. Now it feels so small, but as I hold it, I remember exactly the instructions my grandmother gave me for its use. Kali, I need a thread."

I reached up with both hands open and felt the play of the many threads that warped and weaved their way through worlds and times and dimensions. Waves of sound and colour swirled around us as I searched for the right thread and the right thread sought me out. When we connected and I pulled the thread down, I could see what Remi already knew - before us lay the same landscape and the same path but the scene was ill formed and transitory. If we stepped forward, we would be lost, condemned to walk that same fragment of the path for eternity, constantly searching, constantly collecting treasures and knowledge, but without the ability to remember or retain, unable to learn, unable to grow.

Remi removed a gold needle from the golden case and held it by the point. I passed her the end of the thread and it snaked its way through the eye. She began to sew and as she sewed she sang - lullabies and love songs to soothe the land as she repaired the wound made by the enchanted wall. It was beautiful work - the work of a mother, a weaver, a healer.

Little by little life and order returned to the path. The breath of the land softened and a deep stillness emerged. All but Remi sat, all of us touched by the beauty of her work, all of us aware that this small act of healing would repercuss throughout the world. We had time on our hands and I turned to Dorje and Judith. "Come, let's take a look at our old life - I have a feeling we have something more to do there."

We held hands and our consciousness streamed out as a three, first to the apartment in Paris. It was just as Judith and Dorje left it, everything still in order despite the wind that chased them as they ran.

"Good," I thought, "it is still our place". As we prepared to move on toward London, I thought it better to forewarn Dorje and Judith of the changes to expect.

"Three times you passed through Vril holes as you travelled to rescue me. Although each journey lasted only moments, many years passed in the world we are returning to. Prepare yourselves for some changes."

And then we were looking at the home I first brought Dorje to after Florence. Little had changed since I left in a hurry one night as Dorje slept. Marianne had kept it exactly as it was, waiting for our return. She was there in the kitchen, barely changed for all those years, still serene and fresh as ever, a woman who calmly accepted to do her duty without question, to keep the home exactly as it was and to raise the tulku son fathered by Dorje and left in her care. The boy was beautiful, handsome as his father and serene like the woman who raised him. But it was impossible to tell to which family he belonged. Somebody had thrown a shroud around our home and, although we could look, we couldn't understand. We had to find out who had thrown the shroud and our three-mind search soon revealed the answer. Not far from that home we found Christopher, still playing his medicine game, but in a therapy centre occupying many floors and filled with therapists and healers of every kind.

"Oh god," said Dorje. "I thought Robert took away his power."

"He did," I replied, "but that didn't make him useless. Look."

As we journeyed through the rooms, we saw that each practitioner shared one thing in common. Each in their own way was in thrall to Christopher. Each was taken in by his capacity to manipulate and seduce. Even if he no longer had his powers he acted as if he did and each of his colleagues believed it to be true. They transferred their belief to their clients and, regardless of whatever else they did in their practice, they used the golden needle technique he taught them.

"So that's what they're up to," Dorje said. "They're still building the golden network."

"But bigger and better than before," I replied. "Look who else is here."

And there she sat in the director's office - that bitch of a woman who nearly killed me and who kept Dorje from me all those years.

"I suppose her family's money paid for the centre," Dorje said.

"Of course!" I replied. "But it is much worse than that. I suppose you didn't realise, but Christopher completed your wife's three and also completed her family."

"No way!" Dorje replied in alarm.

"Marisa didn't just want to keep you away from me - she remembered you from before and she knew you had powers, but she was never quite sure of your role. She thought you would complete her three."

"No wonder she grew to hate me so much. I must have been such a disappointment."

"And yet, even as she came to realise that you were not the one, she was still stuck with you, still obliged to keep you from me."

"Why didn't she just kill me, it would have been so easy?" Dorje asked.

"Because you were still useful. She used you when she tried to kill me, because back then even you didn't know whose side you were on."

"Who was the other one of Marisa's three?" Dorje asked.

"Her father of course."

Poor Dorje was so confused he almost let go of the thread that held us all together in Christopher's clinic.

"Is it always that uncertain?" he asked. "Is our fate always such a fickle thing? Could we three be on opposite sides of the war as easily as we became a three?"

"Probably. As you've seen, pulling together a three is not an easy thing. In fact, nothing in this world is easy. Until we reach a certain point in our development we rely entirely on luck. If luck is on our side, someone with knowledge might step into our life - even a permanent if we are especially lucky as we were."

And it really was like that. Life after life, tantalised and disappointed, so close to completion one moment and so far away the next. Fighting for one set of beliefs one life and against them the next. And within each life the same - moments of realisation so profound that it felt like nothing would ever be the same again and yet these could be suddenly swept aside by dreams or distractions that might swallow us up for years. We withdrew ourselves from Christopher's practice just as Remi tied the final knot. We were ready to move again and now we knew our next destination. We moved with exuberance onto the path that unfolded from behind what was once a magical wall. We could move freely, as it would take a while for the people to rediscover this path.

When they did discover it, it would be as if it had been there forever and yet they would no longer be as before. This was one of the many beauties of our work. It was a work without reward, a work without recognition, a work that would most often have effects far beyond our capacity to see. And yet the fruits of our work would often show themselves in other times, other lives, as signs and markers, treasures and teachings, memories and possessions.

4

As we came down from the mountains into the city, life once again gave us what we needed. Mariam led us deep into a warren of back streets - into a complex maze designed to hide all manner of secrets and to ensnare those who were not invited. We stopped in front of a large, ancient wooden door, eaten by insects and time. It had been repaired many times over the years with new wooden pieces cut to replace what was eaten away and reinforced with crudely forged iron.

"Who has the key?" Mariam asked and we all looked from eye to eye, waiting to see whose memory would respond.

"Not you?" I asked Mariam, surprised.

"No," she replied. "I know the door and I remember the key but somebody else knows what lies beyond."

Robert stepped forward with a smile, holding an old iron key high above his head. "Here it is. When I locked this door I never expected to return. I threw the key into a ravine, thinking I'd closed a chapter forever. I know what lies behind this door and I must apologise in advance for the mess - it's been a long time."

Robert turned the key in the lock and the door swung easily open. He was as surprised as the rest of us to see what lay beyond.

We stepped into a sunlit courtyard cooled by a sparkling fountain of fresh spring water. There was a blaze of colour, pots of hibiscus and aromatic herbs, bougainvillea and jasmine climbing the ironwork that supported a first-floor walkway. Fresh cut flowers decorated a table set with nuts, fresh fruit and sweets.

"Not quite as I remember it," said Robert. "I didn't have a maid when I lived here but now, I wish I had. How beautiful is this? You should have seen it when I lived here. But how is this possible?"

"Don't ask," Dorje replied with a wink. "I'm only just getting used to the way our world works now and I'm not sure we really need to understand."

Dorje was right. Little by little we were learning how our life unfolded as many interwoven layers. Every day, so many people walked past the door through which we entered the courtyard and it evoked no interest. Occasionally somebody would stop and look, their curiosity piqued but for no reason they could think of. Sometimes that curiosity might evoke a dream or memory, perhaps a sense of déjà vu. Only a few people held the key.

We had a key and it was clear that others had a key. Somebody prepared this place for us and yet, we might never know each other. Perhaps it was simply something they were asked to do before they left. We were involved in an intimate dance with others we might never meet. We might eat the food they prepared for us, sleep in a bed they had left not long before, wear a coat they had just been wearing. Everything here was shared and each of us could take exactly what we needed. We asked Robert to show us to our rooms but he couldn't. Now there were many more rooms than he remembered.

"When I was here last time, this riad had just enough room for me but now there are rooms enough for us all. It feels almost like a reflection of my mind which used to be so much smaller."

We found our rooms, each one perfectly suited to its intended occupant. Judith, Dorje and I had bedrooms that opened onto a large lounge area, which itself opened onto the walkway. Once we had all finished bathing and changed into fresh clothes we gathered in the courtyard, sitting in a circle. We sat in silence until the old lama joined our thoughts and permeated our sense of being.

"Yes," he said, "your destination is London but the journey will be slow; there is much to do along the way. Sacred paths are opening all over the planet but there is no order. People are travelling, called to the paths but without real purpose. Many people are heading to the north and the west, some fleeing war and violence, some seeking another life but without really understanding what calls them. Other people are heading south and east, searching for knowledge they have heard can be found on the paths but what they seek remains hidden from them, veiled by their habits in thinking and seeing."

We rested in a silence touched only by the music of the fountain.

"The water from this fountain leads to the sea and continues as a pure thread through the brine to the other side. You must follow the thread across the water. Take care - there will be danger and resistance. Not from devolvers, but from ordinary people who do not understand the nature of these times. The devolvers enjoy the confusion; it draws people to them. If the paths are not working correctly, the people will simply travel back and forth and find nothing more than two ends of the same stick. Their confusion will lead to sickness and their sickness will lead them to false teachings."

The old lama's presence receded and we maintained the circle for a while, sharing our thoughts and ideas on how to make the journey. As before, we knew we needed only to make the first move, and the first move was to cross the sea. After that, everything would become clear.

Over the following days we found all we would need, a smuggler and a boat, a forger to make our documents, a healthy pile of ill-gotten money and gold, hidden beneath the kitchen floor in a smuggler's house. Directly above the trove stood his mother - applying all her skills to cook some flavour out of the bones of an old sheep, blissfully unaware of the activities of her only and much-loved son, equally unaware of the wealth he had accumulated as he was too ashamed to tell her his truth.

The stillness workers remained as the rest of us set off in our threes into streets saturated with the magic of the afternoon sun and the faintest hum from the web of information the stillness workers unfolded before us. Within that web we knew all the secrets of the maze. Dorje, Judith and I went to fetch the money and soon found the entrance to the smuggler's house. His mother answered the door as her beloved son smoked and watched football in the parlour. With no more than the slightest nudge she invited us in. Before her son could voice the question that formed in his mind the stillness workers unfolded their spell. As his mother stood in the courtyard gazing into paradise, we lifted the tiles of the kitchen floor and helped ourselves to the smuggler's stash - dollars, euros and gold dirhams. We put some of the gold into the pockets of the smuggler, along with the wish to give it all away.

Some, we hid in his mother's room along with the memory that her husband told her where he left it before he died. We headed back to our riad, feeling again the wonder of working as a family in the ordinary world, glimpsing for moments through the eyes of the others as they completed their tasks. Smugglers would help us all the way and the smugglers we chose were the ones with the best transportation, the ones who moved hashish rather than people across the sea. With a soft veil drawn across their eyes, they sealed our bags to protect them against the sea and loaded them into compartments hidden beneath the seats of the minibus they used to take tourists from the city to the coast.

We tidied the riad and watered the plants, not knowing when we would be back and then, dressed as tourists, headed north with our driver. At the last town before the sea we stopped to eat, taking our time as we waited for the new moon to disappear beneath the horizon and waiting a little more for the darkness to deepen. Our driver summoned us down to the water's edge carrying our possessions with us.

Two men with ropes had pulled the boat to the shore, its four powerful engines silent for now. Once aboard we were instructed to secure ourselves to the deck, using the straps and nets that would usually keep bales of hashish in place. The smell lingered still. The men with the ropes climbed aboard and oared us out into the darkness before strapping themselves into the row of seats that ran along the centre of the rib behind the driver. They stopped and listened, deep into the night, for the sounds of activity ashore or at sea, for the sound of dogs, for the sound of breath beyond our own. They turned, silently concurring. The driver pressed a button and the engines roared into life in unison. He pulled back the throttle and the rib hurtled out into the darkness, too late to follow, too fast to catch.

It was an exhilarating ride of little more than an hour with not much to do but hold onto the nets and soak up the seawater. The journey ended as abruptly as it began. The motors were cut and raised and the oarsmen released themselves from their seat, oars at the ready for the final stage. They listened intently. The driver raised night vision goggles and surveyed the land. At his signal the oarsmen dipped their oars and paddled us ashore, following his direction. We were met by a driver and hurried aboard another minibus heading north as the rib and her crew skulked back to sea.

In that short sprint across the water the smugglers' lives were changed forever. Now they would no longer dedicate their lives solely to smuggling hashish. Now every return trip was spent rescuing those who had fallen into the water on a more perilous trip across the sea. Two kilometres down the road our driver handed his vehicle over to us. He no longer wanted to do this smuggling work. He wanted to be at home with his wife and children. He wanted to wake with them in the morning and walk them to school. "I no longer want to live with this shame," he said.

5

We turned back from where he left us, back to the sea, following the call of the golden stream until we found the place where it left the sea and returned to land. We followed it north until Remi found the first point. “Stop!” she called, and Juan pulled over to the side of the road.

We followed Remi out onto the land, out between broken walls and orange groves, until we reached an ancient stone tower, partly collapsed, infiltrated by wildflowers and lichen. She brought her hand to one of the keystones at the base of the tower and touched, and listened, and waited - until the soft breeze turned into a soft whisper and the soft whisper turned into a hiss. And she continued to touch and listen and wait until the hiss clarified into a tone, into the sound of a singing stone, into the sound of an ancient stone machine coming back to life. Remi stepped back, releasing her touch, tears wetting her cheeks.

“How beautiful is this old technology. Despite all these years lying redundant, forgotten, hammered by the elements and abandoned by the people, still it was ready to work with only the slightest of coaxing, and still it works as well as it ever did. What incredible systems our ancestors left for us.”

We stepped away from the tower and Remi taught us how to feel the stream that led her to this place, that showed us our direction. “Let me ride up front and guide Juan for a while,” Remi said as we walked back to the minibus. “Once we are all completely in touch with the feel of the stream, we can take it in turns.”

As Juan drove Remi taught us the subtle nuances of the stream, giving meaning to each of our body sensations, thought ripples and fluid flows. We learned to read the stream and the energies we could call upon from the land, both the natural and unnatural. From time to time we would stop, usually at a junction in the roads, often at a place marked with an ancient stone - a cross, a pyramid, sometimes no more than the place where something had once been.

These were the places where the stream reached deep into the earth and where, with only the subtlest of gestures, great forces became available to any who knew how to call upon them. We continued learning through the night until the stream led us to a church in the centre of a small town.

Although dawn had yet to break, the square in front of the church was bustling with life, traders setting up stalls for the weekly market and waiters serving the tables at the only café open at that unholy hour. Our work called for stillness and stillness was unfolded. A wonderful hush settled around us, maintained with love and care by Mariam, Rafiq and Hawa.

The rest of us circled the church, following Remi, feeling for the place where two paths meet. Remi called out to me. "Your turn Kali, your turn to find the stone." We continued our walk. My eyes sharpened, looking for something but not knowing what. "But what am I looking for Remi, can you give me a clue?"

"The clue is that you might not need to look; you know there are other ways to find things."

"But what if it's inside the church?"

"They are never inside. The stone marks a place where two paths meet. The churches were built at the junctions. What lies inside has another purpose."

"Does that mean I should search at the corners?"

Remi's smile confirmed what I asked and now, as we continued our walk, I softened my eyes and deferred to my other senses, smelling the early morning dew settling on leaves and stones, hearing the thrushes and sparrows rustling in their nests, called to flight by the first rays of the sunrise, feeling the breeze breath on my cheeks and the stream beneath my feet. Suddenly I was called to turn and retrace my steps by a soft and musical hum that barely moved the air and a smell so fine and subtle it could only be described as the past, not old and musty but of a different time, before cars and machines and burning oil changed the air forever.

We approached the corner we had only just passed and I could feel a soft heat radiating from one particular place an arm's stretch above my head. It was like the heat of a stone caught for an hour in the light of the setting sun, almost imperceptible but distinct when you knew what to feel for. I explained what led me to the stone and each of our family took turns to test the knowledge.

"Now touch it," Remi instructed, and I reached up on tiptoes and brought my fingertips to touch where I could, to feel that fine radiant heat and the softening under the pads of my fingers as a flow of liquid golden light trickled down through my outstretched body to the ground, lighting the path ahead.

"Good work," she called and as one we headed to the minibus as the stillness subsided and the people in the square resumed their tasks, each a little lighter, a little happier, a little more at peace in their work - each reminded of what it was that drew them to work here in the first place.

6

We travelled through the day, stopping occasionally to eat or to lay our bodies on the ground and find again the stillness that we needed so much after the vibration of the road. The way remained clear and golden and the sensation of the stream beneath our feet remained strong. Sometimes Remi led us out onto the land, introduced us to a tree that marked a place where the earth and sky could exchange more strongly or a place by a river where the news of a hundred miles could be heard.

Deep into the night a call came from Robert. "Stop!" he shouted, waking us from our dreams. Juan jammed the brakes and brought us to a halt on the side of a small tree lined road. Moonlight filtered through the high canopy.

"What is it man?" he called back from where he sat gripping the wheel.

"I hear something," Robert continued. "A sound, a strange sound. It's familiar but I don't know from where."

We all stepped out onto the verge and followed Robert over a small brook behind the trees and into a moonlit field.

"What is it Robert?" Remi asked.

"A sound - indescribable but calling to me. Can't anyone else hear it?"

Nobody else could. Remi continued. "This one is yours Robert. We're with you. Show us what you know."

We followed Robert's slow journey across the field, watching him tilt his head, listening to the call, holding our breath as he listened, as if the sound were so feather fine that even our exhalation might blow it away. One by one each of us began to hear something too, but the sound was paper thin and fragile, disappearing as our attention disappeared or overwhelmed by the sound of too much listening.

At last we stopped by a grand old walnut tree. Robert dropped to his knees, crawling around on all fours, scouring the ground. "It must be here somewhere." He said. The rest of us stood and watched, unsure of the object of his attention. He prostrated himself full length, turned his head and brought his ear to the ground. "So close, so close."

Then he was quiet and closed his eyes. We waited, unsure what to do until Robert rolled onto his back, opened his eyes and gestured. "Come. Come and lie down with me." We all lay on the ground, heads in a circle around some mysterious point beneath the magnificent canopy of this ancient walnut tree. Moonlight dappled us where we lay.

"But what is it Robert?" I whispered, still unsure of what I could hear, unable to discern anything specific in the midst of the sounds of drinking tree roots and insects burrowing in the soil. Robert rolled over and brushed away a little leaf mould to reveal a small blue-grey stone. "Is that it? Is that what you were looking for?"

"It's just the tip." Robert replied. "When I first came here, this stone towered above me. We buried it to hide its presence and I planted this walnut tree to guard the place."

"But how did you know it was here?" Remi asked.

Robert sat up and raised a small blue-grey stone between his fingers and thumb. "This told me. I found it in the bag that Mariam prepared for me. It didn't mean anything but I liked the feel and kept it in my jacket pocket. I asked Juan to stop driving because the stone started to vibrate and woke me to a call. I held it in my hand and it led us here. The closer we got, the more I could hear and the more I could hear the more I remembered.

"I remembered the first time I saw the stone. I was a boy on the cusp of manhood. None of the children in our village ever knew of the stone until the time of transition into adulthood. Each child had a guardian and the guardian's duty was to recognise the time to bring them to the stone. My guardian was also my father because my father was the keeper of the stone.

"My father told me the stone came from the sky, but it didn't fall like moon rock. He said it floated down without fire and heat and, as it landed, the earth opened to receive it. For many generations the stone remained untouched by our people. They built the village like a labyrinth around it and kept it hidden like some dark secret.

"One of my ancestors had a dream which called him out into the night. He followed the dream and found himself standing by the stone. It spoke to him. It told him his people were now strong enough to listen.

"He was instructed to dig a passage leading down to the base of the stone, a place no man had ever been. He was told that the base should be excavated so the entire stone was open to the sky, so the people could move freely and touch the stone wherever they felt called.

"My ancestor was a good man and was able to overcome the fear of the people and do as instructed in the dream. The people followed his guidance and built a tunnel down to the base of the stone, a tunnel big enough for the tallest person to walk without stooping. Once the tunnel was complete, they began to excavate both from above and from below until the stone stood in its own special space in the earth and was open to the sky.

"During the period of construction, my ancestor continued to visit the stone in his dreams and was shown its purpose. Once the work was complete he led each member of our community down the tunnel to the stone. He taught them how to find an inner quiet, how to relax their body so it almost fell to the ground, how to follow an impulse to place their hands and how to listen. Through this ritual, the stone brought knowledge from the sky to the earth. Each person who touched the stone was taught according to their individual nature and capacity. Each child was brought to the stone at the appropriate time to begin their education.

"Our people continued to live as simply as before, in a village built with the gifts of nature - with rocks and clay, reeds and bamboo. Our people continued to eat as simply as before - milk from our goats, wild honey, fruits, nuts, berries and some leafy greens cultivated on the land around our village. Apart from that, nothing was the same. Now our people were inspired to travel from our village to other villages, and from those villages to the far edges of our island, from the edges of our island out across the sea to other lands.

"As they travelled, they taught what they had learned from the stone that came from the sky. This continued until my father became the keeper of the stone. During his time, trouble came to our island. Invaders came from across the sea, from a place where our teachers had never been.

"They were not good people who came. They didn't come to learn. They came only to steal and kill and destroy. Like others before us, we destroyed our own village before they could. We filled the tunnel and the space that contained the stone. My father removed this piece from the top and gave it to me look after. We pulled down our walls and towers and fled, leaving nothing but ruins and a sleeping stone. When I was able, I came back to plant the tree."

"Don't tell me we have to dig up the stone!" Dorje said.

"Thankfully not. We only have to turn it on again. If I am right, and I'm sure Remi will confirm, this stone is now a part of the land, connected to other stones through webs of root, mycelium and lichen. Once we turn it on the knowledge it contains will become available again."

Remi nodded in agreement. "It's incredible how each of us carries a memory but how that memory requires the rest of us to make sense of it. My parents talked of a people who came with a teaching written on a stone. Some thought the story referred to the tablets Moses found on Mount Sinai. Some thought it referred to the black stone of the Kaaba. But my parents insisted the stone was blue-grey and the people came from the north."

Remi brought her forehead to the ground in prostration and we waited. After a short while she raised her head.

"You're right Robert, there is an incredible natural web extending in all directions from the stone and now I know how to animate it again."

We followed Remi's instructions, removing our shoes and standing barefoot in a circle. We held hands and waited until we could feel contact between the earth web and our own energy web. It was a new experience for me. I had been so used to working with the sky cords and never really brought much of my attention to the earth. I guess I just took that connection for granted.

Remi had us move in a slow circle around the stone, no longer holding hands but bringing all our attention to our feet and to the way in which the web to web connection adapted to our movement, never quite disconnecting, never holding us back. In the space of a few slow circles we learned to keep that connection without effort, without forcing attention.

Remi asked Judith, Dorje and me to pull down our sky cords and send the energy around the circle as we moved. When we released our grip the energy circles continued to flow alone, one from above from the sky cords and one from below, from the earth web. For a few minutes we played with these forces: combining them, separating them, spiralling them outwards, spiralling them inwards, understanding how to concentrate them through any one of us and send them out into the world.

We stopped all our efforts and let the energies settle into their own sweet rhythm. Remi turned to Robert. "Time for the stone."

Robert stepped forward, dropped to his knees, blew the last specks of dirt from the earth stone and returned the little piece that had been removed by his father so many lifetimes ago. He returned to the circle and we all watched a faint orange glow as the two pieces melded together once more.

Then we felt the force; an immense wave of knowledge flooded our circle and we had to clasp each other's hands again to stabilise ourselves. Our family held together and Remi guided us into the final part of the ritual. We slowly circled the stone and, as each of us faced the walnut tree across the circle, Remi asked us to prostrate and touch the stone briefly with our forehead.

I watched as each member of my family did as Remi asked and each returned to their place in the circle with a drop of blood running down to their brow. With each act of reverence, the earth web pulled stronger on my feet and the sky cord pulled stronger upward until it was my turn.

I dropped to my knees and stretched out in prostration until I could lower my head to the tip of the stone. I felt the piercing, the whistling of air, the pressure change within my skull and, although I knew I lay there for no more than a moment, I experienced an eternity of lifetimes unfold - Kali lifetimes and all the loves and losses, successes and sins they entailed. In that brief moment, so much was resolved, so many lessons learned, betrayals forgiven, failings understood.

I stood again, cleared of so many pasts, elated and free, a warm trickle of blood dribbling down to my brow. Our circle continued until it was Robert who took the final turn, prostrating himself, piercing his forehead on the stone, returning to the circle. A wind swept upward from earth to sky. Autumn touched the old walnut tree and her leaves turned from summer green to lemon yellow and fell in a halo to the ground. The wind swept on up through her branches, clearing the clouds until we could see deep into dark space.

Somewhere up there, the earth wind was met by another wind, perhaps from whatever sent the stone in the first place. The stone rose from the earth until it towered above us. As we remained standing quietly in our circle, the stone expanded and reorganised until we were contained within it. Despite everything that had brought us here - to this place, to this family, to this moment, to this ceremony, to this exchange, we knew we were so small, so insignificant, so impermanent, simply doing what was asked, perhaps even accepting to be used by an intelligence far beyond our realm.

The wind settled and the stone returned to its place beneath the earth, its blue-grey tip no longer visible beneath the leaf mould and soil. The walnut tree budded and leafed and, in the darkness and stillness of the dusk, we gazed at one another around the circle - quiet, open, at peace, in touch with a higher, unknown intelligence.

We broke the circle and hugged our way around our family. On the way back to the minibus Mariam, leading the way with her brothers, stopped and turned back toward the rest of us, eyes bright, face awash with tears. "My father is alive. They told me my father is alive."

7

Back in the minibus the stillness workers took over driving and navigation while the rest of us gave in to a much needed sleep. There was a lot to process and integrate and dream was the best place to do that.

We continued heading north as the sun rose and I remember those hours drifting between dream and awake. Each time I awoke I was still deeply lost in my dreams, so much so that I had to keep checking that Dorje and Judith were still there. Each time I found they were there, I felt safe enough to let go again into dream - dream that refused to be fully separated from waking life. When we stopped in a small town on the southern side of the Pyrenees dream won. I was suddenly cold - afraid. I whispered to Dorje, "hold me please." He wrapped his arm around me and drew me to him.

Judith moved in closer. "What's happening Kali?"

I wasn't sure. For a few breaths I couldn't say if I was still lost in dream life or if the fear was real and belonged to now. Dorje was on alert. I could feel him reaching up for his sky cord. "Perhaps we'd be better off outside," he said.

"Perhaps," I replied and I felt the hackles of my family rise as we stepped out into the car park and spontaneously found our places in the pack. It was a moment of pure exhilaration that cleared me of my dream as I felt the stillness workers searching the air, seeking the danger, feeling for its direction and origin.

Nothing moved around us as we probed and searched further out from the car park, into the streets of the town and beyond the plane trees that marked the foothills and the pathways into the mountains. There was no response.

Our family settled again, breath soft, neutral restored but now I knew how much I wanted to fight, with Dorje and Judith and our family by my side. I thought back to the roadside near Maria's place, my life leaking away as Dorje found his force beside me, found the ability to kill. I wanted to feel him like that again, forceful and furious, ready and willing to kill. I wanted to be there beside him, pulling energy from the sky, pulling energy from the earth, using the new knowledge and connections we had gathered along the road. I wanted to feed him all the energy I could, mixed with all the love I felt, help him extend the distance over which he could kill. Back then was the first time I had seen such skill. I had heard of it but never been witness to it before. Perhaps with a few judicious killings we could end this battle once and for all and settle into an ordinary life.

"It's okay," I said.

I couldn't say the truth. I couldn't mention the wave of disappointment that now flowed through me as I realised that we had no need to fight, at least not for now. I couldn't say how much I yearned to fight.

"We've been here before," I said. "Just Judith, Dorje and me. We took this route through the mountains. It didn't end well for us. Now we have to do it again - this time as a family. There is something we have to complete."

"I know this route as well," Juan offered. "At least the start. I used to come here with friends from Barcelona but we never walked more than two or three hours into the mountains."

"I think I know what lies on the other side," said Mireille. "I used to visit friends near Carcassonne. Our favourite day out was a drive to Rennes-le-Chateaux and a walk in the mountains. We always took the same route, and that was my fault; it was the only hike I ever wanted to do. We never reached the peak."

"My god Juan," Mireille continued, taking his hand, "perhaps I was always looking for you even then. I wonder how close we came to each other."

In town we gathered what supplies we needed for the journey and left what we didn't need with the minibus. Juan, Mireille and Alice led the way, quickly finding a route from the edge of the car park into the mountains. They walked without hesitation as if the path were programmed into their cells. After an hour, the way became no more than a goat track between the rocks and wild olives and we had to walk in single file. A little before sunset Juan led us off the path to a large cave hidden from view from the track. We gathered wood and built a fire. "I never came this far when I lived in Barcelona," he said, "but I knew this cave would be here and I'm sure we will be able to watch the sunrise from here."

As the darkness fell and the cold emerged from the rock we pulled our bedding close to the fire, swaddling ourselves to preserve our heat. Rafiq found his place between the fire and the mouth of the cave and started to turn, catching threads of the sky and earth webs, slowly wrapping them around him, weaving a mesh that he used to fill the opening to the cave, protecting us from the elements, from night creatures and unwanted eyes.

We must have settled into a deep sleep with Rafiq watching over us and I woke from the most comfortable place as the first rays of the sunrise pierced the dark. As the light settled on the ceiling of the cave the memory of my first time here returned complete. I could see the small triangle formed in the stone and the direction it pointed, deep inside the cave. As I looked into the darkness, I knew that the sunlight would soon fall there, would soon illuminate the entrance to a small tunnel, the only way to the other side. I remembered the time we tried to make our way through that tunnel once before. We were being pursued. We had been told of the tunnel by other treasure seekers. We knew it required a key but nobody knew if it was a subtle key or physical. We made the wrong call and found the tunnel closed with no way to move forward. Our enemies built a fire behind us and sucked away the air. Their dogs dragged our bodies out and vultures finished what they left. I woke the others and told them what I now knew.

"There are many ways across this mountain but only one that will work the way we need. We have to crawl through a tunnel to reach a cave. I don't know what's in there but I know I tried to go there once before, with Dorje and Judith. Last time we were in a hurry, with enemies at our heels. This time we have less pressure but we need a key and I have no idea what kind of key it is. Last time we went into that tunnel it was dark and we couldn't carry light with us. All I know is that it feels as if it is cut through solid rock and it ends abruptly. I couldn't feel anything more. Perhaps Dorje or Judith remember something else?"

But no, they could remember nothing more, even if the memories of that terrible end came flooding back to them both and we sought out each other's hands for comfort. The sunlight now lit the place in the back of the cave where the tunnel began. Herve and Remi ventured in, he as bat and she as cat, carrying him on her fur. They moved fast and returned as the sunlight illuminated the entire cave.

"Not the work of human hands," Herve said, "nor the work of the Vril. It is cut in part by water, in part by air."

"And in part by sound," continued Remi, "but not the kind of sound we could make as cat or bat. I have seen something like this before and I think I know the way through."

"We need to be sure," I said. "Once we are in the tunnel it will be very hard to return, there is so little space."

"Does anybody have anything in their bag that could produce that sound?" Judith asked, and I could hear the fear in her voice.

"It's not a thing," Remi said reassuringly. "It's a person. Something tells me Rafiq knows."

Rafiq stepped forward with a smile. "Perhaps," he said. "I can try."

He started to turn and as he turned time slowed down and the air thickened, becoming more visible, moving in waves like the air above a fire. Rafiq modified the mudras of his hands and the tilt of his head, refining the way they stirred the air until he could send waves of liquid air into the tunnel.

A resonance developed, a combination of the rhythm generated by Rafiq in the cave and the rhythm returning to us from the tunnel. The cave vibrated with a slow, deep rhythm adding to the movement in the air. Rafiq caught this new rhythm and drew it into his field, sending the new combination into the tunnel. Dust and small fragments of stone fell from the ceiling of the cave.

Remi organised the air above us so nothing penetrated to where we stood, protecting us from the danger of falling rocks. Robert moved in close to Rafiq. He opened his mouth, drawing in the pulsating air, filling his lungs, opening his throat and the caverns of his sinuses, exhaling a note so deep, so clear we could see it shimmering in the air. Rafiq drew the note into his field and directed it into the tunnel as Robert inhaled slowly again. With each exhalation from Robert, each note thrown into the tunnel by Rafiq, the sound returning from the tunnel grew deeper, from audible to inaudible, to a sensation deep in the pit of the belly, to a movement in the brain.

Storm clouds gathered outside the cave, sunlight replaced by lightning that came in sheets, ripping through layers of darkening cloud. The rhythm of the lightning entrained with that of Rafiq and Robert, and the sound waves of the cave, and the tunnel, until it felt like the whole mountain was being played.

We all gathered closer, brains rocking gently against the inside of our skulls, pulling through inner tissues and fluids deep into the tunnels of our spines. Little by little a path cleared and the sound deepened still further. Slow pulsations pushed their way through fluids, softened membranes, wiped away memories and fears, organised bones, until a clear and polished tube opened to a sound that rose from the slow beat of the air against our sacra.

Together we formed a dungchen and the sound that soared from our throats penetrated the final layer of resistance in the tunnel. It gave way with an immense outpouring of salty air. Rafiq beckoned me with a smile, gently urged me to be the first of our family to enter the tunnel, to complete a task that had cost us our lives before.

I squirmed through that dark and narrow tunnel toward a fluorescing glow in the distance, now freed from the fear I had felt before and carrying the excitement of more than one life. The tunnel opened out into an immense cathedral-like cavern. I raised myself to standing and helped each one of my family to their feet as they entered behind me. Juan came last, pulling our bags behind him with a rope.

8

A voice called out from somewhere in the distance. "At last Kali, you made it through. I have been waiting for you for quite some time."

A figure emerged from the shadows at the far side of the cavern, tall and skinny with chalk-white hair, dreadlocked as if by wind and sea, his small eyes too close together and brilliantly blue.

"Who are you?" I asked.

"I am Auro, wind watcher of the north. Welcome to my home."

Auro walked slowly across the immensity of the cave floor, his long, rickety old bones almost creaking under thin, white skin. As he walked, he hummed, not a tuneful hum but the disjointed hum of a man who spent too much time alone. He stood before us, tears glistening in his eyes, almost smiling. It was the first time I had met a wind watcher, although Dorje had told me something about them. I knew them to be a proud and solitary type but I could not help myself and followed my urge to step forward and embrace him. He sobbed - just once, softened for a moment, took solace in my embrace, pulled back a little, gazed into my eyes and said, "You are everything they said you would be and so much more. I am so happy that I didn't die before I met you."

"How long have you been waiting?"

"I don't know. We wind watchers have no way of counting time, but I built this cave while I waited."

"Are you serious, you built this?" I asked, incredulous as I looked at the immensity of the space in which we gathered. "But what did you do with all the rock?"

"It is easy to dispose of rock on a mountain. And anyway, there was a lot of salt and I just washed that away when it rained."

"How did you do it? Dorje told me wind watchers have a digging stick. Did you dig all this out with a digging stick?"

"No - digging sticks have another purpose, we use them for tunnelling and we use them to talk with the Vril."

"Are the Vril here?" I asked, excited at the thought of being close to the small creatures that were complicit both in the plan to kill me and the plan to save me.

"No. No Vril. There are tunnels but they are not here. There are not so many Vril and they are needed somewhere else."

Auro stopped a moment, stepped back into silence, surveyed our family - one by one, looking deeply into each of us.

"I see you have sound workers in your midst. Let me show you what I do, perhaps there is something for you to learn. Come."

We followed Auro across the cave to a place in the shadows from which he had emerged. There was a row of perfect arches cut into the rock. He asked the sound workers to join him in his arch and the rest of us found a place in the arches nearby. Although Auro addressed Alice, Mireille and Juan he spoke for the benefit of us all. He explained how he cut the first tunnel with his digging stick, until he was right in the centre of the mountain. Then he explained how he used sound within that tunnel, much the same as the sound workers had just done, to soften and dislodge more stones. But it didn't stop there; he had to move the stones as they fell.

"Watch!" he said and all eyes turned in his direction. To begin with we didn't really watch; we listened. We listened to the way his breathing changed, to the way it softened, to the way he exhaled in pulses, to the way he generated a rhythm. We listened as the atmosphere in the cave changed and the echo of Auro's breath bounced around the stone walls. We listened as a new rhythm developed in the air and as Auro's breath was changed by the new rhythm of the air. It seemed as if a dance developed in the air, a dance between the space within Auro's bony rib cage and the space within the cave. And then we watched. We watched in amazement as small stones danced across the floor of the cave, dancing to the waves of Auro's breath, dancing to the rhythm of the air within the cave.

It soon became clear that Auro enjoyed the attention of our audience - perhaps not surprising after so many years digging alone. Without apparent effort, apart from a small change in his breath, a glint in his eye and the redirection of his attention, he gathered all the stones from the floor of the cave into one large circle, had them dance one way and then the other. He brought the dancing stones towards us as a swarm and filed them into an empty arch from where they disappeared.

"Where does that lead?" Juan asked.

"To the outside world," Auro replied. "And then down the mountain as a small landslide."

"Is that how you built this cave?"

"More or less."

Auro went on to describe how he hollowed out the cave using a similar technique to vibrate the walls and ceiling so that whole layers of rock and salt fell to the floor. He even taught our sound workers his methods.

"Something tells me you will need this skill," he said with a slight, knowing smile as if he were capable of looking into our future.

The sound workers quickly learned his ways but he cautioned them to work only with small areas for the moment. "There is only a thin crust of rock left above us," he said, "and it would not do to have this cave fall on our heads."

As Alice finished her second practice, she turned to Auro and asked, "how big a rock can you move?"

"There is no limit - we can move any size of stone using this method."

Hawa stepped forward, agitated, unable to contain herself. "I heard it was the wind watchers who built the pyramids in Egypt. Is it true?"

Remi clapped her hands in excitement. "I had the same question. My people talked of this skill but nobody ever saw it done."

After a long and thoughtful pause Auro responded. "Yes, it was the wind watchers. We moved the stones but we needed help from many others to build the ramps. We can persuade any size of stone to dance but we cannot raise them very high. We danced them up the ramps."

"I knew it, I knew it!" Hawa said, now twirling in circles where she'd stood. "My father whispered it to me in a lullaby one night. I was never sure if he sang it in a dream or if his song made my dream."

And now as she turned she sang, with a face as open as a child. "The wind watchers built the pyramids. The wind watchers raised the stone. The wind watchers built the pyramids. To send a message home!"

"We have gone to great lengths to keep it quiet," Auro continued. "We built many wonderful things around the planet - great walls, circles, pyramids, caverns and canyons - even cities - and all with one purpose, to alter the wind. We used the wind to erode the land, to create deserts, to move human attention from one place to another. We thought that nobody but the wind watchers ever knew but, it seems our secret was not entirely secure."

Auro stopped for a moment, sank deep into quiet reflection. We all joined him in that silence, aware of the significance of the moment unfolding deep in the heart of this mountain. Auro stepped out and turned to face us all.

"The story of your family has been shared between our people.

"Meltemi was the first to recognise elements of one of our great myths when he met you on the island. Shamal confirmed it when he met Mariam and knew there was another to take over the work of her father. But even so, we were still not sure - one of you was missing. Despite Meltemi's help, we did not know if your family would ever be complete. Once you rescued Kali from the cliffside we were sure, and now a new myth begins where the last one became complete. Come, you need to know some things to understand why you are here and why we are teaching you."

Auro led us out through the tunnel that stretched from his cave to the mountainside. It was now a bright, clear sunny day that greeted us and, far below, we could see France.

"Long ago we raised this mountain from the sea to prevent the rising waters from swallowing up the land below. Back then there were few paths of knowledge. The one that brought you here connected to secret places hidden in the High Atlas Mountains."

Auro paused for a moment and let his gaze rest on Remi. "Yes, everything you were told is true. Later, we opened a way through these mountains. Ignorance was spreading like a plague from the north. We wind watchers were asked to help hide knowledge before it was destroyed forever. Some we buried as entire libraries beneath deserts of sand. Smaller treasures were taken through our mountain paths to be hidden away for better times. We closed the paths and changed the wind so no hint of that hidden knowledge would reach the nostrils of those with bad intent. Today all that will change."

Auro asked us to move back away from where he stood and take a safe distance from which to watch.

He raised the digging stick that had now become visible to our eyes and brought the metal tip sharply down against the rock above the tunnel. 'Clack!'

There was a creaking sound from within the rock and a soft fresh breeze arose, as if from nowhere. Auro raised the digging stick again and brought the metal tip to the same place on the rock. 'Clack! Clack!'

A crack appeared in the rock and rapidly zigged and zagged with a crackling sound like arctic ice. The sunny day was suddenly engulfed in the darkest of clouds, seething with lightning that groped upward from the mountains. We huddled closer as Auro raised his stick a third time and brought it to bear on the mountain. 'Clack! Clack! Clack!'

With an immense exhalation of salty air, the enormous dome Auro had carved out of a mountain disintegrated. What was once a mountain peak was now a rockfall. What was once an impregnable barrier was now a high mountain pass. Before the rock fall had settled, the storm broke and a wind that had been thwarted for so long found its way through the mountains.

Down below chaos ensued. Rivers broiled and broke their banks. Windmills spun wildly until safety systems feathered the blades and disengaged the generators. Atmospheric pressure plunged then soared and throughout the country rivers dropped to their lowest known levels. Power stations, unable to draw coolant from the rivers, shut down and in every town and city the electricity flickered on and off as backup systems struggled to cope with the outage. Auro raised his stick and shouted to us through the storm. "It is done. You must go. Mireille knows the way."

"Will we see you again?" I called back.

"I think you will. You have given me good reason to carry on living."

With a final flourish of his digging stick, Auro picked his way back through the new mountain pass and disappeared from our sight.

"Let's go!" shouted Mireille, and we set off in the wake of a woman who had just woken to her role. "I haven't been on this this section of the route but I know where it leads. My friends never wanted to come further than the chapel so they would wait there while I continued to explore alone. I always felt drawn higher into the mountain, as if by a magnet, and now I feel that same allure pulling me downward."

Mireille led the way with the agility of a cat, following a path that she seemed to know with all her being. We followed in the dark, in the wet, into the unknown but with complete faith in our guide. Following Mireille was like following a dance and that dance was passed person by person along our line. It was exact in every respect - which foot to step with next and how far, which hand to use to steady against the rock, which arm to raise to balance the body. As we learned how to follow Mireille's silent instruction, we became more confident, more adventurous, more playful until we were bounding down the mountain with the exuberance of a pack of wolves.

From the land below there was no distraction, the power cut was now total and people hid indoors, unable to access news, fearful of what the blackout might mean, afraid of a darkness they had been shielded from for too long. Few people shared the magic of what was unfolding in the sky that night and those who did, like us, knew this was no ordinary storm and no ordinary wind that brought disturbance to everything it touched. With an ululating yell Mireille signaled our final leap onto a small platform between the rocks.

"It's here," she said as we all settled back into the land, exhilarated by the events on the mountaintop and the free-falling dance down its side. "It's so strange how one event can suddenly make sense of everything that went before," Mireille continued as she sat on a large stone, gazing out over the land below. "This is where I always came. This is where I always sat. This is my throne. I would sit here, staring into the distance, mixing real life with dream, gazing over my kingdom until my friends called, reminding me it was time to go back down and join them for dinner. Now the dream makes sense and I know this stone is no longer what matters. What matters is what I hid beneath it."

Mireille fell into silence, apart from her breath that softly, gently, tenderly found the rhythm of the stone. She smiled as her throne lifted just a little from the place where it had sat so long on the earth. She threw back her head and laughed as she rode the stone, riding on her breath. She yelled another ululating yell as she danced the stone across the circle and settled it back on the earth. Mireille stepped down from her throne and across to the place its dance had revealed. "Just as I dreamed," she said as she bent forward and plucked an old gold ring from the soil. As she raised it to the sky the storm abated.

"Come," she said, "before power returns to the land." And with a leap she led us on down the mountain, first from rock to rock and then as a pack running through a woodland path to the chapel - a simple, unadorned stone building standing alone in a clearing. Mireille removed the ring from the safety of her mouth and spat out a mouthful of soil.

"Few people ventured this far," she told us. "There was already enough to satisfy even the most avid seeker in the village below.

"This chapel didn't even feature in the guidebooks but we liked to come here, it had a special quality. Calmness emerged if you leaned against its walls. The doors were always locked and I never saw inside, but now I know what lies inside is not our business, we need only open an eye."

Mireille slipped the ring onto her finger. She beckoned me, showed me the ring, just like mine but both much brighter now they were close to each other. She pressed her hand against a stone to her side of the door and I mirrored her movement on my side. The effect was immediate, a shudder raked through the rock above the doors and one small stone squeezed from its place and fell to the ground between us. Mireille tucked it into her bag. The clouds cleared, moonlight fell on the eye and another ancient mechanism came back to life.

"Ha!" she said. "Good timing or what?" And once again we were in full flight behind Mireille - but not for long. Soon after we touched the paved road we found a familiar minibus tucked into a lay by. "No way!" I heard Dorje whisper behind me. But it was true, Juan confirmed. The doors were unlocked and the keys were where he left them, under the driver's seat. The mileage indicated an ordinary road trip and not a magical flight had brought her here. Someone had changed the registration plates and left fresh clothes beneath the seats for us all. It was as I had begun to suspect since we arrived at Robert's riad.

"It seems we have another family running with us."

And suddenly each one of us knew it to be true as many small and coincidental things fell into place.

9

The apartment in Paris was not as I remembered. The key Judith carried did not open the door she expected but, instead, the one on the opposite side of the landing. None of us could explain the change in number on the keyring. We had left the minibus in an underground parking, not sure if we would need it again. We gathered under the cover of stillness to avoid the attention warranted by such an unusual family of twelve, all a little dishevelled from such a long and eventful journey. We had no plan but to eat and rest and recover.

In our room overlooking the square, we sat together on the bed and Dorje and Judith told me of the days they shared together in this building, as my life hung suspended on a cliff side far away. I felt so good to be able to rest at last. Since my escape from the monastery we had not relaxed for long and my system was exhausted from so much travel, so many new impressions, so much to learn and understand. I thought back to those days in London with Dorje, remembered a time when I thought we could just stop and be normal. They were such beautiful days but they didn't last long. It was in the peacefulness of our home, in the loving embrace of Dorje, when I heard my inner life again, that I realised something was wrong. To begin with it was no more than my body calling to me in my dreams. The same motif kept repeating - a hole, sometimes through a rock, sometimes through a tree, sometimes in the ceiling of our home. I was always trying to crawl through but there was resistance. Sometimes I simply couldn't reach the hole. Sometimes the way was blocked, perhaps by thorns or rockslides, once even by wild dogs that snarled and bared their teeth. I would wake in a cold sweat and find it difficult to return to sleep.

It was then that I needed Dorje most and it was then that I feared losing him most.

As time went on, the disturbance became more extreme and the fear more real, more definable. I remembered one night when I had to wake Dorje. I wanted him to check me out but he searched and searched and could find nothing wrong. I knew he was missing something. I knew something serious was wrong but I didn't want to frighten him. Now each night when I woke I would sit in meditation, calling out for our lama until, at last, he came. The news he brought was not good - not good for him, not good for me. It was a terrible betrayal but I couldn't tell Dorje, I knew he wouldn't let me go and I was scared of the power he might unleash to try and protect me. The old lama told me it had to be like this; I had to abandon Dorje. If we failed we could try again in another life.

There was still a slim possibility that Dorje would find a solution but we couldn't be sure. Although Dorje had remembered a lot and learned so much he hadn't yet really put his knowledge to the test. The lama told me about the curse but said he couldn't remove it. It was a curse we all shared for our failings in another life. He and I had no choice but to travel to the monastery and do what we were told. He travelled in his own special way but I still had to travel the way of the flesh, slowly, painfully, doing what I knew I had to do but all the time pulled by the desire to turn back, to return to Dorje, to die in his arms if needs be. I remembered so many details of that awful journey, details etched by the pain that enhanced every one of my senses. Alone, my body failing, each section of the journey worse than the one before, until the final stretch as I climbed the mountain pass, my lungs barely able to harvest enough oxygen from the thin air, my failing heart pounding against my rib cage.

By the time I entered the monastery the old lama was already there, back in the lignified body he had left once before. I closed him in by placing a gold coin on his fontanelle and prostrated myself before the discipline master, begging for permission to pay for the failings of my previous life. I was allowed one night to rest, to bathe, to eat and to make peace with myself before I was sealed in the cell and lowered down the cliff side. It was no more than a wooden box with only enough room to sit. The ropes that held the cell were released one by one and, with each release there was a brief pause, a pause in which to adapt my position and posture to balance the construction of the cell until it rested only on the two poles that projected from the cliff side. Each rope released unleashed another wave of terror as my body adjusted and my mind flooded with thoughts that the design would fail and I would fall to my death without completing my duty, lost forever and with little chance of finding again my path in another life. And then I was alone, abandoned by my fellow man, my fate entirely bound to the needs of the abbot and transmitted by the discipline master to the Vril.

The first days were a torture of the flesh. Even the tiniest of movements to ease the pain in my knees or hips threatened to topple my cell. I had to withdraw myself from the sensation of my lower body, struggle against the pain that begged me to move, pleading for my legs that were slowly dying, deprived by their position of blood flow and lymph. The only movement I could make was to lean forward towards the two rivers of life trickling down the rock face before me - fresh water seeping from the rock and honey dribbling in a scant stream from the bee nest hanging from the cliff directly above me. Even so, that movement had to be undertaken with the utmost care, to avoid unbalancing the cell, to avoid unsettling the bees and drawing their attention to me, to negotiate the tendency for the tissues of my lower back to atrophy and to try to find a smoothness and uniformity of action.

The size of the cell offered me no room to move my arms, no possibility to move my hands far from where they rested on my knees. The discipline master had showed me my work, a sequence of breaths, a repetitive counting routine, an inner dance betrayed only by the slightest movement of the fingers as they unfolded a series of mudras.

"Inhalation nine beats," he said. "Exhalation nine beats. Count the beats only with sensation. Every nine beats the fingers take the next mudra. After one hundred and eight mudras lean forward to take honey and water. Drink but keep counting. Count twenty-seven beats and lean back to neutral. Turn the head to the right. Count twenty-seven beats and return to neutral. Turn the head to the left. Count twenty-seven beats and return to neutral. Never stop counting. The bees will know, the Vril will know. When you reach a million, begin again, counting back down to zero. Nobody knows how many millions; the abbot has to complete his work. You have nothing else to do but help him complete his work. You fail and we all are lost."

These were my days, counting the beats, counting the breaths, lean forward, lean back, turn right, turn left. Each error, each distraction, alerted the bees to my presence, invited ruthless stings, tested the balance of the cell, threatened to plunge me deep into the valley. I was so alone, longing for the voice of the old lama, longing for Dorje's touch, unsure I would ever feel it again. I remember the first word from Dorje, reaching out to me from our home in London, no more than a moment, no more than a question, a wish to know I was still alive. Yet that moment was so profound, at once threatening to throw me from my centre, threatening to expose me to the bees, threatening to undo everything the old lama had negotiated. But also filling me with hope, just to know that Dorje had not forgotten me, that he had developed his skills enough to seek me out even when I had been hidden so far from the eyes of his world.

I could answer no more than 'yes'. I could not risk more than the moment of inattention required to send one word. He returned again and again, somehow read my situation, somehow nourished my body even when I had doomed it to slowly die. Sometimes I felt him so strongly, missed him so deeply that my eyes cried as much as I drank. I remember the moment I saw him fly by. Perhaps he had already flown by many times before but this time my head was turned to the right and I saw him crouched low on the back of an eagle, swooping close to the cliff face. That's when I knew he had a plan. I couldn't even wave. Then he came for me with Judith, as Rafiq unturned time, and we danced together for an eternity as their boat plowed the sea and one beat expanded into forever.

In the next beat I was back in our room. Dorje and Judith were walking the circle. "Come," Dorje beckoned, "let's dance together again as three."

I left my reverie on the bed and joined them, my body freer and more relaxed from its remembering. As we walked the circle, Dorje and Judith unfolded everything they had learned from dancing the wind horse together. I followed their breath and their gestures as we walked and felt a sense of softness and joy running through my body like warm honey. Something awakened inside, an old, old treasure I had been saving for this moment. It revealed itself as a ruby red glow that permeated we three. Now we were dancing on the mountain, not far from the dzong. From where we danced, invisible through the veil of our turning, we could glimpse into the courtyard and see the chaos we had caused. The discipline master worked his whip and his tongue with equal force. They had been searching for us, but now they were gathering the sangha together to see who else was missing, who else was involved. We had stalled a process and nobody could understand why - not even us.

Our turning slowed down the world, not to the point of stillness, but close. Our turning extended our vision, out over the wooden shingles of the monastery roof to another peak where another three was turning. It was too far to see clearly but we could feel the connection, feel the synchrony, feel the curious magic that extended way beyond our little dance, beyond our three, beyond their three, until many threes turned as one.

Now as I looked down into the square from our bedroom window, I could see Rafiq, one hand open to the sky and the other open to the earth, in the centre of the park, by the fountain - turning, unseen by any of those he held in stillness. All they could see was the rare beauty of the afternoon, lit by the glow of the late summer sun. Then there was another movement besides our own. On the far side of the square, in a window facing ours, another three was dancing, and then another three appeared, and another until we were aware that a family like ours occupied an apartment on each side of the square, one east, one south, one west, one north, and each family included a three like ours, not all treasure seekers but all in tune with the same dance.

10

As we turned together, the voice of the old lama infiltrated the silence. He was singing - a beautiful and soothing song. He sang in a language I didn't know - not the English he used when he spoke to our family, nor the Tibetan he used when he spoke with me alone, nor the Dzongkha he used when he taught me.

Then I remembered; this was Kapi, the language I heard when my life began again on the floor of a monastery in Kathmandu. I hadn't heard it since then. The song evoked memories, peculiar memories, ill-defined memories, memories of a time when we were a clan, a clan of forty-nine, running behind a flag. The land was wild and natural, little marked by man, apart from a small cluster of yurts and the goats and yaks we grazed. It was late spring and the land was rich and verdant, alive with grasses and wild flowers. We were running - not in fear, not from danger, but with joy. Our dogs ran with us; our eagles circled overhead. Our cats remained with the grazers, keeping them safe from opportunistic rodents who might gnaw at their feet.

We ran in a spiral, widening outward from the camp. At the start of each new circle the flag changed hands, so each of us would take a turn to lead. We continued until we had all led the clan and our spiral touched the foothills of the mountains that now soared above us, mountains we would take to soon enough, in search of new grass. When we gathered again as a family around a fire blazing in the centre of the camp, it was to share what we learned in the dance. There was much to learn as we danced, of the other creatures that also grazed this high plateau, of the plants that sustained us all.

We learned how long we could stay before we stressed the land, before it was time to move up into the mountains for the summer. We learned from the wind what kind of winter to expect, how much wood to cut and store for our return. We learned from the travellers who passed through this land, the stories and knowledge they carried from their village to the towns below and the news of the big world that they carried back home.

We learned something new in that year's run, something that had never been known, never been talked of before. We learned of cruelty and greed, of a people out of touch with nature, of a people who wanted more than they could eat, more than they could carry. We learned to be afraid. We learned to be suspicious. We learned of the need to keep a watch for strangers, to look for signs of their coming. We learned that when they came they came as many, with horses and dogs and ways of killing we couldn't even understand.

We taught our dogs to sniff further than our flocks and herds, to warn us of the approach of strangers long before they could see our smoke. We learned to run from unseen enemies. We learned to hide our treasures. We learned to communicate secretly using the sounds of nature. We learned to build a structure stronger than a yurt, a tower of stone hidden in the mountains, a place where we could protect our treasures - our children, our old and frail, our storytellers and artists. We learned how to keep the tower safe from hungry eyes through the art of distraction.

The strangers came but did not find us. We never saw them either, but our dogs told us when they were near and our eagles showed us which direction they were heading. They never found our tower. They never even found our yurts, and to begin with we didn't understand why.

Each year we built a little more around the tower - dormitories, storerooms for food and wood, meeting rooms - eventually a school. In part we built because some of our people preferred to stay in the stone village, but we also built because we liked to work with stone. It taught us things, things we had never learned from wood or earth. The stone taught silence and stillness to those who lived within it and cunning and resilience to those who lived outside.

Over time, our clan became a tribe and the tribe divided. Some chose to stay in the stone village and some chose to continue the life we had before. Those who stayed in the village learned to work the land without having to move when the seasons changed. They learned to sit together, in silence and stillness. They learned to write, so our stories could be shared beyond the company of the storytellers.

The rest of us became protectors, moving out into the world with our dogs and eagles, constantly working to keep the stone village hidden. We still kept our yurts on the plateau and we still travelled into the mountains with our yaks when the season asked. The stone showed us how to stay in touch with one another through its fine vibrations.

One day, while we were out on our run, we learned a new truth. We learned that, although some of us ran while the others practised stillness, we were really two ends of the same stick. As much as we protected the stone village with our cunning, those in the stone village protected us through their stillness and silence. It was their stillness that hid our yurts as much as our running hid their tower.

11

It was time to move but, before we could travel to London, we had to practise our skills as a family again, now with all the opportunities offered by a city. Dorje and Judith had already showed me all they learned when they played together on the island and I was keen to share the fun. Now, of course, the situation was quite different. Now we knew we were no longer a family working alone. Now we knew there were other families sitting in stillness while we moved and moving when we felt called to stillness.

Dorje and Judith told me how they first noticed this as they travelled through the valley of the scholars, but now the connection was clearer and more powerful. We shared a constant awareness in everything we did of another family watching over us. There was no sense that they could directly help or intervene but the awareness of their gaze was always there and provided support, calling us back to the sense of ourselves when the world became too distracting.

Conversely, we also had a very real sense of other families in movement as we sat together. As we prepared to leave, we knew that what we left behind would directly affect those who would come to use the space. When we stepped out of that cleaned and well-ordered apartment, we were reminded of the curious nature of the world in which we now journeyed. The door was no longer the one through which we entered, but was again the door to which I directed Dorje when I realised that trouble was brewing in our life and he would need a home to run to. We exchanged no more than the subtlest smile as we descended the worn stone stairs into the colonnaded walkway.

Our first steps were under the cover of stillness but, as we walked, we quickly established our sense of connection. We moved slowly between the diners and coffee drinkers, the waiters and buskers, the dogs and their owners. We found the pace of the columns, the sense of the stone beneath our feet, the shape and sound of the arches above us. We tuned into the stillness workers so we could move as the world moved and continue to move with the same rhythm when the world stopped for a breath of stillness. We learned to disappear in the blink of an eye and reappear with the next. If we made a mistake and drew attention to ourselves, Remi and Robert were there to soothe the moment of unease we created for the person who momentarily woke to another reality, and saw the web of interconnection in which they really lived rather than the two-dimensional apparition they had become used to.

Little by little, as with the wind horse, our walk became slower on the outside while inside we ran like the wind through the colonnades, unseen by all but the occasional dog or a small child whose mind was not yet fully cluttered.

Herve became bird and flew, sometimes as a sparrow blending in and gathering crumbs of knowledge, sometimes as a falcon exploring the city beyond the square. Robert ran as dog and Remi as cat, their soft pads feeling the stone, feeling what lay beneath the stone, feeling the connections, gathering information from the great family of dogs and cats that also shared this city and lived a life unknown to their owners. At last we felt the forgotten truth of this beautiful square - a secret monastery hidden within a city, a place of so many layers, connections and possibilities. For some it was no more than another empty bucket, a place to gawp and gasp. Others were momentarily touched by the fantastic design, invited to delve a little deeper, to understand a little more.

For some it was a home from home, a cafe in which to start the day with strong coffee and cigarettes and words of wisdom from a waiter who would spend a lifetime serving these tables with the dedication of a monk. For some it was the shops that mattered most, the refined and familiar attention of the staff, the feel of fine fabric, the beauty of a perfect stitch, a pen finished in shark skin and tipped with a nib crafted in gold, a hand built watch that showed many more cycles than time, a precious tea harvested from a hillside not far from a hidden dzong where I laboured hard to undo the damage of my meddlesome ways.

As we prepared to widen our attention beyond the square, the setting sun emulated the cherry glow of the stone I still carried. A sense of extraordinary happiness settled on all who shared the square with us that evening, an experience they would talk of for the rest of their lives. Now we knew which direction we would have to travel to avoid the devolvers. Now we knew that this square was again awake and active as was intended, reconnected with the path we had opened from the mountains in the south and leading to the channel to the north. Now we knew it was time to leave, without turning back, without visiting the apartment again, aware that each of us had followed the same impulse to bring our leather bags and the precious things that had been gathered for us by Mariam.

By silent agreement we separated into our threes, each three aware of the route that suited their skills. For us, the journey was by road and tunnel. We recovered the minibus from the underground garage and found it cleaned with a tank full of fuel. We set off into the darkening night with Dorje at the wheel and Judith and I feeling the path that now began to open, feeling the liquid thread that would follow us across the sea.

12

Once we gathered again in London, Dorje knew where we would have to begin our work. Our home was cloaked against us so he suggested we stay in his wife's favourite hotel, certain we would find her there, certain we would need to engage with her first. My feelings at the thought of meeting Marisa were complex. I could still recall the pain she brought to me. I could still remember the torment as she seduced my beautiful lover from me, gloating as all hope leaked out through a hole she ripped in the fabric of my heart. But there was also a deep wish to face her again, with Dorje and Judith by my side, to hurt her, to destroy her hope, to watch her suffer as she made me suffer.

It took a few minutes to get what we needed from reception - a suite next to Marisa. Nobody on the desk thought to question how many we were and how we would settle the bill. They were relaxed and happy to deal with people like us who made them feel good and brought a glow to an otherwise predictable day. We took the keys and as we left reception, wiped the memory of the encounter from the minds of the staff so we could disappear into the antique corridors and stairways, exploring at our own pace, taking control as we did.

We found the door to Marisa's suite. While the rest of us hid the corridor from ordinary eyes, the light workers slid their way in to look. When they returned, we followed Robert to our suite to hear what he had to say. "What happens on this floor is strange," he said. "Two times converge here. This floor offers the best suites in the hotel but it is also a devolver stronghold. You are right Dorje, your wife has permanently reserved this suite but you will not find her here.

"Within the rooms that your wife occupies, that the cleaners clean, that room service attends to, there are other rooms, unseen and ancient rooms built of stone and lit by candles and magic, channelling forces from the earth that the devolvers use to enhance their influence. At the moment they are using these forces to keep you from your home. There is another hotel, on the other side of your apartment, and it's there we'll find your wife."

"Of course!" said Dorje. "Her father's hotel. Let's go there now, I can't wait to see them."

"Please wait a little," Juan entreated. "Your wife is out shopping. Let Herve, Remi and me watch them for a while."

We agreed to use the time to recover from the journey. As we showered, Dorje voiced the question that troubled my mind too. "Was our apartment always in their stream? Were they always watching us?"

I didn't know the answer and I was scared that I didn't know. As I rested in the embrace of Judith and Dorje under the shower I tried to figure it out. I thought back to the days when the lama first took me there, first introduced me to Rafa and Christina. He told me then how the place was protected and I realised how literally I had taken his word. But then I remembered, it was hidden only from ordinary eyes. They wanted the devolvers to know it was there, they were hoping to attract people who might lead to the phurba. Suddenly, I could not say if we were safe, could not say if we were on our own path or being dragged into theirs. I pulled Judith and Dorje closer, whispered my fear. "I'm scared. I don't know what's happening."

Thankfully Dorje responded as I hoped he would.

"Don't worry, that's how she wants you to feel. I know her. I know Marisa's game. It's okay, they couldn't possibly have known we were there, what we were doing, how we were living."

I believed what I wanted to believe, felt reassured by the only person who could reassure me, softened deeper into the embrace of our three and said what burned my heart. "How much I would give to stop here, with you two, in this love, in this happiness, forever."

13

We took our love out onto the streets, into the feeling of a normal life, of lovers and families, parents and carers, dog walkers, runners and skaters. We were almost relaxed, almost free. I wanted so much to see our old apartment, to show Judith the streets that Dorje and I walked together before. I wanted to understand what kept us away, from our home, from Marianne and from the boy.

It didn't take us long to feel the answer. Our love was suddenly disrupted, first by a vile and bitter taste, quickly followed by dark and nasty thoughts. The vileness was not ordinary but intended just for the likes of us and, as the world swirled on in a dream around us, Judith wretched and puked. Dorje and I dragged her across the busy streets towards the park, laid her out in the grass, caressing her back to wellness, working hard to clear our minds of the foulness that had found its way in.

When we could sit upright again, we found our circle and within the circle we found our axis, a deep fountain of kindness that extended from the earth as waves of love, cleaning the putrid stench from within our cellular selves.

The afternoon sun softened into sunset and our family gathered. As the stillness workers held us invisible from the people in the park, Robert explained what they now knew.

"Marisa and her father are now at his hotel. Like Marisa's, this one also occupies an ancient place with rooms hidden within rooms.

"We've passed through the boundary many times, testing its permeability, testing their knowledge. They know something is changing in the world but they don't know what. Christopher will join them later, when his clinic is closed. From what we understand, this evening would be the perfect time to visit. We should be able to disrupt their family once and for all and shut down whatever force they use to keep us from your old home."

"Should we wait for Christopher?" Dorje asked.

Remi replied. "It doesn't matter. The main resistance we'll have to contend with will be from Marisa and her father. He has nothing to add to that. If he's there it's fine, if not he will not be able to enter until we're done and by then there will be nothing left for him."

14

When we reached the suites on the fifth floor we formed a line, hand in hand along the wall. We leaned our ears to the wall, listening for what lay beyond. We could discern the different layers of time, the layer against which we leaned and the deeper layer where Marisa and her father stayed, served only by special members of staff drawn from old families, privileged to be called into the service of their dark work.

Then we saw there was an even deeper level, a level that was here long before the present hotel was built, long before the city extended this far, before the palace builders tamed the wild land and moulded nature into a manageable replica of her higher self. As with Marisa's hotel, this level connected deep into the rock, deep into earth forces beneath the city. This level was accessible only to old families. Even if others suspected and searched, they could never find them, they would never know to search for a thread so fine.

By agreement we pressed on through, breaching the walls of the suite, pressing into Marisa's father's world, ready to take them on, ready to change the balance of forces. But something was wrong. I could still feel the fingertip touch of Judith but no one else was with us. I could see into the rooms but I was looking as if from behind glass, as if pressed between two layers of glass. I could see Dorje in front of me but we no longer shared the same dimension. I couldn't reach out to touch him, couldn't engage with his force. Before I could voice a question, I heard Marisa's voice, still so fresh and familiar from our only meeting.

"Papa, come quickly, look who's come back to me. Papa, Papa, look it's my beautiful husband come back to me. I knew he would. I told you he would."

Then her father was there, every bit as disturbing as Dorje described, his long hair swept back, curls and waves subdued by a layer of pomade, a fine roman nose and eyes too close that made him look more like a hawk than a human.

"And who are these?" He asked, gesturing contemptuously towards us.

"Gifts from my husband, Papa; the price he knew he had to pay to come back to me."

Then she was upon him, caressing him, whispering secret things hidden from me and other things intended to be heard. "I knew you wouldn't forget our anniversary, and now everything you dreamed of can be yours."

I felt the force drain from me. How could this be, after all we had been through since Dorje and Judith plucked me from death, how could Dorje have betrayed us? I could feel a tremor of encouragement from Judith's fingertips and was relieved to be reminded I was not alone but nobody else was with us. Somehow, they had failed to press through even this far.

I couldn't reach out to Dorje; he was insulated from us. I couldn't reach out to the others, couldn't even sense where they were. Between us, Judith and I could summon a little force, but it was only personal, ancestral. We could not catch our sky cords or call upon the earth channels we had opened up along the roads and mountain passes and magical encounters that led us to this moment. Our frail force would be nothing against Marisa and her father; they would swot us like flies.

I so much wanted Dorje up there beside us, so much wanted to feel the force of we three, so much wanted to pull down our sky cords and engage with the earth, so much wanted to rip into Marisa, to make her suffer for all the pain she brought to me, to destroy her as her father watched and then destroy him for everything he represented.

Now I would never have that pleasure, would never again feel the force of Dorje fighting for me, fighting beside me, connected with Judith and me. She would finish me as she intended in Florence and take away the love of so many lives for good measure. Everything felt so futile, so ordinary, so easily swept away.

Now I felt relieved, relieved to have it end here, freed from striving and ambition, freed from obligation and responsibility, freed from hope, free to concede all to Marisa. I looked at her and felt love and respect, for her beauty and determination, her patience and persistence. She could have Dorje; she deserved him.

Now Dorje was facing me, held in an embrace between Marisa and her father. Now I could see that Dorje, not Christopher, completed their three. I could not understand how I had missed that. Only the little attention from Judith kept me from falling into a swoon. Nothing made sense anymore. Although Dorje was now gazing into my eyes, I could read nothing of him anymore and it was Marisa who spoke. "Let's kill them now; let's see how we feel as a three."

She raised her right hand towards me. Her father raised his right hand towards me. Dorje raised his right hand towards me and I could see his fist filled with pearls.

As Marisa and her father came to terms with the weakness of their intentions, Dorje gestured toward Judith and me and, in a wave of the most incredible bliss, I felt a new power integrate into my energy web, and I felt a new power integrate into Judith's energy web and I watched in amazement as a new power integrated into Dorje's energy web.

Now we were free again, now we were three again, now the charm was broken and our family was together again. Now Marisa and her father looked small and puny, no longer welcome in this layer of the hotel, now invisible to the staff they had commanded for so long, now confined to the ordinary luxury of their suites, now with only minor aims, wanting for nothing more than to return to their homes and feed their dogs.

As we gathered together, Dorje handed round the rest of the pearls he had plucked from Marisa and her father.

"How did you do that Dorje?" I asked.

"As any treasure seeker would, when in close proximity."

"But you took their powers!"

"Just as Robert showed me. As he told me, it helps to have stillness workers on your side."

"But Dorje, they weren't here. Only you made it all the way through. The stillness workers didn't even make it as far as Judith and me."

"Ah! Then I don't know what to tell you."

I hugged him close. "It was very cool."

Robert stepped up to help resolve the mystery. "We have probably all noticed a change in our powers since our family united, perhaps noticed the development of new skills, felt the connections between us strengthen and the establishment of connections beyond our immediate family. It might even be that Dorje has added stillness to his toolkit. There is a lesson for us all. Dorje acted as if there were stillness because he thought the stillness workers were here to unfold it for him. The certainty of his belief made it so. Perhaps we all need to develop the ability to act 'as if' - to assume we have all the powers we need. I think it's possible that we can now share all our individual powers and skills."

Although I regretted not seeing Marisa torn and ragged there was something deeply satisfying to see her weak and ordinary, to feel her power as my own and to know that there had been no mistake - our family was still complete.

15

We gathered in the dining hall, in the deep layer of the hotel. Juan had called together the staff. "Everything has changed within these ancient walls," he told them, "and everything will soon change beyond these walls. Those of you who wish to go can leave now. Those who wish to remain will have a new life with us, a life that may be contrary to the ways of your families."

Unsurprisingly, most chose to leave and, once their decision was made, the deep layer and the memory of the deep layer no longer existed for them. The only ones who remained were a brother and sister, Gregory and Griselda, orphans with no place else to go. They gave up the jewels that connected them to the devolvers and received gifts from Robert that connected them to us.

It was always surprising and amazing to watch Robert at work, to watch wisdom incarnate, always matching the needs of the moment. With no more than the smallest gesture he freed Gregory and Griselda from the web that bound them to the devolvers. Greyness drained from their cheeks and colour and joy returned to their lives. We agreed they would stay, taking care of the rooms that had now become ours and attending to the deep layer that lay within. They set to work immediately and soon we were all sitting down to a celebratory feast. As we ate, the memories of this space came drifting back, memories of times I had sat here before, in this great hidden hall that had been host to so many shifts of power over so many hundreds of years. Nothing quite made sense in the swirl of images until, at last, one final image became clear and I was able to share what I knew.

"Now I understand this place. I was here long ago when there was nothing but forest. In the middle of the forest, protected by spells and illusions, was a well - a deep, wide well with a spiral stairway set into the walls. It took an hour to reach the bottom, an hour descending by torchlight into the heat of the earth. I was a young woman when I first went there, led by my mother and grandmother and other wise women of our village. When we reached the depth, we stepped onto granite, black granite polished into a perfect dome, the likes of which I had never seen before. We crawled on our knees to the centre of the dome and my grandmother removed a small plug of brass and amber to reveal a tiny fissure in the otherwise perfect rock. She used a delicate silver crochet hook to tease out the finest of earth threads from the fissure, carefully twisting it around the silver hook until the connection was secure.

"We slowly made our way back up to the surface, each of us taking turns to draw the thread - an amazing experience I still feel in my body even now as I talk of it. We no longer needed our torches as the glow from the thread was enough to light our way. By the time we reached the surface the light was so bright we had to cover our eyes. The light was still contained by the spells and illusions the women had woven to protect their sacred space in the forest but the moment it was freed everything on the surface changed.

"The men, who had been bickering and fighting constantly for years, dropped their shields and swords, suddenly woken from their madness by the light, ashamed by what they saw in themselves, by the destruction they had brought to their families and homes. Now they no longer even knew what they had been fighting for. They threw themselves to the ground at the feet of the women and children and asked for forgiveness and for guidance, asked what they could do to make amends.

"The instructions the women gave were clear. The men accepted to melt their weapons to make useful tools and follow the direction of the women. They used their strength and their need for challenge to work with the land and the rivers, building terraces for fruit trees and canals for irrigation. They channelled the urge they had to fight into games they invented - thinking games for the strong of mind and circus games for the strong of body. For generations the women protected their sacred place in the forest and called upon the earth thread whenever it was needed, whenever its light was needed to clarify their thoughts of the future or their understanding of the now.

"I don't know when things changed, it is not part of my memory, but somehow the devolvers infiltrated the sacred place and took control of the earth thread. Somehow, they corrupted the thread and turned it into a tool for their dark intentions. Now, today, we can change that back but we must be careful and we must work fast. All over this island devolver families have been called to action. They know what happened to Marisa and her father. They know their influence is under threat. There are many sources like the one beneath this hotel and the one beneath Marisa's hotel but I think these two are the most important. That's why Marisa and her father retained their rooms here and that's why, over the years, these hotels remained so vibrant regardless of the nature of the time."

Over dinner we made our plans. Judith, Dorje and I would work with the source that lay beneath us. I hoped my memories would ease our task. The rest of our family would return to Marisa's hotel, take over her rooms and find the other source.

16

We took the service stairs to the basement and stilled the staff in the kitchen. We could see through the serving doors into the casino and soon located the roulette table that sat directly above the source.

"They use false hope and disappointment to darken the energy from the source," I whispered to the others as we searched for the way that led beneath the table. "We must change that for a moment. Happiness will subdue the earth thread long enough for us to bring her back into tune."

Dorje spread stillness out across the gaming room as Judith and I tampered with the playing cards, dice and roulette balls. Soon the house was haemorrhaging money and the atmosphere was euphoric for the few minutes it took before the pit manager closed the tables and locked the doors. Already we had found the way beneath the table and located the entrance to the well. We didn't need torches as the way was illuminated with an antique system of ceramic fittings, copper cables clad in rubber and hand-blown glass bulbs. We moved faster than I remembered from before, as the light was better and we didn't have to take account of the pace of the elders. Now, under that warm electric glow, I could see that the entire way was decorated, the stone walls covered in human and animal figures, telling a story we didn't now have time to read. By the time we reached the polished dome, the earth thread was darkening. I could taste the foulness in my mouth again and Judith was weakening and paling under its influence.

"Oh god are we too late?" I heard Dorje say. "Have they already taken back control of the thread?"

It felt like what he said was true. I helped Judith down to the polished surface of the dome before she crashed, doubled up in pain. "No way," she said, "it doesn't end like this." She dragged herself to the centre of the dome, to the fissure, to the thread of corrupted earth energy spiralling upwards toward the roulette table, towards the gaming room, where the winners were learning the truth of the game, that the house makes the rules, that the house always wins, that the only safe way out was empty handed.

Judith wet a finger with her spit and plugged the hole. There was calm. The colour returned to her cheeks and happiness returned to we three. Upstairs the rules had changed and everybody who had won was allowed to keep their winnings in return for silence.

"How did you do that?" I asked Judith.

"I've done it before Kali, but I can't stay here all night. I think you have something we need."

She was right of course and I searched the bag Mariam had prepared for me and found that little plug made of brass and amber. I swapped it for Judith's finger. We lay back on the warmth of the dome, our heads touching at the plug, our fingers touching in a circle, softening ourselves, feeling the earth thread settling and falling back into tune, remembering her purpose.

"She is ours again," I said with a certainty informed by many lifetimes interwoven with this force. "We will let her rest a while until our work in this city is complete."

As we returned to the surface, Judith and I wove a web of magic and illusion and, layer by layer, the dome was hidden by earth. Under the cover of stillness, we stepped out of the hotel onto the dark streets. I wrapped my arms around Judith and Dorje. "We'll be back in our home again soon; I can feel it."

17

We returned to Marisa's rooms and waited, unable to sleep without knowing if the rest of our family was safe. Marisa had left a lot of things behind and Judith and I took what we needed, leaving our own clothes to be laundered. It was dawn before we had word, just a faint call from Juan.

"We've found the source, a well exactly as Kali described, cut deep into the rock under the hotel. We found a similar dome and a fissure but we cannot staunch the flow; we've tried all of our skills and powers. The best we can do is to hold the flow in check but it's costing us all the energy we have. Is there a plug Kali, perhaps like the one you described?"

I scoured my memory but found nothing. The plug I used before was the only one I was aware of and I didn't know this particular well, only the one we had just returned from. Judith suggested using her finger again and it was as good an option as any to begin with. Juan sent directions, leading us down into the basement of the hotel, through the kitchens and laundry rooms, into coal cellars long since abandoned and forgotten, until we reached the rim of the well. It too was lit by weak old light bulbs and it too was decorated by designs that followed the spiral of the stairs. Although we felt the need to hurry down, fearing for the wellbeing of our family, Judith insisted on taking time enough to understand this design. "I have to read it," she said. "I know it means something to me."

Juan agreed and Dorje and I guided her between us, let her set the pace even as we felt the weakness of the others and the vile sensations they had to bear to hold the earth thread in check. As before, Judith was the first of our three to succumb to the foulness and her legs began to weaken. We had to support her on the last of the journey down.

"Don't worry," she said, "I can bear it, now I understand the story. No matter what happens you must get me to the fissure. Even if I pass out, even if it seems I'm dead you must sit me on the dome, hold me there as long as it takes."

By the time we reached the dome, Judith was unconscious and Dorje and I had to drag her as best we could. The others couldn't help, they were exhausted and still working hard to placate the thread. They were seated around the edge of the dome, backs pressed against the wall, leaving space at the foot of the stairs for us to haul Judith into the centre. We did as she told us, arranged for her to sit on top of the fissure, held her up between us. Instantly the fury of the thread subsided and the rest of our family joined us to support Judith, to support the verticality of her spine and balance her head on her neck. She opened her eyes, conscious but soft, allowing us all to hold her tensions, to support the weight of her limbs, to give herself to our support in all directions.

Judith's body became liquid, bones floating like driftwood, muscles swaying like kelp, soft and languid. Her breath settled deeper, her body no longer breathing, just gently breathed, a soft wave through the fluids, effortless. We held together as one, Judith at our core, softening with her, breathed by her. The temperature in the well dropped as our effort became effortless. The well breathed for us all - fresh, cool air rising. And then warmth returned, colour returned, blood and lymph moving, filling our flesh, restoring tension and tone. Now Judith was supporting us, fuller and more vibrant than before, rising to her feet, bringing us with her, a sacred gathering on this polished granite dome.

Darkness was gone from the earth thread; its force now flowed loving and pure. It had found its true channel out into the world. As we followed Judith up the spiral stairway, she read to us her story carved into the walls of the well.

"Long ago, this land was made up of many small islands. They were covered in forest and separated by rivers and seas. The people who lived here were a simple people who left no recorded history to tell their origin. They lived in tribes in close kinship with the rest of nature.

"One day, a warm wind arrived on the islands. Such a thing had never been felt before. The wind brought with it new smells, new birds, new insects. Then the wind brought with it an enormous vessel, almost as big as a mountain, a vessel made of wood, filled with people and all kinds of creatures.

"The vessel was too big to touch the land. It rested a while at sea and some people came ashore on small rafts with leather sails - strange, tall people with white hair, white skin and the palest of blue eyes. When the vessel left, it sailed to the great land across the sea where it could still be seen hundreds of years later. The strangers introduced themselves as wind watchers, sent to this land by little creatures called the Vril. They knew this was the place because the Vril had told them to look for the white island. There were eight wind watchers, each of whom had a wife or two. The wives didn't look as strange as their husbands. They were accompanied by a whole village of children with looks that ranged from quite normal like their mothers to quite strange like their fathers.

“The openness and kindness of the locals made it easy for the wind watchers to settle down. They found people among the locals who could help them with their task, people with eyes that looked into other worlds and ears that heard languages beyond their own. The locals called them ‘the seers’.

“The seers learned the language of the wind watchers and when they discovered their mission, offered them their knowledge of the land and the waterways. The seers built coracles - large circular bowls made of woven willow wood and animal skins that offered shelter at night, protection from the sun and rain and a way to travel across the water.

“The seers made real what was carried by the wind watchers as a mysterious dream transmitted to them by the Vril. After many days travelling, they saw it in the distance as they paddled their coracles across the water, a great hill with a shape so soft and rounded and perfect, like a full moon rising, that it brought tears to all who gazed at it. ‘Nobody landed here before,’ the seers said. ‘The shape was so perfect that nobody wanted to disturb it.’

“When they touched land, the wind watchers already knew what they had to do. They set off with their coracles on their backs to reach the summit. The only route permitted according to instruction from the Vril and now, according to what they felt within their own bodies, was in a slow spiral that took until sunset to complete. By the light of the setting sun they all gathered on the summit, tired and tranquil from the journey, touched by a quality they did not understand. The sky darkened and the stars shone brighter and they felt a gentle breeze circling around them, first like the gaze of an eagle, then touching them with a caress like the love of a mother.

"As night fell and the world became silent, knowledge emerged from the hill, knowledge of the world and its creation, knowledge of the Vril and their origin, knowledge of this hill and its purpose, knowledge of a network of other such places the Vril had created within this land.

"When the sun rose the following morning, the entire group was changed, each according to the place from which they started. The wind watchers were still wind watchers but, overnight they had learned not only mastery of the sixteen earth winds but how to work with the sky winds.

"The wind watchers' wives, who already had remarkable skills in human healing, had learned mastery of the human winds as well as how to heal the wounds of the earth and all her creatures and creations.

"The seers were filled with knowledge and the need to share it. Some wanted to travel to lands beyond these little islands, lands that belonged to languages they already knew. Some wanted to stay, to build places where others could come and learn.

"The wind watchers asked the seers to wait, to make one more journey by water before deciding whether to stay or go. They pointed out across the lake, to another land, a land that resembled a creature with a long tail. Like the moon island on which they stood, the land they pointed to was not forested. It was green and lush with grasses and bushes. Rocky outcrops followed a line, like a spine. 'We call it the dragon land,' the seers told them. 'It's another land on which we never walked - not for its perfection like this one but for the story of the dragon. We have never seen a dragon but our elders told us of them as children, told us they lived on that island, told us never to step ashore.'

"'Let's visit the dragon,' the wind watchers said mischievously and, with great excitement, they carried their coracles to the shore and took to the water. The journey was almost effortless, their coracles drawn, as if by a thread, to the dragon land. They needed only to use their oars to steady themselves. The same excitement carried them up the hill, following the rocky spine of the tail. Once they were on the body of the dragon, invisible forces took control of their bodies, making them dance, making them follow a mysterious pathway hidden within the land. With each twist and turn of the path, new skills emerged in the tissues of their bodies: the skill of charcoal making, the skill of paper making, the skill of making pigments and paints, the skills of writing, of drawing, of painting and the skill of making tools for carving stone and wood.

"When they were almost at the summit, an invisible hand prevented the men from moving further and they sat where asked as the women continued to the top. The gaze of the men was averted as the women learned skills meant only for them. Although the women were asked to bring earth forces to the surface where they gathered, these were intended as their gift to the men. The women were then shown how to find their own rightful energies, from deeper within the earth, brought to the surface by water and the roots of certain plants and trees. When their initiation was complete, the women called the menfolk and taught each of them what they needed to know. To some they taught the skill of moving stones and to all they taught the skill of inner divination. 'Some of you will stay here and build a place for others to come and learn. These are the skills you will need,' they said.

"They all stayed a year on the hill, practicing their new-found skills. They called stones and rocks from the lakes and riverbeds and danced them up the hill, following the long winding path they had been taught when they first arrived.

"They built a long, tall stone-house the likes of which had never been seen before. They built a stone tower for the women, which they used on certain nights to listen to the sounds of the stars. They planted gardens with plants they called to the hill in the same way in which they called the stones. They made papers and pigments and recorded what they knew and what they felt they needed to share. At the end of the year, the women heard a sound from the stars that told them it was time for change.

"On their last day together, each was asked to choose their path. For the wind watchers and their wives, it was time to go, their journey was not yet complete. Some of the seers wanted to travel more with the wind watchers. Some wanted to remain and continue to build the place of sharing. Some wanted to take their new knowledge to their families and invite them to visit the sharing place. The children were free to make their own choice. Some of the older ones chose to stay. The difficulty of letting go of a child is made easier when what calls them away brings them more joy than the habit of remaining.

"The wind watchers continued to travel like this for seven more years and inaugurated eight places of sharing. At the end of the eighth year, it was time for the wind watchers to stay and the women to go. 'We need a year to ourselves,' the women said and their men knew it was true. The sound from the stars told the women more of their own secret work, of the forces they would need to bring to the surface.

"It was a large group that set off that morning, wind watchers' wives, seer women and children of every age. They prepared their coracles on the shore before the sun rose and outshone the stars that still indicated the direction of their journey. Rowan, one of the seers, revealed that she carried with her a guiding stone.

"'It was given to me by my grandmother when I turned fourteen,' she said. 'Grandmother was told the stone was not for her but for a granddaughter yet to be born. Grandmother said a crow brought the stone and the same crow told her to wait for me. She was just a child and had to wait forty-two summers for that moment to come.'

"Rowan brought the stone out from the folds of her bodice. 'I always carried it next to my heart as my grandmother had done before me.' She held it out on the palm of her hand, a small, black oval-shaped stone, patinated with years of body heat and oil. At one end, a small white circle shone out from the black.

"'Watch!' she said as she scoured the shoreline with her gaze. She picked a flat rock, brought it to where we waited, laid it down and asked as to gather round, little ones in front. Then she put the stone down on the rock and we watched in fascination as it swivelled from where she put it to the position it preferred. She repeated this, many times, and each time the stone returned to its desire place. 'My grandmother said when the time was right to follow the circle.' And that is what we did, setting off in our coracles in the direction indicated by the little white circle, Rowan and the pointing stone leading the way. She had put the flat rock in her coracle and from time to time she raised her hand and we stopped paddling. She waited until the movement of the coracles settled and then we waited until she checked the direction again before moving on.

"At night we tied the coracles together like a crown and slept adrift, trusting the water to take care of us. In the morning, Rowan checked again before we continued. Our long journey led us at last to land, to a place where a small river joined the great lake. The stone told us to continue by water and we paddled upstream in a line behind Rowan. Better this way as either side was dense forest that would have been impossible to walk.

"The further we went, the wider and wilder became the river. We stayed close to the bank to avoid dangerous waves and currents that could swallow us up. Finally, the stone pointed to the shore and we stepped onto land again, unsteady from so many days moving like water. Once we were able to walk straight, our journey continued, following a badger path through the woodland. An hour's walk led us to a place from which the pointing stone no longer wanted to move, no longer felt the need to point. The seer balanced the stone on its circle end. 'This is the place,' she said. 'My grandmother told me how to find it but not what to do when I got here.'

"'Don't worry,' said one of the wind watcher's wives. 'We didn't know how to find this place but we do know what to do.'

"The wives found sticks and scraped the earth away from around the pointing stone. They didn't dig deep before they uncovered something solid. The children and seers joined in, scraping the loosened earth away with their hands until they revealed an enormous black dome, at the centre of which stood the pointing stone. They organised a chain to carry water from the river in their coracles and they washed the dome clean of dirt until it shone, like a reflection of the moon on the darkest of nights. All but one stood in a circle around the dome. The one who remained carefully removed the pointing stone from where it stood in the centre.

"She used a crow feather to dust away the last of the earth and a damp cloth to clean. She revealed a small fissure in the rock. A light breeze trembled the trees and bushes around us. She stood and addressed the curious crowd. 'This is the first of two. Let's go and find the other.' She handed the pointing stone back to Rowan who set it down on the flat stone and let it show the way.

“Now they saw what they had not noticed before, another badger path leading in a clear, straight line through the trees and bushes. The stone led them through a circular clearing where they all wanted to rest awhile to enjoy the quality of the light and the sense of peace they experienced there. But the stone had other plans and now pulled hard on Rowan’s hand. They continued until it found the place and they all repeated the process to uncover and clean a second shining dome. Once the fissure was open, the wind watchers’ wives gathered together. One addressed the rest. ‘We do not yet understand what it is we are asked to do but we trust the little creatures that gave us the instructions. They taught our men how to make the wind and they sent us on this journey to find a new land when our own land was no longer able to feed us. They spoke with our men through their tunnels but they spoke to us women in our dreams. Everything we dreamed has come about and we can already see what their instructions have done for us. They have brought us new friends, new knowledge, new ways to live, new ways to make our homes and grow our food, a wish to explore, a wish to share. Now, according to our dreams, we expect three children to come forward. We do not know who they are but we trust they know.’

“And three children did indeed step forward, two girls and boy - seer children from three different families but inseparable from the moment they found each other as infants. Already they knew what they were born to do and they led the group into the clearing and asked them to sit. Mushrooms broke through the soil in a circle around them. The circles extended outwards in both directions along the badger paths towards the domes. While the boy remained, the girls followed the mushroom paths to their allocated dome, each standing in the centre above the fissure. The mushrooms continued to grow until their swollen caps burst, releasing waves of fine spores into the air, highlighting three columns of light that now poured from the sky and enveloped the children.

"We could see that they were listening but we could hear nothing but a low drone that seemed to come from the sky. The sound touched the land, danced the stones, vibrated the earth, shook the mushrooms, released more spores into the columns of light. The girls raised their arms, one palm towards the earth and the other towards the sky. The boy crossed his forearms over his chest and bowed his head. The girls began to turn. The ground around the edge of the clearing loosened and opened. As they turned, the girls sank beneath the earth. We sat, unable to move, and we watched and we waited for the best part of a day until at last, a process was complete.

"When we could move again we all stood, hurried to look for the girls, peered deep into the holes into which they had disappeared, called and waited for the echo to subside. And the calls received replies. 'We're okay,' they said. 'We're coming up,' they said. 'It's a long way up,' they said, 'so build a fire and prepare to dance.'"

18

Dorje took Judith and me by the hand. "Was that us; were we already a three back then? Was that the first time we came together?"

The conversation I had been dreading had arrived. "No, not us. Judith and me yes, but not you. We were another three back then."

I took a breath, prayed I could find the way to say it well, prayed that Dorje knew enough to hear it well. "We were the first three that walked the earth. We didn't know, until the moment we were called out as children by the wives of the wind watchers. We didn't know how different we were, just that we were drawn to each other from the moment we could crawl. We grew up as a three and our families did nothing to interfere with the bond that held us together. You weren't born yet."

"Who was the third?"

"It was Christopher."

We all needed the silence that followed to come to terms with that truth - even me, the only one who knew the whole of it. Thankfully, enough had passed between us for us to swallow the truth without gagging. I addressed the rest to Dorje even if it affected everyone else.

"I had many lives with Christopher, some when you were nowhere to be found and some when you were there as well.

"The more you were there, the more unstable he became. It was impossible to know if your presence affected Christopher, or if your presence balanced out a change that was already happening within him. I met him again in London before I knew where you were. He came into the shop wanting to buy a bell. He was specific and precise when he described it, a unique altar bell entrusted to me by the old lama and hidden upstairs in the dressing room. His request unsettled me and I could not lie to him freely. He laughed and played with me and made me feel at ease. He told me not to worry, just to bear him in mind if ever a bell like that came my way. When he left, he left me with a longing to see him again.

"The next time I saw him I now know it was contrived. A supposedly chance encounter in the street but one that he, not I, was well prepared for. He knew too much of my story, too much of Rafa's story, too much about Christina and her father. I wanted to run, to call for the old lama, but I couldn't get away and the more time he kept me there the more at ease I felt. Over coffee, he held my hands and read the nuances in the pulses beating at my wrists. He revealed our past and predicted my future, invited me to his home to learn the answers to questions he had awoken within me. Once more, he left me with a longing to see him again.

"At night the lama came to talk with me, told me I had time to spare and I should use it to find out what I could. The lama didn't know whose side Christopher was on but he knew he was important; how else could he have known about the bell? He assured me that Christopher had no idea of my training but I was not so sure. The next time we met he left me confused. He talked of our previous lives together, as friends, as allies, as lovers.

"But the truth is Dorje, he was not describing my lives with him but the lives I lived with you. The strange thing is, the more he lied the more the truth revealed itself and the more I saw the truth, the better I could lie. By the time I knew he was one of the first three with Judith and me, I knew he was not to be trusted and I hid that knowledge from him. By then he was convinced that I was his dakini - his 'sky dancer,' as he called me, and I used that obsession to get what I needed.

"Thanks to the time I spent with him, Dorje, I remembered you. I remembered how you saved me from myself in London, remembered our agreement to meet again in this life, remembered the son we had agreed to bring through. Like you, I went to him pretending to learn, but actually I taught him what I needed him to do. I became his consort and I brought Marianne to him and told him she was our third. I convinced him that the new knowledge coming into his life was due to the completion of our three. By the time we left to find the phurba in Tunisia, I knew I would also find you there. I also knew the danger that lay ahead for me and realised the possibility that you and I would not have time to bring the boy through. That's why I had to leave Marianne to complete the process."

"So the boy is born of Marianne and me, not you and me?" Dorje asked, trying to make sense of the mess I was describing.

"Her womb, my seed, our love," I replied and quickly returned to telling my story before Dorje could drown in too many questions.

"I brought some special knowledge with me. I taught Christopher to do what I needed and I taught him what he had to do with you.

"The most important part was not the seed from my body that Marianne nurtured within her womb, but the energy thread that allowed the boy to find his way, to tether him to Marianne and you. I couldn't risk losing him and I couldn't bear the thought that he might be born lost, like you and me. The only thing I didn't take account of was you. You were a hard man to seduce, Dorje. Poor Marianne had her work cut out. In the end she had to drug you to get you to comply."

"Ah! I always wondered about that. The night by the river?"

"Poor Dorje, what I put you through. But I was there with you, there to help you through the night."

"The deer?"

"Yes, the deer. I love you Dorje. Sorry it could not have been more simple."

I embraced him, kissed the tears from his cheeks. "So, our family is getting bigger all the time."

"Christopher included?"

"Not really - although we do need him a little longer. He was one of the first three and it's no accident that we are all back together again. We need him to complete something before we can leave this city."

19

We had to make our way back to the river. The badgers were long gone but feral cats and city foxes still marked the path wherever they could. Buildings and roads often cut the way, but our memory ran deep and, with the combined skills and treasures of our family, it was little surprise when we found ourselves at the riverside, facing a stupa on the other bank. I teared up as I remembered when Dorje took me there, brought a moment of brightness to my dull spirit and our sad and confusing relationship that, even then, I knew was pulling him apart.

Dorje reached out to take my hand, nothing to say. Those days were past and here we were again by this river that had seen so many precious moments in our story. I reached out and took Judith's hand and, once again, a memory of our three came back. Across the river a familiar figure emerged from behind the stupa. We ran across the bridge to meet the old lama, embraced him in that special way reserved only for permanents. Now we could see how this stupa had been built, waiting for a day like this.

Christopher sat on a ledge beneath one of the golden figures, gazing out towards the river, happy and contrite. He didn't belong with us but we needed him for now and it wouldn't cost us much. He had lost everything that came with Marisa's family and he was happy about that. "Too much pressure," he said, "and her father scared the shit out of me."

We all sympathised with him and it made me smile to see him again at his most vulnerable. How many journeys had I taken with this man and now, despite all that had happened, I still loved him!

"I am finished playing with greed," he said. "I just want a little love, a little kindness, just enough to get me through this life. I only hope I can learn enough, can remember enough, to live it better next time round."

From the handful of jewels Robert held out I took two, one to help us in our work and one for Christopher to keep. The deal was simple; first Christopher would help us and then I would pay him his fee. The only power he wanted back from those that Robert had taken was the one that would bring a woman's love, an emerald green stone that would ensure he would attract a remarkable woman who would pay his way and help him on his path.

The old lama opened the space beneath the stupa and Dorje took his place. We would depend on him to coordinate our work. The thin layer of gold leaf on the figure above him was not simply some decorative pretension but, rather, a way to connect to the earth streams through which we would communicate once we were deep in the ground.

Judith and I took Christopher to his place. In his hand he held the other jewel, the one he had carried many times before, the jewel that reminded him of his origin, of his real duty on the earth. When I opened the garage door, I was happy to see my old Mercedes waiting, brought back from Barcelona where Dorje left her long ago. The car had been cleaned and polished and sat there ready to go. She was accompanied by two others, same year and model but maroon rather than black.

I prised open the panel that led us into the space beneath the cars and Christopher set off down the stairs to his place in what was once, long ago, a clearing in a forest. Judith and I went to our respective hotels, to return to the wells hidden deep beneath them. Dorje remained at the stupa, holding the thread of communication between us all as the old lama and the others summoned up stillness and secrecy, spreading it across the city through a wave of fine fungus spores.

Deep beneath my hotel I dashed down the stone staircase into the well, exhilarated that this moment had come once more. I read the story as I ran, read a story I had read so many times before, read the story that I wrote so many lives ago. When I reached the dome, I removed the brass and amber plug that held the thread in check and took my place above the fissure. I opened myself, softening the channels through my body, expanding the space between organs, muscles and bones, until my body became looser, more liquid, with just enough tension to keep me from collapse but no more resistance than that.

I felt the earth thread rise through me. I raised my arms, turning one palm up and one palm down, tilted my head, turning one ear down and one ear up. I heard a drone like sound, something between the beating wings of a wood wasp and deep tectonic growl. I felt the sky thread seeking its way down through me, the meeting and mingling of the threads, an exchange that required nothing more of me than to let go and to witness. I accepted to do my duty without understanding its true purpose, as I had done many times before.

As the blending of forces strengthened, I felt my human fears arise, the fear that the forces would be too strong for me this time, that my body would be too frail, that I would disintegrate and the process would be left incomplete.

I remembered the words that were written on the last section of the journey down.

'Don't worry. Let your fears come to the surface. Become aware of your body's wish to run. Feel the way in which your muscles engage, the way your attention streams away, searching for safety in familiar faces, familiar places. Feel the wish to go back to them, to abandon this duty. Notice the fear that you might never see them again, that this will be the ultimate sacrifice. Carefully, softly, draw your attention back, away from those thoughts and images, to the sense of your body sitting here. Become aware of the forces running through you, sensations of heat or cold, a sense of pressure on your muscles, the pulse of your blood, the winding and unwinding of your heart, the blood shimmying through your arteries and veins. Let your attention rest softly on your breathing, simply observing the way your body is breathed, inhaling, exhaling, without any effort.

'With that same softness let your attention seek a spacious place within, a place between bones and muscles, between muscle and muscle, a place where fluids flow, where heat flows, a place where awareness and attention can flow. Allow that spaciousness to expand, beyond the boundary of your body, now aware that you are more space than matter and that your space connects with all space. You are not alone.'

20

The city slept and the city dreamed - all that is but the foxes who remained alert as always, sniffing the air for any sign of devolver activity. The city shared a dream that night, a dream from which all would awaken a little softer and slower and kinder.

All along the sacred paths, sickness spread like a virus. The walkers felt their hunger, felt the weight of their bellies, filled with desires but devoid of satisfaction. They felt the need to purge, abandoned their bags, their shoes, their books, the hollow teachings that now caught in their throats like dry crumbs.

They broke their malas and rosaries, letting the beads tumble into the earth. Their tears poured silent, without a sob, into the soil. Within the mud, fine liquid threads revived, connecting with the threads we had opened on our journey north from the High Atlas Mountains.

After the purge came purification and through the naked soles of their feet, they felt the fluid flow beneath the earth, felt the fluid flow through the fine capillaries of their bodies, through the bodies of their companions on the path, clearing away tensions, patterns, postures, the automaticity of their life.

Now their eyes could see space, their ears could hear silence, their bodies could feel the continuity between all things, all beings, all times. Now they could taste the truth. Now they could smell the fake. Now none of them had anything left to teach, none of them had any more need to learn.

They felt us where we stood by the stupa on the riverside, where we stood on the black domes buried deep beneath the bedrock of the city. Their wishes became real, no longer some idle thought but a real desire that had form enough to reach out to where we stood. They called on the forces that now found their way to the surface through the bodies of we three, gathered and condensed by Dorje, available to all who knew how to ask.

As the city dreamed and the people on the path were taught to watch, the lights shimmered through clouds of spores and one of the great paths became active again. Now the people on the path were free. Free from the need to take and free from the need to give. Quietness settled as the truth of the path revealed itself.

The people on the path turned, suddenly aware of the folly of their ways, now aware that there was no right direction, no destination, not even a need to walk, that anywhere on the path was as good as anywhere else and the challenge they had been led to seek was no more than a sweet, sweet lullaby rocking them to sleep.

As they felt the real purpose of the path and deepened into the silence it offered, they saw the trickery that had been laid along the way - the false destinations, the false goals and false suffering, the promise of rewards, now clearly visible as no more than trinkets and tat.

Now they sat where they were, no place more precious than any other, no view more worthy, no moment more significant. Now they were aware that their bodies served more purpose than to carry their thoughts around from place to place. They felt an exchange. They felt the nourishment of impressions, pouring in through all their senses as they relaxed deeper into awareness.

They felt the excitement of their responses - the feelings and emotions, the impulses and urges to move, the constant flow of things to think and things to say. As their sitting became quieter and more still, they felt another quality, a third force holding the other two in balance and now, as they found a place within, neither lost in impressions nor lost in activity, they felt how that third force connected them to all things, all times.

21

Nobody could say how many people sat that night along the paths as Judith, and I retuned the great wells but, as dawn touched the towns and cities through which we had travelled on our journey north, there was a great awakening. Not something spectacular, but a fine shift that would pass almost unnoticed by most.

All along the paths, in ancient squares and historic cafés the waiters awoke. For some it had been a whole lifetime of waiting, for others just the beginning as they took over the role from their elders. As with the square outside our window in Paris, the waiters now felt the sacred design beneath their feet and the precious knowledge they had learned through the gestures of their families. The call to attention with each short journey from table to bar. The precision of their movements. The fine, alive balance required to carry the tray - an oasis of stillness in action. Outwardly little had changed but, for the regulars in these establishments, enough had changed to bear comment - perhaps a reference to the spring in their step, a softening of their expression, a sense of peace that seemed to emanate from within.

As the spore cloud settled over the city and the world awakened from stillness and sleep. we gathered together again by the riverside near the stupa. The lama confirmed what we already felt; the city was ours again and the devolvers had nothing with which to oppose us.

"They will try again," he said, "but now we have many things in our favour.

"These ancient wells are restored and the channels through the mountains are open. For now, you have a safe place in this city and a safe route to follow when you have to go. As with so many of the great and sacred wells given to humanity, there was no longer one place to gather, no possibility to contain or manipulate them. Now those forces will find their way to the surface through a multitude of threads that require no more than a moment to stop and remember. Take your time to put your human lives in order, the time to leave will come for you soon enough."

All along the paths the walkers were heading home. All felt called by the preciousness of their loved ones: their parents and children, their families and friends, their neighbours and the creatures that shared their patch. Within them they carried a sense of the deep inner stream that flowed through them, through everything. They would resume their ordinary lives without the need for anything more, barely even aware of the difference they made on the lives of all whose paths they crossed.

The waiters would continue their work. They came from old families and their history was now beginning to make sense - the odd stories told to them by their grandparents as their parents walked from bar to table, from table to bar, where often as children, they went to eat a pastry before school or a fruit sorbet on a summer's afternoon. It was there they learned the rhythm of the walk, a little slower than everyone else, with a little more awareness of what flowed beneath their feet. It was there they developed a memory that never forgot an order, never forgot a face.

It was there that they learned to divide their attention, with one stream focused on the order, never missing a table to wipe, the smallest gesture calling for the bill, a newcomer acknowledged and put at ease with the subtlest of nods.

The other stream of that attention was not theirs; it simply found its way through them from a higher source.

For us, it was time to go home, to join Marianne and the boy.

22

The apartment was still so familiar even if its atmosphere now betrayed the presence of a strong young man. Marianne was as beautiful and self-effacing as ever and had prepared our room for us when she first knew we were coming home. The boy remained in his room as we drank mint tea with her in the kitchen.

"He said he needed a little more time to prepare," she said. It wasn't hard to appreciate that. Marianne said there had been no secrets. "He is clever. There was no point in hiding the truth from him. You'll see what I mean."

My heart swelled with the love I felt for Marianne, for her purity and simplicity. She was like a fountain of goodness in my life, there as a sister when the old lama first brought me to London, taking care of Rafa and Christina and me with such kindness, holding our home together when we travelled, stepping into the shadows when I returned with Dorje, and loving him on my behalf when I had to leave.

It was not until the evening that we met the boy. The whole of our family was gathered in the sitting room, sitting silently after tea. He came and joined our circle, squeezed his way in between Dorje and me. We all immediately felt his force, felt a surge within the group. He betrayed no sense of the special quality he had, simply sat there nodding to each member of our family in turn.

Then he took our hands, Dorje's and mine, and spoke.

"At last I meet my parents and have the possibility to thank you for everything you did to bring me here, for all the sacrifices you made to keep me safe and for the struggle it must have taken to come back, to finally let me meet you. Thank you for leaving me in the care of Marianne. She is a jewel and words cannot express how much gratitude I feel. Not only did she care for me with such kindness, she reminded me every day of my parents, never sought to take your place but nurtured the love I so naturally felt for you both. I already knew exactly how you would be, long before this moment when I finally meet you."

We sat in silence. I don't know what I expected - not that. Perhaps I thought he would be a child, in need of a laugh and a cuddle. Yet here he was, this extraordinary young man, bright and clear and pure. In the end I could do no more than laugh, rise to my feet, draw him up and hug him with the love that saturated my entire being.

The boy continued to amaze us as he moved around the circle, from me to his father and then to each of the others. With each new member of his family, he gazed into their eyes until the tears flowed and they gave themselves to his embrace. With each embrace I could feel him learn the skills and knowledge of each one of us, until he embodied us all. When the circle was complete, he made a request. "I'm sure we're all starving but can I ask just one thing?"

We nodded our agreement. He turned to Marianne and asked, "Can the food wait another ten minutes?" Her smile said yes and suddenly the boy was a gleeful youngster. "Can we dance the wind horse please?"

None could resist his excitement and we moved the zafus back and danced, beginning with the simple circle with which our three always began, but soon adding a little something extra from each member of our family in turn: a nod of the head, a flick of the wrist, a side-bend, nostrils flared, eyes up, a spin, an internal counter-turn. With each new gesture, our pace slowed down until the turn touched Rafiq. He crossed his arms at his chest and lowered his head. The air thickened and the room became more porous. As Rafiq held a still point, the boy led us into a run beyond the sitting room, beyond the apartment, into the streets of London.

We ran as a tribe through the streets, our dogs running with us, our eagles soaring above, all sharing the joy. We dashed through the city and could now feel the delicate change effected by our work - a softening in the people, a slowing in their pace, a little more kindness in their gestures and words. We could also feel the change in our family, the way we all stepped back and let the boy lead the run, the sense of ease we felt to have him show the way, as if we had all been waiting for this moment to follow our true leader. The boy brought a freshness and naivety to our run, allowed us to see the city as we'd never seen her before, sparkling under our gaze, long hidden treasures suddenly catching the dusky light or glistening with the evening dew. A gargoyle that once looked grotesque and scolding now called us to look deeper into ourselves with a mischievous grin and a glint in its eye. A copper curlicue on a drainpipe seemed suddenly to have emerged from the shadows and revealed itself as an ancient and secret sign.

As our circle extended as a spiral out to the edge of the city, we learned to read those signs, to understand the knowledge woven into the fabric of the city by our elders, to see the way the buildings were organised to reduce the wind to subtle breezes that carried knowledge and news from afar. We also saw the devolver influences, the buildings built to irritate the wind, to create disturbances that distracted people from their purpose, to make them forget what lay just beneath their feet.

Now we knew our work here was complete. The wells were working as intended and the force of their goodness now protected the city from the devolvers. Beyond the city there would inevitably be opposition but, for now, the city could dance more freely.

The boy led us back into the apartment just as Marianne finished laying out the feast. Barely ten minutes had passed but as we sat to eat, we could all feel that everything was now different, both in the outer world and in our inner worlds. For me, a new awareness emerged and I let that awareness settle on each member of our family in turn as we gathered around that abundant table. At last, my gaze settled on Marianne where she sat at the head of the table, as always closest to the kitchen door, as always poised to check on something cooking on the stove.

For Marianne, the process of cooking didn't end with the meal on the table. She once told me that her cooking continued regardless of what else she was doing. She sourced ingredients on her walks, perhaps from a shop she was lured to by the smell of a particular spice just arrived from a distant land, perhaps fresh herbs grazed from a garden or one of the many wild meadows she had hidden in the city parks. She imagined flavours and combinations of flavours as she danced, and she remembered every jar pickling or fermenting in the kitchen, knew the exact moment they were ripe to eat. Marianne had been so many things for me: a sister, a childhood friend, my confidante, a shoulder to cry on, my lover, my lover's lover, the mother of my son.

Now I saw her afresh, no longer though the eyes of all the needs she had satisfied for me but for who she was, this remarkable and powerful woman, hidden by a cloak of humility and service, holding the stillness that allowed us all to fulfil our roles.

For a moment I saw her as I had seen her once before, her hair unplaited, right arm raised, holding a golden sword to the sky, holding a point around which the world could spin into chaos, a point around which the world could be called back to order.

The feast and celebrations lasted until the early hours and Marianne filled me with her wonderful food and the wellspring of love I felt in her presence. Our week together passed too soon. The boy had already warned us that we would need to move and we used much of that week to prepare, to load the cars with things we would need for the journey.

In the dressing room I found Dorje searching through the watch collection. He convinced us all to choose one. He was right, they could still be used to grease a palm along the way.

23

We set off early, before the sunrise called the workers to the city, before the commuters realised that this was not just any other day. We had checked the cars the night before and planned the route. Each car carried a stillness worker. Rafiq came with us. He and the boy had become inseparable since the night of the run. Marianne had prepared supplies for the journey: fresh bread, preserves, pickles and ferments, flasks of coffee and a couple of bottles of calvados made by her grandfather. "Call me when the time is right," she said, "and I'll join you all wherever you are."

The journey south unfolded as a limitless love affair. My love for the boy grew hour by hour as I listened to him chat with the others in the car or when we stopped to picnic. There was an amazing wisdom in his observations and words. Not the wisdom we might expect from a tulku, carrying the knowledge of many lives, but that of a young man who watched and listened and felt from a neutral place and responded from a place of love, unburdened by history. As my love for him grew, so too did my love for the woman who carried him and nurtured him and let him be, the woman whose presence I now felt more and more. In any moment I could close my eyes and see her there in the kitchen, with her baskets of fresh vegetables and bundles of herbs hanging to dry. Other times I could see her alone in the sitting room. But now I understood that Marianne was never alone. A great family populated her inner world and she never forgot any of us, not even for a moment. She shopped and cooked and cleaned, ready for any of us to knock at the door. In this life she didn't need a sword to hold the stillness.

The boy constantly reciprocated my love for him. Whenever he felt my gaze, no matter how fine and glancing, he would bathe me with his sweet attention. Although he loved his parents as much as we could possibly want, another love was growing, between the boy and Rafiq. Rafiq had never been one for idle chat but in the company of his new companion he was unstoppable. Somehow, he was capable of meeting the boy on any subject he cared to discuss. When we stopped driving their conversation became silent, words and sounds replaced by movement. They took time apart from the rest of us and I was fascinated to watch Rafiq teach the boy his ways. I had seen Rafiq at work so many times but now, watching him teach the boy, I realised there was a whole encyclopaedia of nuances in his movements and gestures. I could understand very little but I could clearly see the joy and passion the boy brought to his learning.

When we were able, Dorje, Judith and I tried to make sense of what we saw, of the obvious fact that Rafiq had more to teach him than did we. Was he a stillness worker rather than the treasure seeker we had been expecting? Not far into France the boy answered some of that question himself. We were following a familiar road, one that had brought us north not so long ago, when the boy leaned forward and whispered in my ear, "Mama, would you mind taking the next right, there's something we need to do."

Without hesitation I followed his directions to the sea, to a beach that now, in the dark, became known, the beach where Dorje and I waded out to a waiting boat so long ago. While we three paddled by the water's edge and the others drank coffee and watched from the dunes, Rafiq and the boy began to dance on the sand. It was a fascinating dance, a conversation the likes of which none of us had ever seen before.

As Rafiq squatted on the sand looking out towards the sea the boy started circling him, eyes closed and left ear turned to the earth, arms raised to chest height, thumbs and forefingers tapping a rhythm. There was nothing regular in the rhythm, nothing regular in his walk. He seemed to be feeling his way, searching. Something caught his attention and he set off along the beach. Rafiq remained squatting until the boy called him. He leapt to his feet and ran to stand by the boy's side amongst the dunes and beach grass. Hawa and Mariam brought tools from the car and helped them dig away the sand.

The rest of us felt the need to hold the beach safe while they dug, we three at the sea and the others by the road. We were not disturbed and we all ran to look as Rafiq and the boy dragged a wooden case to the beach and cracked it open with a wheel-brace. Out rolled a vase I had not seen since the night Marisa left me dying on my bed in Maria's house. It was the dark vase, the last one Dorje found, carved by Ennio and hidden by him beneath his studio.

"Marianne told me where to find it," the boy volunteered.

It had lost none of its special quality and we all gazed, captivated by its darkness, not even noticing as the boy raised the wheel brace above his head, not until he crashed it down, shattering the marble, destroying the magic of its form, releasing a light contained within.

"Phew!" the boy exhaled. "I'm glad she was right. I'm glad we don't have to look for another one."

"What do you mean?" Asked Dorje.

"Marianne wasn't sure if it was the eighth vase or the ninth. It seems it was the ninth."

"I don't understand," Dorje continued.

"Marianne told me about the vases, about the work you and Mama did to find them and bring them to London. Marianne's task was to deliver them. She brought this one here."

"And she told you where to find it?"

"More or less," the boy replied, "although she couldn't say exactly where. Her only involvement was to bring it to this beach. Thankfully, I inherited some skills from my parents."

"But what now?" Dorje asked. "What about the vases? What about the network?"

"Their job is done," the boy said as he bent down, picked a shining object from the rubble, held in it his fist. "Now all that matters is this." And before we could see what it was he integrated the brightness into his web.

"Come," he said, "time to get moving."

24

We continued our journey, travelling back roads and lanes, taking our turn to drive, taking our turn to sleep, stopping only when Remi asked, always near to some sacred place or object. "Just a little tune up," she would say before applying her skills, which became subtler the more she used them.

I expected to return the way we came, travelling south through Spain to the sea and then taking a boat to Africa. A stop just outside a small village put pay to that idea. Remi led us along the riverbank to an ancient church built into the rock, showed us a corner that marked a junction.

"Two great paths meet here," she said. "One leads to Rome and one to Jerusalem. The path to Jerusalem is closed. You can still go there but it's meaningless without the walk, it just leaves people confused. The devolvers have created so much agitation around the well that nobody can feel the truth there anymore. The stretch of path we opened from our mountain home is all that matters now. Jerusalem is fading."

Remi led us from the corner, along a cliffside marked by cavities and ledges carved long ago into the rock. I felt the tug of the web beneath my feet. "As you can feel, the path to Rome is still open but the destination is no longer important. The devolvers built a citadel to contain the well but they could not staunch its flow. There are many places along the path where the threads reach up to touch the sensitive soul.

"There is another path that matters to us now - the path to the valley of the scholars, but we cannot afford to take the fast route as we did last time in our search for Kali."

The boy interrupted. "Remi is right, you cannot travel like light this time, there are things to complete along the way. First, we have to go to our home in Italy. There is something there I must find."

For a moment I was awash with emotion, so many memories invoked with that one short sentence, memories of Marisa and her father attacking me, the violence on the road which took us to the brink of death, Dorje's awakening and the experience of the extraordinary power that flowed through him. The boy called me back from my reverie. "Mama, it's fine if you want to wait, I'm happy to go alone."

We all protested as one. We wanted to go back to the place that marked an awakening for us all.

25

With great caution, we approached Ennio and Maria's house following Peppi's secret way, the stillness workers and the boy walking ahead of the cars, feeling into the distance. The place remained broken and abandoned, doors and shutters left open, windows shattered, weeds growing where once were beds of vegetables and herbs. It was strange that it remained like this, that nobody had returned to repair the damage. But I guess after Marisa and her father discovered what had been going under their noses it must have been impossible to use it again for our work. I couldn't imagine what the boy could possibly find in the wreckage. Surely they must have searched it thoroughly?

Dorje and I wanted to show Judith around. We left the boy dancing with the stillness workers and took her on a tour, to the room where Dorje brought the nine vases together, to the tree where Dorje found the ring hidden for him by the old lama, to the kitchen where Maria worked magic with food and fire, to the studio where Ennio worked magic with iron and stone and where Robert worked his magic with us all. Although the rest of the property had lost its charm, the studio affected me just as it always did. When I first went there, I was told that the walls were imprinted with Ennio's presence, carrying a memory of his skill and attention. Later, I felt that Robert's work added to the effect, touching all who entered there. When Dorje discovered the vases embedded above and below the studio I realised that their presence must have had a profound effect on the space. But now, so many years later, so many years since we left with the vases, since Robert tuned us all, since Ennio produced his work, the feeling remained.

"Do you feel it too?" I asked the others. They nodded. We fell into silence, listening to the sound of the room, the stillness of the air, feeling the stillness it brought to our bodies after so many days on the road. The quietness extended outwards, beyond the studio to the farm, to the land around the farm, across the valley and onwards towards the sea.

Now there was no longer the sound of birdsong, no more rustling of leaves in the breeze, no voices from our family, no sound of farm machinery harvesting in the distance. Now the silence became unsettling and, as one we moved towards the door, looking out with caution as we realised the silence was wrong and there was danger. What we saw took many slow breaths for us to fathom - a standoff between our family on one side of the field and Marisa, her father and their mob on the other. Between them stood the boy. Nobody moved. All were held in stillness, all including our stillness workers, their intentions and gestures frozen in time.

But who was holding the stillness, and why was it that we were untouched when it quite clearly extended far into the distance? The answer came soon enough as the boy turned in our direction and the rest of the players remained frozen. I couldn't help myself, had to show myself, had to call out to him. "Are you okay my love?"

"Yes Mama, I'm fine, don't worry for me."

I walked out to the place where the boy was now facing Marisa, in this field where she seduced the boy's father away and tried to kill me. I felt my rage, at her brazenness, daring even to look at my son after what she did to his parents. I called upon all the forces available to me, from earth and sky. I could feel how our journey to this place had prepared me for this moment.

But as I stepped between Marisa and the boy, I found myself caught up in the web of stillness, unable to resist, unable to protest.

My attention was drawn away from my frozen inner state, away from the frozen dance in which our two families found themselves, far away from the farm, to a monastery perched on an austere mountainside, to a stone tower where I lay on my belly, spying on the terrace below. Two brothers, one my lover, were locked in a fight. Inside the monastery the sangha was gathered, preparing for the passing of the abbot. A great moment was stalled, a moment the abbot had prepared for over many lives, a moment the discipline master, whose fingers now played nervously with the double dorje, had prepared for over many lives.

I wanted to shout at the brothers, to stop the fight, to remind them of their duty, to remind them of all the people who depended on them to do what they had spent their entire lives preparing for. But I was torn between my love for the sangha and my love for one man. When I saw Christopher about to strike Dorje down with his staff, the man won. I threw a coin to distract their attention. But in the same moment I was distracted by a sound, like the call of a bird.

As chaos unfolded in the courtyard of the monastery, I ran to my hiding place in the mountains and watched as the discipline master lashed out with his whip and his tongue, demanding answers from the confused and fearful members of the sangha.

Dorje and Judith joined me in my secret place and, as the discipline master continued his interrogations, we danced - hands, hearts and heads raised to the sky, slowly turning.

Beyond the shingles of the monastery roof, on a mountaintop in the distance, I could see another three were dancing, hands, hearts and heads lowered. One of them raised her hands to her mouth and called, a high pitched, wavering call like that of a red kite and now, I could see it was Marisa.

Back in Maria's field I found myself face to face with Marisa, both of us freed from the stillness, Marisa without her power, both of us without our family.

"Do you understand now Kali? Your love for one man doomed everybody else. We were moments away from the great awakening and you ruined it. All these lives later you were given a second chance and you ruined it again, dragging Dorje and your family of fools halfway across the planet just to save you. Why did you betray us Kali?"

"What do you mean 'betray'?" I asked, far from understanding what Marisa was talking about. "I was never with you; how could I betray you?"

"You keep on refusing to see, and that is why you're here. That's why you keep coming back here. It was Dorje who was with us, not you. You were just his lover, nothing more. If you'd let him do his work, humanity would have been free and it would have ended there. Just look at what's become of him, tail tucked between his legs, scared to death that he might have to fight, that you'll ask him to kill again. When he was with me he was beautiful. Even without his power, he was beautiful. Now he's shabby, wearing other people's clothes. The only thing he has of value is a Rolex and even that doesn't belong to him. If you loved him you would set him free. With me he would be magnificent. With his power and my love, we could finally put an end to this human stupidity forever. With you he's stuck chasing a fantasy, your fantasy, that humanity can be saved, if only you can 'wake them up'.

"Don't you see, after all these lives, after all these deaths, they don't want to wake up. They like their sleep. They like their dreams. They like the squalor they create around themselves. They can't wait to screw everything up. Even now you think you've won, Kali. You've taken away my powers. You've taken away my father's powers. But we can still muster an army of supporters to find you and confront you. Dorje left me with one jewel and it is that jewel that allowed me to find you. Why would he do that?"

I could not answer, could not piece together everything Marisa said. Some of it felt true, true enough to leave me incapable of responding.

"Let me share a story with you," she said.

"Many years ago, long before anybody thought of countries and borders there was a people who lived high up in the highest mountains. They lived in a stone village, hidden amongst the rocks and clouds. In the centre of their village was a great hall in which the people gathered. These people had been taught how to make paper and tan leather, how to sew and how to bind, how to make pigments and print, how to write and illustrate, how to make silver hasps and gold leaf. Around the walls of the great hall were shelves filled with the books they made - the greatest library on earth.

"A labyrinth of corridors and alleys surrounded the great hall, linking dormitories and kitchens, gardens and storerooms, water tanks, byres and stables. The people were divided into two types. There were those who enjoyed the crisp, thin mountain air and the beauty of the sky. These people maintained the village - building with stone, channelling water, keeping gardens, preparing food, teaching children, tending animals, listening, reading, writing, illustrating, story-telling and, when called upon, sitting in silence.

"The others preferred to live outside the stone village. In the spring they led the yaks and goats down from the mountain to graze them on fresh grass. They gathered wood to bring back to the stone village for the winter. As well as the yaks and goats, they also kept dogs that gifted their sense of smell and eagles that gifted their vision. These people liked to run. They ran as a tribe with their dogs and eagles and gathered knowledge of the world to bring back to the scribes. They also ran because there was danger. There were people who travelled the land in hordes, who destroyed whole villages for no purpose, who killed for no good reason, who carried away more than they could eat, more than they could ever use in an entire lifetime. When the hordes came, the scribes would sit in silence and stillness, drawing attention away from the runners. The runners used their cunning to lead the hordes away from their pastures, away from the mountains and away from the stone village.

"Long ago, twin sisters were born in the stone village. They grew up inseparable - eating together, studying together, sitting together and coming of age together but, during the ceremony to mark their coming of age, they separated. One twin, like her father, preferred the silence and stillness of the stone. She liked to listen and to learn, to illustrate and to write and wanted nothing more than to fulfil her purpose in the stone village. The other twin was more like her mother and could barely contain her excitement when the day came that she could leave the stone village and run with her mother.

"By then the stone village had already existed in the mountains for hundreds of years and its library was immense. Over these years the scribes had learned much more from the stone than just silence and stillness. They had learned how to move rock, how to open fissures, how to cause rock-falls, tremors and quakes, because the threat from the hordes had grown and knowledge of a secret citadel hidden in the mountains and filled with treasure had leaked out into the world. The scribes could no longer be sure that the runners alone could protect them.

"The runners had come to love the chase and, although they still brought the herds to the stone village for the winter, they preferred to live permanently outside its walls. They didn't tell the scribes that they had learned how to kill. The hordes had become too many and the runners feared that the stillness of the scribes could no longer protect them, and their own cunning and resilience would soon be overwhelmed. One day, they lured a horde into a mountain trap and killed them with arrows and rocks. At first, they were ashamed of the pleasure they felt for the killing but quite soon they experienced a desire for more.

"The sisters grew old and each became the leader of her type but, by now, the scribes and runners had little understanding of each other. The scribes still felt called to sit in stillness but no longer knew why. The runners still loved to run but now took so much pleasure in killing those whose greed exceeded their need that they forgot the real purpose of the run. The hordes were now so many that the runners were overwhelmed and the hordes were able to take to the mountains in search of the apocryphal citadel filled with treasure. The scribes kept them at bay with earthquakes and rock-falls until there was nothing left to fall but the village itself. Before destroying the village, they took all the books to the shores of their sacred lake and sacrificed the library and themselves to their fires."

I dropped to my knees, overwhelmed by Marisa's story, overwhelmed by the effect of the truth on my being. Marisa joined me, close enough to touch, bended knee to bended knee. She reached forward to take my hands. "Sister," she said, "look what's become of us!"

I wrapped my arms around her, nuzzled my nose into her neck, soaked her shoulder with my tears as she soaked mine. "Two ends of the same stick," I said, "but we lost sight of the stick. I destroyed everything, all human history and knowledge, hoping I could bring it back in better times."

"But you cannot bring back what matters most. You cannot bring back the memory of a time before envy, a time before greed, a time before violence. Nobody believes that anymore. I love you Kali."

"If you loved me why did you try to kill me?"

"I didn't want to kill you Kali; if I had you would be dead and Dorje would be mine. I did what I had to do. I wounded you so deeply, so invisibly that nobody could heal you, so you would have to come back to the monastery and complete the sacrifice."

Three

1

When the stillness subsided, we ran out to the field, to the place where Kali was still kneeling, the place from where the boy had held the stillness. Marisa and her family were leaving, walking towards their cars, betraying nothing, neither threatening nor defeated. As they drove away, we gathered, clamoring for an explanation, desperate to understand the nature of the stillness, the nature of the confrontation between Kali and Marisa. The boy was the first to help with a piece of the mystery that had unfolded before our eyes. He reached into his energy web and brought out something that glowed so brightly it was impossible to discern its form. "From the beach in France," he said. "Try it."

He passed it to me and I integrated it into my web. A soft wave of warmth passed from my feet to the top of my head. He beckoned me towards him as he stepped back. "Come, take my place."

As we switched places I felt a vortex swirl upwards through my body. All at once I could see the warps and wefts between all things. Through the swirls I could hear the boy say, "call for stillness," and I did as he said.

The experience was not as I expected, not what I had imagined it would be after seeing stillness unfolded by others so many times before. As I looked around at my family, I could understand everything that brought us together, the strengths and weaknesses, the previous lives together, the wishes, aims and agreements. Despite such a richness of information I was at peace, resting in a simple place, simply watching, simply aware, unperturbed, unattached, enfolded in love.

"Extend the stillness," the boy said and I allowed my attention to flow outwards. Everywhere I looked I could see the effect of my call. I could see Marisa and her family in their cars on the road to their villa. I could see the villa in the far distance with its high walls and gates and a small army of security guards and domestic staff all captured in stillness. I could see the relief that stillness brought to each one of them, momentarily freed from their own inner machinery and outward obligations, all senses open to receive without the pressure of action.

I could see that the stillness I called for did not freeze the world in time - rather, it involved a deepening of my own attention, of my own sense of time, until what was contained in each moment was unlimited. I could peer into the hearts of Marisa, of her father, of the entourage of workers and helpers from ancient families who supported them. All at once I understood their purpose. Whereas before they had been aiming for a final cataclysm, to release enough energy to tear the earth apart, enough energy to free all those like us, who were already in the final stages of our lives, now they were involved in a subtler transition.

I saw how cunning they were, how they had arranged to win regardless of what we did. If we'd failed to save Kali and she'd fallen to her death as agreed, the process we'd stalled once before would have been completed. Kali would have willingly died, the discipline master would have willingly killed, the abbot would have completed his last exhalation and the breath of the dzong, entwined as it was with the breath of the abbot, would have continued to exhale until the walls failed and collapsed. The fault line on which it stood would have ruptured and the earth would have come apart at the seams. Although we thwarted that plan, the devolvers used the time we travelled through the Vril holes to instigate another, and it was a brilliant plan. They built a new web, still using gold as before, but finer than anything ever seen.

The web we had worked to restore seemed so old and gross in comparison, the illuminations in manuscripts, the thin gold leaf on holy objects. Every religion had integrated the same golden network into their sacred places, using it to call the gaze, to focus the attention, to connect people to the threads and streams and paths, to draw their eyes and hearts to a higher level.

The devolvers had spread their network so far and so fine that the gold was no longer even visible and yet, it infiltrated every aspect of people's lives - their homes, their cars, their pockets, even their bodies through so many different devices. Now, when people had even the slightest moment of inspiration or felt a call to conscience, their first impulse was to turn to the network the devolvers had created around and within them, away from the heavens and the true origin of that call. Now the people were truly asleep, and as they slept, they dreamed. And they dreamed that they were awake. And they dreamed that they had access to knowledge and truth. And they dreamed that they were magicians and prophets. And they dreamed that they were free.

I inhaled again and the stillness subsided. My breath rested before the next exhalation and I removed the jewel from my energy web and passed it back to the boy. Marisa's family inhaled again and all memory of the events on Maria's land drifted away. Nothing was left but Marisa's longing to embrace her sister again.

The boy pressed the jewel into the ground as our family gathered. "Maria can come back now, her home just disappeared from devolver awareness," he said. "When you took away the vases this land was no longer protected. Now it is hidden again. Now we have a home to return to."

"But what about their plan?" I asked. "You saw what they've done! How can we ever counteract that?"

"I don't know," he said. "All I know is that we have to return to the valley of the scholars."

2

We continued our journey by car, following the boy's directions. We had no idea if the devolvers were tracking us. Although we had made Marisa and her family forget their encounter with us at Maria's house, we could not make them forget us entirely. Our lives were intricately woven together and, in this life, they would always be devolvers and we would always be a threat.

Although we never lost touch with each other and continued to travel as if together, we kept some distance between each car, taking it in turns to lead. There were many places where we had to be seen, to buy food, to refuel, to wash, to cross borders. It was better to do that one car at a time with the others standing by in case of emergency.

It wasn't until we were halfway across the Bosphorus strait that we were suddenly called into action. The traffic had stopped. There were police, soldiers, sirens, blue lights, people running and shouting, helicopters either side of the bridge, strafing the darkness with search-lights. We abandoned the cars, gathered together, drew down our sky cords, pulled forces from deep within the land at both ends of the bridge.

But we had no need to fight. We felt the power of choice, the power of stillness, the power of disappearing from view, of deflecting attention, of standing calm and free as the world fell into chaos around us. "Devolvers?" Kali asked but nobody knew.

The cars were lost, abandoned to the jam, attracting all the attention of the soldiers and police as we walked through the melee towards Asia, towards a solitary figure beckoning from the end of the bridge, unseen by all but us. We climbed aboard the minibus and set off into the darkness. Meltemi's son introduced himself as he drove, told us how he had turned out more like his mother than his father.

"My way is not the way of the wind," he said. "My way is the way of the road. It is not often I can be of service to my father and it brings me great happiness when I can."

3

The gates slid open as we arrived outside Meltemi's house and stepped down from the bus. Although Meltemi greeted us all like family, he reserved a special quality of attention for Kali.

"An auspicious moment for us all," he said to her. "Your family is complete and, as Auro has already told me, it was worth the wait." He hesitated a moment. "But there is one more than I was expecting."

"My son," Kali said, beckoning the boy forward.

Meltemi rested a hand on the boy's shoulder, gazed at him a moment, then guided him toward the entrance. "No matter; I rarely eat and my body is better suited to moving than sitting. Come in, prepare yourselves for lunch."

We reconvened around a large dining table set for thirteen. Meltemi, true to his word, remained standing and, when the food was served, walked slowly around behind us. His presence was so light that he was able to chat with us without ever disturbing the rhythm of the feast. Kali and the boy sat together and many times Meltemi hovered behind them, a little distracted, a little lost in thought, as if searching for a misplaced memory that might make sense of what he saw.

Finally, when the meal was done and the table cleared, Meltemi excused himself. He returned with a bottle of booze in his hand. The cook followed, carrying a tray of glasses and a jug of iced water.

"Raki!" Meltemi said. "To celebrate."

"What are we celebrating?" I asked, as Meltemi poured the raki and the cook topped up the glasses with iced water.

"I'm not yet sure but the raki will help us to know," Meltemi said and he brought a glass to each of us in turn before taking one for himself and raising it high. "The cook's husband sent the raki; he thought I needed cheering up. Now, before even a drop has passed my lips, I can feel its effect. To happiness," he said, and took a sip.

"To happiness," we all agreed and sipped the icy, milky drink that tasted of aniseed and cleared away doubt. As we finished our glass and basked in the inner warmth the raki brought to our bodies, Meltemi invited us into the kitchen. "Come," he said, "we have to make a journey."

He must have seen our hesitation. "Don't worry, I know about your bags, they will be waiting for you when you return."

Meltemi explained to Kali and the boy about the process involved and led them both to the corner. He took the boy by the hand. "Come with me. Just press on through." In a moment they were gone and we gathered around Kali and encouraged her to follow. One by one, we pressed on through and one by one, we found ourselves in a completely different place to the one we expected. What we found was not a tunnel through the lava as before but another room, wood panelled, smelling of beeswax and cloves, old leather sofas arranged around a large hand-woven rug, lit by candles and a soft green glow that seeped around the edges of the panels.

"Let's agree to meet back here when it's time to return and share our stories," Meltemi said, and we nodded our half-hearted agreement, not quite sure what he meant. We followed him through a door at the far end of the room, into a passageway carved through the rock. Meltemi cut no slack as he walked and we had to jog to keep up with him. I whispered to Kali. "See, this is the red light we told you about! Beautiful isn't it?"

Unlike the journey we took with Meltemi before, there were no junctions to worry about, just a long tunnel cut straight through the rock. We continued down that tunnel for more than an hour. When we stopped at last it was in a cavern where Meltemi had turned to face us. He motioned us to sit and we sat in a large circle that started and ended with Meltemi.

"Let your eyes rest a moment," he said, "and then tell me what you see."

We told him as one with our expressions, without need of words, our faces radiating smiles with as much brightness as the golden light that filled the space. There were no words to describe the experience, just a question spoken by Remi on behalf of us all. "Is it gold?" she asked.

"You call it gold. We call it god."

"But what is this magical place?" she asked.

"It's a gift from the sky," Meltemi replied.

The answers we received didn't even wet the edges of our questions but Meltemi let us sit a while, our smiles stretching our cheeks, our sense of awe greater than any that had gone before, our chatter utterly silenced.

When the silence itself became silent and, between us we held a void so enormous it threatened to swallow us, Meltemi spoke.

"We don't know how these places came to be and we don't even know how many there are. The Vril show us how to find them when they are needed. The Vril told us that they let us listen to the sounds from the sky. When the first wind watchers left their island and travelled the earth, they were directed by the Vril to some of these places. They were told to keep them secret and they were taught how to draw out golden threads and create wells that would become places of learning for the people they met on their travels. Last night I was asked to share this knowledge with you. I was asked to leave you here and meet you back in the sitting room when you are ready."

Meltemi left us there, sitting in our circle, inside that golden space. Our silence gave way to sound, to the sounds of the sky gathered and transmitted to each of us in our own individual way.

We were given a glimpse of a network of golden threads that spread around the planet, connecting together these golden spheres.

We were shown the places where gold was first thrown to earth, long before life, and how it was used to establish the conditions that could support life.

We were shown the threads of gold we had revived as we made our journey north from Mariam's home in the mountains.

We were shown the threads that connected us from where we sat to the valley of the scholars.

We were shown how the air we breathed was filled with a gold dust so fine that it was invisible to the untrained eye.

We were shown that gold dust infiltrated all space, hidden within light, unseen, because our eyes were taught only to see emptiness between things.

We were shown how gold had been used by all teachings, all religions, to call the attention, to induce a state of awe, to open a listening space within people through which they could receive knowledge.

We were shown how the great human teachers were always bathed in golden light, a light that shone from within, from the gold they had accumulated within their bodies thanks to their learning.

We were shown how some people had fallen for an illusion, how they had come to search for gold, to steal it and horde it as if it had some intrinsic value.

We were shown how that illusion had brought greed and violence to so many sacred places.

We were shown how real knowledge had to be constantly moved.

We were shown what was expected of us.

4

When we returned to the sitting room, Meltemi was waiting for us. Our positions had been decided in advance, marked by our leather bags on the sofas. Nobody objected and, when we took our places, the arrangement felt perfect. Meltemi didn't sit but hovered discretely behind our circle. It took a long time before any of us could talk. The experience in the cave had been deeply moving and we carried the silence back through the tunnel to the sitting room. It was difficult to find words again, words precious enough to describe what we had seen.

The boy was the first to speak, but now he was more man than boy. He turned to Mariam, with whom he shared a sofa, but could say no more than her name before they were both weeping, then standing, then embracing, then holding hands, facing each other, gazing into each other's eyes.

"Papa," Mariam said.

"Sweet, sweet Mariam - I never thought I would see you again. It's so strange, even though these are different eyes that I look through, you are exactly as I remember."

While still holding Mariam's hand the boy turned to where I sat between Kali and Dorje on the sofa and, as he did, his face softened to become more like the boy and less like Mariam's father.

"I know this is going to be strange for us all," he said. "Although I am still the son of Kali and Dorje I am also Mariam's father. My name is Atal. I hope you don't mind to call me Atal; I think it will be easier for us all and it's the name that suits me better for this part of our journey."

Atal walked around the circle, just as he did when we all first met him as a boy in London. At each member of his family he stopped, reached out, took them by the hands, led them to their feet where they embraced. And for each member of our family his appearance seemed to change just a little, somehow integrating the boy, Atal and the one he faced and embraced. When we were all standing, he raised an arm and led us in a dance and as we danced, he told us a story, and as we listened and turned, we could see everything he said.

"Long ago there was a time when it was possible to walk safely from Istanbul to India. There was a path - not an obvious path nor a busy path but a path nevertheless for those who knew how to find it. The ones who travelled the path were taught the rules of the road, taught to invent a story that aroused no suspicion, a story based on the place they just came from and what little they knew of the place they were going to next. Oftentimes, they posed as couriers carrying a mundane message for somebody nobody knew, sometimes as a farmer in search of a particular seed. As well as the simplicity of the story they told, they learned a simplicity of manner, betraying no sense of learning, attracting no more attention than a sparrow.

"Hidden along the path were places of refuge, perhaps a home offering a clean bed and a warm meal, perhaps a secret meeting place where knowledge was shared, perhaps a place on the land where people were invited to stand and feel the exchange between the earth and the sky. The path was designed to prepare the traveller for the truth they would face when they finally arrived.

"Not so long ago, the path was opened for many more travelers. There was a need. The devolvers had come close to achieving their aims and the world was left sad and bitter, with little sense of connection or hope. Out of the ashes, a new world began to emerge, a world seemingly filled with all kinds of opportunity, of education and work, easy access to money, things to buy and do, an artificial abundance in which people could lose themselves, lose all sense of purpose.

"A movement began, a wave of young people dissatisfied by the life that was offered to them. There was nothing obviously wrong. They had homes, food, education, opportunities and money and yet, they walked away from it all, drawn by a call but with no clear idea from whence it came. There were no guide books or maps back then, just a word on the road, a destination picked up in some particular cafe or hotel, perhaps on a beach hidden from the world by the difficulty of the walk, or a place by the river where a sandwich of fresh fried fish was served from a boat, where a pickle vendor would offer a word of direction along with a plate of sour gherkins.

"It was on this path I met your mother, Mariam, and it was on this path you called to us, asked us to bring you through. We met in a coffee shop popular with travellers like us, a curious place that served sweet rice pudding washed down with Nescafe, not the dark, dusty Turkish coffee we had gone there for. Your mother begged a cigarette from me and from that moment never left my side until she was sent away, sent to find a place to hide you from the world. Although at that time there were many other paths, the one we travelled was the most important. It didn't last for long; the devolvers saw the threat to their plans and laid traps and sent out tricksters. Hashish seduced the smokers while false teachers seduced those who still searched in spite of the smoke.

"In the lounge of our hotel we met marijuana farmers who travelled north from their fields to sell their crop in the city. They brought pouches of pollen that they rubbed into tola with their leathery hands. Despite our disinterest, one farmer pressed a tola into my hand as we prepared to leave the lounge and find our room in the warren of corridors on the upper floors. We were woken by the sound of banging and shouting, the sound of police and dogs, the sound of travellers dragged protesting from their rooms. We fled with our bags through a window that opened onto the roof and found ourselves following a young boy who hissed and waved, beckoning us to follow him over the rooftops and into a yard, into the back of a small truck that left as soon as we were aboard.

"We were taken to the valley of the scholars. It was not on the path that most travellers followed but ran parallel, protected from the uninvited by stories of bandits and madmen, stories of tribesmen with rifles so long, so finely engineered that they could end the life of a traveller a full three seconds before his companions heard the shot, and could end the lives of the others as they struggled to make sense of what had happened. The only people to survive the journey to the valley of the scholars were those who came invited.

"We were lucky Mariam, we made it just in time for the spilling days. The City of Wisdom was opened and books and treasures spilled out into the valley. Teachers had been prepared around the world and scholars were sent out with treasures that would complete their initiation. We learned amazing things while we remained as guests but, when the eternal war began, your mother was given a treasure and guided from the valley. She was instructed to return to her land to find a safe place to hide you. I was asked to stay with the scholars to help them protect the remaining treasures until they could be carried out from the valley.

"Some of us sought refuge in the mountain, travelling deeper and deeper into labyrinths and caves that had hidden the treasures so many times before. As we travelled, we learned, not only from inscriptions on the walls but from the proportions of the walls, of the stairs and the corridors - spaces and dimensions that shaped and educated our very being. When we could travel no further, we had to dig, leaving our own inscriptions on the walls we created.

"The devolvers were persistent. They stirred the minds of men, troubling their spirits, clouding their eyes, teaching them ever more hateful and destructive ways to be. As they followed us, they raided the libraries and burned the books.

"When the Vril left we thought we were finished as we could dig no deeper; not even a wind watcher's stick could cut the rock that marked the beginning of their world and the end of ours. The devolvers set fire to the sky above the White Mountain, sucked the air from the caves and tunnels. But the Vril left their tunnels open and used them to supply us with icy air and abundant water from the north and an earthy tasting paste that nourished us for months as we hid, waiting for a time we could return to the surface.

"The Vril came back to tell us there was no hope of returning the way we came; our tunnels had collapsed and they could not sustain us for the time it would take us to dig our way out. They offered us another way, to abandon our body to the mountain and allow the Vril to draw our spirits out through their tunnels, to a new body, to begin again. We all, apart from Shamal, gave ourselves to the Vril. 'I will stay,' he said. 'I am Shamal, wind watcher of the White Mountain. This is my place but I will help you leave.'

"One by one, the scholars followed Shamal's instruction and lay down with the back of their head resting over one of the Vril holes.

"One by one, the scholars departed and those of us remaining removed their lifeless body to make room for the next. I was not the last to go; I knew whose hands would carry my body away. I lay down in the place and felt the little bump at the back of my head fit comfortably into the Vril hole. Shamal brought the tip of his digging stick to a point between my eyebrows. There was a strange sensation, painless, like a tube sliding through the bone, between the membranes, toward the centre of my brain. There was a little heat, a pure white light, a hissing sound as the machinery of my thinking slowed down and settled into neutral. I could hear my breath softening - exhaling, exhaling, exhaling. I could feel myself floating within a river of life. I could feel the river of life merge with another river through the opening at the back of my head. I could feel myself float out from my body into the river the Vril had prepared within their tunnel. I floated out from the valley of the scholars. It was not until I sat inside the golden sphere that I remembered, and now I remember what it is we have to do. I ask you all to put your faith in me as I lead you on this part of our journey."

Atal turned toward Meltemi. "Please come with us, you are needed in the valley of the scholars."

Meltemi agreed to his request without hesitation. "Of course," he said. "I have been waiting for this moment for a long time and, like you, my bag is already packed."

5

Before the day was out, we were boarding the bus again, setting off on a journey we had done before with the help of the Vril; this time driven overland by Meltemi's son. The presence of Atal and Meltemi in our family added something we had never known, a smooth and effortless freedom to do what we wanted without any conscious effort on our part. It was as though we were helped and, in return for that help, we were used as participants in an unknowable process. We were free from any sense of external threat, seen by all, yet able to take whatever we needed, as everybody and everything we touched, unconsciously felt a wish to support us.

Our journey took us through many lands, through great cities built to draw people to them, away from their farms and forests, away from their orchards and rivers, away from their deserts and mountains. We visited shrines and sacred wells, places of worship, places of remembering, places for the dead - all abandoned, but by the few too old or poor to move to the city or aware enough to know that there would never be anywhere better than where they were now.

As we travelled, we felt the constant movement of the golden threads, a living network that used us to reform, to connect to the spheres, to open the wells, to draw an intelligence to the surface, to draw an intelligence from the sky.

The devolvers' aim was to spread need, greed, ignorance and hunger to every corner of the world. They encouraged the hordes to bring violence and fear, to invade the lands of others, to destroy the holy places and steal their relics.

They encouraged them to dig and search for treasure but all they ever found was gold. They would never find the threads. They would never find the wells. They would never find the golden spheres. They would never understand the nature of the treasures.

They could take down a mountain and sieve it and wash it and all they would ever find was gold, and as they stirred up the dust it integrated into a web they could not see.

6

By the time we reached the mountains that led to the valley of the scholars, Meltemi's son had swapped our vehicle several times. Now we travelled in a truck built for high altitude and unpredictable mountain roads. It was decorated with stories painted in bright colours, laden with charms cut from tin, belching black smoke with every change of gear. We had no need to hide and we could enjoy the beauty of the mountains, standing looking over the cab, sitting on one of the rows of benches or lying on a sheep wool mattress.

When the truck stopped suddenly I was standing at the front with Kali and Dorje. "What the hell is that?" Kali asked of the white, demonic figure dancing in the road before us. What would have been a terrifying sight for the ordinary traveller brought laughter to those of us who knew.

"It's Shamal, wind watcher of the White Mountain," Dorje said and Kali, reassured, joined the laughter. A moment later Meltemi jumped from the truck and, taking on a similarly bizarre appearance, joined the dance, both holding their digging sticks aloft, both digging sticks ablaze.

We all jumped down from the truck and rallied around the flaming sticks, dancing with the divine madmen, sharing an opportunity so rare that none could pass it up. As we danced, the wind watchers' sticks shed their charred wooden scabbards and became the white-hot swords that heralded action. And action came as clouds and thunder, lightning and torrential hail, a deluge that stalled the truck and washed away the road.

"Time to go," called Shamal through the gale and we followed him onto a mountain path that led to a large cave, a blazing fire, freshly cooked bread, and a red bean stew.

7

We moved freely under the noses of the strangers who now controlled the valley, moving amongst them, listening to them, taking from them whatever we wanted, disturbing their thoughts, disturbing their dreams. We felt no need to make amends; these people didn't belong here. They were here to satisfy their greed and there was nothing good to be gained from their presence. Eventually they would go home and disturb their own people.

The food stalls, book shops and zikrs that once lined the road were gone, replaced with devolver machines and the cruel and ignorant strangers who preferred to kill than to listen, who preferred to steal than to open their hearts to receive.

After a day's walk we found our guide, hidden far from the road, in a cave that reached deep into the rock, his breath and heartbeat so slow that he barely betrayed any signs of life. Atal knew where to find him and, although the Atal who found him was quite different in appearance to the Atal who taught him how to hide, they recognised each other in an instant, just from the sound of their voices and the secret song they shared through the rhythm of their speech.

As we shrouded him in stillness, Gorbat the guide breathed deep again, pumped heat to his muscles again, resurrected his dormant nerves, dragged himself to the surface through a tunnel that looked barely wide enough to fit a fox.

Atal had brought him clothes and a bottle of soup prepared from freshwater algae by Meltemi's cook. We afforded Gorbat some privacy while he purged and dressed.

"He has a lot of sludge to clean out," Atal said by way of reassurance. "Once he's ready, he'll help us find the scholars."

Gorbat the guide joined us and, as Atal held him in a long embrace, tears streaked his dirty face. "Is today the day?" he asked.

"If you are ready, then today is the day," Atal replied.

"I am ready."

"Then let's wake the scholars."

Gorbat led us further into the mountains, slowly to begin, as his legs hadn't moved for so long. Once he found his pace it was not much faster, but it was light and graceful. We emulated his rhythm and found it offered an economy of movement and energy that allowed us to climb upwards for hours without stopping, until we were high enough to enjoy a view over most of the valley. From our vantage point we could see just how much the hordes had infested this land. There was a constant movement of men and vehicles along the road and into the foothills. Helicopters clattered through the air below us.

"They don't like to bring their flying machines up here," Gorbat told us. "The air is thin, our gods are strong, and they are scared their wings will fall off. I learned to like their flying machines. They are noisy and, when they came, I used the time to breathe deep and shake my body."

When we were here before, the valley was so quiet and the people so attentive that we had to use prayer time to move. Now the hordes were so in thrall to their machines, so distracted by them, that crafty people like us could do what we wanted. As the sound of the departing helicopter slapped against the valley walls we gathered our family and agreed our roles.

Atal, Dorje and the stillness workers continued to shroud our presence, while Shamal and Meltemi stood together, swords raised, listening to the wind, ready to call a gust from any direction at the first sign of danger from the valley floor.

"We can empty the air so their flying machines fall from the sky," Shamal said, "or we can bring a dust so fine that they are blinded and their engines choke and stop. Without their machines they are lost."

Juan, Mireille and Alice listened deep into the valley while Robert, Herve and Remi followed the eyes of Gorbat. When he pointed out a place in the rock, Herve flew out as an eagle to confirm what he saw. If his memory was correct, and it was correct every time, Remi ran to the place as a fox, calling the scholars back to life, guiding them to the surface. She couldn't carry clothes and soup and, once she had shown them where we were, they had to find their own way to us. The stillness workers hid the scholars as they made their way over the rocky terrain to where we waited. Kali and I gave them clothes and soup. When they were fully revived, we awakened the treasures that lay dormant within them, and this alone more than made up for the years of hibernation.

When all the scholars were awake, we led them to the cave, to the fire, to the food, as the wind watchers unleashed another tempest over the valley. We let the scholars sleep under our gaze, protected by our presence, free to dream deeply, to shake, to twitch, to whimper and call out, to free their bodies of the horrors they had seen, of the violence they had done as the spilling days called upon them to do their duty.

When they woke again, their bodies soft and receptive, we taught them how to feel the path, how to walk the path, how to avoid drawing attention to themselves. We taught them how to bury their treasure deep, to hide any sign of learning, any sense of value, to dull their eyes, to dull their spirits, at best to attract pity, at worst disdain.

While the wind watchers brought more floods and fear to all who remained, we led the scholars from the valley. There was nothing of value left for the hordes but they could not leave. They still did not understand the nature of the treasures and they were more confused than ever from the time we spent playing with them. For some, that confusion would become an inspiration, for others a curse.

Once we were sure that the scholars could feel the paths, we sent them on their way with a last embrace and tears in our eyes, knowing that the paths we had opened would guide them, knowing that along those paths they would meet people who would protect them and care for them until they reached their destination.

As we watched them disappear into the distance, the old lama entered our thinking, told us of the wave of people now moving across the planet. As the hordes brought ignorance, violence and greed to so many sacred places, families like ours were sending the treasures out along ancient paths in the hearts of the humble, the uninteresting, the overlooked and the mistreated.

The world remains in a curious state of balance that the devolvers cannot understand. They continue to develop their web. They continue to build new devices. They continue to integrate their devices deep into the lives of the people wherever they might live. All around the planet more and more people fall under their spell, into their sleep, into dreams that are not their own. They continue to encourage greed, carelessness, waste and ignorance, pushing the earth to its limit, hoping that the day will come when she will wash us all away.

What they do not understand is that there is another web, one with a higher origin than theirs, with a purer intention, with a greater reach, too fine for the devolvers to see, impossible for them to control.

Now there are no more sacred places; all places are sacred. There are no more sacred days; every moment is sacred. There are no more sacred beings; all beings are sacred. The treasures the hordes search for are gone, carried to every corner of the planet, to every town, to every street. But the treasures are no longer on show, no longer dazzling people with great words, great teachings, great presence or beauty, charisma or style. They are carried in the hearts of the humble, the simple people who bring a smile to the street, whose eyes are open to see you if you look, whose hearts are open to touch you if you feel.

If you ask kindly, they might even tell you a story - of a time before envy, a time before greed, a time before violence.

Printed in Great Britain
by Amazon

75970671R00220